Praise for the novels of Christie Ridgway

"Delightful." —Rachel Gibson

"Tender, funny, and wonderfully emotional."
—Barbara Freethy

"Pure romance, delightfully warm and funny."
—Jennifer Crusie

"Smart, peppy." —*Publishers Weekly*

"An irresistible read!" —Susan Wiggs

"Funny, supersexy, and fast paced . . . Ridgway is noted for her humorous, spicy, and upbeat stories." —*Library Journal*

"Christie Ridgway is a first-class author."
—*Midwest Book Review*

"Christie Ridgway's books are crammed with smart girls, manly men, great sex, and fast, funny dialogue. Her latest novel . . . is a delightful example, a romance as purely sparkling as California champagne." —*BookPage*

"Ridgway delights yet again with this charming, witty tale of holiday romance. Not only are the characters sympathetic, intelligent, and engaging, but the sexual tension between the main characters is played out with tremendous skill." —*Romantic Times*

*Titles by Christie Ridgway*

HOW TO KNIT A WILD BIKINI
UNRAVEL ME

# Unravel Me

CHRISTIE RIDGWAY

BERKLEY SENSATION, NEW YORK

**THE BERKLEY PUBLISHING GROUP**
**Published by the Penguin Group**
**Penguin Group (USA) Inc.**
**375 Hudson Street, New York, New York 10014, USA**
Penguin Group (Canada), 90 Eglinton Avenue East, Suite 700, Toronto, Ontario M4P 2Y3, Canada
(a division of Pearson Penguin Canada Inc.)
Penguin Books Ltd., 80 Strand, London WC2R 0RL, England
Penguin Group Ireland, 25 St. Stephen's Green, Dublin 2, Ireland (a division of Penguin Books Ltd.)
Penguin Group (Australia), 250 Camberwell Road, Camberwell, Victoria 3124, Australia
(a division of Pearson Australia Group Pty. Ltd.)
Penguin Books India Pvt. Ltd., 11 Community Centre, Panchsheel Park, New Delhi—110 017, India
Penguin Group (NZ), 67 Apollo Drive, Rosedale, North Shore 0632, New Zealand
(a division of Pearson New Zealand Ltd.)
Penguin Books (South Africa) (Pty.) Ltd., 24 Sturdee Avenue, Rosebank, Johannesburg 2196,
South Africa

Penguin Books Ltd., Registered Offices: 80 Strand, London WC2R 0RL, England



UNRAVEL ME

A Berkley Sensation Book / published by arrangement with the author

PRINTING HISTORY
Berkley Sensation mass-market edition / November 2008


Cover illustration and hand lettering by Ben Perini.
Cover photo of "Woman's Legs" by Altrendo Images/Getty.
Cover design by Rita Frangie.
Interior text design by Laura K. Corless.


For information, address: The Berkley Publishing Group,
a division of Penguin Group (USA) Inc.,
375 Hudson Street, New York, New York 10014.

ISBN: 978-0-425-22485-4

BERKLEY® SENSATION
Berkley Sensation Books are published by The Berkley Publishing Group,
a division of Penguin Group (USA) Inc.,
375 Hudson Street, New York, New York 10014.
BERKLEY SENSATION and the "B" design are trademarks of Penguin Group (USA) Inc.

PRINTED IN THE UNITED STATES OF AMERICA

10 9 8 7 6 5 4 3 2

*Dear Diary:*

*Tonight I met the man I'm going to marry. He brought me you, this diary, that has a cover like a watercolor painting and with pages that feel like butterfly wings. It's a grown-up diary, not something bubble gum pink that you'd buy for a little girl. He said, "Happy thirteenth birthday."*

*My throat felt like I'd swallowed an Easter egg whole so I sounded whispery when I thanked him. He told me I was welcome and didn't pay any attention to me after that. He's a friend of Dad's, but he doesn't have Dad's bald spot or that spare tire around his waist that Mom teases him about. The man I'm going to marry looks like a movie star and my mom says he's going to be a general some day.*

*Everyone will say he's too old for me. I'm not so dumb that I don't know he'd think the same thing if he knew what was in my heart tonight. But my parents have always treated me more like an adult than a kid so I'm certain no boy could ever make me feel like this.*

---

*Dear Diary:*

*Today I buried the man I married. It seems only fitting to chronicle it here, in another of the diaries he presented to me over the years. God, I hope this one has waterproof pages, because I'm sure it will be filled with more tears than confessions.*

*It's been eighteen years since we met, eight since we married, four since he was first diagnosed with cancer. Our years together are over and part of me wants to slip under the covers and sleep for the next one hundred.*

*Can I build a new life all on my own? I suppose I'll have to, because I think no one, no man for certain, could ever make me . . . well, feel again.*

# One

Love is like war; easy to begin but very hard to stop.

—HENRY LOUIS MENCKEN

*Eleven months later . . .*

Driving from the shop by the beach to her home in the Malibu hills, Juliet Weston peered through the deepening dusk and weighed the merits of bathing in Super Glue. A dab would repair a fingernail. She'd read a line of the stuff could close a wound. What she faced was more dire, however. Would immersion in a tub of maximum-hold adhesive keep her from fracturing into a thousand little pieces?

She needed her protective shell. It kept her emotions contained and it kept away the rest of the world. But the jarring information she'd been told twenty minutes before had tapped her surface, a single hammer blow to porcelain, and she sensed the cracks in her control.

She arrived home to find her foyer shadowy, her kitchen just as dark, but she didn't flip a single switch. Bright lights, a deep breath—who knew what might trigger the ruin of what had held her together for the last eleven months?

With slow, careful steps, she made her way across the terra-cotta tiles in the kitchen, her gaze brushing the butcher-block island, the whitewashed cabinets, the gleaming sink, to land on the window overlooking the flagstone deck and the pool that stood between her and the guesthouse. From there she took in the stretch of Pacific Ocean that was her western view.

It was an incredible vista, worth every penny she'd paid for the place, and though she'd lived here a week, its beauty wasn't sinking in, any more than the news she'd been told at the yarn shop by the beach. That was the downside of her shell—it kept her distant from the good as well as from the bad.

"Who am I?" she said out loud, and at the same instant she voiced the question, a light flashed on outside. Startled, she jerked, stumbling back so she had to catch herself from falling by slamming her hand onto the butcher block.

Some idiot had left a knife there, a small one that the same idiot—Juliet herself—had used to cut up an apple earlier in the day.

It cut *her* now. Without thinking, she lifted her forefinger to her mouth, her attention shifting out the window again.

The pool lights were glowing, turning what had been dark waters into a tranquil, turquoise lagoon, a lovely contrast to the now-descended night. This time, the beautiful sight struck her, a second hammer blow.

And then the surface rippled, the lagoon was invaded, the tranquility shattered.

A man was in Juliet Weston's pool.

Her finger was still bleeding. The blood was salty on her tongue, giving an earthy flavor to a further realization.

A *nude* man was in her pool.

She should turn away. At least shut her eyes.

Instead, she found herself staring at the naked, novel sight.

Against the turquoise light his figure was a dark silhouette with an aquamarine outline running along the edges of his body like veins of neon light. He was tall and lean, his shoulders wide. He had strong arms that reached out as if to gather life closer to himself with each stroke.

He swam away from her, and as his long legs fluttered with lazy kicks, she detected the shift of muscles in his rounded buttocks, the muscles tightening to create a scoop on the right, then a scoop on the left. She watched, fascinated at how every movement, how every line of that big body exuded power. And sex.

*Sex?*

Embarrassment flooded Juliet's face with heat, but something was burning inside her, too, burning so hot that the blast of heat was the final blow to her compromised defenses. As her gaze stayed focused on that masculine specimen of sinew and skin, her shell crumbled, the pieces flaming as they fell to land as ashes at her feet. Her flesh was left behind, still clothed, but hypersensitive to the gentle scrape of fabric against its surface. It left her hyperaware of that swimming man, turning now.

Coming toward her. Inexorable. Inevitable.

Climbing the steps, climbing out of the pool, his all-male nakedness part threat, part magnet.

His right foot breached the deck. His left.

Her heart expanded, pressing against her chest wall. *Get back!* her instincts screamed. *Get away!*

Air rushed out of her lungs. She leaped in retreat, even as she knew he couldn't see her through the darkened windows. Her hips crashed into the square butcher-block table, shoving it along the terra-cotta pavers with a piercing screech. The knife clattered to the floor, followed by the shallow wooden bowl that held the rest of the ripe, red fruit.

*Thump-thump-thump-thump.*

Apples rolled unevenly along the floor, mimicking the jerky beat of her heart.

One darting glance showed that the dark figure had frozen, but then it thawed in an instant and made a dash for the kitchen door. The too-flimsy door that was the only thing keeping them apart.

It was wrenched open. The overhead light blazed on.

Juliet resisted the urge to hide from him. What good would it do?

She kept her focus steady on his face, not glancing down, not letting him realize that she realized that his big male body was dripping on her floor. His big, dripping, naked male body.

He didn't acknowledge his nakedness either. Instead, he stared, his gaze running over her. She felt it like a hand, his hands, big like he was, strong and sinewy. She hadn't felt anything in so, so long. Goose bumps rose in the wake of that imaginary touch and her breasts tingled inside her bra as again her face burned.

"You're hurt." His voice was rough but he reached toward her slowly, one of those hands lifting in her direction, heavy veins standing out on the back of it. The dark hairs of his forearm were plastered against his tanned skin and drops of water still moved along his muscles like a man sweating after hard work . . . or after making hard, satisfying love.

Forgetting her cut, she put her hands over her eyes, appalled by the direction of her thoughts. Shocked by the heat of a flush on the back of her neck, by her swelling breasts, by the sensitive pinpricks that rose on the flesh of her inner thighs.

The air in the room shifted, so she supposed he was moving, but for a man so big, he was graceful and silent. She'd never noticed that about him before.

"Juliet." Closer now, his voice. "Juliet, honey."

*Honey*. When was the last time a man had murmured an endearment to her? This man had never. This man must be rocked to the soles of his size twelve feet—God, somehow she'd even noticed his feet and made a determination of their size!—if he was talking to her like that.

And touching her like this. Because he was peeling away one of her hands. The hurt one. Like a coward, she only squeezed her revealed eye tighter shut.

His palm cradled her fingers. The calluses on his skin

made an erotic scratch along her knuckles. "You've cut yourself. What happened? Did something startle you? Did some*one* startle you?"

*You. Me*. She had no idea which was more accurate. But she did know she couldn't keep pretending she wasn't standing in her kitchen with a naked man.

Her heart still whomping inside her chest, she opened her eyes. Oh. Not naked. Not naked any longer.

He was staring down at her, a line between his black brows and concern in his blue eyes. Around his neck was the strap of a butcher-style apron. It was printed with green vines and red roses. It barely covered the flesh between his dark nipples and its ruffled hem hit him at mid thigh.

She remembered buying it at one of the boutiques in the Malibu Country Mart, thinking it would look cheerful hanging in her kitchen. Wrapped around him, it should have looked ridiculous. The sight should have made her smile, if not out-and-out laugh. Instead, she could only think that on the other side of the apron he was—no, don't go there.

Too late. His first-class buttocks were back in her memory, that vision of him as he churned, naked, through the water. His muscles flexing, creating a tantalizing scoop on the right, scoop on the left.

"Oh, God." She put her free hand to her forehead.

One corner of his mouth ticked up. "I know, I know. I'd be ready to thank the Lord, too, if someone presented me with such primo blackmail material. If I let you take a picture, will you tell me what's going on?"

"I have absolutely no idea what's going on," she answered, with all honesty. Her voice came out a little rusty, and his fingers tightened on hers, like a brief embrace. "Not beyond the fact that there's a man dressed like Rachel Ray in my kitchen."

One of his eyebrows winged up. "So *she's* the one they call 'The Naked Chef?' "

"No." She rubbed her forehead again. "No. It's . . . oh, it's all so complicated." So completely unexpected.

"Not so bad. Nothing we can't fix with a Band-Aid."

He was looking at her cut hand again. While all she could think of was that what really needed fixing wasn't going to be helped by any item stored in her medicine cabinet.

Because something momentous had just happened to her tonight. Her defenses had dropped away, and the resulting clatter had awakened something inside her—or perhaps it was she who had awakened. In any case, Juliet Weston didn't feel like herself, which made sense, after all, since she'd just learned she wasn't who she'd always thought she was.

But the why of this current situation didn't matter, not when the what was so clear to her. The what—*oh, God*—was this: With her protective shell gone, she was overcome by a sudden and raging sexual attraction for the naked non-chef standing on her tiled floor, holding her shaking hand. He affected her just that much. Her whole body was trembling in reaction to him.

Him. Noah Smith.

The man who lived in the guesthouse across the pool. The man who worked for her and who before that had tended to her dying husband.

The younger man.

He shouldn't go back to her, Noah thought, pulling on jeans and shoving his feet in a pair of ragged running shoes. He should stay in the guesthouse and mind his own business, leaving Juliet alone to deal with whatever it was that had spooked her.

But hell, before finishing college and attending three years of law school, the Army had schooled him long and schooled him well in keeping focused on the mission. And his mission—but no, not his obsession, damn it—was Juliet Weston.

For her—no, for the *mission*—he'd done some things,

and then not done some others that were secrets he expected to take to his grave. He didn't regret a one, but he was now bound to her in a way she didn't know. That's why when he'd heard the strange sounds from her supposedly vacant kitchen—she'd said she was going to be gone for a couple of hours—he'd rushed in wearing nothing more than his protective instincts.

Probably scared the bejesus out of her, a big wet body decorated by only an infantryman's meat tag tattoo. Naked Noah.

Except he couldn't claim she'd looked at him with any particular awareness then or before. From the pleasant yet detached manner she always exhibited he supposed she considered him along the lines of a convenient piece of furniture.

While she'd never struck him in the least like a chair or a table or a desk.

Just another reason to keep to his side of the pool.

He glanced out the window to assure himself all was well. There was no reason to go back there. To her.

Except a stealthy figure was just now creeping over the wall to position itself outside Juliet's kitchen windows.

Christ! What now? Kidnapper? Peeping Tom? Didn't matter. His Army training said OP-FOR and he was going after this particular opposition force with everything he had.

Noah was through his door and across the flagstone deck before the intruder could take another step.

"Hey!" he yelled, grabbing the stranger by his shirt collar to yank him around. "What the hell do you think you're doing?"

The lights from the pool glowed greenly on the other man's face. Like Noah, he was close to thirty, and dressed in jeans, the cotton shirt that was crumpled in Noah's fist, and lightweight hiking boots. Two cameras hung around his neck. Noah twisted the shirt collar tighter and the guy stumbled closer.

"What are you up to?" he demanded again.

"Easy, easy," the stranger said, not attempting to fight Noah's grasp. "I'm a friend of the lady's." He gestured toward the kitchen windows. "She invited me over."

"You and your cameras?"

"She . . . she asked me to take some pictures." The stranger's voice was low, his smirk suggestive. "You know."

Noah didn't want to know, but hell, he had to find out, didn't he? "Juliet?" He pitched his voice louder. "Juliet!"

The fixture over the back door flipped on and then she stepped out, hesitating there as the light turned her wealth of fine, straight hair from its usual caramel color to a brighter gold. When Noah had blasted into the kitchen earlier, it had been down around her shoulders, but now it was pulled away from her face by a thin band. It looked damp around the edges as if she'd just splashed water on her skin. The lashes surrounding her amazing eyes—one green, one blue—were spiky with wetness.

She blinked as she gazed at the two men. "Noah?"

"Is this a friend of yours?" he demanded, not easing his grip on the other dude's shirt. "Did you invite him over?"

Juliet blinked again.

*Shit,* Noah thought. *Maybe she had.* For God's sake, she'd been a widow for eleven months and her husband had been dying for many, many before that. It would be natural to want someone to spend time with, and there was no reason to be pissed that if she wanted a man she hadn't turned to him. She was the quintessential uptown girl and officer's wife, while he, after all, was the hired help, the enlisted guy, the piece of furniture from across the pool. But did she have to torture his imagination by wanting pictures, too?

Because, God, imagined freeze-frames were overtaking his gray matter. Juliet out of her pants and sweater and into a black teddy, lace playing peek-a-boo with his gaze so he glimpsed a shell-pink nipple here, the crease that separated her long legs from her hips there. Now a backside shot, Juliet peering over the creamy, elegant blade of her shoulder, the sweep of her delicate spine leading to the taut hump of her ass. One set of ruby-tipped toes in the air.

Trying to banish the thoughts, his eyes closed and his hand tightened on the photographer's collar. He barely recognized the grating sound of his own voice. "Well?"

"I've never seen him before in my life."

"I've never seen her before in my life."

Juliet and the stranger spoke together. Noah's eyes popped back open. "What?" Loosening his grip a little, he shook the man he held. "I thought you said she invited you over."

"I thought she was somebody else!"

Noah's eyes narrowed. "You forgot your friend's address?"

"She used to live here, anyway. I know this used to be her house."

Puzzled, Noah stared at the guy for a long minute.

"Oomfaa," Juliet put in quietly. "Remember, Noah? She owned it before me."

Oh, Christ. The realtor had revealed that "One of the Most Famous Actresses in America," nicknamed Oomfaa by the Malibu community, had lived here before Juliet had moved in. Which meant that the guy with the cameras was likely one of the—

"Paparazzi," he said with disgust, letting go of the man's shirt and shoving him away at the same time. "I hear they guarantee celebrity sightings at the Malibu Starbucks. Get out of here."

The man shrugged his shoulders and pulled on the placket of his wrinkled shirt. "Wrong. Now the best spot is The Coffee Bean & Tea Leaf. But I'm looking for Oomfaa in particular. Do you know where she moved? I heard she's for sure in Malibu."

Noah rolled his eyes. "As if I would tell you."

The guy slid his hand in his front pocket. "There'd be money in it for you. I sell my stuff to that website—I'm sure you know it—Celeb!.com. I pay for tips that pan out."

"I don't want your money," he said, shooting a glance at Juliet. They both knew that the actress had moved just across the canyon.

The paparazzo followed his gaze. After a heartbeat, his pose went from casual to alert. He pivoted to face Juliet. "Wait a minute. I *do* know you."

When his hands moved toward his cameras, Noah wrapped his fingers around the straps hanging from the guy's neck. "No pictures. Don't even think about it."

The photographer pointed his forefinger at Juliet instead. "You married America's Hero."

That's what the media had dubbed General Wayne Weston—America's Hero. With his Hollywood looks, his West Point education, and his well-documented bravery, he'd been a military man that the populace—and more important, maybe, the politicians on both the right and the left—could be proud of. When he'd retired, the world assumed he was going to run for public office. The highest office.

And win.

"They called you the Deal—"

Noah's hand jerked to the other man's throat. "That's—"

"Okay," Juliet interjected. "Let him say it. And let him go."

Shit. He gentled his stranglehold, but didn't completely ease off. "Juliet . . ."

"Then I'll say it for him," she put in, her voice matter-of-fact. "They called me the Deal Breaker."

Shaking his head, Noah dropped his hand. It was true that when the general had married his very much younger wife, both of the parties had dropped him like a hot political potato. Where before they'd been courting him to run on their tickets, now they couldn't back away fast enough. Rumor had it that when he'd mentioned his plans to wed a woman thirty years his junior the national committees had said the bride was out or their support was gone.

Wayne Weston had chosen marriage.

The media and the people hadn't taken very well to losing their favorite presidential contender. But had they blamed the hierarchies of the parties or even their hero himself? Hell, no. They'd blamed Juliet.

"Then they called me the Happy Widow."

Every muscle in Noah's body clenched. He hated that part of the story most of all. He'd been there in the last months of the general's life and in all the months since. Not once had Juliet been happy.

Not goddamn once.

But because she hadn't been at Wayne Weston's side in his last hours, unfounded, anonymously sourced rumors had been swallowed by the hungry-for-content twenty-four-hour media machine, to be regurgitated into cruel sound bites like the Happy Widow. And here, right beside Noah, was a representative of that slanderous, libelous, salacious fourth estate.

*Hey*, he thought, cheering a little. *And I've been trained to kill.*

"You'd better leave," he told the man in a low voice, deciding even a dolt like this one deserved a warning. "Now."

The guy was smart enough to shuffle back.

But Juliet intervened once again. "Celeb!.com, you said? Don't they have a companion TV show in the new fall lineup?"

"Well, yeah," the photographer replied, shooting Noah a wary look. "*CC! on TV*. Celeb!.com on television. You a fan?"

"We happy widows have to fill our hours somehow," she answered, without a hint of irony in her voice. "Maybe they'd like to do a piece on the general's book."

Noah rocked back on his heels. It all made sense to him now. General Wayne Weston's autobiography was hitting the shelves next month. Apparently Juliet wasn't above chatting up a slimy paparazzo if she thought it might gain attention for her late husband's book. Noah knew she counted on the publication of the general's life story repairing the damage to his reputation that had been the result of their marriage.

Christ. Noah rubbed his chest. He really wished he hadn't left the guesthouse now. He hated seeing her like this—because it made him worry that what she wanted so badly wouldn't come to pass.

"How about if I take a couple of shots of you?" the photographer asked.

"Now?" Her hand went to her hair.

"Sure. Why not? I'll bet people would like to know what you're up to." He jerked his chin in Noah's direction. "And *who* you're with."

The overhead light clearly illuminated the flush shooting up Juliet's slender neck. "That's not . . . we're not . . ."

*Yeah*, Noah thought. *I'm the furniture. The enlisted guy. The hired help. Not good enough for her, and I know it.*

Her gaze flicked to his face, then jumped away. "Noah is . . . Noah was my husband's assistant. He helped Wayne as . . . as my husband declined. He helped him dress, helped him with his meals, helped him with the book he was writing."

Noah refused to let any feeling show in his expression. He'd helped the general in ways that Juliet would never know about. In ways that she would never thank him for if she ever found out.

Which she never would.

The paparazzo shrugged. "None of that means you two aren't an item."

Juliet was shaking her head, her cheeks bright pink. She glanced over at Noah again, and licked her lips.

*God*, he thought, staring at her mouth. She was so effing beautiful, sometimes it hurt to look at her. And maybe it hurt a little more to see her total rejection of him as a romantic interest.

Of course, they were miles apart and he accepted that. And he also knew her well enough to realize it would be difficult for her to verbalize this to some dumbass from

Celeb!.com. With a sigh, he stepped closer to the photographer.

"Listen, bud, the lady said we're not . . . intimate or whatever the hell you're getting at, and that's a fact. She's . . ." He ran out of steam, and just lifted his hand to where she stood under the light, her pretty hair, her delicate build, her slender limbs all glowing golden. "She's . . ."

"Too old for him," Juliet said.

Noah froze. He was hearing things, right? There was water in his ears from his swim. Because he *knew* Juliet Weston. Of the many things to keep them apart, the *very* last thing that would ever stand in the way was . . . was . . .

He moved his head to stare at her. She couldn't have possibly said . . .

But then she said it again. "Noah's younger than me."

All right. He hadn't left the guesthouse and come back to her after all. Instead, he'd fallen across his bed and then into a deep sleep, dreaming.

A really odd, odd dream.

# Two

You can no more win a war than you can win an earthquake.

—JEANNETTE RANKIN

Noah was back in her kitchen. He'd ushered from the premises the Celeb!.com photographer who'd left after trying to wheedle her phone number out of her. With disapproval blasting from Noah's parade-rest position a few feet away, she'd reconsidered her impulsive proposal of a tabloid TV segment on Wayne's book—she must have been really rattled to suggest it in the first place—but the paparazzo had persisted in trying to set something up.

She'd held firm to her refusal though, and while the stranger with the cameras was finally gone, Noah's dark mood hadn't dissipated. Trying to ignore it, she moved about the room, making up little tasks for herself like refolding the dish towels and straightening the salt-and-pepper shakers. Normal activities. Normal activities that she hoped would put their relationship back to normal.

There'd never been tension between herself and Noah, and now the air seemed thick with it. From the corner of her eye she stole a look at him and—*bam!*—another jolt of sexual heat rocked through her. Oh, boy. Her response to him wasn't anywhere near normal either.

But was that her fault? Who could ignore all that uncovered skin?

"Aren't you cold?" she blurted out.

He glanced down at his bare chest. "No. Do I look cold?"

From the shield of her lashes she glanced at him again. Leaning against a countertop, he wore only jeans and shoes. The denim was nothing special, worn almost white in places, and slung low across his hips to reveal yards of healthy male abdominal muscles, curved pectorals, and heavy shoulders. Those sinewy arms. There were his dark nipples that had caught her attention earlier in the evening. The centers were gathered into tiny, hard-looking buttons. Her nipples only tightened like that when she was chilled, or . . . or aroused.

Her right arm clamped over her breasts and she clutched her upper left with tight fingers, a little noise sounding from her throat. She tried to disguise it by faking a cough.

Noah wasn't so easy to fool. "Juliet?" His voice sounded puzzled. "What's going on?"

"Nothing." Everything.

"Juliet."

She looked up at him. He was still propped against her counter, but he'd folded his arms over his chest in a no-nonsense attitude that went along with the no-nonsense narrowing of his blue eyes. Noah was handsome—she'd always known that on some faraway, objective level—thanks to his chiseled cheekbones and square jaw. Wayne had been a good-looking man, too, her lean silver fox. But Noah was made of more rugged material and there was nothing subtle about the testosterone that seemed to ooze from his pores.

"C'mon, Juliet. We're friends, aren't we?"

Her throat tightened. "I thought we were."

Something flickered in his eyes. Oh, God. Had she hurt his feelings? This was all her fault, she thought, looking away. This unseemly, inappropriate, unlooked-for reaction was something that was entirely on her shoulders. "Noah . . . It's not you."

He laughed. "I've heard that one before."

She met his gaze again. "Somehow I doubt that."

"What?"

"You forget how long I've known you. Remember all those months when you were in the apartment over the garage at the house in Pacific Palisades?" While attending law school, he'd lived with them and aided her husband as his illness progressed. Noah had stayed on with her after the general's death, taking care of a thousand details, including helping her move to this much smaller place in Malibu.

She found a smile for him. "Don't think we didn't notice the blondes, the brunettes, and those redheads who came and went from your apartment. I think your social life gave Wayne more than a few vicarious thrills."

"Now I'm the one doubting. Not only am I not nearly the player you're making me out to be, we both know the general had the only woman and the only thrills he was looking for."

Juliet looked away again. Maybe not. She'd felt an inexplicable distance between herself and Wayne as he neared the end of his life and it still bothered her.

"Juliet." Noah had made another of his silent moves. Without her detecting his travel across the terra-cotta tiles, he was beside her, his body radiating warmth. One of his fingers slid under her chin to lift her face. "What's going on with you tonight?"

Thoughts of the past evaporated as goose bumps shivered over her flesh from the point of his contact. Her heartbeat throbbed in the cells of her skin as she stared up at him. She'd never, ever, been so aware of her body, but she couldn't let this man know what he was doing to her. She couldn't! They were supposed to be getting back to normal.

His finger curled in what seemed to her overheated self as a short caress. "What are you thinking about?"

"You." Oh, God, her brain was set on blurt again. She coughed, then lied to explain herself. "I was, um, thinking that since we moved here I haven't seen a woman at the guesthouse. You . . . you need to know I don't expect it to be a monastery." Maybe if she saw him with some pretty young thing she'd get over this weird reaction to him—if a night's sleep wouldn't do the job on its own.

He dropped his hand and stepped back. "I don't need to bring a woman here."

"But, Noah—"

"It's only temporary, remember?" Turning away, he ran his hand through his dark hair. "I'm only living here for a short while. Until the automatic sprinklers are set right and the gazebo is painted, and we've figured out how that damn built-in barbecue works."

Then he'd be gone. And she'd be alone. There was Wayne's daughter, Marlys, of course, but they'd never been close. Even after Juliet had told her she was moving from the Weston family house in Pacific Palisades so that Marlys could have it to herself, the other woman hadn't warmed up. No doubt she blamed Juliet for everything from her parents' divorce—that had occurred years before Wayne's second marriage—to her father's cancer diagnosis.

Or maybe Marlys believed all the ugly rumors about Juliet. How she'd been callous over the fact that her husband was dying. How she hadn't cared enough to stick by him when the very end came.

Yes, Marlys wasn't going to provide much friendship. When Noah vacated the guesthouse across the pool, there'd be no one who—

This time the information she'd learned at the shop that night hit with the weight of a brick and sank straight to her consciousness. "Oh." She put her hand over her mouth. "Oh my God."

Noah spun. "Now what?"

"I think I need a glass of wine." She headed for the refrigerator. "How about you?"

He caught her arms and drew her to him. "I'm not a wine kind of guy, honey. Surely you know that."

*Honey.* The soft word made her feel all warm again, but she couldn't be distracted by that, or by the smooth skin of his tanned, muscled chest such a very few inches away. "Noah . . ." She tried pulling free.

He only drew her closer. "Juliet . . ." he echoed. "I'm done dancing around this. You're acting very unlike yourself."

"That's the problem." She looked up into his eyes. "I don't know who I am anymore. Not really." That was the truth. And not just because she was smelling Noah now, taking in his scent, and feeling her inner woman instead of her inner widow responding with another wash of heat.

She tried pushing him away, but Noah's grip firmed on her upper arms. "I'm not letting you go until you come clean with what's set you off-kilter tonight."

It was like trying to move a mountain. With a sigh, she went ahead and told him some of what had her teetering on her feet. "I'm not my father's daughter."

"Yeah?" His thumbs drew a pattern over the flat knit of her silk sweater. "What makes you say so?"

"It's what my sisters told me."

Surprise showed clearly on his face. "You're an only child."

"That's what I thought. But tonight—just an hour or so ago—I found out that isn't the case." The notion seemed incredible, but the words coming from the mouths of the two women in the yarn shop had held the distinct ring of truth. "Cassandra Riley and Nikki Carmichael told me we are all products of a single sperm donor and our own separate mothers."

"Whoa, whoa, whoa. Where did this come from? How did these women contact you?"

Juliet thought of the knitting shop on the Pacific Coast

Highway, a short drive away. She remembered walking in and looking at the two women sitting together on a couch and how their jaws had dropped when they'd looked back.

"Cassandra—she has a business in Malibu—did some Internet research into her biological father. Her mother told her from childhood she was the product of an anonymous sperm donor, but only recently did she try to discover who that donor was."

"I thought you just said 'anonymous.' "

"It's the age of the Internet. I could probably find out your deepest, darkest secret given my flying fingers and a few hours with 'the Google.'"

He didn't crack a smile at her little joke. As a matter of fact, at the mention of "deepest, darkest secret," his body had tensed. A muscle in his jaw ticked.

"Noah?"

"So you're telling me that this Cassandra . . ."

"Used her own flying fingers. When I was still living in the old house, she sent me an invitation to her business in Malibu. I dismissed it as some generic direct mail advertising, but when I was out for a drive tonight I saw the place and it jogged my memory. I was curious enough to stop by." She shrugged. "I thought it was a whim at the time, but maybe fate was giving me a little nudge."

"And inside you found your two supposed sisters."

Sisters! It really was a strange thought. But . . . "I'm inclined to believe we're related. If you listened to them, if you saw them, you'd understand why."

"Well, I *am* going to see them."

"Noah . . ." She shook her head, realizing she should have expected this. "There's no need to go guard dog on me."

"Yeah? Is that what I'm doing?"

"Yeah, that's just what you're doing. It's written all over your face." She lifted her hand to touch his hard cheek, then pressed it to his chest. "And all over the tension I can feel right here."

Beneath her palm, his heartbeat quickened. Then her skin registered a surge of heat in his and she heard the jerky hitch in his breathing. She couldn't continue to meet his eyes.

Instead, she shuffled back, a new burn spreading across the nape of her neck. But her hand stayed glued to his chest and she stared at it, willing it to move, too. *Now*, she commanded. *Stop touching him now.*

The stubborn thing finally obeyed, but slowly, so that her fingertips took a lazy path down the hard plane of his abdomen. When they brushed his denim waistband, she jerked, and her hand dropped to her side.

They both let out a breath.

She whirled toward the refrigerator and opened it, staring at the shelves while the cool air wafted over her. Oh, it would be good to crawl inside right now, not only to bring her temperature down, but so that she didn't have to face him again. What must he be thinking?

"It doesn't matter what my body's telling you, Juliet. I've got a job to do, and I'm going to do it."

"Noah—"

"You know the general would expect me to check this out for you."

"*I* can check this out for me." And she definitely would, she decided. "Tomorrow I'm going to back to the shop to find out more about the situation and the sisters."

He touched her shoulder, and she turned. "For me, then," he said. "Let me look into this as your friend, to set my mind at ease. There are people out there who might like to take advantage of you."

And he was a soldier, under orders from the general. That part went unspoken, though she suspected a deal had been struck between the two men during the months Wayne lay dying. She could hear him now, officer to subordinate. *Get Juliet settled, soldier. Make sure she stays safe and has everything she needs.*

She'd understood that everything about Wayne—his upbringing, his personality, his career—had given him a great need to protect the ones he loved. Unfortunately, his illness had robbed her of the time to fully dispel the fragile flower image he had of her—and had apparently passed on to Noah.

She frowned at the younger man now, irritated by the thought. "Look—"

"Please," he said with a smile—and oh, yeah, despite his denials he was no doubt a lady-killer, because she felt her irritation immediately start to seep away.

"Please," Noah said again.

And he asked so nicely, too. "Okay," she heard herself answer, but she grumbled it, trying to make clear she was no gentle geranium.

He smiled a second time anyway. "So tomorrow we'll visit this business and these self-proclaimed relatives of yours together," he said. "We'll go to lunch first."

"Fine." She watched him head toward the door.

With his hand on the knob, he paused and looked over his shoulder. "Wear something pretty."

Startled by the request, she let out an awkward laugh. "What? That sounds like a date."

He flashed his lady-killer grin again. "You can call it what you like. By the way, how old are you, Juliet?"

Surprised again, she answered automatically. "Thirty-two."

"I'll be thirty on my next birthday."

"August fourth." Where had that come from? She knew his birthday off the top of her head?

"Yep."

Apparently she did. "So . . . ?"

"So stop thinking you're older than me. Come next summer, we'll be in the same decade darlin', both of us over the age that anybody can trust."

Then he left, which gave him the last smile and the last word. But not the last thoughts.

Those were racing through Juliet's head as she stared at

his retreating, half-naked form, the muscles of his strong back shifting as he walked away. She'd definitely failed at getting things back to normal, hadn't she? Because normal for this lonely widow definitely wasn't a lunch date with a virile, muscled young man who suddenly made her sweat just looking at him.

On the day they'd carried boxes into Juliet's house on Mar Vista Drive, the movers had told Noah there were three kinds of people in Malibu: the beach people, the canyon people, and the view people. As he and Juliet ascended the road in the direction of the Pacific, it made sense to him that she'd chosen a hillside home. She'd always struck him as someone who stayed above the fray.

Composed and serene in her beauty, her feelings always seemed to be held carefully close. While her love for the general had been palpable and her grief over his death truly deep, she'd never betrayed any wild swings or passionate bursts of emotion. He'd never seen her less than graceful. Not once had she ever fidgeted in his presence.

Until last night, when he discovered she'd bumped into her butcher-block table and cut her hand.

Until now, when her fingertips were drumming a ceaseless percussion against her left leg. Letting his gaze linger on her a moment, he smiled to himself. She *had* dressed pretty. Not that she ever looked anything less than classy. Today she had on a pair of leg-hugging, biscuit-colored jeans covered by a V-necked tunic-y thing that was mostly the same color as the pants and splashed with vibrant blue, green, and gold flowers. She wore low-heeled strappy gold sandals on her feet.

Her toenails were painted a matching shade the color of twenty-four carats and the whole outfit made her look expensive but approachable.

And yet, oddly nervous.

He put out his hand to still her fingers, flattening them

against her warm thigh. She twitched at his touch, and he slanted her a glance. "Why so tense?"

"I didn't sleep well last night."

"Yeah?" With a final pat, he slid his hand off hers and gripped the steering wheel again. "I'm sorry to hear that."

His sleep had been shitty, too. He'd kept dreaming of Juliet's fingertips drifting down the bare skin of his chest, leaving four hot, pulsing brands in their wake. Then his eyes would open and he'd find himself in his dark bedroom, alone. After a groan, he'd bury his head in the pillow . . . and hope to find his way right back to where the dream had left off.

"What kept you up?" he asked.

"I had a lot on my mind. This, especially."

He glanced over. "This . . . lunch? You and I sharing a meal?"

Her face flushed. "I mean meeting my sisters again today. I didn't spend much time with them last night. After their initial revelation, I just turned and walked out of the shop. Shell-shocked, I guess."

They'd reached the Pacific Coast Highway. Noah turned left on PCH, following Juliet's directions. Malibu & Ewe, the business owned by Cassandra Riley, shared a parking lot situated on a bluff overlooking one of the area's famous—and surf-friendly—south-facing beaches. When they pulled in, he realized that the adjoining business to the yarn shop was an eatery he'd noted on his own previous explorations.

His eyebrows rose as he pulled into a parking spot. "This is where you want to have lunch?" It was more his kind of place than hers, with the appetite-tempting smell of something sizzling in a deep fryer already reaching his truck. There was a small number of tables within the café proper, and then a stand-alone shelter harboring plastic-covered picnic tables. "I don't think it runs to Asiatic pear and goat cheese salads."

She wrinkled her nose, which made her look fifteen. "Goat cheese. Yuck."

He laughed, and then followed her from the car and toward the restaurant's screened door. Even though it was October, here in Southern California the temperature was summer-warm, the sky clear, and the view spectacular. The sound of the surf hitting the sand below mixed with the cars whooshing by along the coastal highway.

Inside, she claimed a table next to a window while he ordered at the counter, lingering there to wait for the fish tacos—his—and the shrimp salad—Juliet's choice. With a smile, he watched her pull a paper napkin from the table's holder to brush the plastic surface free of unseen crumbs. Then she plucked plasticware from a foam cup and grabbed other napkins to set them each a place at the table. Such a lady.

To a guy who'd eaten MREs from a ditch dug beside a Stryker combat vehicle, and who'd found those haute cuisine compared to some of his childhood meals, it was no wonder he was fascinated by her fastidious habits and elegant appearance. The slightest whiff of her top-shelf perfume could make his head spin.

When he slid their tray of food on the table and dropped into his plastic seat, she was staring out the window across the parking lot. In the direction of Malibu & Ewe.

He moved her paper plate and iced tea in front of her. "Should we have gone over there *before* lunch?"

"I don't mind putting it off a little longer." She drew her drink toward her with a frown.

"Juliet, no law says you have to have further contact with these women, legitimate claim to sisterhood or not."

"You want the truth?" Her gaze lifted to his.

There were those eyes of hers, arresting in their difference, and just as arresting by their own individual quality. One was as blue as the Iraqi desert sky, the other the green that he'd dreamed about all those months of his deployment, when sand had been his second skin. "Sure I want the truth."

"Part of me is excited. Startled, sure, and I'm going to

proceed with caution, I promise you, but if I'm honest, I'd have to say I'm a bit thrilled at the idea of siblings."

He raised an eyebrow. "Thrilled?"

She nodded. "My two best friends don't live in the area. One's a new mom in Seattle and my friend Kim's opening a dance studio in London. It would be nice to have some people nearby who are on my side."

She said it as if she was all alone in the world. "What, I'm not people?" He tried smiling, but it felt forced. She was always so composed: He hadn't considered how lonely she might be. Or how lousy he might feel hearing that he wasn't enough for her.

"Of course you're people, Noah. It's just that . . ."

He groaned. "Tell me you're not going to play the age card again. Even if you overlook my time in college and law school, before that I spent four years working for Uncle Sam."

"I know." She looked down at her plate. "But at the risk of repeating myself, it's not about you. Think, Noah. I was married to a much older man. After he became sick, there wasn't much socializing, but while he was well, it was mainly with *his* peer group. So it's not that you seem young, it's just that maybe I feel . . . older than my age."

Noah had admired the general. Considered him an out-and-out genuine American. But damn it, had the man ever stopped to consider what their marriage might do to his young wife?

Irritation made Noah's voice caustic. "Shall I find some yellow pages so we can shop for walkers on the way home?"

Her eyes widened, and he felt like a stupid, snarling dog. "Forget I said that." He grabbed his taco and stuffed it in his mouth to prevent another careless comment.

"If that's an apology, I accept." She pierced a shrimp with her fork. "And I'm not ready to sign up for the retirement home just yet. What I *am* going to do—I was thinking about this last night, too—is look for a job."

His mouth was full, so his only reply was a strangled, "Armph."

"Don't look so shocked," she said. "I have a perfectly good college degree that has surely prepared me for a job doing . . . doing . . . well, I haven't quite figured that out."

He swallowed. "What did you study?"

"Dance. I have a bachelor's degree in dance." She made a little face. "When I was small, my dad called me his 'Dreamy Balleriny.' I either had my nose in a book or my feet on the dance studio floor."

He could see her willowy body leaping and turning and . . . doing whatever it was that dancers did. "So you wanted to be on a stage somewhere . . ."

She was already shaking her head. "By the time I was a senior in college, I'd figured out I didn't have what it took to be a star. But before I could decide on what I'd do instead, my parents passed away and Wayne came into my life."

The general had once told Noah that he'd spent five minutes with Juliet at her parents' funeral and had been a goner after two minutes and thirty seconds. Gazing on her golden hair and unusual eyes, Noah could sympathize.

He toyed with the edge of his plate. "For the record, I wasn't shocked about you wanting a job. It's just that I hadn't considered—"

"That I'm actually capable of something other than looking pretty and playing hostess?"

*Whoa, whoa, whoa.* He hadn't seen that coming, but from the way Juliet had narrowed her eyes and was staring him down, she had a little tender spot on the subject about, oh, a mile wide and two miles deep. Noah wiped his mouth with his napkin. "Didn't the general . . . ?"

A flush crawled up her neck and she looked away. "It's just that . . . that sometimes I feel like he didn't think I was competent to handle things."

*Shit.* This was a conversation Noah didn't want to continue as it came much too close to secrets he'd promised to keep. So he attempted to jump the train onto a different track by pasting a cheery smile on his face. "Okay, well. A job. Sure. We can—"

"Noah, there isn't going to be any 'we.'"

Cheery, along with his smile, died a swift death. "Of course I didn't mean 'we' we, I meant—"

"I know what you meant. But have you forgotten? You've taken the bar exam, Noah. You told me you have feelers out for jobs and that you're ready to interview as soon as the test results come in."

He could have been interviewing without the test results, but he'd put off spending those hours away from her. "Yeah, but—"

"It's your time now. You'll move on, move away. Before long there'll be a woman who'll stick, and you'll get married and have a family."

He tried to picture that. Tried to picture the she who would stick, the she who he'd want to stick by, but no image came into his head. He'd never considered himself the marrying kind—Christ, dear old Daddy had been one hell of a husband example—and Noah had been satisfied with the sort of temporary relationships that brought a woman to his bed but not trouble to his life.

So he shook his head. "Maybe the one who'll get married is you." And then he decided he didn't like the sound of those words either. Juliet, with some other man watching out for her when it was Noah's mission.

"No," she said, her voice implacable. "I won't marry again."

He could read the certainty in her expression and because he knew how much she'd loved her husband, he figured it was likely true. There wouldn't ever be room for another man in her heart. And didn't that just strike a sour note, too? But hell, he could be wrong about that. She could be wrong.

She could fall for someone else someday.

As he stared into her face, he saw her gaze shift over his shoulder. Her spine stiffened.

"What?" he asked.

"There," she whispered. "At the counter. That's one of them. It's the one named Nikki."

Noah glanced over his shoulder. A woman stood by the cash register, dressed in checked chef pants and a starched tunic. Her brown hair was streaked with gold and worn in loose braids on either side of her head. In that baggy getup, it was hard to say if she had the same sleek body as Juliet. It was impossible to tell if they were related at all.

A trickle of relief coursed through him. If Juliet was wrong about being related to the chick at the counter, then she could be wrong about never loving ag—

The woman he was watching turned. As her gaze roamed around the room, Noah's thought process seized.

He stared.

Oh, hell. It looked as if it was going to be like Juliet had said after all. She'd go on with her life, he with his. And she'd be the ghost that haunted him forever, the ache that he'd remember every morning as he woke from his dreams.

Just that.

Only that.

Because she was certainly right about this. That woman at the counter, the woman with braids and with one blue and one green eye, just *had* to be Juliet's sister.

# Three

Love is an irresistible desire to be irresistibly desired.

—ROBERT FROST

Malibu & Ewe's front door was propped open and as Juliet and Noah crossed the threshold she detected a faint chemical smell over the salty ocean scent pouring through the sliding doors at the rear of the shop. Lingering a few steps inside, she could see what she'd missed the night before. Those sliding back doors led to a balcony overlooking the sunlit expanse of the Santa Monica Bay.

Yet while the outside view was stunning, the store's interior had its own charms. The afternoon sun bounced against the sand-colored walls and lit up like jewels the many-hued skeins of yarn that were tucked in wooden bins stacked on the floor and reaching to shoulder height. A seating area of overstuffed furniture took up the center of the room, each piece draped in a knitted throw of lush colors and textures.

Last night, she'd wandered in, a stranger. Today, the store felt almost familiar. Familiar . . . like family. Is that what she'd truly find here?

She'd missed the closeness of other women. As the

media dubbed "Deal Breaker" and "Happy Widow," not to mention the wife of a man with a daughter near her very own age, she'd come up against blatant criticism. But there'd been subtler snipes from the older women in their social circle as well.

Put their distrust together with the onset of Wayne's illness early in their marriage, and you ended up with the fact that she'd become reclusive during the past few years. Over the last eleven months it had only gotten worse.

But no longer! As the sun rose that morning, she'd resolved to make changes. Changes like a job. Changes like taking real action to ensure Wayne's book succeeded. And she could do both of those with or without sisters.

One of whom seemed to be MIA anyway, she realized, as she made another perusal of her silent surroundings. The shop appeared to be absent its owner.

Noah walked up behind her and she glanced at him. "Maybe we should visit another time."

Before he could answer, a woman's voice drifted from a back hallway. "You're amazing," she said with a little laugh. "Who would have thought we could be together like this?"

A male grunt responded. "It's because you're following orders for once, just as I like it. Now rub."

In the telltale silence that followed, Juliet's face burned. The front door was open, they were here during regular shop hours, yet still it sounded as if she and Noah had walked in on something very private indeed.

"Rub harder."

At the second low growl of command emanating from the hallway, Juliet shuffled in retreat, only to be stopped by the warm wall of Noah's body. She wobbled, and his hard forearm clamped across her hips to steady her.

Oh, God, she thought, swamped by the sudden awareness of his heat, his height, the maleness of the muscles cradling her. It was happening to her again, just like it had been happening since she'd seen him naked in her pool.

That deep, undeniable consciousness that she was a woman and he was a man.

A hard, virile man.

"Damn it, Cassandra, I said rub harder."

Juliet jolted in Noah's arms, trying to get away from her own response and the images the disembodied voices were painting in her head. With a hard swallow, she pulled free of the strong arm holding her.

"I think we should go," she whispered, darting a quick look at him. "And come back later." After a cold shower or something.

"What?" Noah's eyebrows rose. "Why?"

Another "Rub harder," echoed in the room, turning up the heat on her face.

Noah gave a sudden grin, as if now he could see the story playing out in her imagination. "Juliet Weston. Get your mind out of the gutter." Still grinning, he returned to the front door, where he grasped the string of bells hanging from the handle. At his tug, they rang out.

From the hall, the woman's voice instantly responded. "Be with you in half a second," she called out.

"Thanks a lot." The unseen man groused. "It might take a little longer than that."

The woman laughed, and from his renewed place beside Juliet, Noah did, too. For her part, the situation seemed serious. Last night her shell had crumbled, freeing at least one thing she would rather have stayed safely under wraps. Before now, her mind had never wandered into the gutter!

Clearly she needed another focus in her life besides Noah.

On that thought, Cassandra came hurrying around a corner. "Juliet!" Her big blue eyes widening, she stopped short and her fall of rippling brown hair settled about her shoulders. "I didn't expect to see you so soon."

"We didn't have anything else going on today," Juliet said.

The other woman came closer. "And you wanted to make sure you hadn't dreamed it all up?"

"Something like that."

"I know *I* wondered," Cassandra said. She was dressed in a pair of jeans and a sleeveless cotton hoodie sweater that she had surely knit herself. "You can't imagine the jump my heart gave when you walked in last night and I glimpsed another pair of Nikki's eyes looking back at me."

It had been a jolt for Juliet, too. But it had taken a naked Noah to bring her completely awake. She carefully kept her gaze away from him now. "We just saw Nikki at the fish place next door. They're still the same blue and green as mine."

Cassandra nodded, a smile playing around her full mouth. "The same. Though I think I see something of myself in you, too."

"Yes? Well . . ." Juliet hesitated. "I hope we're not interrupting."

"No, no. Gabe and I are rewallpapering the bathroom. It's going to look so cute when we're done."

"Cute?" A dark-haired, dark-eyed man came around the corner. He was very lean and his hair was scruffy. It looked as if he hadn't shaved in a few days and his whiskers only made his scowl appear fiercer. "Tell me you're kidding."

Cassandra lowered her voice and leaned toward Juliet and Noah. "I think he's color-blind. I told him the pale blue and yellow stripes are black and silver—he's a Raiders fan and it seemed to make him happy."

Juliet didn't think the whiskered man would ever be happy, even with a bathroom inspired by his favorite football team. Especially as his scowl was only turning more menacing as he stomped over to confront the other woman.

"Damn it, Cassandra. Cute is going to drive my property values down."

"Nonsense," she said calmly. "Your nasty temper does that all by itself."

He sucked in a breath and stiffened with what looked like outrage.

Cassandra ignored that, too. Reaching out to balance

herself on one of his heavy forearms, she came up on tiptoes to kiss his bristled cheek. "Just kidding."

At the touch of her lips, he arched back, as if her mouth was fire. "I'm outta here," he muttered. "The last strip is up and holding."

Cassandra called to his retreating back. "That's two dinners I owe you then."

He waved without turning or even slowing his stride. "For your information, I see colors just fine. Which means if the rice is that brown crap, I'll know it. I want red beef and white starchy stuff, Froot Loop." Then he was out the door.

With a little sigh, Cassandra returned her attention to Juliet and Noah. "I hate that nickname. It's a toss-up as to whether it's his diet or me that will kill him first." Then she reached out toward Noah. "I'm Cassandra Riley, by the way."

He gripped her hand. "Noah Smith."

Cassandra's gaze shifted to Juliet's face, and then to the hand that Noah had placed on her waist when Gabe had come marching into the room, trailing his black mood along with him. "Your boyfriend?" she asked Juliet.

She felt Noah's hand drop, as if she was as fiery to him as Cassandra's lips were to Gabe. "My friend."

"And no boy," Cassandra added. Then she lifted her arms to gesture around the shop. "Welcome to Malibu & Ewe."

An awkward silence descended over the trio. Juliet's stomach jittered, her nerves reminding her she'd made a promise to be cautious. She was here on an exploratory mission only, she told herself—not to forge any formal ties.

Cassandra broke the silence. "Why don't you come sit on the couches where we can talk more comfortably."

The cushions *were* comfortable, and Juliet darted a glance at Noah as he took a seat beside her. His chiseled face and calm expression didn't betray a clue to his thoughts, even as Cassandra crossed to a big basket and drew from it needles, yarn, and a half-started swatch that she held out to Juliet. "Do you, um, knit?"

Obviously Juliet wasn't the only one feeling nervous, and that settled her a little. "Not for a long time," she said, taking hold of the big needles and the soft wool. "I think I learned in Girl Scouts."

"It'll come back to you." Cassandra plopped down on the couch across from her and grabbed another piece from the basket. "It's calming."

Her needles started clacking away, but she could stitch without looking at them. Her gaze met Juliet's. "Whatever you need to say, to ask, I'm here. Ready."

With that, Juliet plunged ahead. "You said you began some Internet research a few months ago," she said. "Why did you start then, if you've known all your life about the artificial insemination?"

The corners of Cassandra's mouth lifted. "Wait until you meet my mother." Then she quickly went on. "That is, if you want to meet my mother someday."

"She discouraged you from finding out more about your roots?"

"Not quite that. While I was growing up she was adamant that we didn't need anyone but the two of us—mother and daughter."

Juliet let her needles and yarn fall to her lap because she couldn't focus on them and Cassandra at the same time. "She's changed her mind?"

Cassandra shook her head. "She's changed continents. A two-year backpacking trip around the world. I got to feeling a little lonely . . . so I started looking into who else I came from. Does that make sense?"

As a widow, a little lonely was something Juliet knew a lot about. She leaned forward. "I—"

"Why didn't you make a phone call to Juliet?" It was Noah, his voice not suspicious, exactly, but not warm and friendly either. "Or you could have sent her a letter with a few Internet links so she could have pursued the information herself if she was interested."

The flush deepened on Cassandra's face. Her needles stilled. "I chickened out. I couldn't make myself directly contact a stranger out of the blue. So I sent invitations to both Nikki and Juliet, hoping to entice them into the shop where I could get a look before making my approach. Underhanded, I'll admit."

Noah folded his arms over his chest. "How did Nikki take it?"

Cassandra looked away. "Not as calmly as Juliet—but that was partly because I delayed telling her until after we were becoming friends. That's why Nikki and I told Juliet right away when she came into the shop. Before I told her about her parentage, Nikki had never suspected the truth—"

"If what you say *is* the truth," Noah interjected.

Juliet put her hand on his arm. "Noah, seeing Nikki, do you really have doubts?"

He hesitated, then shook his head. "I see you in her," he nodded at Cassandra, "as well."

The other woman—God, she truly was Juliet's *sister!*—released an audible breath. "I can show you what I found on the Internet. I'd be happy to let you see the steps I took and how I linked we three—and it's only we three, by the way—to our father. Donor 1714."

Donor 1714. That sounded so sterile, Juliet thought. So without feeling. But she'd had a father. And a mother. Both had loved her and she'd yet to figure out what she thought about them keeping this from her. "Like Nikki's, my parents never hinted at anything unusual about my conception—other than they'd waited a long time for it."

"Most families of that era didn't talk openly about infertility. Many donor-inseminated kids don't come to find out their biological beginnings until they're into adulthood, like you and Nikki."

Nikki. Nikki and Cassandra. Two women that she knew so very little about.

"Tell me . . ." *Everything.* She hesitated—would the request signal a closeness she was unsure of pursuing?—but then gave into the urge. "Tell me about Nikki."

Cassandra grinned. "Oh, stick around and be entertained. Our little sister is the prickly one. She's a professional chef and she recently had knee surgery that's going to allow her to do some great things in whatever kitchen she chooses. For now, she's heating up the life of one of Malibu's natives and its one-time überbachelor Jay Buchanan. They're engaged and would be married tomorrow if he had his way."

"And you're not?" Noah asked. Juliet could tell that he was trying to get a clearer picture of the situation. "Married, that is?"

"No." Cassandra seemed perfectly comfortable with the idea. She eased back against the couch and raised her brows at him. "Never. How about you?"

Juliet froze, then darted a glance at Noah. God, she'd never thought . . . never considered, even though she knew he'd been in Iraq and it wasn't uncommon for young soldiers to marry their girl before deploying to a battle zone. Had he ever . . . ?

"Thought about it at twenty-one." Noah's expression was as noncommittal as before. "Then thought better of it."

Juliet's tight chest loosened, and wasn't that just a warning in itself about the trouble a lonely widow could get into? What kind of person didn't want the man living across the pool to have once fancied himself in love enough to marry?

She put the yarn and needles aside and got to her feet. "Maybe we should go." New to this awake-and-in-the-world business, her emotional state was rocky, as these weird responses to Noah proved. She had her answers from Cassandra so it was time to leave.

"Good idea," Noah said, rising. "But before we take off, Cassandra, I want to make something clear."

Juliet's donor sibling stood, too. "All right."

He crossed his arms over his chest. "I have Juliet's back."

Juliet swallowed her groan. Great. Here they went. "Noah—"

"No matter where I am, no matter if it's today, tomorrow, or ten years from now, I'm there," he said over her protest. "Someone tries to take advantage of Juliet—whether it's of her wallet or her heart—well, just understand I won't stand by and let that happen. I'll always be watching out for General Weston's widow."

*General Weston's widow*. Good lord, did Cassandra even know that's who she was? Juliet thought. But of course she did. There was the Internet. Not to mention all the media attention during the last year. Cassandra would know as well as Noah that Juliet was the object of derision and suspicion by some.

And pity by others. Is that what Noah felt toward her? Is that why he'd just made his declaration?

"I understand," Cassandra said. "And I'm glad my sister has such a loyal champion."

Out of nowhere, tears burned the corners of Juliet's eyes and she blinked them back. She didn't need a protector, damn it, and despite what Noah claimed, he was only her temporary "champion" anyway. He would move on to his own life, and soon, just as she'd told him at the restaurant.

She swallowed, feeling a desperate need for fresh air. "Good-bye," she told the other woman, already moving toward the door. Noah had his fingertips at the small of her back, even as she looked over her shoulder. "I'll . . . I'll talk to you, um, soon." Caution, remember? No need to be more specific than that.

Cassandra's smile was bright. But her eyes were, too. Bright with unshed tears that matched the ones Juliet felt gathering once more.

Just like that, her resolve broke. "Come to dinner," Juliet urged. "The day after tomorrow. You and Nikki. Ask her." Without even looking, she felt Noah's dismay at her rash words.

"Are you sure . . ." the other woman started.

"I'm sure." Of course, Juliet wasn't, but she couldn't make herself take back the invitation.

"All right," Cassandra replied. "I'll call Nikki."

Noah had Juliet's fingers now and was towing her out the door toward his truck. Even though she sensed his concern, she couldn't help but appreciate the secure warmth of his clasp.

*So be careful about Noah, too,* Juliet warned herself, trying to tug free of him. While it might be too soon with her sisters, it was too late to become attached to the man who held her hand.

Juliet surveyed the selection of cookbooks spread on the kitchen's butcher-block island, and tried remembering her last impulsive action. If she didn't count the act of inviting her sisters to dinner, before that there was . . . there was . . .

There was the night she'd decided to marry Wayne. When she was thirteen years old.

A rap on the glass of the French door behind her made Juliet spin around. Obscured by the mullions stood Noah, who had been repainting the flaking backyard gazebo for the past few hours. She gestured, and he swung open the door to step inside, bringing with him a blast of outdoor-scented air and the unsettling, electric presence of raw maleness.

Barefoot, Noah was dressed in a pair of ragged camouflage pants.

And nothing else.

So right there in the room with her were his uncovered powerful arms and shoulders, not to mention the rippling board of his abdomen. Above that, his naked chest, with all its muscular bends and fascinating dips. Pressing the small of her back against the edge of the island, she put more room between herself and his skin, though she couldn't keep her gaze from inspecting every tanned inch. There was a streak of clay-colored paint under the curve of one pectoral, just three shades lighter than the hard-centered disc of his nipple.

She yanked her attention to his face, even as heated pin-pricks washed from her nape to her heels. "What, um, what can I do for you?"

"I thought I heard the mail truck a while back."

"Mmm. Yeah." There was another scent in the air besides the green-and-fresh smell of the outdoors. She took it in, and then wished she hadn't. The other olfactory note invading the kitchen was the toasty, soapy scent of a sun-drenched Noah and in a flash she saw herself putting her mouth to that smooth juncture of chest and shoulder and breathing him in, deep into her lungs. The tang of his sweat salty against her tongue.

"Ma'am?"

The polite prompt jarred her back to reality. Punishing herself by pushing back harder against the edge of the butcher block, she forced out a laugh. "'Ma'am?' You haven't called me that since the first few weeks you came to work for Wayne."

"I work for you, now," he said. "Just trying to remind myself of that."

"I'd appreciate it if you wouldn't."

He crossed his arms over his chest, bunching his pectoral muscles. "You'd appreciate if I wouldn't what?" Noah asked. "Remember that ours is purely a boss-employee relationship?"

Those prickles burned another path down her torso and then reversed direction to rush toward her face. "Of course it's boss-employee," she reassured him. "I could do without the 'ma'am,' that's all. Makes me feel a hundred years old."

One side of his mouth kicked up and she stared at his lips. He hadn't shaved, and the contrast of dark stubble to smooth skin only made it harder to look away. "Ah. It's the older woman thing again."

No. She didn't care that she was older than he. Wasn't it she who had pointed it out, after all?

And right now she didn't feel older. Right now she just felt . . . different. Female to his male. Uncertain to that knowing gleam she thought she detected in his eyes.

With a whirl, she turned to her open cookbooks again. "The mail's there in a stack by the sink. I haven't yet separated yours from mine."

"Then my *Playboy* renewal form is free from your prying eyes."

She ignored the teasing gibe and left it to him to sort through the pieces. After a moment, though, the rustling ceased and she registered an odd, suspicious silence. Curious, she glanced over her shoulder.

Noah stood as if carved from stone, a manila envelope in his hands. Her gaze ran across the heavy bones of his shoulder blades and down the groove of his spine and she didn't think he breathed.

"Noah?"

He didn't respond, so she hurried to his side. Call her nosy, but she couldn't stop herself from peering at the correspondence that had fixed his attention. "The California Bar? Noah, are these the results of your exam?"

"I don't know. They weren't supposed to come back until November."

"Well, open it!"

He hesitated.

She jostled his elbow. "What are you waiting for?"

Sliding a glance at her, he gave a little smile. "You've never struck me as the impatient type. This is a whole new side of you, Juliet."

"Yes, well, I've been surprising myself a lot just lately." There was her sexuality, suddenly awake and somehow fixated on Noah, the man who'd just ma'amed her. And then there was that impetuosity she'd noted earlier, too. Clamoring desire and impulsive dinner invitations. "And I'm not sure I like the new me."

"I think I do." He tapped her nose with the envelope.

Tapped her nose with the envelope! Bubbles broke in her bloodstream, making her feel girlish and woozy and startled all over again. She shuffled back a step and his gaze returned to what he held in his hand.

He didn't appear any more eager to open it than he had a minute ago.

"It's a big moment," she said. "Been a long time coming."

He nodded. "Years."

"Did you always want to go into law?"

"Nah. For a long time I didn't have any direction at all. But there came a day . . ."

Curiosity got to her again. "There came a day . . . ?"

"Before they send you into a combat zone, the Army makes you write a death letter. You're supposed to have them ready to be mailed to a loved one in case, well, you know. When I wrote mine, that's when I started thinking about becoming a lawyer."

Cold trickled down her spine. Death letter. "And yours was going to . . . ?"

"I didn't know my mother's address. She moves around a lot. But my dad's I knew—he'd been in the same prison since before I enlisted."

"Oh." Well. She didn't know quite how to respond to that. "You decided you wanted to be a defense attorney? So you could help get your father out of prison?"

He looked over at her and laughed. "Hell, no. I wanted to be one of the guys who could put a man like my free-with-his-fists father away a lot sooner. So it was going to be either law or order—and frankly, after three years in the infantry I'd had it with guns. Police work was out."

*Free-with-his-fists father*. "I don't know what to say. It sounds like you had a rough childhood."

"Yeah. You could call it that. You could call it—" But then he shrugged, his jaw tightening. "Never mind. I don't want you to think about that. As a matter of fact, I'm damn sorry I mentioned it."

As if somehow the knowledge soiled her. Juliet bristled. "Noah. Listen, I won't faint if—"

The sound of the envelope ripping open swallowed the last of her words. He pulled out the papers inside and scanned the top one. "The board has a new scoring mechanism that enabled them to get the results back a month early—more in line with other states that generally return theirs in October. If the damn cable company hadn't left us hanging, we'd already have Internet access and I would have known what was going on."

Did he have ice in his veins? "Well, what *is* going on? Did you pass or didn't you?"

He shuffled the sheets in his hands. Then his gaze met hers. "What do you know? It appears I did."

His offhand tone didn't match this kind of news. She had to replay the words in her head. Then ask again, just to be sure. "So you passed?"

"Yeah. I passed."

Juliet stared. "You don't seem all that thrilled," she started, then light dawned. "I guess that means you're not so surprised by the results."

He shrugged, still Mr. Cool. "Not so much. It ends up that I'm pretty good at taking tests."

" 'Not so much!' " She whacked the side of his arm with her hand. " 'Pretty good at taking tests.' " She whacked him again.

When he didn't react, she grabbed his forearms and tried to shake him. "You could show some happiness here," she said, smiling. "Excitement might even be in order. Noah, you did it!"

"You're right. I did."

But his slow-growing grin wasn't good enough for her. "You really did it! Congratulations." The moment called for a hug, and in keeping with her new habit, she went with impulse, throwing her arms around him.

And then it was just as she'd imagined. Her mouth at that smooth spot where chest met shoulder. His sunshine, soap, and sweat smell in her lungs, her tongue . . . her tongue she kept imprisoned behind her teeth, even as his arms came around her in a return embrace. The papers and the envelope fell around their feet.

She was so close she could hear the slam of his heart against his chest. The bubbles were dancing through her blood again, and the woozy was back, but there was nothing girlish inside of her now. Now it was a woman pressed against a strong, virile, healthy young man.

When was the last time she'd been held like this?

"Juliet." Noah whispered the syllables against the top of her head and then let out a soft groan. "Oh, God. *Juliet*."

Her head tipped back to look into his face, to see why he sounded so tortured. His blue eyes were fixed on hers, and the look in them wasn't pained—it was a look that made her hot all over. Her nipples tightened and her thigh muscles clenched. Desire burned across her skin like a hot wind.

She should move away. Cautious Juliet would defuse the moment and then promptly forget it ever happened. But now, now she had that impulsiveness. She was reckless with that burn on her skin and that effervescence in her blood. And she couldn't regret it, didn't want to even worry about it, because she hadn't felt alive like this in years.

His big hands came up to cradle her face as his head lowered. "So you know," he said, his voice whispery-hoarse, his breath warm against her lips. "*Now* I'm excited."

# Four

War does not determine who is right—only who is left.

—BERTRAND RUSSELL

Noah's kiss wasn't tentative or gentle or sweet, but as confident and masculine as the man himself. Against hers, his mouth was hot and hard. His whiskers scratched the skin surrounding Juliet's lips.

*I shouldn't . . .* sailed across her mind, but then fell right over the edge of her consciousness, shoved aside by all things Noah.

His sun-and-man scent.

The breadth of his chest in the circle of her arms.

The warm, sure thrust of his tongue.

She gasped, drawing him farther into her mouth, and his fingers cupping her face tightened, biting into her scalp. It was all so real, so here-and-now, so *corporeal*.

So much different than cold sheets and quiet memories.

She pressed harder against his solid heat, and felt his body shudder. An answering shiver shot down her spine as pleasure softened her knees.

Who could ever want this to stop?

"Juliet? Hello!" The rattle of the front door closing followed the woman's voice. "Juliet?"

Noah jerked back, breaking their embrace. Ducking her head, Juliet put her feet in reverse, too, her hand coming up to cover her burning lips.

"*Juliet*?"

"In here." She coughed to clear her clogged throat, and didn't know whether to curse or bless herself for leaving the door unlocked after retrieving the mail. "The kitchen, Marlys. I'm in the kitchen."

Her husband's dark-haired, twenty-five-year-old daughter entered the room with all the jerky speed and tightly wound energy she brought to every task. "What's up?" She dumped the large cardboard box she was carrying onto the butcher block, heedless of the arrayed cookbooks. Her gaze flicked from Juliet to Noah, who was squatting on the ground to retrieve the scattered papers from the California Bar.

Marlys's lip curled in what was more sneer than smile. "Hey, Private," she said. It was an obvious put-down instead of a personal nickname, and everyone in the room knew it. For whatever reason, early on she'd taken a dislike to the man who did so much for her father. Wayne's death hadn't changed her attitude one whit.

Noah ignored it, as he always did. "Marlys," he said, nodding in her direction as he came to his feet. "I'll talk to you later, Juliet."

"Okay. Later." Her view of his back didn't give a clue as to how he was feeling. Or how she should be feeling now that their scorching moment was over. Or what she should do or say when "later" came about.

Closing her eyes, she rubbed her temples with her fingers.

"You look like crap," Marlys observed, with her usual tact.

Juliet lifted her lashes to stare at her husband's daughter. "Gee, thanks."

The other woman wasn't deterred by her dry tone. "Really. You should try combing your hair and using a little powder. You've got a rat's nest going on there and your face is too pink."

But Juliet had bigger worries than what the kiss had done to her appearance—such as what she was going to do about the kiss. "It'll be simpler if I just wear a sign when I venture out in public. 'Not Looking My Best.' "

"I wouldn't go that far. Frankly, nobody expects widows to be candidates for *InStyle*."

"Right." But at the mention of the magazine, her gaze sharpened on Marlys. With sleek hair and dark eyes, she was gymnast-sized and sprite-tempered. As the owner of a successful boutique in Santa Monica, she made a living out of looking like a fashion layout.

Today, though, she was in boy-styled jeans with rips at the knees and a sweatshirt that read "Bayridge Bengals." "Marlys? Have you been digging into the boxes of your old junior high clothes?"

When she shrugged, the overstretched neckline of her sweatshirt slid to reveal some of her olive-skinned shoulder. "Last night I might have been rummaging through some stuff I dragged down from the attic."

"Oh, Marlys," Juliet said, though she wasn't surprised. The house in Pacific Palisades had belonged, originally, to Wayne's parents. Though the time had felt right for her to move out and leave it to Wayne's daughter, it didn't seem healthy for the younger woman to use her new solitude as an unfettered opportunity to fixate on the past. In the months since the funeral, she'd often found Marlys sifting through cartons of military memorabilia as well as even less worthy flotsam of Weston family life.

Despite Juliet's best efforts, she'd never been close to Marlys. But because of her love for her husband, she couldn't overlook the old clothes or the shadows under his daughter's eyes. "Have you been sleeping?"

Another shrug.

"Maybe you shouldn't be rattling around that big house," Juliet started. "Maybe you should think about sell—"

"No." The word was fierce. "Maybe you can walk away so easily, but I can't. I won't."

*Grrrr*. Juliet wanted to smack her forehead against the nearest countertop. Marlys never once gave her a break. Of course it hadn't been easy for her to leave the house where she'd spent her married life. Of course it hadn't been easy for her to . . .

. . . kiss another man. The moment caught up with her in Technicolor, with surround sound and full tactile memory. Noah's muscles, his heat, his soft groan, and then the taste of his tongue in her mouth. God. *God.* Hardly more than a week after she'd left the house where she'd lived with the husband she still loved, she'd kissed another man.

"By the way, your ex–grief counselor called."

"What?" Juliet blinked, trying to follow Marlys's next thread of conversation.

"That woman you used to see after Dad died. Did you tell her I needed help?" Marlys looked ready to spit fire at the idea.

"What? No, of course not. She has the home number and was probably just checking—"

The other woman cut her off with a slash of her hand. "Yeah, yeah. That's what she said. Checking on you." Marlys leaned over to toy with a tail of denim fringe on the edge of her ripped kneehole, so that her shiny dark hair hid her face. "Did you get anything out of that? The counseling?"

Mercurial was a good way to describe Marlys's moods, and Juliet found her hard to keep up with on her good days. But now, rattled by Noah, rattled by that kiss—*oh, God*—she was struggling more than usual. "The counseling? You want to know about the counseling?"

"Yeah." The dark-haired woman jerked upright and folded her arms over her chest. "Tell me about it."

"I went for just a few weeks," she answered, not sure what information the other woman actually wanted. "It let me know that my feelings were entirely normal."

Feelings like the ones she'd been experiencing lately, Juliet realized. During their last session, her counselor had gone over what to expect in the upcoming months.

Deep loneliness and isolation. Check.

Then a lessening of the heavy grief. Check.

Finally, the renewal of sexual drive.

At the time, that possibility had seemed remote. Due to Wayne's cancer and treatment, the physical side of their marriage had ended long, long before his death. She'd believed her urges in that direction were dead, too.

Okay, she thought, taking a deep breath and letting it out. So what had happened today wasn't crazy or weird or even unexpected. Wayne would be the first one—as a matter of fact, he *had* been the first one. "Juliet," he'd said. "You're too young to have your future end with my life."

But there wasn't room in her heart for anyone else. There wasn't.

"Well, I'm at least as normal as you," Marlys declared.

*Not even close*, Juliet wanted to retort, but she'd managed to play peacemaker for this long so she swallowed the words. "If there's anything I can do . . ."

"It's too late for that, don't you think? With the anniversary of Dad's death coming up, the rumors are swirling again, you know. I hear it at the club, in the shop, around all the old family friends. Deal Breaker. Happy Widow."

"Marlys—"

"If only you'd been there for Dad on the day he died. But I forget where you were again? Oh, yeah, a *spa*."

Spa. How Juliet had come to hate those three letters arranged in that particular order. It had been all over the cable channels. They'd run footage of the place's fancy double doors, zeroing in on the discreet placard that read CELL PHONES OFF BEFORE CROSSING THIS THRESHOLD.

Without thinking, Juliet had complied with that order. So when she returned home to the terrible news, she'd been glowing from a facial and sporting a fresh pedicure.

"Marlys, of course I didn't know what would happen." This wasn't the first time she'd defended herself. But Marlys, the press, and many in her social circle had continued to look on her with suspicion.

"It hasn't helped that you don't talk to your old friends. Aunt Helen said you won't return her calls."

"Aunt Helen" was Helen Novack, a contemporary of Wayne's, someone he'd known since childhood, and who'd never warmed up to Juliet. So Marlys was right, she had been dodging Helen's calls and ignoring others. The "old friends" had been Wayne's old friends and not hers. Without him, would they have anything to talk about? And if they got together, wouldn't the "without him" be just that much more painful?

But the grief counselor had told her she'd have to push herself to be sociable. And while she might not yet be ready for Helen and that circle, she could look at the dinner tomorrow night as practice.

The sense of purpose lifted her mood a little. A dinner party. Tomorrow night. She turned toward her cookbooks.

Marlys's box sat in the way. She slanted the brunette a look. "What *is* this?"

"Showed up at home and addressed to you," Marlys said. "From the publishing house."

"The books." Juliet's mood bobbed higher. "It must be the books."

Ignoring Marlys's blasé shrug, Juliet armed herself with a knife and sliced through the packing tape, anticipation making her breath come faster. Beneath the flaps and a wad of crumpled paper were two stacks of hardback books, their covers gleaming. *General Matters: My Military Life & More,* by General Wayne L. Weston. Juliet stared. Here it was, Wayne's dream.

Here it was, Juliet's hope. Her hope that whatever tarnish their marriage had brought to his reputation would be polished away by his life story in his very own words.

Despite her casual attitude, Marlys crowded in for a look. It was she who reached in to take hold of the top copy to survey the front cover with eager eyes. It was a dark silhouette of a man, the red, white, and blue of the American flag rippling behind him.

Slowly, Juliet reached inside to retrieve her own book. Her palm slid across the sleek front, and then she turned it over. *Wayne.*

It was a wonderful photo of him, black-and-white, which played up his silver hair and dark, watchful eyes to their best advantage. With her forefinger, she traced the edges of his military brush cut and then let it fall to find the curve of his black eyebrows and then the line of his firm lips.

*Oh, Wayne.*

Was it really natural? she wondered to herself. Was it really natural or forgivable, that though her gaze drank in her beloved's face, the rest of her was still humming in reaction to the warm, sexy resilience of another man and the pulse-jittering thrill of his kiss?

Noah gave Marlys plenty of time to clear the premises before heading back across the pool. The general's daughter didn't take rejection well, even though he'd been as tactful as he could in rebuffing the feelers she'd sent out when they'd first met.

She was beautiful in a petite, devilish sort of way, but Noah hadn't been moved by either her lures or her ensuing vitriol when he'd turned his back on her. Marlys was a powder keg and he was careful to keep any sparks away from her.

Even the sparks that had been generated by Juliet's body against his. By his mouth to hers.

The memory caused his pace to quicken as he skirted the pool. That kiss wasn't something he could ignore. He was going to confront Juliet . . . and then follow her lead. Through the kitchen windows, he could see her figure, back turned toward him, and his hands curled inside his pockets.

God knows, it was going to be hard to let her direct their what-came-next discussion. He'd gone back to the guest-house with her high-class scent on his hands and the taste of her hot mouth in his. Hell, she'd sucked on his tongue! The memory of that was enough to have him going hard again as his libido geared up for a second round.

But blowing out a breath, he forced himself to slow his stride and rein in his sex drive. Yeah, he was a man trained for action, but Juliet deserved more from him than his thuggish sexual impulses. She'd seemed to enjoy herself—hell, he thought all over again, she'd sucked on his tongue!—but she was still the officer's wife, the officer's *widow*, and he was still the enlisted guy she'd hired to live across the pool.

He shouldn't presume that anything more would come of this—but he couldn't ignore it either. He had to find out what she was thinking about their kiss.

So he rapped on the French door, then opened it, pausing at the threshold to take in the sight of the sleek fall of fine hair draped against her elegant back. It was a straight swathe the color of the caramel used to cover autumn apples. Today she was in a matching caramel shirt and plain jeans.

"Juliet?" he said softly, even as his inner gangster itched to take what he wanted. His hands would close over her shoulders and spin her to face him so that he could plunder her mouth all over again. From there he'd touch, he'd kiss, he'd taste everything. He could see it all in his head, but he didn't stir a muscle to make it happen.

His body tensed as she remained frozen in place. His voice roughened. "Juliet?"

She didn't turn, just talked, and in a decidedly—deceptively?—cheerful tone. "I heard from Cassandra. She and Nikki can make dinner tomorrow night. Nikki's bringing along her fiancé, Jay, and Cassandra asked if she could tell Gabe—that's the wallpaper guy—that I wanted him to join us as well. That way she can ensure he eats. Apparently she sees herself as his nutrition guru."

"Ah." He didn't know what else his response should be.

"I thought maybe you'd like to come as well."

As Juliet's date? "Sure." Confidence surging, he took a step toward her—

"It will even out the numbers."

—and then halted his forward movement. Shit, there he was again, unsure of himself, and hating every moment of the uncharacteristic hesitance.

So stymied about his next move, he was still standing halfway between the door and Juliet when she at last turned to face him. The jewel-brightness of her blue and green eyes hit him like a one-two punch in the gut. His palm over his heart, he inhaled a hard breath, and then realized his pose mimicked hers. Except her hand was used to hold an open book against her body. *General Matters* by General Wayne L. Weston.

Noah's gaze flicked to the cardboard box behind her. So that was what had brought Marlys to Malibu. Irritating woman. Thanks to her, now he couldn't bring up what had happened in the kitchen, could he?

"So it's here," he said. "Those are your copies?"

She ignored the question. "He wrote about me." Her voice wobbled a little. "He said he would, but I was never sure."

Noah's eyebrows rose. The general had asked her not to read the book in manuscript form, and obviously she'd kept her promise.

"Wayne wrote about the day we met," Juliet continued, "the day we re-met, I should say."

"Page three hundred and forty-three." By the time the

galley form of the manuscript had arrived—the last step before publication—it had been Noah who had checked through each sheet because the general didn't have the energy. " 'She was everything fresh and fine this jaded soldier had forgotten about the world.' "

Juliet gave a little shake of her head. "I can't believe he wrote something so . . . so . . ."

"Sappy?" Noah tempered the word with a little smile. "When it came to you, there wasn't much the general wouldn't do." Or ask of Noah, either.

"It was at my parents' funeral. He was a friend of my father's. I hadn't seen him since I was a kid, but there he was again."

Noah nodded. "He remembered you as that child, but when he saw you at the funeral service . . ."

"I was twenty-two, yet he thought he needed to take care of me." She wore a half-sad smile.

"He fell in love with you," Noah corrected.

"And I'd daydreamed about a handsome prince since childhood. In dress uniform, he was about as close to one as a modern American man could get."

Great. On the one hand there was common-as-dirt Noah, and on the other was a highly decorated, wife-adoring ghost. Why the hell for even two seconds he'd let his imagination run to images of refined Juliet going sweaty skin to sweaty skin with him, he didn't know. For a smart guy, he sure could be as dumb as the next box of rocks.

"What did you think the first time you met me?" she suddenly asked.

His surprise made him step back. "Huh?"

"I don't remember it. Do you?"

Christ, was the question a test? It felt like a test, and hadn't he told her he was such a good taker of them? Now he felt tongue-tied and buffalo-footed, while the man she'd married had written: *She was everything fresh and fine this jaded soldier had forgotten about the world.*

If Noah wanted his tongue in her mouth again—he did—and if he wanted her scent on his hands, on his chest, and every other inch of skin he could manage—he did—then his answer was crucial. Still, his mind was as thick as a custard milkshake and refused to stir.

It was the truth or else risk looking like he suffered from some sort of brain damage. "If I recall correctly, we met on the front porch as you tore out of the house screaming at the top of your lungs while chasing after Marlys's dog with a plastic bag full of dog shit."

As if all the air leaked out of her, she sagged back against the butcher-block table. "Oh, my God. What must you have thought?"

If he hadn't been there to interview for a job that seemed perfect for his circumstances, he probably would have laughed his ass off. "I thought I better not have an accident on the carpet in the master bedroom."

" 'Accident,' " Juliet scoffed. "That dog takes his attitude cue from his owner." She narrowed her eyes at him. "And just in case you think I'm mean—I happen to love dogs."

Noah had had more than one run-in with that unruly canine himself. "I know you're not mean, Juliet. You don't have a mean bone in your body."

Body. See, he shouldn't have said that word, because it put her body in his mind, and he was pretty sure he was wirelessly broadcasting those fantasies he'd been suppressing for longer than he cared to remember. Those fantasies that had come roaring to life along with his hard-on the instant he'd touched his tongue to her bottom lip and felt her mouth opening for him.

Here came a few now . . . Juliet, dressed only in a swimsuit, on that armless chaise lounge beside the pool, her long legs parting to wrap around his hips as he came down over her.

Juliet, wearing those jeans she had on now and nothing else, walking toward where he was sitting on the edge of a bed, the hard nipples of her pale breasts at the perfect height for his mouth.

Juliet, in a hot shower, her naked body obscured by the wavy glass door, then only covered by steam as he opened it to step inside.

In the fantasy, her eyes widened. In the now, they widened, too, and Noah curled his fingers into fists again, trying to keep himself in check. Yeah. He was definitely broadcasting, and it was hard to determine what she thought of the waves he was sending out because though there was a pink flush riding the edge of her cheekbones, she was clutching that book in front of her like a shield.

"Maybe . . ." She cleared her throat. "Maybe that's just what I need."

"What?" His voice cracked like an adolescent's. He cleared his throat, too. Damn. Was she saying that she needed a little flesh-on-flesh time? "What is it you need?"

She blinked at him. "A dog." The "What did you think I meant?" went unspoken, but it was there all the same.

Kee-rist. She was talking about a dog, which meant the person who needed to get something was him. He needed a life. New fantasies. A woman in his bed. Juliet was right, it had been a monastery around his place for too, too long.

"I've gotta go," he said, before he made a further fool of himself. He was at the door when her voice caught him.

"Noah. Are you all right?"

He paused, wrapping his hand around the doorjamb. His gaze took in the pool, and didn't sweep around to her, because he didn't want to tempt himself again. The woman had just received copies of her dead darling's autobiography—*She was everything fresh and fine this jaded soldier had forgotten about the world*—and now wasn't the time for another man to be coming on to her. Still, he had to find out what was going through her mind.

"That should be my question," he said. "I took something that wasn't exactly offered. Are you okay about that?"

"I'm okay."

He hesitated still. Were they talking about the same thing? Because putting himself in her place, he could see that she might be feeling bad, guilty or something, and he hated the idea.

"Look, I have to ask. About what happened, about our, uh, hug. I hope you don't feel, didn't feel . . ." He still couldn't make himself turn around and face her. But he heard her just fine anyway.

"Hmm," she said. Her voice was threaded with gentle amusement. "You're sure you want to know the truth?"

"Sure, I'm sure," he answered, because he suspected he might need to soothe her spirits.

She let a second go by and then she slayed him. "The truth is, Noah, what I felt when I kissed you was horny."

# Five

The hunger for love is much more difficult to remove than the hunger for bread.

—MOTHER TERESA

*The truth is, Noah, what I felt when I kissed you was horny.*

Juliet had said those words, trying to make light of that impromptu embrace in the kitchen. She hadn't wanted Noah to worry that she'd taken it too seriously. But it wasn't possible for her to entirely understand how *he'd* taken it because after her half-laughing remark, he'd made tracks for the guesthouse across the pool.

She'd even wondered if he might not make it back to her place for dinner the following night, but he did, entering through her open back door just as she heard commotion coming from the direction of the front one.

There, she pulled on the doorknob in time to see a man stride around the curve of her walkway, carrying a laughing woman. It was Nikki, and, presumably, her fiancé. Her arms were thrown around his neck, and to go along with his blond good looks the guy wore a grin that declared all was right with his world.

He stopped short when he caught sight of Juliet. His low whistle pierced the air. "I'd recognize those eyes anywhere."

"Well." Made nervous by his intense regard, Juliet rubbed her palms along the skirt of her new, knee-length dress. It was a silky, paisley mix of turquoise, pink, and black, with three-quarter sleeves, a V-neck, and a sash that tied around the empire waistline. Was it too matronly? Too young?

"Come on in." From behind her, Noah's deep voice gave the welcome she'd been too preoccupied to utter. His hand landed on her shoulder and gave it a supportive squeeze.

It helped her find her voice. "Yes. Welcome," Juliet said, stepping aside to let the man—still carrying his fiancée—inside. "Did something happen, Nikki? Are you hurt?"

The woman kicked her legs, bared by a little skirt and ending in a pair of strappy sandals. "Jay likes me in high heels, but he doesn't like me walking in them because I had recent knee surgery. So we've negotiated. I wear, he walks."

He set her gently on her feet. "Oh, yeah, right, as if you don't like your girly shoes just for yourself."

"I like my girly shoes because of what you'll do to get me in them—and then back out again," she retorted, but the hand that moved up to adjust the collar of his shirt was gentle. She patted his cheek with her palm. "Jay Buchanan, meet my sister, Juliet Weston."

Her sister. She was Nikki's sister.

Biologically, yes, they were connected. But she was still cautious about extending that into a relationship. Though what if it could fill these empty, lonely places she'd woken up to find were in her life?

The arrival of an arguing Gabe and Cassandra distracted her from her thoughts. "If you weren't such a flake, you wouldn't have forgotten to feed those wild cats of yours before we left," the dark-haired man said, shaking his head. "Then we wouldn't have had to backtrack, which caused us to be late."

"The cats aren't wild," Cassandra replied. Looking like an earth goddess in a leaf green, off-the-shoulder sweater she'd surely knitted herself, she smiled a greeting at the other two couples.

Gabe barely appeared to register her protest. "And why I had to be the one to pour the food into their bowls and then endure their annoying ankle-winding—"

"Because they miss you, Gabe. They like your attention and you haven't been by in a couple days."

He narrowed his dark eyes at her. "Don't think I don't know what you're doing, Froot Loop."

"And yet you let me do it anyway," she said softly. Then she took him by the shoulders and turned him to face the rest of the party. "Meet the nice people, Gabe. You forgot to say hello when they came into the shop the other day. This is Noah Smith. And this, this is the last of the three sisters. Juliet Weston."

After shaking Noah's hand, he turned to Juliet. When he smiled, he went from good-looking to good-God good-looking. "Three witches, you mean," he corrected, taking her hand in his. "Because it must be some spell that allows all three of you to be so alike . . . and so damn attractive."

Cassandra's eyebrows headed for her hairline. "Gabe? Compliments? And smoothly done at that. I'm shocked."

*Me, too,* Juliet thought. So alike? Yes, she and Nikki had the same dual eye color, but did she and her—okay, use the word—sisters, really have anything more in common?

Again, it was Noah who stepped in to move the evening along. He put his hand on her forearm and drew her away from Gabe. "Drinks, everyone? What can I get for people?"

With Juliet's silent thanks, he continued in that vein, taking on the role of host. Before long he'd provided the beverages and helped her retrieve the hors d'oeuvres. The group gathered near the pool, settling at a table set beneath a radiating patio heater where they could enjoy the last of the sunset view.

"I thought the ocean couldn't look as beautiful as from Jay's beachside house," Nikki said. "But this comes pretty close."

"Oh? You live on the beach?" Juliet asked. "You, too, Cassandra? Gabe?"

Cassandra's hair rippled as she tossed it over her shoulder. "We're canyon dwellers. Gabe and I live in separate houses on his property. It's perfect for Gabe. He has the same seclusion as the most privacy-obsessed celebrity, while I'm close enough to make sure he doesn't turn feral."

Gabe toasted her with his bottle of beer and sent a gleaming smile Juliet's way. "And I'm close enough to make sure she's really as celibate as she claims."

Noah coughed on his latest swallow of Sam Adams.

"Not that I'm surprised, you understand," Gabe continued. "But yes, she is."

"New topic, please," Nikki ordered. "Quick, before the children start squabbling again."

Cassandra straightened in her chair. "Hey, I'm older than you are, little sister. And Juliet—oh."

Juliet looked up from the scrap of cocktail napkin she'd twisted into a small circle and slid onto her left ring finger. Upon moving to Malibu, she'd removed her wedding band and her unadorned hand still looked odd to her. Both her sisters were staring at her fingers as if they looked odd to them, too.

Jay did a fair rendition of the *Twilight Zone* theme. "Do do do do, do do do do."

Puzzled, Juliet glanced over at Noah. He nodded toward Cassandra. "Check out what she's been doing with her napkin."

On the other woman's left thumb was a rolled ring of paper. Juliet's gaze jumped to Nikki. She shook her head. "I have a ring, thank you," she said, flaunting the boulder of an engagement bauble on her left hand. In her right, though, she held out a little snake of paper. "I was thinking maybe a bracelet?"

"No." Juliet frowned. "There's no way."

Cassandra shrugged. "Nikki and I noticed our common quirk when she lived with me after her surgery. Looks like you have it, too, big sis."

"That's not possible . . . is it?" Juliet looked to Noah again.

"If it's a legal question, I'm your man. But genetics? You're going to have to find some other expert."

"Actually," Jay put in, "it's not all so surprising to find commonalities like that among siblings . . . even those who grew up apart. There are dozens of separated sibling studies that support the notion that nature can hold its own against nurture. I notice the way you three smile is the same, too. Starts on the left first, then makes its way to the other side."

Nikki swung her napkin snake in little circles. "Though I hate to swell his already oversized and too-handsome head, he's probably right. He edits a magazine, and so vast quantities of information cross his desk every day. Some time you should ask him about weasels."

Bemused, Juliet's gaze drifted around the circle of people. The men had common qualities, too: They looked to be close in age and were all attractive examples of their gender. But nothing more. And that's how it had been for her and every other woman—every other person—since her parents had died. There'd been no one with whom she shared a genetic link.

Now, according to Jay, she smiled like her sisters. She knew she played with napkins like her sisters, too. Were these signs that she should let them into her life?

Unsettled and still undecided, she excused herself and hurried into the kitchen to finish the dinner preparations. A few seconds later she felt another presence behind her. "Noah, would you mind—"

"He was out of his seat by the time you were two steps toward the kitchen," Nikki said. "But I wrestled him back to his chair by playing the professional chef card."

Turning, Juliet grimaced. "Yikes. I didn't think about that when I asked you to dinner tonight."

"No worries. It smells terrific." She hesitated, then took a breath and rushed on. "I came inside because I want to talk to you about something."

"What?"

Nikki glanced over her shoulder to where the others

were gathered on the patio, then looked back, her expression serious. "I want you to be careful with Cassandra."

Juliet frowned. "Be careful with her how?"

"Be careful with her feelings, with her dream."

" 'Her dream'?"

Nikki pulled a stool away from the butcher-block island and dropped onto it. "Argh. I'm not good at this touchy-feely girl-talk stuff."

"What dream are you talking about?"

"When you were a kid, did you sometimes make up wild fantasies for yourself? You know, like pretending you were really the progeny of a roguish pirate and a runaway princess?"

Juliet thought of herself at thirteen, of how she'd met a dashing man in uniform and given her heart to him. She smiled. "I had a fancy or two."

Nikki's voice lowered and she leaned toward Juliet. "Well, this is Cassandra's fancy. The dream she's had for as long as she can remember. Her mother had always told her she was donor-inseminated and that big old marshmallow heart of Cassandra's has caused her to wonder her entire life about siblings that she could meet and make a family with."

"Nikki—"

"Hear me out. I'm just asking that if you're not interested in forging anything with us, if your curiosity is satisfied tonight and from now on you'll only want to exchange the occasional Christmas card, that you'll let our sister down easy."

"Nikki—"

"Just be gentle, okay?" The blue and green eyes so like Juliet's own held her gaze. "Be gentle with her heart. Like I said, it's soft and it's bigger than that ocean out there and she cares too much, too fast."

Juliet stared at the younger woman, her own heart feeling too big for her chest. If nothing else had swayed her to get to know these two, then that impassioned little speech would have done the trick. This is what sisters could give to each other, Juliet thought. Loyalty. Understanding. Caring.

She wanted that, she decided. She wanted that bond with them.

Nikki spoke once again, her voice hoarse. "Please." It was easy to see she wasn't used to asking anyone for anything. "Please be careful with Cassandra."

Smiling a little, Juliet tilted her head. "And not with you?"

The youngest sister waved the concern away with a swipe of her hand. "I can take care of myself."

"Now where have I heard that before, cookie?" Jay was suddenly behind his fiancée, and his fingers sifted through the wavy tangle of her sun-streaked brown hair.

At his touch, Nikki looked up with a glowing smile that caused Juliet's chest to ache. Maybe it did something to Jay's, too, because he bent down to press an affectionate, but prolonged kiss on the mouth of the woman he was engaged to marry.

Juliet didn't look away. It was so tender—and so telling. Another rustle of movement caused her gaze to shift. Noah filled the doorway and maybe the kiss affected him, too, because he was staring at Juliet's lips. They tingled and her skin flushed, as she remembered their embrace the day before. Noah's heat. The bite of his fingers and the thrust of his tongue.

Jay's mouth had lifted from Nikki's now, but he was murmuring something to her. *Oh, yes*, Juliet thought. How tender and how telling.

And the bittersweet truth that it told was this: As much as a relationship with her sisters might come to mean to her, she knew now it wouldn't fill every empty space. It couldn't meet every need in her life.

Noah decided the evening was a success. Juliet's vegetarian lasagna had been enjoyed by all—even Gabe, who was a strictly red meat man, appeared to like it—and after serving dessert, it was evident as they sat around the dining room table that Juliet was more relaxed and happy than he'd maybe ever seen her.

That should have made him happy, too, right? The fact was, he'd been glad for this further opportunity to study Juliet's sisters—a claim that he really couldn't harbor a doubt about any longer—and now he knew he liked Cassandra and Nikki. They were smart and pretty and the men they'd brought with them tonight were the kind he didn't mind having beers with.

He particularly liked the engaged one, Jay.

Regarding Gabe—well, the jury was still out there, to be honest. Not that he triggered Noah's streetwise sixth sense, but he couldn't forget how Gabe had held Juliet's hand a beat too long upon meeting her.

"So damn attractive," he'd told her. Well, damn him. He shot the guy a dark look as Gabe leaned over to murmur something for Juliet's ears only.

The intimacy of their positions led Noah's mind straight back to the kiss he'd shared with her in her kitchen. *The truth is, Noah, what I felt when I kissed you was horny.* She'd said that. Elegant Juliet Weston had said "horny" with a little laugh in her voice that he suspected was her small payback for the audacity he'd shown by turning her friendly hug into a fiery interlude.

But now he wondered . . . Was she really horny? And would Gabe try to take advantage of that?

But Noah was distracted from the sour thought as someone else asked him a question and the conversation moved to old surf movies and the part Malibu had played in their making. From there conversation turned to books. After that, Noah helped Juliet clear the dessert plates then serve more coffee. His tension eased away as she sent him a private smile in thanks and resettled in the seat beside his.

With a clack, Jay Buchanan placed his coffee cup on its saucer, and then caught everyone's attention by clearing his throat. "Juliet, there's another book I'd like to discuss," he said. "Your late husband's autobiography."

Her eyes widened and Noah's tension returned. Oh, hell. Not once had the general come up in conversation and he'd thought that omission had been good for Juliet, too. She needed to be more than a widow. He wanted her to think of herself as more than a widow.

"What about it?" Juliet asked. Her fingers started toying with the cloth napkin in her lap. Not paper this time, so there wouldn't be any impromptu jewelry, but that didn't stop her from worrying the fabric. "It's coming out next month."

"I know. I saw an advanced reader's copy bouncing around my magazine's offices."

Juliet's gaze dashed around the table. "No one mentioned . . . I wasn't completely certain any of you knew . . ."

Cassandra smiled. "Those cursed tubes of the Internet. Nobody has privacy anymore."

Nikki's voice was soft. "We're very sorry for your loss."

Across the table from Noah, Gabe shifted in his chair. "Uh, fill me in?"

"Oh." Cassandra squirmed in hers. "I guess I didn't tell you."

"I guess not. Tell me what?"

"Well, uh . . ." Cassandra looked to Nikki in mute appeal, and then gave a little shrug. "Juliet's husband died about a year ago, and, um . . ."

An awkward silence descended over the table. Cassandra tried again. "And, um, it must have been an especially tough time for Juliet because . . ." She glanced at her newfound sister and then back at Gabe, obviously uncomfortable with the subject matter. "Uh, because the press got involved and, they, um . . ."

Juliet jumped to her feet, bumping the table to set the cups rattling against their saucers. "They called me the Happy Widow," she said, her voice tight.

Cassandra reached across the table. "Juliet—"

"And before that," she told Gabe, ignoring the other woman, "the press called me the Deal Breaker. So you can take your pick. Or use both. I really couldn't care less."

Noah stared at her in surprise, noting the bright color in her cheeks and the telltale tension in her posture. Until this moment, she'd kept her feelings about those nasty nicknames buried beneath what must have been a blanket of snow. Now, however, she was experiencing a major meltdown. He rose, a wary eye on her. "Juliet . . ."

She ignored him, too. "Excuse me," she said to the table at large as she grabbed a half-empty wine bottle by the neck. "And I'm sorry," she added as she rushed for the kitchen.

Noah got to her first. "Whoa, whoa." Under his hands, her shoulders were stiff. "You don't have to apologize to anyone. Not for anything."

Her fingers white-knuckled the wine bottle. "Not even to my—these two women who I'm sure are less than thrilled to find themselves related to an infamous widow?"

He squeezed her shoulders. "Juliet . . ."

"Face it, Noah. It's ugly. Ugly and infuriating. I didn't deserve it. Wayne deserved better."

Now Cassandra rose. "Nothing about you is ugly. We don't think anything like that."

On the other side of the table, Nikki glared at Jay. "Look at what you've done. This is all your fault."

"Hey—"

"If you hadn't decided to bring up the book—"

"*Hey*—"

"Would someone please explain to me what's going on?" Gabe asked again.

Crossing her arms over her chest, Cassandra shot Jay her own hostile look. "Ask Big Mouth over there."

He appeared wounded. "You're usually on my side, Cassandra."

"You're usually not so oafish."

"Would someone please explain—"

"Fine." Jay looked over at Gabe. "Juliet's husband? He was General Wayne Weston."

"Ah. *Aaah.*" The dark-haired man nodded, as if understanding was dawning.

"That's right," Jay nodded back. "You remember now. They called her the Deal Breaker when they married."

Flames shot from Nikki's two-toned eyes. "Did you have to say that stupid name again, Jay?"

"It's not her fault, of course," the man continued. "Though that Happy Widow claim was even worse."

Nikki and Cassandra griped together. "*Jay*!"

"Jeesh." He held up both hands. "It's not my fault either. I'm just laying out the facts. You girls are so touchy."

The two women met each other's gazes. "He called us girls," Nikki said.

Cassandra waved her on with a sweep of her hand. "You're engaged to him, so I'll let you kill him."

Jay leaned away from the table as his fiancée grabbed up a stray fork.

"Good God," Gabe muttered. "I think I'd rather be spending the evening with Cassandra's cats."

And with that Juliet started to laugh. It bubbled out of her throat and even made its way past the hand she clapped over her mouth. The brewing argument assassination subsided as all gazes turned on her.

Nikki's fork clattered to the tabletop. "What's so funny?" she asked, her voice cautious.

Temper apparently neutralized, Juliet stepped away from Noah's hands and dropped back into her seat, still laughing. Then she tilted her head and took a healthy swallow from the bottle of wine clutched in her fist. She wiped an errant drop off her lower lip with the back of her hand. "You know what?" A smile played around her mouth. "This is the closest I've ever been to a family argument."

Nikki grinned back. "Yeah."

"Yeah." Cassandra's smile was just the same and then

her gaze relighted on Jay. "And it's even better that the three sisters can all blame it on the same dumb guy."

Beleaguered Jay Buchanan didn't share the joy. Maybe he was still reeling from his near brush with death. "I think we men should do the dishes while the"—he paused—"*women* drink more wine."

And with that, the XY chromosomes beat a hasty retreat from the dining room.

Weathering that storm seemed to put the sisters at complete ease with each other, Noah decided as the clean-up wound down. Well, that and another bottle or two of vino. But it didn't take a genius to realize that Juliet had held some concerns about how Nikki and Cassandra might regard her unwarranted notoriety. The fact that they already knew of it and had actually attacked one of their own for introducing the topic, obviously put the hostess in a celebratory mood.

A little later, the celebratory mood called for another pot of decaf coffee. A slightly tipsy Juliet managed to grind the beans and start the maker, but then she was called out onto the patio where her sisters and Jay and Gabe were enjoying the view by moonlight. Noah watched her unsteady walk and smiled to himself. The fresh air would be good for her.

The whole evening had been good for her.

He was collecting the last of the items on the dining room table when he heard Gabe and Juliet's voices drifting through the open window. He couldn't see them from where he stood, but the quiet tone of the conversation told him they'd wandered away from the others. Just the two of them. Alone.

"So," Gabe was saying. "A widow."

"That's right."

"I . . ." He cleared his throat. "I lost my wife three years ago."

"Oh." Juliet said, and Noah could hear the surprised sadness in her voice. "I'm sorry."

"Yeah. Me, too." Gabe's voice lowered. "I know it's tough."

"But it gets easier?" The note of hope sliced through Noah's gut.

"I'll let you know," Gabe answered. "I haven't figured that out yet." There was a moment of silence, and then he went on. "It was a car accident. Sudden."

Juliet's voice was a whisper. "Wayne suffered for a long time. Knowing his pain is over . . . that makes it more bearable."

"But it doesn't take the loneliness away."

"No. And now I find myself wanting, actually craving—God." She broke off and embarrassment was clear in her voice. "Never mind. Obviously I've had way too much to drink."

"Way too much to drink because . . . ?"

"Because I must be drunk if I even started such a conversation. Forget I said anything."

"But so far it hasn't been much of a conversation at all," the other man pointed out. "Let me guess, though. You find yourself wanting, craving—well, let's call it 'contact.' Touch. Skin."

Noah's senses went on high alert. Even through the walls and the darkness, he could hear the guilty catch of Juliet's breath. He imagined there was a flush rising on her cheeks, too, and it was the warmth of it that was releasing a tantalizing note of her classy perfume into the night air.

"That's it exactly," Juliet confessed, her voice still low. "You, too?"

"Yeah. I've had my moments. My advice—don't beat yourself up about it. We're still human, after all." Gabe hesitated. "But, Juliet, if that little itch . . . that is, if you need . . ."

Shit. Noah's body went rigid. What was the bastard about to offer? And how quick could he get through the window and introduce Gabe to his fist? He was inches from the screen when Cassandra's voice halted his forward momentum.

"Gabe? Oh, Gabe?" she called from across the patio. "I just spotted a falling star. I'm wishing something for you."

"Froot Loop, didn't anyone ever tell you to be careful what you wish for?" As he spoke, his voice drifted away from the window and in the direction of Cassandra. "My heart's desire is to get you out of my hair, but I can't ask you to wish yourself right out of Malibu."

In what appeared to be their usual style, the two traded insults that Noah barely registered. His focus, his thoughts, were on Juliet, standing just a few inches of plaster and insulation and stucco away. He knew she was still there, he could still smell her perfume and still sense her confused emotions.

She needed, wanted, *craved* contact. Skin. Touch.

Was that true? In his pocket, his cell phone vibrated, and Noah absently pulled it free. Was Juliet really itching?

*The truth is, Noah, what I felt when I kissed you was horny.*

Well, if that was the case, then the platonic hired help from across the pool had just added a new task to his mission. Because for damn sure the one that was going to be doing the scratching would be nobody other than Noah.

# Six

War is the only game in which it doesn't pay to have the home-court advantage.

—DICK MOTTA

Marlys wound through the hills above Malibu. Her dog, Blackie, part black lab, part who-knew-what-else, had his head out the passenger window and was drinking in the morning air with a toothy grin on his face.

At least one of them was in a good mood.

In the trunk of her Miata was another package for Juliet with the publisher's return address in the upper left. Marlys had already placed a call to the Big Apple that morning and had been polite but icy when informing them that her father's wife had had a change of residence. Her tone had gotten her through to her father's editor, who had blah-blah-blahed an apology followed by a promise to take permanent note of the information. So this should be the last occasion that Marlys was forced to play delivery chick.

And Marlys could hope that keeping clear of Juliet would mean she'd be freed from the acid bitterness that welled in her belly every time she came in contact with the other woman. The knowledge that marrying his second wife had dirtied the general's reputation continued to fester inside the general's daughter. However, if Juliet stayed in hiding here in the hills of Malibu, maybe Marlys could let go of her—yeah, she knew it—sometimes juvenile resentment.

Her foot tapped the brake as she caught sight of the house. The garage door was closed, but a mean-looking motorcycle was parked in the drive. *Huh?*

Instead of zipping in beside it, she made a more cautious and uncharacteristic choice. She parked the Miata against the curb across the street.

But Blackie, being Blackie, didn't curb his reckless impulses. The minute she opened her door, he shouldered past her hip and dashed out and up the street at a four-legged lope.

"Damn." She didn't even try calling back the dog. From experience, she knew that would only spur him on. The animal was so focused on his own selfish concerns, he didn't care a whit about pleasing the human who fed, watered, and walked him.

Knowing he'd eventually wander back, she popped the trunk and tucked the thick package under her arm. With a last curious once-over of the motorcycle, she headed along Juliet's curved, lushly landscaped walkway.

Rounding a corner, she halted at the bottom of the graduated porch steps. On the white wooden bench near the front door, a man was sleeping. He wore battered blue jeans, a white T-shirt, and black motorcycle boots. His long legs were draped over the far arm of the bench and a leather jacket that looked like it had been run over a time or two was bunched under his head as a pillow. In contrast to the rest of his Hells Angel persona, his hair was cropped fairly close to his head and was matched in color by the black stubby lashes that rested against his high-cheekboned, very tanned face.

A burn started bubbling in her belly. Had Juliet gone from Marlys's war hero father to men who looked like they sold drugs on East L.A. street corners?

Perhaps her outrage made a sound, because the stranger suddenly woke. His lashes lifted in a beat, their color a cold, alert silver that immediately focused on her face. She'd seen only one other man come awake with just that same instant awareness.

The comparison to her father pissed her off. "Who the hell are you?" she demanded.

With a lazy movement belied by the sharpness of his gaze, he sat up. With his scarred boots planted firmly on the flagstone porch, he tilted his head and took his time taking her in. "What mushroom did you stroll out from under?"

Marlys narrowed her eyes. "I'm short, not some stupid troll."

He shook his head. "It's fairies, not trolls, who use mushrooms for umbrellas." Lifting his face, he squinted up at the sky. "But I don't see any clouds."

"Yeah? Well I'm about to rain on your parade, buddy. What the hell are you doing here? Should I be calling the cops?" For some stupid reason, it now irked her even more to think that this . . . this darkly handsome guy might be linked to Juliet.

"I'm here to meet someone. Arrived early."

Hah. So he *was* linked to Juliet. And didn't that just show how shallow the other woman was? She was a widow, for God's sake, and she had no business hooking up with a man as gorgeous as this. Sex appeal clung to him as closely as that T-shirt hugged his ripped chest.

Not that she'd noticed.

"Are you sure you have the right house?" she asked, freeze-drying the edges of her voice.

He shrugged, then craned his neck to glance at the address marker posted on the wall behind him. "This is the number my friend gave me when I called him last night. Noah lives here with a lady. Is that lady you?"

Marlys bristled. She couldn't help it. Everything about this man, his lazy posture, his cool eyes, his hot body, the whole package rubbed her the wrong way, as if she was a cat being petted from tail to ears. "Noah doesn't 'live' with my . . . my stepmother." She never referred to Juliet in that manner, she'd never thought of her as a maternal figure, but she kind of liked the idea of giving the leggy blonde an older, not to mention evil, image.

Bad Marlys.

The Hells Angel's eyebrows rose. "Ah. That explains the brat part."

"Brat?" Marlys echoed, offended. She'd been called a lot of things in her time, but nothing so childish as brat. What a jerk. She straightened her spine and threw out her A-and-a half cups. "I might be the size of a kid, but I'll have you know I'm twenty-five years old."

One side of his mouth kicked up. "Sorry. Didn't mean to imply you needed a babysitter. But if Juliet Weston is your stepmama, then you've got to be the general's daughter. I meant Army brat."

"Oh." Army brat. A soft sense of nostalgia bloomed in her chest. That's what she'd been a long time ago. Until she was twelve years old and her mother had tired of military life and divorced her dad.

The motorcycle man was looking at her like he could see every thought in her head. Marlys prided herself on her tough exterior, so the idea he found her transparent incensed her all over again. "Did you say you had business here?"

"I have some time off. Thought I'd find myself a fairy whose wings could use a tug or two."

She rolled her eyes. "You tug the tail of a puppy. You strip the wings off a butterfly."

His smile was as lazy and slow as every other move he'd

made. "Strip? When I get you naked, I promise I'll leave the wings just as they are."

*Strip. Naked.* Marlys's insides heated again. But it wasn't that bitter burn she'd become familiar with. Not that she'd let him see that his flirtation was getting to her, not when, dressed in a long-sleeved T-shirt and a pair of old jeans, it had to be a knee-jerk reaction he had to women, any woman, not particularly her. She slammed her hand on her hip. "Give me a break. That kind of line might work in a biker bar, but around here—"

She yelped as her feet were swept from beneath her. She found herself up in the air—and, no fairy wings, damn it—then down, painfully, on her ass. Blackie—selfish, unrepentant, and wiggling with doggy delight—breezed up the steps, then back down, stepping on her hair as he circled her prone, breathless form.

"Sit." The rough order from the man on the porch had Marlys struggling to obey. "*Stay*."

Blackie plopped down. Froze.

In the same position, she and the dog looked at each other with astonishment. It's why she didn't see the biker guy move down the stairs. He was quick for a lazy man.

"Are you all right?" He lifted her to her feet with big palms beneath her elbows. His hands ran down the cotton knit of her shirt to her wrists, then transferred to her waist to cop a feel along the denim covering her hips.

"Hey!" she snapped, stepping back.

"Just checking for injuries," he said, giving her an unrepentant smile.

She scowled, because every inch he'd touched was tingling, even through 100 percent cotton fibers. "You should be checking the dog," she said, glaring at Blackie, who, miracle of miracles, was still down on his haunches. "Because there's a rolled-up newspaper with his name on it."

"Jesus." The stranger frowned. "Don't hit the dog."

A flush shot over Marlys's face. She wasn't perfect by

any means, she knew that, but she'd never actually strike Blackie. It mortified her that the man would think it. It mortified her that she cared what the man would think.

"He's my dog," she mumbled, looking down at her feet. Good Lord, she was wearing her Keds from seventh grade. "I'll do what I want."

"He needs some discipline," the man advised. "Enroll him in obedience school."

"We're kind of free spirits, Blackie and I," she said, reaching out to stroke the dog's head. Blackie whined.

"I get it now." The Hells Angel crossed his arms over his chest. "You're both spoiled."

"That's *not* what I said."

The silvery eyes of his had warmed up. Apparently she amused him. "The principles are easy. Let him know what to expect. Reward the behavior you want, and when he crosses the line, withdraw your attention. A little time locked outside and he'll come around."

"I'm not sure Blackie gives a flying fig about my attention."

"Beautiful fairy like yourself? Any male would be ready to knock himself out for you."

Marlys cast him a look through her eyelashes. All right, she was human, wasn't she? And when a man this good looking called her beautiful—even when wearing her junior high Keds—it wasn't a crime to be flattered. Or tempted.

Didn't he imply he was going to be around for a while? With the foul mood she'd been in lately, she could use a distraction, so maybe a flirtation—or more—wouldn't be such a bad idea.

Then she remembered. This particular temptation was here at *Juliet's* house, a place she'd been looking forward to avoiding.

"Where is my evil stepmother anyway?"

Motorcycle man shrugged. "I told you I arrived early. Noah's out, she's out, I don't know where either is."

She guessed she should be grateful he hadn't broken into the place.

"I'm Dean Long, by the way." He stretched his hand toward her.

Without thinking, Marlys put her palm against his.

*Zap.*

Electricity shot to her elbow as her bare flesh met his. Her gaze jumped upward to clash with his surprised silver eyes.

"Wow," he said.

She yanked her hand away. "It's the crisp October air."

His smile dawned slowly. "Yeah, must be about seventy-five, seventy-eight degrees out here."

Oh, what the hell. She found herself smiling back and enjoying the exhilarating feel of her blood zipping through her body. "Like I said, crisp."

"Mmm-hmm. Snap, crackle, pop." The flirtation in his eyes heated to seduction. "I don't know your name."

"Marlys." She took a step back, and bumped into Blackie. He whined, and her fingers stroked the fur on the top of his head. "Marlys Weston."

Dean watched her retreat a few feet more, Blackie pressed to her thigh. "Are you going to come back and see me again while I'm here, Marlys Weston?"

"I think I'm going to have to," she heard herself murmur, then she turned like a coward and hightailed it to her car.

Once there, though, she realized she'd only been telling the truth. She still had Juliet's package.

Noah ran across Juliet at Zuma, the two-mile stretch of sand situated at Malibu's northern end. It was the kind of beach that symbolized California. The hundred yards from parking lot to waves were strung with dozens of volleyball courts and along the horizontal stretch lifeguard towers squatted like giant toddlers hunkered over plastic pails.

Whether it was thanks to fate, or instinct, or just dumb luck, his eye had caught on her car in the near-empty lot as he cruised along the Pacific Coast Highway. Though he knew Dean was waiting for him at the house, Noah hadn't hesitated to turn off PCH and into the parking lot at the next opportunity.

He braked his truck beside Juliet's Mercedes and then trudged through the sand in the direction of her solitary figure. She didn't move or shift her gaze from the horizon across the water, even as two bright yellow lifeguard vehicles trundled past with rescue surfboards strapped to their racks.

From twenty feet she turned her head and looked at him. The breeze off the ocean had dashed pink color against her cheeks and onto the tip of her elegant nose. It had made her mouth rosy, too.

The mouth he'd kissed.

The mouth of the woman who last night had confessed her longing for a man's touch.

He stumbled on nothing, tripping over his own feet like a skid row wino. One of the lifeguard trucks slowed beside him. "You okay, pal?" the driver called out, lifting his Ray-Bans to scrutinize Noah's face.

"Fine," he said, waving with the hope the gesture would be enough. Sure, he was publicly intoxicated, but he didn't feel like explaining that he was drunk on memories of those reddened lips and that beautiful woman in his arms.

Her hair had smelled sweet and the smooth strands had slid against his cheek like water. She'd looked up when he'd groaned her name and without thinking, without weighing, measuring, worrying, he'd taken her mouth and given back the kiss of a starving man.

He wanted that again. He wanted to be the one who assuaged her need—"craving"—for skin. Contact. Touch.

The lifeguard glanced over his shoulder and took in the focus of Noah's attention. Juliet was facing the men now, her hands stuffed in her pants' pockets, her jeans stuffed in a pair of knee-length sheepskin boots. A long-sleeved white T-shirt clung to her slender frame.

"Ah," the lifeguard said, with a grin, as the truck started moving again. "Break a leg, buddy."

But nobody was going to get hurt, Noah assured himself, as he continued toward Juliet. This was about helping, not hurting. With several inches still between them, he halted.

She spoke first. "What are you doing here?"

"I . . ." Well, hell. He hadn't thought it through that far. He'd spotted her car and formed a plan that only went so far as finding her. Throwing her down in the sand and having sex in the surf like the famous scene in *From Here to Eternity* wasn't suitable for someone like the high-class blonde now staring him down.

He shoved his hands in his pockets to disguise the way his cock had already warmed up to the idea and tried shrugging away his uneasiness. He liked women. Women liked him. Before now, he would have claimed to know all the steps to the dance and how to easily flow from one to the other until two bodies went from the first moves of foreplay to the last throes of a satisfying fuck.

But this was Juliet. And from that night he'd rushed naked into her kitchen, nothing between them had been easy.

"Noah?"

Since he didn't have an answer, he asked his own questions. "Are you all right? What are you doing out here?"

She swung back to gaze at the ocean. Her profile was so damn classically pure it made his still-stiff cock ache. The banner the breeze made of her caramel hair had his palm itching to fist his hand in the stuff and draw her close enough to once again heat those reddened lips.

"I need to take care of Wayne's ashes," Juliet said. "And here might be the right place for them."

Cold dashed over Noah's libido like a winter wave. Oh, Christ, he thought, wanting to kick his own ass to hell and back. Here he'd been certain she was considering her next move to satisfy her skin craving when instead she was contemplating what to do with her dead husband's remains.

"Insensitive jerk," he muttered, cursing that sexual thug inside himself.

Juliet frowned at him. "Noah? Are *you* all right?"

"Yeah. Fine." *Just moving my brain back from my little head to the big one.* "So, about the general's ashes . . . ?"

"Maybe this is their right resting place."

As usual, she'd been pale but composed on the day he'd accompanied her to meet with the funeral director. Juliet had made all the arrangements according to her husband's wishes. Marlys had been there, too, her gaze never lingering long on anything or anyone. The only time the general's daughter had spoken was to request she be given some of her father's ashes in a tear-shaped silver pendant—though Noah had never seen her with it since.

Maybe his thoughts of the younger woman transferred to Juliet. "I thought Marlys might have an opinion, but she says she doesn't want anything to do with it."

"You should decide for yourself."

"That's what I was thinking." Juliet turned to watch another wave wash in. "Here is pretty."

"Here is pretty," he agreed. "It's quiet now, on a weekday autumn morning, but in the summer it will be crowded with people. Volleyball players, surfers, bodyboarders."

"Kids," Juliet said, her voice so quiet it was nearly drowned by the crescendo of the latest wave. "Children playing in the sand and dipping their toes in the water."

Children. God, that was something that had died for her, too, hadn't it? Noah had never considered that she and her husband might have wanted a family, but from that wounded expression on her face, it looked as if she believed there were no green-eyed, blue-eyed babies in her future.

For himself, he'd never given the next generation much thought, but it seemed like a damn shame to him now, no silky-haired towheads trailing like baby ducks after their lovely mama. Clearing his throat, he pressed the heel of his hand into his chest.

"In Iraq," he started, driven to redirect the conversation with the first thing that came into his head, "there are soccer fields in the middle of the cemeteries. Families picnic there, too. It sounds weird, but I liked it. Those that had gone before were part of what was going on now."

"Wayne would like that, too." Juliet sank into the soft sand and drew up her knees to wrap her arms around them. "He'd want to be part of where people are living and laughing and enjoying nature. That works, I think."

Noah joined her and they sat in a silence almost as companionable as they had once been. Before he'd kissed her.

A better man would regret that too-brief embrace. But a childhood when hunger gnawed at his belly more often than not had trained him to snatch the goodies whenever he could. A breeze kicked up and caught Juliet's hair, its ends flying against his face.

He let them tickle his skin. He let them tickle his libido to life, too, as he imagined himself twisting his fingers in her hair and bringing that soft mouth toward his so he might kiss the sadness from her face. He'd kiss her, hold her, run his hands over all that smooth skin and those slender curves until she didn't remember anything, anyone but him.

Everything but the two of them would be taken out to sea on the waves of what he wanted from her—what he had wanted for years but had made do instead with other kisses, other curves, other faces and skin. He'd wallowed in other perfumes to cover his desire for the only one that called to him.

She wanted touch and he wanted to touch. Couldn't it be as simple as that? For as short as it lasted?

"Tell me about Iraq."

The sound of her voice jerked him from his thoughts. "What?"

She held her hair back with her hand and gazed at him with that unbalancing combination of blue and green. "Death letters. Cemeteries. I feel bad. I've never asked you about your experiences as a soldier."

"You were dealing with your husband's situation," Noah responded. "That was enough."

"But not now. Not anymore."

Now she needed more?

Contact. Touch. Skin.

"Juliet . . ."

"Tell me, Noah."

He didn't tell anyone. There hadn't been anyone to tell. His mother never left forwarding addresses and his correspondence to the old man had started and ended with that stupid-ass missive he'd written but which never had to be mailed.

Except she didn't look as if she was ready to let it go. So what the hell? "It was boring most of the time," he said. "It was scary as shit some of the time. I was never so glad in my life as when we got on the bus that would take us out of Iraq to the airport in Kuwait. To be honest, I was scared as shit then, too, because there were a hundred stories around the sandbox of guys who bought it with leave orders in their pocket or who were blown up the day before they were due to depart the theater for good."

So there it was. He hadn't been any big war hero like the general. For four years—the last one a tour in Iraq—he'd been an everyday grunt with a job he'd signed on for without thinking much about what it entailed. An ordinary grunt who'd learned right quick that there wasn't the whiff of a death wish in his body, despite the adrenaline that flooded him during dozens of night missions. Despite the many times they rode out on the Strykers with "Get some!" still hoarse in their throats and the beat of apocalyptic heavy metal music still ringing in their ears.

He thought of his buddy Dean's reckless grin and the angry red shrapnel scars on his sergeant's neck. He remembered Tim, "Tiny Tim," the kid from Tacoma and his roommate at the FOB, whose scars now cut across his forehead and ran behind his skull and who couldn't grin at all anymore.

Juliet's eyes scanned his face. "You weren't hurt?"

"No," he murmured, his gaze on the Pacific, but his mind back at the hospital and the way Tim's hands—the ones Noah'd seen grasping an iPod, a Gatorade, a girlie magazine—were now curled tightly toward his wrists like the seashells an uninjured, lucky SOB like Noah might come across on a beautiful California beach.

Juliet touched his arm, her fingers cold, her voice insistent. "You're sure you weren't hurt?"

"Of course not. I'm here, aren't I?" He smiled down at her, at that perfect oval of her face, her caramel hair, her leaf-and-sky eyes. Nothing should touch that, he thought with sudden conviction, damning himself for telling her anything about war. He doubted the general ever had, and like him, Noah didn't want anything unpleasant to touch her.

"Noah?" she questioned again.

But despite what he wanted, he felt his smile die and he heard himself start talking, as if she'd ripped off a scab with just his name on her lips, with just that sensation of her fingertips against his arm. He found himself telling her that while he was unhurt, that his friend Tim—his brother in arms—would never walk or talk or see again. He told her that an IED had taken away everything but Tim's capacity to breathe, so he lay in a hospital bed, a husk of the man he'd been. Noah spilled about Walter Reed Hospital and the guys he'd seen in the hallways when he'd gone to visit Tim—men with prosthetic arms or prosthetic legs or men with prosthetic arms *and* legs.

Then, appalled at all that he'd revealed, appalled at the emotion he saw in her eyes, he jumped up. His feet stumbled over nothing again.

"I've got to go," he muttered, already backing away from all the angst he'd laid at her feet. Christ! What was wrong with him? This wasn't the kind of contact he'd wanted to make with Juliet. Not this kind of touch.

He hadn't wanted this kind of closeness at all.

Love is friendship set on fire.

—JEREMY TAYLOR

It was Knitters' Night at Malibu & Ewe, and Juliet was dropping by the shop again, this time fully aware of what—who—she'd find inside. Her sisters.

But it was Noah on her mind. He'd done so many things for her over the past years. Even when Wayne was still alive, she remembered Noah arriving on scene as she struggled to lift a flat of pansies from the trunk of her car. On another occasion, he'd laughed at the crooked result of her picture-hanging attempt and taken the hammer out of her hand to line the frame straight on the hallway wall.

For such a long time, she'd merely considered him her husband's helper, another set of hands, a better eye than her own. But now . . .

Now she was seeing him as more—as a man. A complex man—an attorney, a soldier, someone who overcame a tough childhood with a compassionate soul still intact. When her very own dinner party had hit some snags just days before, it was Noah who had stepped in to smooth and soothe.

As penance for her previous blindness, or at the very least to show him her gratitude for how he'd helped during the party, she wanted to give back something in return. She hoped Cassandra and Nikki could help her brainstorm a suitable gift.

The door to the shop was half open, so she slipped in without a sound. It was not yet 7 P.M., but Cassandra was ready for the knitting group. The lights were blazing, Juliet could smell coffee brewing, and on a small table sat sweating bottles of water and trays of baked goods.

But at the register, the shop owner was cursing. "Nikki, can you give me a hand?" she called out after another string of frustrated swear words.

From somewhere unseen, Nikki called back. "I don't do register tape, you remember that."

"No, I remember that you bragged about the ability to do every and any job found in a restaurant. Surely—"

"Can I help?"

Cassandra started at Juliet's voice, then looked over to beam a distracted smile. "You're here."

"And willing to do what I can."

The other woman flashed another quick smile. "No offense, but I doubt you have the moves to tame the Accucount 480. Or, in layman's terms, my uncooperative cash register."

Cassandra couldn't know how Juliet resented being seen as nothing more than an attractive decoration, so she ignored the little sting and instead made her way behind the counter. She shouldered Cassandra aside even as the woman sent out another smile—indulgent, the kind you'd serve the silly village idiot.

In ninety seconds this village idiot had the paper tape replaced and the register ready for business. She glanced up to give the shop owner a pointed look.

Nikki came around the corner at the rear of the shop. "Hey, lookie. She's not just another pretty face."

Juliet nodded. "I'll have you know I put in my share of afternoons at the Palisades Women's Club thrift store."

Though once it was out she decided it sounded closer to boasting about flower-arranging classes than she'd like. "Okay, it wasn't running a business or running a restaurant kitchen or—"

Nikki signaled a time-out. "Don't apologize. While *I* might have talents truly worth admiring, the Froot Loop here isn't good for more than weaving nothing into more"— She pointed upward, at an exquisite, knitted string bikini displayed on the wall—"well, more nothing."

Instead of taking offense, Cassandra laughed, making it clear the two were easy enough with each other to take teasing with good grace.

*I've never had that*, Juliet thought. No sibling to laugh with, let alone pester.

"You'll regret your insults after you've seen your Halloween costume, Nikki." Cassandra turned to whip a white plastic dry cleaner's bag off a dressmaker's dummy. "Ta-da!"

"Oh. My. God." Nikki stared at the figure, then clapped her hand over her mouth. "Oh. My. God," she repeated, her voice muffled and her eyes blue and green platters.

Juliet figured her own were at least saucer-wide. It was the most outrageous Halloween costume she'd ever seen. The skirt was a belly-baring knitted tube of silver-shot seaweed-green that curved in at the ankles and then flared out again in faux-flippers. The top . . . well, the top was really just two starfish-colored and starfish-shaped pasties. Thrown over the shoulders of the dummy was a sort of poncho in sky blue that looked like a fishnet.

Cassandra's mouth curved like a satisfied cat's. "Jay's always calling you his mermaid."

Nikki's hands dropped from her mouth, but her gaze didn't leave the getup. "He'll never let me out of the house in those starfish," she said. "What am I saying? I don't have the guts to leave the house in them."

The costume designer shrugged. "I can whip up a bikini top and we can sew them on it."

Nikki's two-colored eyes gleamed. "A *string* bikini top in a flesh-colored yarn, yes? Jay won't notice that until after he's felled by lust. I love a man on his knees."

"You're very bad, little sister," Cassandra said.

"And God, does it feel good." Nikki turned, grinning, to Juliet. "Shall we get Cassandra to make you something memorable, too?"

"Not like that." Juliet couldn't imagine. "I don't have anyone to wear something like that for, and not anyplace to go on Halloween."

Nikki waved away the objections. "The second we have covered. We bought tickets for a charity thing on the thirty-first and we have extras. As for the who to wear it for . . . not Noah?"

Noah. Juliet's face burned, thinking about wearing something like that mermaid costume. For Noah. Beneath her cotton blouse and matching buff-colored pants, her skin prickled as if chafed by wool.

"Are you okay?" Cassandra asked.

"Noah," Juliet managed to get out.

Nikki shot Cassandra a look. "What about him?"

"I . . . he's one of the reasons why I came here tonight. I thought you two might help me think of a present to give him."

The sisters glanced at each other again.

"He's been nice." Juliet objected to the blatant speculation on their faces. "And I haven't noticed quite how nice until lately."

"Okay." Cassandra sounded cautious. "What kind of gift are you thinking about?"

"I don't know." Juliet spun, looking for inspiration about the room. "Maybe I could make him something. Knit him a sweater."

"No!" The sisters said together, their voices horrified.

"No?"

Cassandra took Juliet by the arm and steered her toward the seating area in the middle of the shop. "It's a curse," she said, pushing her onto the soft cushions. "The Curse of the Boyfriend Sweater. You start to make your man one and he'll be out of your life before you bind off."

"But Noah's not my boyfriend." A little shiver tracked along Juliet's spine. Was the open door inviting in a draft?

Cassandra must have spotted the telltale tremor. "Let's brainstorm gift ideas later. For Knitters' Night, we'll get you started on making something warm for yourself. A wrap, maybe."

Nikki watched her bustle about the shop collecting needles and yarn. "Hey, you wouldn't allow me to attempt anything like a wrap until I was stuck on your couch after surgery."

"Because I had to keep such a close eye on you when it came time to increase and decrease. Juliet strikes me as a person good at taking direction and following rules."

*Is that truly how they saw her?* Juliet wondered. Good at taking direction and following rules? It sounded so dull and conventional. But she didn't have time to explore the idea because Cassandra handed over a pair of knitting needles and a luscious yarn the shade of a midnight sky.

"Nice," Nikki said, complimenting Cassandra. "She needs a color stronger than tan."

Obviously referring to Juliet's outfit for the evening. Again, dull and conventional. That wasn't who she was, was it? Frowning, she shoved away the thought in order to take in Cassandra's instructions.

"Start by casting on three stitches. Then knit one row, purl one row. On row three, increase one stitch at each end of the work. Do you know how to increase?"

Juliet nodded, though she hoped there were some instruction books lying around or that an experienced knitter would sit down beside her.

"After the increase, purl a row and keep on like that, increasing on each side of the knitted row until your piece is as wide as you want—since you want to wrap it around you, make it about as wide as the length of your back. Once you have that, you simply knit a row, then purl a row until the wrap is as long as you'd like."

"Then I just decrease, I suppose," Juliet said, to show she could change cash register tape *and* anticipate simple knitting instructions.

Cassandra beamed at her, even as her attention was divided by more women entering the shop. They were typical Malibuites, dressed in jeans that came with three-digit price tags and casually chic boots that sold for three times that. "Exactly. You knit two stitches together on each side of the knitted rows until you're down to three stitches. Then you bind off. Easy."

"Easy," Juliet echoed.

"For someone so good at taking directions and following rules," Nikki said, plopping onto the cushions with so much energy they both bounced.

It still sounded like faint praise to Juliet.

But she still couldn't dwell on it, not when she needed to focus on her knitted piece as well as the conversation flowing between the Tuesday Night Knitters. The dozen or so women who seated themselves in Cassandra's shop were at various stages of projects that ranged from simple to difficult. Nikki dispensed with any concern over introductions—Juliet wasn't sure how the Happy Widow or surprise sister would play with this crowd—by announcing, "Everyone, this is Juliet. Juliet, this is everyone."

The declaration allowed her to sit back and quietly work on her piece—and work on her ability to increase her stitches—as she listened to one woman despair of completing the tree skirt she was knitting by Christmas—the tree skirt she'd started two summers before. Another nimble knitter seemed to have no trouble at all adding to a stack of sweet stars made out of a glittery yarn and intended as tree decorations. Nikki and a couple of others were working on sweaters for the men in their lives.

It didn't occur to Juliet to question that until the knitting session had ended and the three sisters were once again alone in the shop. As Nikki bundled her work into a canvas bag, Juliet frowned. "Wait a minute. How come you're ignoring the curse and making Jay a sweater?"

"*Boyfriend* curse. Not father or brother or fiancé."

Juliet fingered the soft, pretty wool in her hands and felt a little puffed up by the progress she'd made in just a couple of hours. "But I could do it then. Knit a sweater for Noah. He's like a brother to me."

Nikki froze, then called over to Cassandra. "Um, help here?"

The other woman stopped her tidying to join them at the matching couches. "What?"

Nikki pointed at Juliet with a knitting needle. "Noah's like a brother to her. That's what she just said."

"Oh." Cassandra dropped to the opposite couch.

" 'Oh'? Oh, what?"

Cassandra's voice was gentle. "He doesn't look at you like he's your brother . . ." she started.

"And you don't look at him like he's your brother either," Nikki finished in a rush.

Heat flashed over Juliet's skin and up her neck. "I don't know what you're talking about." They hadn't been there that night in her kitchen when she'd stared at him, naked, in her pool. No one but Noah and Juliet knew about the accidental kiss that had come out of her celebratory hug.

It had been a mistake, she'd decided days ago. An aberration. And the fact that she'd felt a resurgence of sexual feelings wasn't something personal to Noah, just something she was experiencing as another step in the grieving process.

"I'll tell you what I'm talking about," Nikki said. "The man's hot. He stares at you like skinny women stare at slices of chocolate cake on a restaurant's dessert tray. Why don't you give both of you a present and do something about that?"

"Nikki," Cassandra protested, a laugh in her voice. "Sex isn't the answer to everything."

"I didn't say so. I just don't want two celibate sisters. That's no fun."

Cassandra shook her head, leaving Juliet to sputter. "I can't . . . I'm not . . ."

"You're not what?"

She tucked her hair behind her ears and took a breath. "I'm a widow. My husband and I . . . I loved him very much."

"Oh." Nikki sank back into the couch, her exuberant expression gone. "It's not that I forgot . . . it's just that . . . it's just that . . ." Her eyes filled with tears.

Alarm made Juliet slide closer to the younger woman. "What's the matter?"

Cassandra tossed Nikki a tissue box from a nearby table. "It's okay, Nik. Everything's okay." She glanced over at Juliet. "Our chef's been a crier since the night Jay got her cornered and made her promise to marry him. Turned her romance-crazy, too. She wants everyone to be part of a committed couple."

"God," Nikki said, wiping her eyes. "I'm mortified to admit I resemble that remark. But I'm so sorry, Juliet. I wasn't thinking about you losing your husband."

"It's all right." She smiled, remembering herself as Nikki was now. Giddy with new love and wanting everyone to have their own taste of that incredible dish. "But I've had my turn as half of a committed couple. I'm not expecting to find that again."

"Well," Cassandra mused, "it doesn't have to be about commitment, now, does it?"

Nikki popped upright on the cushions and hooted, tears all dry. "No way! Ms. Takes-No-Man-to-Bed is suggesting Juliet shag Noah for . . . for . . . just for the fun of it?"

For the fun of it? Juliet remembered his hot mouth, his hard hands, the breadth of his chest and the solid weight of his muscles. Would getting close to all that be *fun*? With a shiver, she gathered her knitting against her chest.

"He's going away soon," she said. "In three, four weeks

tops, he's going to leave the house and move on to his own life."

"Maybe that's all the better," Cassandra responded. "Because there is that way you two look at each other. If he's leaving soon, nobody gets hurt, but you still get—"

"Laid." Nikki interjected, an unholy grin taking over her face. "Perfect. I think you should let that gorgeous guy strip you right out of those beige clothes you're wearing tonight and bring you back to life."

"Nikki!" Cassandra laughed. "I said it before, I'll say it again. You *are* bad."

"And I like it," she said, wiggling her eyebrows. "Bet Juliet will, too. We're sisters, after all."

God, the women were crazy. Juliet Weston—rule-following, instruction-adhering widow Juliet Weston—couldn't just hop into a brief affair with the guy across the pool . . . could she?

Wouldn't it be a betrayal? She'd loved Wayne with all her heart.

But . . . this wasn't about her heart.

It was about her body, her tingly, womanly, okay, *aroused* body that was put in that state just thinking about . . . about . . .

Shagging Noah.

But she'd come here tonight to figure out something to give him. How could she walk out thinking about possibly giving *herself* such a present?

And now that Nikki and Cassandra had put it into her head . . . how could she not think about it?

Noah jolted awake, just in time to catch the glass in his hand from tipping over and dumping the two inches of whisky it held onto the flagstone deck.

Behind him, he could hear the rhythm of one of their old Iraq anthems, Metallica's "Seek and Destroy," beating like a headache from inside the guesthouse. After some

Mexican takeout, he and Dean had cranked up the volume coming through the speakers and toasted old times with a full bottle of booze. They'd siphoned off more than half when Noah's old Army buddy had leaned back in the recliner and z'd off for a little rack time.

Considering that half-bottle gone, Dean had just as likely passed out. *Hooah.*

Noah was slightly better off, because he'd left the guesthouse to head outside, and because he'd semi-controlled his intake so he'd be coherent when Juliet came home.

*Juliet.*

His head snapped around and then he figured what must have woken him. When last he'd looked, the place across the pool had been dark except for the security lights. Now the kitchen was lit and he could see her moving about. Apparently she'd returned from Malibu & Ewe. Standing, he shook his head and took a minute to let the liquor settle in the lower half of his brain. Then it took only seconds for him to reach the French door leading into the kitchen.

She jumped at his rattling knock on the glass. Then she crossed to the door and through the double panes he could see she was wearing boxy, man-cut pajamas in some satiny fabric. They hid everything from below her throat all the way to her ankles, but he'd already conceded the singular sexiness of her elegant, gold-tipped toes.

"Noah?" she said, as she opened the door to let him inside. "What's up?"

Yeah, there was a dangerous question. With that classy scent of hers in the air and now in his head, he was forced to shove his hands in his front pockets, working on the good ol' denim stretch. It took so little of her to get to him. "I just wanted to make sure you're okay with Dean bunking with me across the way."

"I told you so when you asked after he called the other night. That's your place, your decision." Despite the speech, there was a new pink flush across her cheekbones and her gaze kept sliding away from his.

Frowning, he tucked his forefinger under her chin. "Juliet? What's wrong?"

She gave a wry smile and then lifted her hands to pluck at the lapels of her pajama top. "I realize I'm in beige again."

His glance flicked down. Beige? On her, to him, everything looked golden. Out of reach. He let his finger drop and he stepped back. "Uh, I guess I should go then."

She was grasping those silky-looking lapels with white knuckles. "So soon?"

He frowned. "Well, I . . ." His throat closed down as he looked into her eyes, their unmatched color making him unsteady on his feet.

Of course he remembered her confessing to Gabe that she craved contact, but since then he hadn't been able to convince himself it was true. Except now, now there was something in her eyes, or maybe just something he wanted to believe he could see . . . In any case, that damn weather vane in his pants was suddenly declaring clear skies and hot nights ahead.

God, he probably was an idiot. He probably was an idiot who had sucked down too much booze, yet he still couldn't stop himself from taking a step closer to her. Then another, telling himself that when she backed up he'd take the hint and leave. Surely that would happen any second. Yet her pretty bare feet stayed stuck to the floor.

His head lowered toward hers and her breath rushed out, warm, and he detected the slightest scent of chocolate.

A song he remembered from the sandbox floated through his head. Not the boost-your-shit-kicking-attitude heavy metal music he'd been reminiscing to with Dean back at the guesthouse. What he heard now was one of those oozing, aching, gotta-get-me-a-girl songs that could have all the guys groaning and heading off for the showers or off for some private time with a pinup or just their personal prurient fantasies.

The words of the song slithered like seduction through

his head. They reached into his pants like a slim, warm hand. "I smell sex and candy," he heard a voice croon in his brain, and then he had to taste it. Taste sex and candy, and the most dangerous taste of them all.

Hers.

Without more thought, his mouth found Juliet's lips and they parted on another little whoosh of sweet, decadent breath. His belly clenched, hard, harder, because this kiss was no damn accident. He couldn't tell himself this time that it was just a harmless, unintentional tail end to her friendly hug.

This wasn't friendly. And when his hands slid down over that slinky fabric to find her elegant ass and draw her hips against his, well, that wasn't any hug.

That was hell-o, hail Mary, thank Jesus for being born a man so he could press the stiff weight of his cock into the softness of her female mound.

He didn't hesitate sliding his tongue into her mouth. It was wet and hot inside, more than he remembered, and it had him thinking of the other wet, hot place of her body he could explore. But he might not get that far, he might not have that long, so he hauled her even closer against him and pressed his hip bones into her belly and damned the consequences.

She opened to him, she softened to him, and heat flashed like fire down his spine and rushed around to his groin. Though his head was buzzing with sexual glee, he recognized the yielding give of her breasts against his chest and his hand slid upward to cup one's supple weight. Her nipple stabbed his palm and they both groaned.

His fingers tightened and she did that signature Juliet move on him again—sucking on his tongue and shattering his sense so that he was only about *sensation*, the stiff nub of her nipple under the brush of his thumb, the sweet taste of her chocolate-Julietness on his taste buds, the velvety smoothness of her belly skin beneath his fingertips.

Yeah. He was going for the gold.

Oh, Christ. But he couldn't stop himself, even as he wrenched his mouth from hers to press kisses to the corner of her lips, the edge of her jaw, the sleek velvet column of her neck.

She was holding her breath, he thought. He could feel the trembling tension in her body as his forefinger flirted with her belly button. "Relax," he said, though his voice was rough and tight and he couldn't command his own muscles to let go. "Relax."

Of course she didn't. And of course he was at the whim of his lust, so far gone that as his fingers found no obstacle on the way to the curls at the apex of her thighs, he couldn't stop himself from testing his teeth against the edge of her elegant chin. She jerked into both touches, and then his mouth found her wet mouth again and his fingers—

Also found wet. Heat.

Her outside flesh seemed to flutter around his fingers, and against his other hand, her nipple tightened further. In another second he was going to explode. For the first time in all these damn months of half-guilty fantasies, he had Juliet as he'd imagined.

At the mercy of his lust, of his l—

He halted the thought by moving his middle finger lower, deeper. Her breath hitched. More heat, more wetness flowed into his hand, and then he was inside her.

His tongue thrust into her mouth and she held him there . . . and *there*. Sucking, tightening, taking. They had each other. It was sweet and carnal and more than he'd ever expected out of life.

*I smell sex and candy* . . . Then that croon made way for another voice.

*Warning! Enemy in area!*

And like that, he was in Iraq. In the Stryker, with that calm, yet urgent female voice that automatically sounded when an opposition force was within the armored vehicle's battle space. *Warning! Enemy in area!*

Noah wrenched himself away from Juliet.

Juliet, the general's wife.

Widow.

Whatever.

Blessing that mean, fucked-up little flashback, he backed away from the beautiful woman who stared at him, her chest heaving. Despite how he'd touched her, all her secrets remained still covered by gold satin.

Shit, and all his secrets still remained damn good reason to retreat now and forever keep his distance. While he'd imagined this, fantasized about it, the reality of getting this close would create a tangle he couldn't fight free of. He shouldn't have forgotten that. Cursing himself, he took another step back.

The classy woman didn't utter a single sound as he left.

# Eight

The quickest way of ending a war is to lose it.

—GEORGE ORWELL

Juliet's house looked quiet and no one answered Marlys's ring. Congratulating herself that the world was going her way for once, she pushed through the side gate and ventured around the pool to the guesthouse. Its door swung open following her knock.

She gazed coolly at the dark-haired, silver-eyed biker standing on the other side. Dean Long. "Trick-or-treat."

He leaned a shoulder against the doorjamb and returned her same unruffled stare. Then he reached out a big hand to tap the wire and white gauze that made up the wings of her Halloween costume. "So, you decided you're a fairy after all."

"Nope." From behind her back, she drew out a sequined halo and popped it on top of her head. "I'm an angel."

"Now why do I find that hard to believe?"

She shrugged, her wings shifting on her shoulders. The truth was, she'd never angled for sainthood. Mom didn't care and Dad hadn't been around to appreciate the achievement. "Are you going to pony up a Snickers or a Tootsie

Pop, or am I going to have to pull out the eggs and shaving cream?"

He mocked a shudder. "Scary. You better come in while I scrounge up something from Noah's cupboards."

She grinned. "Fab. I've never been inside the private's private quarters."

Dean sent her a look over his shoulder as she followed him in, but he didn't comment on the nickname. "You've known him awhile."

"Mmm." Marlys didn't want to talk about Noah, though, except to find out how long she had before he returned. "Where is the big guy?"

"He went to some charity Halloween thing. Same party Juliet's attending, I think."

Marlys frowned, distracted. "Juliet went to a party? With who? The Evil Stepmother doesn't socialize."

This time when Dean gave her a look her neck went hot and she had to shift her gaze. He continued on to the narrow galley kitchen and she perched on one of the stools drawn up to the short breakfast bar that separated it from the living area. Her white and sequined tutu poofed up in front, exposing even more of her legs in their matching white tights. She tried pushing the layers of tulle down, but gave up when Dean handed her a beefstick.

Frowning, she inspected the plastic-wrapped tube of meat-colored preservatives. "Ick."

"It's the best I can do." He didn't look sorry about it.

"Guy candy," she said with disgust.

"Wrong." His gaze ran over the old dance costume she'd found in the attic, from its little satin bodice to the white ballet slippers she wore. "You in that skimpy outfit—now *that's* guy candy."

She pretended to be displeased. "Again with the biker-bar come-ons."

"If we were in a biker bar and you were dressed like that, I wouldn't come on, I'd come over and get you out of there before the fights broke out over who got to bend your halo."

"I never need rescuing."

"I was talking about saving the guy who got first dibs."

She had to laugh. That was the thing about this Dean Long. She knew men. She knew their approaches. But he was different, disarming her just when she thought she had all her armor in place. "So despite all the soft trimmings"—she reached up to flick a wing tip—"you think you see all my sharp edges."

He came around the end of the bar to take the other stool, at the same time twisting hers so they ended up facing each other, knees to knees. "Maybe." With humor warming up his silver eyes, he considered for a short moment. "Yes."

"Must be hard to sleep at night, you and your arrogance all crowded together in one bed."

Another speculative gleam entered his silver gaze.

Oh, hell. She had to mention beds and sleeping, which led to her thinking of sleeping—with him—and damn if he wasn't looking at her again as if he could see right through her skin. Right through her skin and to her cardiovascular system that had suddenly become a supersonic speedway.

He touched her knee and she jumped. The skimming contact felt like a sting.

"Ouch." He looked down at his fingers. "You burn."

"Then keep your hands off," she grumbled.

Rubbing it against his jeans, he glanced back up at her face. "Not sure that's possible."

Yeah, well, she wasn't sure that was possible either. After she'd left the other day with Juliet's package, distance and her common sense had kicked in. True, she was impulsive, sometimes incautious, hyperenergetic, and often caustic, but she wasn't stupid. Instead of making plans to head back to Malibu and chance running into Dean again, she'd slapped a new address label on Juliet's package and remailed it at her local post office.

And yet, here she was again.

She had to figure out why this man—from the moment he'd gazed at her from those cool silver eyes—fascinated her. She didn't fascinate easily. Hell, she didn't think she'd ever been fascinated.

Until Dean Long had looked at her. Especially after Dean Long had touched her.

There had to be an explanation, she thought, rubbing her knee and surprised to find he hadn't burned a hole clear through the fragile mesh. So far, she was betting on that mystery factor. He'd gone out of his way to be all he-man inscrutability. Getting to the bottom of him would surely end her overblown interest.

She propped an elbow on the breakfast bar and sent him her most winning smile. "So why don't you tell me every little thing about you?"

"I'm the strong and silent type."

Okay, so she wasn't all that practiced at winning smiles, but did he have to be so uncooperative? Curbing her normal impatience, she only jiggled one foot while trying to look sweet—even with her teeth clenched. "Well, let's start with your birth date. Or gee, if you find that's just too personal, how about your astrological sign?"

"Who's trying to pick up whom now?"

She snorted. Whoops, there went sweet. "Just give me the info, damn it."

Leaning into the back of the stool, he crossed his arms over his chest and grinned at her. "Now that's more like it. No point in faking the sugar when vinegar looks so good on you, angel."

"Why won't you just answer my questions?"

"Because you look so cute when you fume."

Beyond annoyed, she launched out of her stool. Maybe he thought she was going to get violent, because suddenly he stood, too, and his big hands curled around her wrists. "Don't hurt me," he said, grinning again.

His fingers were bands of heat and that warmth was shooting up her bare arms, leaving prickly goose bumps in their wake. Instead of struggling to be free, she went still. "Maybe," she heard herself say, her voice quiet, "that should be my line."

Alarm bells sounded in her head. No, no! The words sounded female and weak and it was as if he'd already managed to rub away her sharp edges and evaporate the acid from her tongue. With a yank of her hands, she tried pulling free of him, but he ignored her struggles and jerked her closer.

White satin bodice met white cotton T-shirt. She was aware of the little silver teardrop she carried with her always, now tucked between her breasts, but she was even more aware of Dean's heartbeat. It thumped, steady and strong, against the double-time that was her own.

He smelled like laundry soap and then, as his mouth descended, she caught the scent of cinnamon. And then she tasted the red-hot flavor as his breath brushed against her lips. "Shall we try this, Marlys?"

No!

Yes.

Certainly not.

Please now.

Never in a million years would she admit it, but she didn't have the voice to utter a single one of her conflicting responses. So she threw each to the wind and answered in the only way left to her. Marlys-the-Brash went on tiptoe to close the gap between them.

His kiss burned, too. She opened her mouth to cool the flames and his tongue took up the invitation. He stroked inside her mouth, strong and sure. Oh. Oh, wow.

To bolster her sagging knees, she pressed against his chest even as her head dropped on her neck, letting him take what he wanted.

He didn't take enough. With a small groan, he lifted his head to press a gentle kiss to the corner of her mouth, her nose, her chin. "I'm thirty years old. Aries. April second."

"Stubborn," she said.

"You've got to be kidding." He dove in for another wet, deep kiss that had her clutching at his shirt. His hands slid over her back and then down, to tilt her hips into his. She went on tiptoe again to make the fit more gratifying. "I wasn't planning on telling you anything," he said.

She managed a laugh, even though with every unsteady breath, her breasts rubbed against his shirt. "I meant your astrological sign. The goat."

"It's not a goat." He looked offended. "It's a ram."

"That's a kind of truck. Your sign's a goat. As in old goat. Or Billy Goat Gruff or—"

"Ram," he said again, with heat, and then caught on. With another groan, he shook his head and then snatched the halo from her hair and sailed it toward the living room couch. "Brat, not angel. I was right the first time we met."

It gave her a moment to rearrange her sagging armor. She mentally pulled it up around herself, and then scooted back so that her butt met stool again. Dean's arms dropped, and she discovered she didn't like the chill that distance afforded.

He didn't look happy either. "You're not going to make this easy, are you?"

The skinny satin strap of her costume dropped, but before she could draw it back, he ran his forefinger along the newly naked spot of her skin. "Are you, Marlys?"

"I don't know what you're talking about."

"Uh-huh." He shook his head again. "You big on denial, angel? Because we've got some crazy-ass chemistry going on here, and I, for one, am all for exploring it."

Well, Marlys wanted to explain it. "I don't . . . I'm not . . ." While no fainting virgin, she didn't know how to deliver the message that Marlys Weston didn't fall into strangers' arms. She didn't casually sleep around or even have a congenial fuck buddy on speed dial.

She didn't like men that much.

Or women, either, for that matter.

Marlys Weston took no prisoners and not lovers very often. Her last best friend had been lost to her in seventh grade, and there hadn't been anyone to fill the gap since. So how could this man so quickly get under her skin? There had to be a logical answer.

"Let's start over again, Mr. Aries. So you have an April second birth date. Where exactly are you from?"

He hesitated, sliding back into his own stool. Was he playing obstinate man of mystery again? But no, he didn't look cagey, he looked . . . confused?

Or unable to answer.

With new eyes, she took in his muscled physique and the close haircut, and then remembered that moment when he'd gone from asleep to alert. Like her father. Like a soldier.

"You grew up military, too," she said. Military kids couldn't name a hometown because they'd never had one. Two years here, three years there, they moved from place to place, base to base. "Army then, army now?" she hazarded a guess, and then thought, duh, he was a friend of Noah's. That crazy-ass chemistry had scrambled her normal deductive skills.

He nodded, a little smile quirking his lips.

Yeah. That crazy-ass chemistry all made sense now, she decided. It must be because Dean was part of her tribe, the one and only group she'd ever belonged to. The one and only group that she'd felt completely comfortable in her skin around—until she'd been yanked from base life and had gone from soldier's daughter to misfit civilian in one fell swoop.

As another who'd grown up military, he was one of her own. Almost like family—she found she was staring at his mouth, so, okay, not like family. But that was all right. Because he was military that meant he knew the score, too. An organization of the brats had assigned themselves a flower, like governments did. The U.S. national flower was the rose. The state of California had the poppy.

The military brats had adopted the dandelion.

Like them, it was resilient. Like them, it knew how to move on.

Which meant that she and Dean were alike and in their sameness they were safe. When—no, *if*—she decided to do something about this crazy-ass chemistry, they could go ahead and enjoy the experiment until the inevitable wind blew off its blossom . . . or blew out its flames.

Nikki bumped her elbow into Juliet's ribs and gestured toward the costumed crowd gathered on the restaurant's glass-screened deck overlooking the ocean. "What do you think it says about men when a disproportionate number of them came dressed for Halloween as kings?"

"It could be a superiority complex, I suppose," Juliet said, pitching her voice over the sound of the crashing surf and the rendition of "Monster Mash" from the band in the corner. "But my guess is a big basket of fake crowns right next to the checkout at the Rite Aid."

"Okay," Nikki said, nodding. "Laziness over a supremacy wish. And it explains why Jay is here telling everyone he's Don Ho when he's really just dressed in his own pair of cargo shorts, flip-flops, and one of his collection of vintage Hawaiian shirts."

Juliet smiled as she spotted the man in question threading through the crowd and carrying drinks for the three of them. The deck was lit by the lights on the small patio tables and the tiki torches ringing it. "The ukulele is a cute touch. And the costume does kind of go with your most outstanding mermaid getup."

Nikki reached for the lemon drop martini Jay handed to

her and ran her gaze over Juliet. "You're looking good, too. I like the Shakespearean slant."

"Credit Cassandra's creativity once again," she said, running her hand down the long blue velvet robe the other woman had pulled out of her own closet. Underneath the half-open garment they'd paired a white peasant-style blouse and a long cotton petticoat. "It took her fifteen minutes and a glue gun to make the 'Juliet' cap." In a darker shade of velvet, it hugged the crown of her head and was edged with colored "gems" as big as her thumbnail.

And it had taken less than fifteen for Cassandra to convince Juliet to attend the Halloween event. After a few days of stewing over Noah, she'd realized she needed the distraction. A little fun.

Nikki sipped at her drink and leaned closer so she didn't have to yell over the music. "The only thing missing is Romeo."

*Romeo, Romeo, where for art thou, Romeo?*

Juliet sighed. Recently, she'd only caught glimpses of her across-the-pool-neighbor—always accompanied by Dean. He'd nodded. She'd fluttered her fingers.

They'd both looked away.

After that last interlude in her kitchen—she was beginning to wonder if the location was bewitched—she'd gone to bed flustered. Okay, frustrated. Not to mention hurt. How could he touch her so intimately and then retreat with such speed and without so much as a word?

But after a few hours of flopping back and forth on her mattress, she'd started to look at it from his point of view. Why would a man—handsome, intelligent, and used to a variety of women—want to get involved with a widow who carried enough baggage to weigh down both of them?

Not to mention that she hadn't spoken a word to him either. Before that kiss, after those touches, neither time had she assured him she was only contemplating a brief affair. Maybe if she'd been up-front: *I just want your skin, your heat, your manness, no more—*

But thinking about that wasn't distracting or fun, so she turned away from it all by turning to her sister's fiancé. His gaze was trained on Nikki.

"So," she said. "How are things with you, Jay?"

He started. "Huh?"

"How are you?"

He shook his head. "Sorry, I was just congratulating myself on my choice of future wife."

Nikki rolled her eyes. "Right. You were congratulating yourself on my cleavage, Hef."

He grinned. "If you say you didn't wear those starfish with just that in mind, then you lie, cookie."

Without bothering to hide her own shameless grin, Nikki shot a look at Juliet. "Can't get much by him, I tell ya."

"Which reminds me," Jay said. "I've been meaning to follow up on that conversation I started about your husband's book."

"Jay . . ." Nikki groaned. "We're at a party."

"Exactly. So if you try to murder me again, this time there'll be plenty of witnesses."

Wayne's book, Juliet thought. She'd yet to come up with any concrete plan to promote its success. "What do you want to know about it?"

"I'm thinking of featuring the autobiography in *NYFM*'s online edition."

"*NYFM*?" Juliet's interest sparked. Now she recalled that Jay was a magazine editor, but she hadn't known it was *that* magazine. For men, mostly about men, the publication could bring to the book the kind of attention it deserved. "You work for *NYFM*?"

"Yep," he said. "So what do you think about your husband's book? Does it capture the essence of the man?"

She closed her eyes and breathed in, for a moment almost conjuring up the essence she remembered so well. She almost, almost, had it, the smell of starch on Wayne's shirt mixed with the slightly caustic scent of his dry-cleaned dress uniform. Then it was gone, and she looked at Jay again, with a pang realizing how alone she still could feel, even at a party attended by more than a hundred people.

"Juliet?" Jay prodded. "I wouldn't take up much of your time."

Time wasn't the issue at all. All she had now was time, unending, empty stretches of it, and she had to force that thought away as another sharp ache pierced her chest. "But why would you need me?" She must have missed something.

"I said I want to do an interview with you."

"No," Juliet said, her answer automatic. "Not a good idea."

"Have you read the book? Are you worried about what it reveals?"

"I've read it. And I'm not worried about what it reveals at all." She'd pored over every printed page. What Wayne had said about their romance—*She was everything fresh and fine this jaded soldier had forgotten about the world*—had torn new holes in her heart, but in the end it was only a very small part of Wayne's story. The rest of the book had been devoted to his experiences in the Army and at war.

"So why not?" Jay pressed.

A knot of tension tightened at the back of her skull. Was she having fun yet? "*General Matters* is everything I want people to know about my husband, but I don't think it's wise to remind them of my connection to him."

Though she'd give anything for the book to be a sensation, giving an interview surely wasn't the right way to make that happen. She made a face. "We're both aware I'm not the public's favorite person."

Jay frowned. "Yes, but I think—"

"*I* think you need to take off your press pass." Nikki placed her hand on her fiancé's forearm and sent Juliet a look of exasperated sympathy. "Jay, now is not the time to discuss business-type things."

"But—"

"No." Nikki's voice was firm. "Now is the time for entertaining things. Things like ogling guys. Juliet, behind you and to your left. Check out that dude dressed like Tom Cruise in *Risky Business*."

Grateful to drop the subject of the interview, Juliet glanced over her shoulder. "Oh," she said. "Um."

"I know," Nikki answered. "Kinda cute face, but those caveman legs would do better without tighty whities. Ankle-length boxers, maybe."

Jay grabbed Nikki's empty glass from her hand and then Juliet's. "We're all going to need another round if we're to survive the cookie's critiques. I'll be right back."

Nikki smiled at his retreating form and sidled closer. "Okay, now it's just us again. So . . . how's it going with Noah?"

"Not." Juliet admitted, without meeting her youngest sister's gaze. "Not going."

The other woman shrugged. "Oh, well. As we mermaids say, there are plenty of fish in the sea." She lifted her right hand and using the shield of its palm, pointed her left forefinger at a man standing a few feet away. "That guy over there. The one in the kilt? Jay knows him. Well, Jay knows everybody, but I'm pretty sure he's single. Look! He's giving you the eye."

Juliet didn't look. She was still staring at Nikki and her hands, the shield, the pointer. She hadn't seen anyone do that since high school and a bubble of laughter caught in her throat. More of her tension slipped away. "I've always been suspect of men in dresses."

"That isn't a dress, it's a kilt. A kilt is like a uniform, and you like those."

The laugh slipped out. "Nikki . . ." She glanced at the man this time and decided that it wasn't the skirt, but the knee socks that really turned her off. "I don't think he's for me."

"Well, survey the crowd. Jay and I will steer you clear of the sharks."

Juliet had to laugh again, even as she followed orders.

Maybe there *was* something to what Nikki said. She'd told herself her reaction to Noah wasn't personal. Of course she didn't see herself hopping into bed with some stranger—instruction-adhering, rule-following widow Juliet probably wouldn't go that far—but what was the harm in looking?

However, not one of the men milling about the party caught her eye. Not the guy in the kilt, not the hirsute Tom Cruise in his white dress shirt, not the several pirates, or the many fans of plastic crowns. There was an elegant gentleman in a Clooney-worthy tux, but as he was hand-in-hand with a cowboy wearing chaps and a ten-gallon hat, she slid her gaze right over him.

Then the crowd shifted and she caught a glimpse of a tall male. It was just a flash of his shoulder, in a darkish T-shirt, but something about him caused her to pause. She narrowed her eyes and kept her focus pinpointed there. Another movement of the knot of people and there was that shoulder again, then the flat plane of a masculine back.

Two people strode off in the direction of the bar leaving a larger gap that revealed Cassandra in a knitted, naughty schoolgirl's outfit, her wavy hair in two long pigtails bound by more yarn. Next to her was Gabe, wearing his characteristic grim expression and regular street clothes. The both of them appeared to be talking to the man with the shoulder and back that had caught her fancy.

He was wearing his T-shirt tucked into a pair of camouflage pants. Costumed as a soldier. Maybe that's what had caught her attention, she thought. Except her attention had been caught by him before tonight. It had been captured the instant she'd seen his naked body swimming in her pool. At that moment, she'd awoken to the world around her.

As if he could feel her regard, Noah turned. There was thirty feet between them, but neither of them blinked, even as a couple drifted past, and a young woman dressed as a Dallas cheerleader skipped by.

"Juliet?"

She managed to turn toward Nikki.

The mermaid smiled. "This feels like that song, you know, 'Some Enchanted Evening.' "

"Noah's no stranger," Juliet protested.

"Convenient, that."

The sensation of his gaze on her back was impossible to ignore. Prickles of heat cascaded down her spine and she could actually feel her blood surging through her veins. Awareness, attraction, sex—call it what you will, but it had never found her from across the proverbial crowded room.

"I don't know what to do," Juliet confessed in a whisper.

The band had segued into a loud version of *Rocky Horror Picture Show*'s "The Time Warp," but Nikki seemed capable of reading lips.

"That's easy," she replied, pushing on Juliet's shoulder. "Just turn around."

She did, and he was there. Broad, and so tall that she had to tilt up her head to meet his gaze. Behind Noah, someone pushed by and he stepped nearer, the warmth of him mingling with the warmth of her.

They stood together in a bubble of combined body heat.

"Hey," he said.

"Hey." She couldn't pull air into her lungs.

"You came to the party."

She swallowed. "A woman has to get out sometime."

His gaze moved from her eyes, to her mouth, down her neck to her pulse point. There was a wealth of bare flesh between her throat and the edge of Cassandra's low-cut peasant blouse, and Juliet was aware of each millimeter of hot-chilled skin as he took that in, too.

"Nice costume," he said.

She swallowed again. "You, too." Of course his was leftovers from his Army days. She'd seen those ragged camouflage pants before, and the cotton knit of his T-shirt looked soft and worn, so thin that it couldn't hide the curve of his pectoral muscles and the tight points of his nipples.

New heat flashed over her body and she was sure her

skin flushed with the sudden change in temperature. Her fingers curled so that her nails dug into her palms and she didn't know what to do with her gaze. What to do with herself.

Her skin pulsed with each beat of her heart and she didn't think she'd ever felt more alive.

"Juliet?"

She met his eyes. They were intense, their blue color hot. His hands were fisted, and she could sense his restraint. There was power in those flexed muscles, but she knew he had every impulse leashed this time.

This time, there would be no hug ending in a kiss. No kiss ending in a touch.

There wouldn't be any fun to be had with this fire-breathing attraction unless she did something about it herself.

Unless she wanted it.

Unless she asked for it.

# *Nine*

> Love is the wisdom of the fool and the folly of the wise.
>
> —SAMUEL JOHNSON

Juliet took a breath. Then took a chance. "Want to take a walk?" she asked Noah.

He hesitated a moment, and she could see his muscles bunch beneath his shirt. Then he shrugged, as if forcing himself to relax. "Sure."

A small breath eased out of her tight chest. She led the way—that was what this was about, wasn't it?—and he followed, closely, but not touching her, even though the small of her back twitched in expectation. Around her, people parted for their progress, until a man dressed as a cannibal—wild wig, "bone" in his nose, painted skin, and brandishing a big fork—leaped into her path.

"Yaahh!" he yelled.

Swallowing her surprised shriek, she jolted back, bumping into Noah. He drew her close, twisting to put himself between her and the happy carnivore.

"Damn," the other man said, looking crestfallen. "And I wanted to make a meal out of this morsel of sweet meat myself."

"She's not a morsel, she's a *lady*," Noah said through his teeth. "A widow, for God's sake. Show some respect."

The cannibal's painted face turned even ghastlier at the word "widow" and he backed off in a big hurry. "Sorry. Excuse me. Uh, gotta go."

Juliet felt as embarrassed as the other man looked. "I didn't need saving," she protested.

"From that guy?" Noah responded, enclosing her hand in his and stepping through the restaurant's back exit that opened onto a bluff. From there he towed her down a narrow, gritty trail that tracked through low-lying ice plant toward the beach below. "Yeah, you did."

The steep path quickly dropped them beneath the level of the restaurant. Juliet glowered at his back as annoyance joined the arousal inside her. "Because I'm a poor little widow?" she asked.

Or worse, was his protective response because he considered her such a "lady"? No wonder Noah hadn't followed up on those kisses in the kitchen. No wonder he'd backed away. He probably pitied her, the poor, desperate widow lady.

As they continued down the path, the annoyance grew, smoldering embers of it flaring into the fire of real anger. It was cool outside, but dressed in her velvet robe and thorny mood, she barely noticed. Trying to keep up with Noah's longer strides, she stumbled over the root of a scruffy bougainvillea, and the graceless movement stopped her short, her bad temper spiking.

"Damn it," she yelled, kicking at the scrubby brush. "Damn it all to hell!"

Noah turned to stare at her, and she yanked her hand from his then kicked the bush again. Twice. She glared at the offending plant and then at him. "And don't you dare look at me like that."

"Like what?"

"Like you didn't think I knew any swear words. Because, hell yes, I do, and when I'm mad I'm going to let them loose."

Noah's voice softened. "Juliet, what's the problem? What's made you so upset?" In the bright moonlight, she saw his expression soften, too. It only made her madder.

"I'm not upset." She took another swipe at the bush, and its barbs caught the hem of her robe so she had to reach down and jerk it free.

"Okay." His placating tone did nothing to help matters.

She kicked the bougainvillea once more instead of stomping her foot like she wanted to. "I'm enraged, all right?" And before he could ask the obvious question, she let the answer tumble out from wherever it had been packed away all these months. "I'm enraged at Wayne. What was he thinking? How could he have done this to me? How could he have left me alone?"

"Ah, honey—"

"And then how am I supposed to do this . . . this thing we're doing now?" Her throat tightened, but the ball of anger inside her was growing and it pushed the words up and out. "I barely dated before I was married—did you know I didn't have one date in high school?"

"Uh—"

"Well, I didn't. And so guess what? It means that here I am, over thirty and unmarried, with no idea of how to play the game or read the signals or where to find the rules. There are rules, aren't there?"

"I'm not sure I know . . ."

She rolled her eyes. Six plus feet of soldier muscle and a law degree and he was trying to play dumb with her? Before Wayne's death, she'd watched the leggy girls, the curvy women, the feline females Noah had escorted in and out of his above-the-garage apartment. "Oh, you know the rules all right, which is why I'm furious with you, too. Sure I'm angry at Wayne for leaving me, but you, you're worse because, damn it, you've been leading me on."

Noah jerked at the accusation and stepped forward. "Now wait a minute. Now wait just a minute." His hands closed over her shoulders.

She wrenched back. "Don't touch me. Don't touch me unless you're prepared to follow through."

His arms dropped.

Now she did stomp her foot. She stomped her foot and fisted her hands and addressed the swathe of stars flung across the night sky, her frustration pouring out of her. "Damn it all! Is it too much to ask that I could have just a little time with a man I admire? Is it too much to ask that I could have a man to hold me through one simple, single night? Is it too much to ask that I could find some way to prove that I didn't die, too?"

As the last words echoed in her ears, the desperate note in her own voice doused her anger. It subsided as quickly as it had built, leaving her still hot and bothered—but only by distinct embarrassment. And Noah was staring at her, silent.

Aghast, most likely.

"Oh, God," she said. She covered her eyes with her hands. "Oh, God. Now you not only think I'm a pitiful widow, but a crazy pitiful widow."

The ground didn't open up and swallow her. Noah didn't back away as she was sure he wanted to. Instead, his fingers circled her wrists and he yanked down her hands, leaving them eye to eye, toe to toe.

"That's it? Someone to hold you through the night?" At Noah's guttural tone, her eyes widened. "That's what you want?"

But he didn't wait for her answer. Instead, he jerked her hard against him. Her feet slipped on the sandy ground, but that didn't matter, because he held her with a grip that wouldn't allow her to move, let alone fall.

Then he kissed her.

The last dregs of anger evaporated. Embarrassment fled. Everything but the feel of him against her dropped away. Juliet stepped closer to his solid strength and moaned into his mouth, parting her lips so that his tongue could push inside. Sweet, heady intrusion.

Her fingers curled around his biceps and she hung on as he took her mouth, took it without hesitation or doubt. It was all confidence and need and when he sucked her bottom lip, she could only press into him with her hips and breasts.

His hand slid upward to cradle the back of her head and hold her steady for more searing kisses, one after the other, creating a string of perfect, burning sensation. She dug her fingers into his resilient skin and opened her eyes to marvel at the moonlight on his face, his eyelashes feathery shadows against his cheekbones.

His mouth was coarse-edged with whiskers and she reveled in the rough burn of them against her chin, her cheeks, the corners of her lips. "Juliet . . ." It wasn't a question, she thought, it was just her name, an extension of the desire she could feel running through his veins. Noah desired her.

Noah desired Juliet.

A woman, not a widow.

And suddenly the kisses and the embrace weren't enough. They were hot, but still too chaste, and remembering the other times they'd kissed, she worried that she might only have this moment, this chance. Grabbing his hand from her shoulder, she yanked it down to cover her breast.

His groan made her womb clench.

Her head fell back and his whiskers abraded her skin as his mouth followed the column of her neck. She felt the prickly burn everywhere, could imagine it everywhere, on her shin, behind her knee, against the tender flesh between her thighs.

His hips pushed against hers and she felt the heavy weight of his erection along her belly. She tilted the cradle of her pelvis toward it—taking the heavy male thrust of him against her softer abdomen, wishing right now that she could take him into the softest, hottest part of her.

"Noah." How far was a car, a couch, any comfortable flat surface? "Noah." His hand kneaded her breast and her urgency only flared higher. "*Please.*"

His hair was cool against the palms of her hands as his head dipped toward her breasts. Flat surface forgotten, Juliet only thought of more. More of his touch, more of this pressing desire, more man against her.

More knowing she was, indeed, alive.

His fingers brushed over her nipple. Not enough, not enough. But then she realized he was pushing the edge of the velvet robe away, tucking it below her left breast so that it was only covered by sheer blouse, sheer bra. The surf below them roared, but her blood was louder in her ears as she waited, breathless, for what he would do next.

His mouth latched onto her breast. With his tongue, he wetted the fabric. His lips drew hard on her nipple.

Her knees buckled. Her womb clenched. Wet heat rushed between her thighs and she wanted to cry with its goodness.

His arm was a steel band around her back, and his mouth was as relentless at her swelling breast. She felt her flesh there expand, as if it wanted to fill his mouth like she wanted to be filled by the erection pressing heat and life against her belly. Her fingers bit into his scalp and he nipped her in return.

Her hips jerked against him, helpless against the sweet sting. He nipped again, and it wasn't so sweet, only better, and she yanked his shirt from the waistband of his pants so she could touch skin. Noah's hot, smooth skin.

He lifted his head as she explored beneath the soft cotton. His mouth was full, redder than usual, and his eyes were intent as he worked on the other side of her robe. "More," he said, glancing up at her. His eyes glittered in the moonlight. "More."

"Yes."

At the word, beneath her palms, goose bumps rose on his skin. Her blood raced, guessing the physical reaction meant he was as turned on as she, and then she was certain he was, because he jerked the blouse down, taking her bra with it, exposing her breast to the night air.

To him.

He stared at it a long moment. She clutched his sides, feeling a matching set of goose bumps rise along her flesh from the top of her head, over her exposed chest, and down the sensitive insides of her legs.

Noah's gaze lifted as his mouth lowered. He was watching her, she thought, excitement a booster rocket to her already speeding pulse. He wanted to see how she reacted when he took her bare nipple in his mouth.

Heat and wetness closed over her tight bud. His tongue stroked, drawing a delicate circle around her areola. She heard herself whimper. Surely he could see the plea in her expression.

Yet still he kept up the subtle strokes. Had she imagined that earlier bite?

*Could* she have imagined it? No man had ever touched her with less than gentleness. During lovemaking she'd always been treated like a breakable piece of expensive crystal.

She dug her fingers into Noah's scalp and his gaze intensified.

"More," she whispered the word this time, desire and the desire to be more than a precious object making her voice husky. Demanding. Would he understand what she needed? "More."

His lips locked onto her flesh.

She bowed in his embrace and gave herself up to the fire and pressure of his mouth. A shiver raced through her, shaking her bones, her thoughts, her understanding of herself. After years of living with a dying husband, she'd considered herself a woman of mild desires and low-level libido, but now she only wanted strong sensation after strong sensation: the rasp of a beard, the clutch of strong fingers, the stinging edge of a man's teeth.

Then she could be sure she was living.

Suddenly, Noah's head jerked up. She jerked, too, startled

by the movement and how much she already missed his mouth. The night air was cold against her wet nipple.

"Someone's coming," he said.

She whimpered, less disturbed about being seen than being cut off from this dark, delicious round of sensation.

A grimace crooked the corners of his mouth. He bent his head swiftly, and then there it was, that little sting.

She moaned, her nipple throbbed, Noah yanked her clothes back into place. Then he pulled her to him, tucking her face against his chest. "That's what you want?" he asked, repeating the question he hadn't let her answer earlier.

Her arms wrapped around his waist and she shivered again, reacting to all that she desired and all that she was being denied—at least for the moment.

"That's what you want?" he said, again.

She lifted her face to look at him. "It's a start."

Noah pushed through the doors leading into the restaurant, towing Juliet behind him. He had to get her somewhere, somewhere private, before he woke up. Because if this was merely a dream, he intended to stay within it as long as he possibly could.

Juliet pulled back on his arm.

*Should have known this was too good to be true.* He closed his eyes a moment, then looked back.

Her eyes . . . the Iraq sky, the green of spring. Her cheeks were pink from the cool breeze and her mouth was reddened, the edges blurred from the scrape of his whiskers. He couldn't stop himself from reaching out and using his thumb to outline her lips. "Second thoughts?"

Her tongue darted out to taste his skin. He hissed in a breath, then his hand shifted to cup her chin. "No second thoughts?"

She shook her head. "I came with Nikki and Jay. I need to tell them I'm leaving."

"I'll do it." He was already scanning the crowd, looking for the couple. "You stay right here."

Catching his hand, Juliet squeezed his fingers. "I'm not going anywhere without you."

And wasn't that just another sign he was asleep? But he wove through the crowd anyway, in case it really was Juliet he'd been kissing outside, in case it really was her unspoken demands that had caused him to tighten his hands and his mouth on her. Perfect, classy, golden Juliet had begged him in every way for a rougher touch.

Hell, his body was telling him he was well on his way to wild monkey sex with Juliet Weston. He *must* be dreaming.

But there were Jay and Nikki, dancing, and he shouldered past a Raggedy Ann and Andy to tap the mermaid on the shoulder. She turned her bicolored eyes on him, the ones so like her sister's, and it halted his thought processes.

It was Juliet's face he saw, full of frustration and unexpected anger. *Is it too much to ask that I could have a man to hold me through one simple, single night?* She'd said that.

*A man I admire.* She'd said that, too.

"Noah?"

He shook his head, and focused again on Nikki's questioning expression. So that she could hear him over the band's rendition of "Thriller," he leaned in. "I'm taking Juliet."

The younger woman glanced back at Jay. He was all innocence and no comment—practically gazing up at the ceiling and whistling. She turned back to Noah and narrowed her eyes. "*Taking* her?"

"Yes." Then he realized how that sounded and amended his response, eager to get back before Juliet disappeared like the soap bubble he was afraid she might be. "Taking her home."

Nikki put her hand on his arm as he started to turn.

"I've only known her a short while . . ." she started.

He could read her concern, and because he cared for

Juliet, too, he was grateful for it. His biological family had given him nothing, but he'd found brothers in the Army and he knew how valuable those bonds could be.

"I'm not going to hurt her," he told Nikki. Juliet only wanted a simple, single night, and he could do that, without jeopardizing hearts or secrets.

*Is it too much to ask that I could find some way to prove that I didn't die, too?*

He had to do that for her.

It took him moments to get back to the spot where he'd left her. She wasn't there.

The soap bubble had already burst.

But no—no, *there*. There she was, in the restaurant foyer. He hurried through the archway and took her hand. "I thought I'd lost you."

He registered the frozen look on her face and her odd, stiff posture, and wondered if he just might be right after all. She glanced at him, her expression that careful blank, then slipped her fingers from his as she directed her attention back to an older woman standing nearby.

"Noah, you remember Helen, don't you? Wayne's—our—old friend?"

Helen. Helen Novack. In her early sixties, the woman had the chic but no-care haircut of a woman who spent her days on tennis courts and golf courses. Her face was tanned but relatively unlined and her eyes were a shrewd brown. Noah had grown up without learning shit about high society, and if he'd thought about it at all, he'd have figured that the southern end of wet-behind-the-ears California would be without such pretensions anyway. But then he'd met the general and the old-moneyed families like the Westons who called places such as San Marino, Bel Air, and Pacific Palisades home.

There was the new-ink reek of the money made by studio heads, movie producers, and the DUIs-by-the-dozen actors, and then there was Helen Novack's money that smelled like century-old bricks of cool adobe and acres of orange blossoms.

Juliet was still speaking. "And, Helen? I'm sure you recognize Noah Smith, my . . . um . . . Wayne's assistant?"

"That's right," the older woman said, acknowledging Noah with a flick of her eyelashes. "He's working for you now."

Noah didn't give Juliet a chance to reply. "Correct, ma'am."

"Only until I'm settled in the new house," Juliet added, her lips curving in a pale imitation of her usual smile. "Noah just passed the California Bar exam."

Helen Novack's brows rose a fraction. "But for now he's your—what exactly? Driver?"

"Um, well . . ." A flush rose up Juliet's neck.

"Driver, gardener, house painter, whatever's required," Noah injected himself into the conversation again, not that he thought for a moment that Juliet would confess she wanted him to be more. And not that he considered for a moment that Helen Novack herself would ever dream that the general's beautiful wife would go slumming with the likes of an enlisted soldier who hailed from some scrub-and-sand desert hamlet—law degree or not.

Staring him down, Helen's eyebrows rose a half-inch more, but he'd never withered under the disdain of his drill sergeants and he didn't twitch now. After a moment, she transferred her gaze back to Juliet. "Well, it's convenient we ran into each other."

"You said your niece persuaded you to join her tonight."

"A charity event, she told me." Helen frowned as the band took up an old party song and the crowd shouted for *Tequila*! "I didn't expect it to be quite so raucous, though I should have known. *Malibu*."

It was said in the same tone as Noah imagined she'd use when uttering, "Drugs." "Rock 'n' roll." "Sex."

The crowd yelled again—*Tequila!*—and Juliet glanced

over her shoulder then sent Helen another one of those half-hearted smiles. "I was just leaving myself."

"I must say I'm surprised to see you out *partying*."

The older woman's obvious disapproval made Noah's hackles rise. The general had been gone for nearly a year and Juliet had devoted herself to him during his long illness before that. Wasn't she entitled to experience a little music, a little laughter, a little—

*Tequila!* the crowd shouted.

—even a little of that, too, if she liked?

"I'm sorry, Helen," Juliet said, her voice low.

Noah stared. Sorry? Sorry about what? Why was she apologizing?

"Never mind," the other woman replied. "But as I said, it's convenient I ran into you. I want you to know that I'm planning a party—a party to launch Wayne's book."

Juliet brightened. "Oh, how fabulous. When?"

"The twenty-first of next month. Invitations have already gone out and I've been promised press coverage as well."

"Really fabulous." Juliet's smile was genuine this time and he saw her shoulders relax. "But my mail's been spotty catching up with me at the new house. Where and what time is your party? I'll put it on my calendar."

Helen didn't bat an eyelash. "Juliet, I didn't invite you."

"Oh." A single syllable, that's it. Besides the death of her smile, she showed no other reaction to the verbal slap.

"Surely you understand," Helen continued. "I didn't think it was a good idea, when the focus should be on Wayne and all that he accomplished."

"Surely," Juliet echoed, giving a jerky nod. "I've had similar thoughts myself."

"But don't worry." Helen was tucking her handbag beneath her arm and seemed prepared to move on. "The rest of our group will be there, all Wayne's friends, Marlys, of course, and everyone else who knew and loved him."

*Except Juliet. Except the general's wife.*

As she took a step past them, Helen's head whipped toward Noah, and he realized he'd said the words out loud.

"As his wife," the older woman responded, quiet, yet oh-so-cold, "don't you think she's done enough?"

# Ten

In war, there are no unwounded soldiers.

—JOSÉ NAROSKY

Juliet's defensive shell was back in place, the same shell that she'd thought had shattered for good the night she found Noah in her pool. She tried welcoming its return, because it was better to feel nothing than to feel the pain of Helen's cuts, wasn't it? *Juliet, I didn't invite you.*

An event to celebrate and honor Wayne's life and his accomplishments, and everyone who loved him would be there, except Juliet. *Surely you understand.*

No, no she didn't. But she'd lost the opportunity to say it a moment ago and she didn't have the energy to track down Helen and say it now. *Why?* she thought, suddenly so weary. *Why bother?*

"Choose your poison," a male voice said.

She looked over. Noah. Noah was gazing down at her with a look on his face she couldn't read. "What?"

"Choose your poison."

"You mean arsenic or cyanide?"

"No." He rubbed the edge of his thumb against her cheek. She didn't feel one millimeter of the short stroke.

"I'm thinking either a shot of booze in the bar over there, or maybe we get out of this place and find ourselves a cup of hot coffee. Black with sugar."

*Both beverages for a person in shock*, Juliet thought. She tried drumming up some concern about her looks—obviously pale—but couldn't bring herself to care. "I'm okay."

On second thought, though, getting out of the restaurant was a definite priority. "I take that back . . . I could use the coffee."

The Coffee Bean & Tea Leaf was just down the highway, and even on Halloween night it was busy with customers, some in their everyday Malibu casual—those tight dark jeans and expensive boots—while others were costumed for the holiday, including one Jacques Cousteau wannabe in a neoprene dive suit, complete with black booties, black hood, and an underwater camera.

She found them seats at a table hardly bigger than the lid of one of their cups while Noah stood in line. When he came back with their beverages on a tray, she immediately grabbed hers to bring the paper cup to her lips.

"Whoa, whoa, whoa," Noah said, snatching it from her and dropping it to the tray again. "They're out of those wrappers that keep you from burning your hand and the coffee's hot."

As he sat down across from her, so close their knees bumped, he took up her right hand and inspected her fingertips. "Scorched?" He pressed a light kiss to them.

She hadn't sensed the heat. The light caress didn't register either. She didn't feel a thing, when not an hour ago she'd been baring her soul and baring her breasts to this man.

Maybe he was remembering their interlude on the path to the beach, too, because he dropped her hand and sat back.

"So, what's this about you in high school?" he asked, his voice light. "I never pegged you for a Dateless Debbie. Not with your looks."

Juliet shrugged. "I didn't fit in."

"It was high school. Who really thought they did?"

There was that, so she had to nod. "Still, on top of the usual teenage angst, when I was thirteen I developed a huge schoolgirl crush on Wayne."

He straightened in his chair. "*What?*"

"It was all on my side. I told you I was a romantic bookworm and when I met him . . . it was like meeting a movie star or royalty, you know? He fueled enough innocent daydreams to get me through high school without dates or boyfriends."

"What did your parents think about your feelings for him?"

She ventured for her coffee again, and because Noah didn't protest, figured it was safe to cradle in her palms. "If they'd known about it, I suppose they would have figured I'd grow out of it. Which I did. He wasn't the only man I ever went to bed with. He was the man I fell in love with, though, really in love, when I was twenty-three."

Noah busied himself collecting his own cup from the tray. He took a sip, then stared down at it. "What would your parents have thought about that?"

"Hmm." Juliet tasted her drink. Black, with lots of sugar, just as Noah had promised. "That's tougher to answer. They were older, quiet, very conservative."

"And they never told you about the circumstances of your conception?"

"Not a peep." A movement behind Noah caught her attention, but it was only Jacques Cousteau changing seats. Now he was across the room from them and fiddling idly with his big camera. "It's hard to say if they would have told me at some later date. I've actually been thinking a lot about that."

Noah took another swallow from his cup. "Are you angry they kept the truth from you?"

Even for those few days when she'd been capable of emotional highs and lows, she'd not been angry. Not exactly.

But . . . "I hate secrets," she said. There was that nagging sense that Wayne had held something back from her, and now there was this. "It bothers me more, I think, because of what happened to them."

"What was that?"

"My parents got this big idea of crossing the country in an RV. They weren't experienced, and during their first cold night, they were having trouble keeping warm. Someone lent them a portable gas heater and it didn't work properly. The carbon monoxide poisoned Mom and Dad in their sleep."

"Sudden and shocking, then."

"Yes." Looking down, she saw her fingers tighten around the coffee cup. "They were in good health and in good spirits. So I was unprepared . . . and devastated to find myself without family. We were close, I was an only child, my college friends were far away. But if I'd known the circumstances of my conception, I would have known I still had sisters."

She watched, surprised, as liquid plopped onto the back of her hands. When she touched her fingertips to her face, she came away with more wetness.

Tears. She was crying and yet she still felt nothing.

Jacques Cousteau was on the move again, choosing another table, and she grabbed up a napkin to blot her cheeks. Nevertheless, the tears continued.

"Juliet?"

She saw Noah's arm reach across the table and his hand find hers. Then she watched his fingers flex, tightening around her own, but she could only see the action, not feel it, not with that brittle barrier between her and the world re-established. When Wayne had died, she'd appreciated the protection.

But now it worried her that though Noah was just inches away and leaning across the table with a look of concern in his eyes, he seemed as far from Juliet as the creepy guy in neoprene across the room. And if she couldn't change this, she knew with sudden certainty, then she would never achieve closeness with anyone.

Even her newfound sisters wouldn't be able to reach her—or she them. If nothing else, if no one else, she needed to be able to connect to Nikki and Cassandra, to reach out to them so that she wouldn't be alone in her empty rooms with her cold heart forever.

There had to be some way to break free again . . . and she thought she knew what that way was.

Afraid to leave time for second thoughts, she pushed back her chair. It screeched against the floor, but even the sound seemed muted. "I need to do something," she told Noah. "I need to do something right now."

He set his cup on the table. "Tonight?"

"Yes." It had to be tonight. Immediately. "Will you come with me?"

It never occurred to her that Noah would refuse to comply. He'd been her ally, her companion so often on this journey that she couldn't imagine taking these particular steps without him.

He did all that she asked. He drove her home. He waited outside her house in his truck while she changed into sweats and flip-flops and gathered everything she needed, including a beach blanket, into a large tote bag.

He kept his thoughts to himself, even after she gave him their destination. *Just like a man*, she thought, a little burst of amusement catching her by surprise. Their lack of curiosity about people and their motivations could sometimes astound her.

But she didn't want to answer questions anyway. And so she kept quiet, too, as she led them down the beach at Zuma, past a couple of concrete circles roaring with bonfires and ringed by revelers. When the flickers of the flames were far away, when the only light came from the big, fat harvest moon overhead, she reached into her bag for the blanket and spread it on the sand. Then she reached in again and brought out the container of Wayne's ashes. Handcrafted from recycled paper, it was shaped like a clamshell and colored the same blue-green as the Pacific waters. With careful hands, she set it on the olive-drab wool of Wayne's old Army blanket, the one that had accompanied them on dozens of beach trips and just as many forest picnics.

"Oh, Juliet." From the mix of resignation and concern in Noah's voice, she realized he'd guessed why she'd wanted to come here from the instant she'd mentioned the place. Likely he'd been silent on the trip over because he'd been wishing so hard he was wrong.

But this was right.

The time was right.

The place was right.

And this was the way she'd achieve what she needed.

She kicked off her sandals and then pushed the elastic hems of her sweatpants up past her knees. Now in knickers, she stepped onto the cool, silky sand.

Already she was feeling something.

Noah was nothing more than a dark statue as she bent to retrieve the ashes. "Juliet . . ." He whispered her name into the darkness.

She crossed her arms to hold the container against her chest, close to her heart. It was beating . . . beating . . . beating, yet it felt more like a death knell than a sign of life.

And she wanted to live again.

She couldn't do that with this task still left unfinished. Wayne had never wanted to be her burden, and now she had to set them both free.

"Juliet . . ." Noah whispered again.

But she couldn't let the ache in his voice stop her. With that moon shining overhead, its color the orange marmalade shade of the cat that had adopted her and Wayne in the first year of their marriage, she took resolute steps toward the surf. The water washed over her ankles, her shins, tickled her knees, and then wet the cotton of her pants as she waded farther out.

She hesitated a moment. She listened hard for Wayne's voice and she breathed deep, hoping to catch the scent of his presence one last time. But the shush of the waves was the single sound she heard and the sole scent was the salty wet that smelled only of eternity.

Now.

*Now.*

Obeying her instincts, Juliet lifted the clamshell away from the cradle of her body and flung it from her and into the cradle of the sea. The shell settled with a gentle splash, and rocked there on the surface of the water.

Snippets of images flipped across the movie screen inside her head: the shiny button of a dress uniform, the cover of the original diary, navy blue pajamas hanging without a slouch from a hook in the closet.

For another five minutes, more images joined that inner slideshow as she watched the shell float on the surface of the Pacific. Then, as it was designed, as Wayne had wanted, it slowly sank, where over time it would become part of the ocean and part of some child's sandcastle and—most important of all—part of the whole.

She focused on the last place she'd seen the shell, not blinking for fear she'd lose it. Five minutes more passed or fifty minutes, she didn't know.

"Juliet," a voice called from behind her. Called her back to shore.

She turned. Noah was wading out to her, his rolled-up pants already trailing in the water.

"I'm coming," she called. "I'll be right there."

Her hot, salty tears found their own eternal home as she made her way back to the beach. The breeze was brisk, the ocean arctic, her hair whipped across her eyes and caused more tears. By leaving the shell of Wayne's ashes in the water, she knew that just as she'd hoped, she'd left her own shell behind, too. It was gone for good this time.

Noah grabbed her as she stumbled out of the low surf, keeping her upright and pulling her against him. He was warm and strong and so alive that she cried harder at the pain of it, as if her icy feet had been plunged into heated water.

With her still in his arms, he dropped to the blanket and wrapped its ends around them. Her back to his chest, she sat between his legs, and buried her face in her hands, shuddering against the raw ache that reached her now that there was no longer any shield but the tattered blanket and Noah's body.

She thought of that old marmalade cat, already ancient, according to the vet, when it had found them, and how it had disappeared one day, never to be seen again. She remembered how she'd cried, how Wayne had held her, promising other cats, other pets, a whole zoo, just to assuage her grief.

"I'll never love another," she'd said then.

"I'll never love another," she said now.

Dawn came late to Malibu, because the Santa Monica Mountains blocked the sun's earliest light. But the sky overhead was turning from midnight blue to morning gray as Noah pulled in front of the house on Mar Vista Drive and turned off the engine. When Juliet didn't stir, he steeled himself and glanced over.

She was looking at him.

He almost jumped out of his skin.

They'd been together for hours, first on the beach, and then at a twenty-four-hour diner where he'd plied her with little pots of lemony tea and stacks of rubbery pancakes doused in sticky syrup. Juliet had been her customary courteous self, quick with her usual "please" and "thank you," but he wasn't certain she'd even been fully aware of his presence. They'd not spoken beyond the polite phrase or two.

He hadn't known what she was thinking. For his part, he'd been preoccupied with the memory of her shaking and sobbing in his arms.

*I'll never love another.*

Echoes of that whisper had raked at his insides.

But he didn't want to think about that anymore. Somewhere between that stark whisper and the final drip of maple syrup, he'd made a decision. Juliet had taken her big step last night, and today was a new day. His new day, the day he would take his first step away from her.

He couldn't think when she was looking at him like that, though. "What?" he asked. "Do I have jam on my face or something?"

She shook her head. "No. I'm just realizing I haven't thanked you."

"Not a problem."

"I just assumed you would go with me to do that last night."

He shrugged.

"I wasn't surprised to see you wading out to get me, either. Or to find myself comforted in your arms."

A night without sleep hadn't dimmed her blue and green gaze. As usual, their bicolors unsteadied him, and the fragility that the faint purple shadows beneath them added only made him rockier. He jerked open his door before he did something stupid like draw her into his arms again. It was that new day.

They both followed the front path leading to the door. He stooped for the morning paper, then stood back as she put her key in the lock. Yeah, he could have gone around the side gate to get to the guesthouse, but it was quicker to go through her place, and having seen her this far, he decided to go the whole nine yards.

In the kitchen, he hesitated before the back door, the newspaper still in hand. "Juliet," he started.

"Noah," she said at the same time.

They both went silent for so long, deferring to each other, that the moment turned awkward. Awkward enough for Juliet's face to go pink. He wondered if what she wanted to bring up was as uncomfortable as what he wanted to say, and that's why they were both still mum.

But he had to get on with his life. "Mind if I take the classifieds with me?"

She blinked. "Oh, sure."

Glancing down to separate the sections, he took the plunge. "I'm going to look for another place to live."

Her answering silence told him nothing. He had to shift his gaze upward. Their eyes met. Again, the silence stretched thin.

Finally, she turned away. "Orders all carried out then?" she asked, an odd tightness to her voice.

Noah frowned. "What are you talking about?"

"Wayne's orders. He issued them, didn't he? That's what this has been about these months, I know that. That you helped me with everything after his death, that you helped me move here, that you thought you needed to check up on the situation with Cassandra and Nikki, that you . . . that you . . ." She made a vague gesture with her hand that seemed to encompass all manner of things. "That you did everything I asked for or needed."

Hell. This wasn't a conversation he wished to have. He'd merely wanted to make his plans known and then escape. "Of course the general talked to me about you and . . . what would come after. He was concerned."

"So he came up with a plan. Told you how to carry it out."

Noah tossed the newspaper onto the nearby counter. "I'm not here because of what the general wanted."

Her head whipped toward him so fast her hair flew out like a golden banner. "Then why?"

Shit. And he'd been thinking he was so smart. *Walked*

*right into that one, Smith.* He ran his hand down his face. "Juliet—"

"Be honest. How did it go?" she asked, her voice rising. "Because I'd really like to know. Did he say something like, 'Give her time, soldier.' Did he say, 'Watch her, watch her closely, and there'll come a day when you'll feel free to walk away'?"

"It wasn't like that." Christ, didn't she know he'd never be free? The rest of his goddamn life he'd remember her, he'd remember every moment with her, from the day he spotted her chasing after that feckless dog to those hours last night when he'd held her against his heart.

Her whole body pivoted to face him and she crossed her arms over the chest of her snowman sweats. They were thick, white cotton and so unsexy that his mind shouldn't be drifting that way at all, but just the mere glimpse of the slender column of her neck had him thinking about how it had tasted under his tongue, how she'd slid her fingers through his hair and brought his head lower . . .

"Then what was it like?" she demanded.

Sweet, he remembered. And hot. So damn arousing. His mouth tingled and he almost felt the stiff nub of her nipple against his tongue.

"Noah?" Her voice was sharp.

He tried snapping back to the question at hand, but she was too quick for him. "Never mind," she said, turning her back on him again. "It doesn't matter."

"Juliet, I'm sorry—"

"I said it doesn't matter!" Then her voice cooled, slowed. "And I'm sorry, too. I had no right . . . not when you've done your job. You should feel good about that."

He felt like shit about that comment. "It hasn't been just a job, Juliet."

She nodded. "I know. I get that. You've been a good, um, pal. Not just to me, of course. There was all that you did for Wayne, too."

*Pal*? God, this was torture. Noah closed his eyes. "I liked your husband very much."

"He was a worthy man."

"The best." Better than Noah, that was sure.

She turned to face him again, so damn beautiful whether it was in snow-sweats or Shakespearean velvet or bare-naked between the sheets of his imagination.

"Juliet . . ." There was so much he wanted, and so much he wanted to say.

She plowed on. "I hope you realize how much he thought of you, too, Noah. I know he considered you a real friend."

"Yeah?" A real friend? Christ, he couldn't take this. And worse, she was gazing on him as if he was some sort of self-sacrificing, decent-minded Dudley Do-Right.

"Yes," she said, a little frown digging a line between her eyebrows. "A real friend."

"God!" He shoved his hands through his hair, then let his arms drop to his side. "*God!*" He really didn't think he could do this anymore. He really didn't think he could play noble Noah for one more moment.

And who could blame him? Just hours ago he was inches away from wild monkey sex with the woman and he'd ended up with ashes instead—another man's ashes. Jesus Christ, it was enough to provoke even the Boy Scout she considered him to be.

"Noah?" She moved forward and placed one cool hand on his forearm.

He steeled himself not to react to the touch.

"What's the matter?" she asked. "Did I say something wrong?"

It was him, he was all wrong. But with her hand on him, with the thousand fantasies he'd had of her flooding his head, he couldn't hold back an instant longer. "Christ, Juliet, do you suppose he'd still consider me a 'real friend' if he knew the truth?"

"The truth?" she echoed.

"Yeah." He laughed, but there wasn't an ounce of humor in it.

"What truth? What are you trying to say?"

"I'm trying to say I doubt the general would consider me a real friend if he knew how goddamn much I've always wanted to make love to his wife."

There. That should do it. Those words and her shocked reaction to them would surely give him the push he needed to walk away from her.

Except she was only staring at him, as her hand slipped off his arm. "W-What?"

He shook his head. Christ. No wonder she was confused when he was still prettying it up. "Let me be clear, Juliet. I don't want to just kiss your cheek or hold your hand. I want to go to bed with you. I've always wanted to go to bed with you. Bad."

She blinked. "You have? You do?"

"Oh, yeah. And I wouldn't be what you're used to, honey. I'm no officer and gentleman outside the blankets or underneath them either. I'm a guy from the streets who likes his sex sweaty and raunchy and more intimate than you can imagine."

Still looking like twenty-four carats of class, Juliet stared up at him. Why wasn't she throwing him from the house or at least running, screaming, from it herself?

Noah dropped the veneer he struggled so hard to maintain when he was in her presence. "I want to touch every inch of your skin . . . I want to lick it with my tongue and roll across it with my cock, and when I'm done I want to use my mouth and teeth to mark every place I've been like a tagger marks a street corner."

Now she stepped back.

Well, good. Good for her. Good for him, too. He took it as his invitation to leave. Gritting his teeth, Noah turned to the door. But then something caught at the back of his ancient Army T-shirt.

Over his shoulder, he saw Juliet's fist in the hem. He

didn't want to stay for what else she had to say. Eye on the door, he made to yank free of her hold.

*Riiip.*

His shirt gave way, and at the sound, so did his resolve. He spun, jerked her into his arms, and covered her mouth to take one last kiss before he left.

# Eleven

To love is to place our happiness in the happiness of another.

—GOTTFRIED WILHELM VON LEIBNIZ

Except, Noah realized right away, this wasn't a good-bye kind of kiss. Juliet had her arms around him, holding him close with the same kind of desperation that was driving him, and then when he took the kiss deeper, she did that thing that fired his blood and thickened his already-hard cock.

She sucked on his tongue.

He groaned, and when she sucked harder, he had to wrench his mouth away from hers before he did something more drastic like wrenching all the clothes from her body. His chest heaved as he stared down into her blue and green eyes, desire burning like fire in his blood and his erection pressing like heated iron against his belly.

It should be a crime to want this much and have no chance at getting the prize.

Except—no chance? Because Juliet was still clutching his shoulders and her breathing was an erratic rhythm as she gazed up at him. She looked confused, maybe even bewildered. Dazed by surprise to find herself again in his arms or . . . dizzy with desire?

*Is it too much to ask that I could have a man to hold me through one simple, single night?*

She'd wanted that earlier, she'd wanted that man to be Noah, but he'd assumed the events that came after—Helen's rejection at the restaurant and what Juliet had done at Zuma—had put that wish right out of her mind.

*Is it too much to ask that I could find some way to prove that I didn't die, too?*

But now, now that the long night had passed, perhaps her need for proof had resurfaced.

Or maybe he was just kidding himself. Two-and-a-half years of fantasizing about the unattainable could fool a man.

She shivered, and hell, there was his answer. Time to go. So he moved back—but then she moved with him, her fingers digging into his muscles and her belly ghosting a kiss against his cock. Even that brief stroke sent lust punching through him like a syringe of adrenaline. Without thinking, he reacted to it by hauling her hips against his and taking her lips again.

She didn't protest, no, not at all, because as he sank his tongue deep into her mouth, she sank against his body. Wasn't nature amazing, he thought, his arms steeling to keep her upright. When he went pole-hard, she went pliant. When he needed in, she went open. And God, wasn't that yin-yang opposition just so damn good.

As was that message her sweet pliancy, her sweet yielding delivered.

She trembled against him, but he knew what that signaled this time, and he petted a path up her back to tangle his fingers in her long hair. "It's okay, baby," he said, putting an inch of space between their lips. "I've got you. I'll give you what you need."

She buried her forehead against his chest and through his palm on her back he felt the hitch in her rapid breaths. "You know?" she asked, her voice a throaty whisper.

The husky note traveled down his chest to wrap like a

hand around his dick. "Oh yeah, baby, I know. And I'm going to do you so good."

At the bawdy words, she jerked against him, and he smiled over the top of her golden head. He'd laid it out for her before, he'd told her without a dab of sugary icing and in the crudest terms how and what he wanted, and he refused to back away from it now—because she hadn't. Maybe part of what Juliet needed was a little slumming with Noah so it wouldn't be anything like the sex she'd had with . . .

. . . in the past.

He wasn't going to think of her with another man.

He sure as hell was going to do his best to make sure she didn't either. Noah had this one time to make her feel alive and he wasn't going to let anything or anyone get between them.

And he wasn't going to hesitate to get started.

Peeling her hands from his shoulders, he stepped back. There was color on her face, and her mouth was as rosy as he planned to make her nipples. His eyes on hers, he brought her fingers to his lips and ran his tongue along her knuckles.

"You're cold," he said, taking in their icy temperature.

Her breath hitched again. "Nerves."

The word tightened down his control. While the thug inside of him clamored for sex as quick and dirty as a streetfight, Noah wrapped the urge in strong, thick chains. From the size of Juliet's dark pupils and the continued tremor in her limbs, he figured he could take her down as fast as he wanted, but with only this one shot to have her, he knew he better savor it.

Oh, yeah, he was going to go so slow, inch-by-silken-inch, that she'd never realize how much of her she let him have, touch, taste.

He kissed the back of her hands. "I know a way to warm you up."

"I should wash the salt and sand away," she said quickly, looking down at her feet, still in rubber-soled flip-flops.

"Just what I had in mind," he answered. "Shower or bath?"

A flush rose on her cheeks. "Not . . ."

"Together?" he kept his tone mild and tried to put out of his head all the questions starting to gather there. When was the last time Juliet had had sex? Had she ever stepped into a shower or slid into a bathtub with a man? And how slow could he take it if he had her naked and slippery and slick with soap? "We're in California, right? Shouldn't we be doing our part for water conservation?"

Biting her bottom lip, her head bobbed and then she let him lead her toward the master bedroom suite. Morning had finally found its way to Malibu, and sunshine poured like transparent gold paint through the trio of arched windows in the hallway and onto the hardwood floor.

"It's awfully bright," she worried aloud. "Maybe we should wait . . . maybe tonight . . ."

*When there was darkness to hide behind,* he finished for her.

His hand tightened on hers. "It's a new day, Juliet." This day that he thought was his, had become theirs. *It's our day.* "And unless you've changed your mind—"

"No."

"Then it's like I already told you, honey. I'm no gentleman." He gave her a wolfish grin and wiggled his eyebrows. "Your modesty doesn't stand a chance against my wicked ways."

She laughed like he wanted her, too, and it got them to the bedroom. On moving day, self-preservation had mandated he avoid any space so personal to her, and now he took in the pale walls and amber area rug as well as the queen-sized bed with its vanilla-colored bedclothes.

Juliet halted, staring at it with a frown.

Noah swallowed his groan. It was going to kill him if she balked now. If she tried, swear to God, he was going to summon every touch he knew, every technique he'd ever tried, to seduce her back into the mood. He did know there was a big whirlpool tub in the attached bath, and he could already see both of them inside of it, bubbles up to her breasts, his hand sneaking beneath the camouflage of the frothy stuff to explore the soft layers of her sex.

Yeah, it was going to take an agony of persuasion, he figured, an hour of kisses and surreptitious touches to get her there, but he would. He wanted it that bad.

Taking a careful breath, he squeezed her hand again. "Juliet? Okay?"

She glanced at him, and then around the spacious room. "It's just so . . . so *beige*."

Noah blinked at the disgust in her voice. "And, um . . ." Um what? "And?"

She dropped his hand. "And I'm sick of it." In a sudden flurry of movement, she spun to face the massive mirror hanging over a long chest of drawers crafted from some light-colored wood. "And look there," she said, pointing to herself in that white sweatsuit. "More colorlessness."

Without a pause, she reached down and whipped her sweatshirt over her head. "I never want to see myself in these again." She threw the top across the room. Then she shoved down the pants and flung them away with her foot, one flip-flop going along for the ride. The other she tossed, too, and it thunked against the wall, marring the pristine paint.

She stared at the mark, her chest heaving again, and it gave him time to appreciate the underwear. She was wearing a matching—and demure—lace bra and bikini panties in an understated buff color.

He toyed with mentioning it, certain they'd be the next victims of her unexpected ire, but he wanted to save some unwrapping for himself. His mind spun off, thinking how best to accomplish that. Should he ease up behind her right now, or lure her into the bathroom? How many kisses until he could walk his fingers to the back clasp of that bra?

Would he slide her panties off at the first opportunity, or instead slip his hands underneath the stretchy fabric to cup her sweet little ass?

She whipped around while he was still deep in the selections of his imagined sensual buffet. "I'm ready for sex now," she declared, and marched past him to the bathroom. "Are you coming?"

Startled, he stared after her. Was he coming? Shit, he hoped so. But man, even that might be in question, because by the time he'd reeled his tongue into his mouth and beaten back his surprise to hurry in her wake, she was already not only in the dim bathroom but was a shadowy figure behind the wavy glass of her two-will-fit-just-fine stand-alone shower.

The beige lace underthings lay flat on the floor like she'd removed then in haste and then stomped on them at leisure.

He flipped the switch to illuminate the stall and then he could see her better . . . still blurred by the shower glass, but that was definitely Juliet's curvy outline and Juliet's elegant back, the cleft between her perfect peach cheeks the only shadow that remained. *God.* His balls drew tight and more lust poured into his blood. Noah fisted his hands, holding himself back as the sexual gangster inside of him urged for a simple smash-and-grab.

Over the soft fall of water from the showerhead, Juliet's unsteady voice reached him. "Those nerves I told you about . . ."

"Mmm?" His gaze glued on her unmoving figure, he started shucking off his clothes.

"I lost them."

He smiled as he leaned over to unlace his boots, and was surprised by the sudden clumsiness of his fingers. "Maybe you misplaced them during your little strip show out there."

"No," her voice thinned. "I mean, I think I *lost my nerve.*"

"Ah, honey." Naked, he put his hand on the stall's door handle. "It's just me."

She let out a shaky laugh. " 'Just you.' Oh, Noah."

The door opened with an audible click and steam washed over him like hot breath.

Her head jerked around and she looked at him over one wet, creamy shoulder. "Oh, *Noah*."

Her gaze whipped back around to the wall, but from that first, wide-eyed glance of hers, he knew it was going to be okay. He'd thought about this moment for years, showered with just this very fantasy more times than he could count, and though the hoodlum inside him wanted nothing more than to vandalize all that smooth and elegant skin with urgent touches and rough kisses, he found the control to approach her slow and steady.

One forefinger reached out to trace the bumps of her delicate spine. She shuddered, and he moved closer to lower his head and sip the water off her shoulder blade. Another shiver wracked her body and he chased goose bumps up the slope of her shoulder to the side of her neck. He took another lick.

Her body bumped back, out of the shower's direct spray, and her ass brushed his cock. They both sucked in breaths. "I've never showered with a man before," she confessed.

"Yeah?" Smiling against her skin, he reached for the liquid soap that sat in a nearby niche. With one hand, he managed to pump his palm full of the stuff. It smelled like her, classy and clean, and he took the scoop of his hand up to his nose for another heady inhalation. "I've never washed anyone as beautiful as you."

"Like this . . . the light . . . naked . . . *Noah*." His name soughed out as he pressed his slick hand to her belly. He rubbed in little circles and felt her press back against him again for support. With his other arm, he anchored her to him, not even trying to avoid the rounded pillows of her ass. He pressed himself there, distracting her from the way he was insinuating himself between her softness by the unceasing circles of his hand moving from hip bone to hip bone.

She moaned. "I'm a little embarrassed."

"You're turned on."

"I know it's ridiculous, but I'm a little embarrassed about that."

It wasn't ridiculous. Elegant, aloof Juliet Weston wasn't used to letting someone so close.

"Noah, at the moment, I'm not even sure I can look at you."

He rubbed his cheek against the sleek wet fall of her hair, and let his soapy hand travel upward. "At the moment, you don't have to look at me, baby. You just have to feel me." Feel alive. He cupped her breast, capturing it in the cage of his hand as if it was a wild bird. Against the edge of his thumb, he felt her heart beating erratically and the sensation delivered another blast of lust to boil his blood.

She squirmed, and his cock nudged deeper until he had to tighten his hold on her breast to keep her still and keep him sane. At her needy whimper he kneaded her breast again, and then he drew his fingertips together and outward, drawing them to the areola and then farther, tugging on her hard little nipple.

Another sweet, plaintive moan had him pressing his cheek to hers, and he noted her eyes were squeezed shut with enough force that lines fanned from their corners. He kissed her there, and then leaned around her to sweep his tongue across her lashes. "Relax."

"I can't."

"You can." Both of his hands cupped her breasts now, and he played there, gentle on the full flesh, and less so on the tight buds. As he plucked them, her head fell back against his shoulder, but there was nothing boneless about her body. Even as he saw the flush of arousal suffusing her face, he could feel the fine tremors shaking her tense frame.

"Noah . . ."

"You have a seventy-gallon hot water heater, we have plenty of time." A quickie wouldn't be enough for either of them, would it? Him, to exorcise the fantasies with real-life Juliet sex, and for her, didn't she deserve a prolonged reintroduction to man-woman pleasures?

But her body was getting more rigid by the moment and then he saw her teeth bite down on her bottom lip. This wasn't making her bloom, he realized, it was making her hurt.

Shit. How long since she'd let herself have this little taste of life? She was reaching for it and battling against it, both with such force that she was shaking with the dueling purposes.

And then Noah knew.

Juliet wouldn't have orgasmed on her own. Not by her own hand, not with some naughty-girl toy. Not when her husband was dying, not while she was grieving, not ever in . . .

Years?

For himself, he wanted to play with the possibilities of that for hours. For her, he was going to have to give her a fast, ruthless push over the brink.

The gangster inside of him grinned, but he told the bad boy to settle down. This could be his single chance at her climax and he was going to let her fly solo.

With the fingers of one hand still rolling a berried nipple, he shoved the other into the shower spray to rinse off the soap, then brought it down between her thighs. He didn't take it slow, she was needy enough. Instead, he speared his middle and forefinger through her wet curls and between her swollen layers to trap his quarry.

She froze, every muscle tight. Like her heart, this little organ was beating too, rising toward his touch and hungry for what he offered. In his fantasies he spent hours getting to know this sweet morsel of flesh, but now, he accepted he might only have these few moments.

Wrapping her with his left arm, he used the middle finger of his right hand to draw a snug circle around the stem of the hard bud. All her muscles tightened, her spine as stiff as if he'd lashed her to a pole. But her support was his body behind her, her bond his left arm circling just below her breasts, her instrument of torture the firm ring he drew around her with his finger.

On his next pass, new wetness met the tip of his long digit. He jolted, heat rocketing through him at the slippery sign of her surging desire. Without thinking twice, he brought his finger to his mouth, sucking off the flavor of her, sucking her essence into his mouth.

She whimpered, and he glanced down to see she was watching him, her face flushed and her blue and green eyes wide and trained on his mouth. Oh, yeah. He dropped his hand and dipped it in her softness again. Then he lifted his finger to her lips, offering to feed her that distinct proof of life. "Try it," he urged her. "It's as good as your next breath."

He painted her lower lip and his blood burned again as her tongue crept out to taste. He rubbed the rest of the liquid arousal along the velvet surface and saw her flush deepen.

"My turn," he said, his voice hoarse as he lowered his hand. "This next taste is mine."

Seeking the lush well inside her, his fingers brushed her erect clitoris, and just with that small nudge, she flew. With a low moan, she pressed back against him. Her shoulder blades dug into his chest, her back bowed, and the cheeks of her ass tightened along the length of his cock.

He would have lost it, surely should have lost it, but to his eternal shock, his instinct to support her writhing body overrode the sexual demand pounding in his blood.

Miracle of miracles. Maybe he was noble Noah after all.

She moved through shudders, to tremors, to the sweetest little shivers, and he went along for the ride with her, his finger easing up on her sensitive flesh as she quieted. Then she turned in his arms and buried her face against his chest.

"Baby." He backed her into the shower spray again, intent on keeping her warm now that her climax had passed. His hand caressed her shoulders and she shivered again, her face still hidden. Shit, was she crying? Under where she pressed, beneath his skin, his sinew, and his skeleton, beneath all those protective layers were four aching chambers that twisted and squeezed at the thought of her tears.

At the reality of her regrets.

At the realization that he'd never have more of her than this.

Then, in that same spot, a sharper pain stung. For a minute it didn't register as separate from the other hurt. Then it came again, another small bite of sensation and he looked down, pushing her away at the same time.

Her eyes were half-mast, her mouth swollen. She reached up to his chest, tracing with her thumb the shallow tracks of her teeth. "I did that," she said.

Astonished, he stared at the marks and then at the smug expression of the woman.

"I want to do it some more," she said.

His skin flashed hot and then he was on the move, dragging her from the shower and then dragging a towel over their flesh, the entire time battling the elegant woman whom he'd always assumed didn't have a whiff of warrior inside her.

But she went heads up into a skirmish with him right now. Apparently she wanted undelayed, unfettered access to his body and she fought to touch him, taste him, crawl over him even when they were standing, even when he was trying to do something as uncomplicated as getting her across the room and horizontal on that whipped cream–colored bed.

"Take it easy," he said, holding her by the shoulders so he could move without their feet tangling and taking them both to the floor.

"I want it hard."

Shaking his head, he laughed. "Really, baby. Relax."

"Not till I get what I want." She lunged for him, and twined her arms around his neck and one calf around his hip. The hot, melting center of her body scalded his thigh. Groaning, he bent his knee to give her some friction.

She moaned, and licked across his pecs to find one of his nipples. He hissed in a hard breath, then gathered his resolve and folded her up in his arms.

She made a muffled protest against the side of his neck and rubbed one of her nipples along the hard plane of his chest. Striding for the mattress, he dropped a kiss on the top of her head. "You're a maniac, do you know that?"

"Maniac for your body."

He laughed, dropping her to the mattress, then following her down as soon as he managed to get on the condom he had in his pants. She went wild again, writhing under him, delivering hot kisses, scratching his back with her nails.

Lust slammed into him again, harder this time. Desperate to slow things down, he reached back to close his hands on her wrists before the sharp edge of her fingernails had him coming over her belly before he could make it inside her.

He pressed her hands to the mattress and reared onto his knees to put space between them . . . and to let him look at her creamy skin, her pretty curves, the pink-tipped breasts and the pink wetness waiting for him between her splayed thighs. She was breathing hard.

He didn't think he was breathing at all.

"Noah. Noah, please."

There was desperation in Juliet's voice, renewed tension in her quivering body. His inner sexual thug was gleeful, urging him on in single-syllable words.

*Fuck her. Fuck her fast. Fuck her hard.*

But this was Juliet. *Juliet!*

The woman he'd watched, the woman he'd wanted, for something like a hundred years.

So he closed his ears to that low-life gangster and treated her like the lady she was. He penetrated slow, sliding against hot, tender tissues at a pace that had him gritting his teeth. She moaned as he seated himself as deep as he dared, but he didn't let that little sound hurry him either.

Instead, he took his time and took her with the caution and care that she deserved. He used a gentle rhythm and shallow strokes, but still pleasure burned. When his climax could no longer be denied, he wet his thumb and touched her again, sending her on a soft, sweet journey. As her body quaked against his, he ground his teeth harder and resisted the urge to plunge deep. Holding steady, he didn't move another inch, but let her squeezing contractions around his cock do the work to bring him off. His body shaking, he swallowed his groan of satisfaction until both their bodies were still.

As he pulled away, Juliet's eyes were closed and her mouth looked bruised. Guilt swamped him—those kisses had been too damn rough—and he tried to apologize by pressing his lips to her forehead. She made a little murmur and shivered, so he drew the covers over her and went off to deal with the rubber. When he came back, she was sound asleep, and he stood there, watching. The sun was higher in the sky and now flooded the room. When its rays burnished the gold of her hair, Noah closed his eyes and turned away from the almost-painful brightness.

# *Twelve*

All war is deception.

—SUN TZU

Marlys stood by the door of her boutique, wrapping up her good-byes to one of her few former bed partners. A pharmaceutical rep, Phillip dropped by when he had some minutes to burn between appointments. She figured he had other, ulterior motives as well: He liked the coffee at the bakery next door, and he loved congratulating himself on having never offered her the flashy diamond and marriage proposal he'd planned.

When his brother couldn't help himself and gossiped the news to her first—not such a surprise since he was a SoCal stringer for the tabloids—Marlys had dumped Pharmaceutical Phil that very night.

Another woman might have let him go through with the one-knee moment, but she'd spared them both the experience. Not only didn't she want to be some man's wife, she didn't want to sleep with a marriage-minded one either. Smacked of codependency.

Then the shop door swung open and Dean Long stepped in. She took the jolt of pleasure at the sight of him like a stab to the belly. The sharp sensation made her suck in a hard breath, and then she hid her sudden flush of yearning by grabbing Phil by the ears and planting a searing kiss on his lips.

She put tongue into it.

And a little panic.

When she let him go, she dried her bottom lip with the edge of her hand and then pushed her ex toward the door, feigning surprise at seeing Dean standing in the way. "Oh!" She hid her smirk behind her fingers.

Dazed, Phil wandered around the other man and outside without a word, but Marlys waved at his retreating back with an aspartame smile. "See you!"

Then she swung her attention to the newcomer. "And I didn't expect to see *you*." Her hands tugged on the wrap dress she wore with a pair of sleek riding-style boots and then adjusted the little cardigan she had on for extra warmth. "You didn't mention it last night."

He shrugged. "The way you scampered off clutching that beefstick, I thought I'd given you enough to worry about for one evening."

"Worried? You don't worry me." After a little more light-hearted flirtation, she'd left him without a care in the world. He was cute, she'd decided once she was safe at home with her dog, but of no concern for a woman like herself.

"Then how about a late breakfast or an early lunch? Can you get away—or did you already spend all your free time on the guy you just poleaxed with that out-of-the-blue tonsil inspection?"

Crap. He hadn't bought her act—and it made her mad, because she wasn't completely sure of what she'd been trying to sell. Was she trying to prove to Dean that she could attract other men? That she could manage any man?

"Well?" He looked as if he couldn't care less what she answered and that made her mad, too. But he was here, wasn't he? Maybe he was a better actor than she was, but he hadn't sought her out without reason.

Maybe he wanted his own tonsil inspection.

That now-familiar belly burn ignited again and Marlys glanced around the shop. She had plenty of excuses if she wanted to refuse, but her clerk Leeza knew the ropes nearly as well as she did. And there was only a couple of browsers besides the woman who'd taken some outfits into the fitting room. Through her lashes, she made another quick assessment of Dean.

Not cute, handsome. Sexy. And the way he was looking at her, all silvery cool, felt like a direct challenge. *Angel, show me what you've got.*

Marlys could never resist a dare, and this one didn't have a downside. The upper hand was always fun, and she'd show him that to her, lunch with a gorgeous man like himself equaled pure playtime.

"All right." The shop was so small it was only two hops and a skip to retrieve her purse from behind the counter. "Leeza, you'll be okay?"

The clerk said she would, and Marlys was headed for the door and Dean. With only five steps to go, the woman who'd been in the fitting area blocked her way. In a long-sleeved, knee-length cotton knit tunic over leggings, she held out her arms. "What do you think?"

Marlys didn't hesitate. "You'll need to lose ten pounds before you can wear that without looking pregnant."

Over the crestfallen shopper's head, she caught Dean's wince. She ignored the little poke of guilt at her plainspokenness, and while she would have done it anyway, she hurried on her detour to a freestanding rack. There, she pulled a different top off the metal stand. "This one will look fabulous with your great skin."

Cheering some, the woman took the hanger, and Marlys continued on her way. Outside, Dean slanted her a look. "How the hell do you stay in business with that kind of customer service?"

"I stay in business because when I tell them something's

right, they believe me, and don't think I'm just trying to make a sale."

"Ah," Dean said, nodding. "I've been to a restaurant in Atlanta where the waitresses regularly curse the diners and roundly criticize their selections from the menu. The line is out the door."

"The top I picked out cost twice as much as the one she'd tried on."

"Marlys!" A laugh was startled from him.

She gave him a cheeky grin. "What? It will look twice as good on her. Really."

He laughed again, and slung an arm over her shoulders. Her little shiver of reaction was easy to cover by drawing her sweater closer around her. "I can't decide if you're wicked or fun," he said.

"Wicked fun," she answered. See? Playtime. Nothing to worry about.

It was cool enough to choose the table under a patio heater at a nearby café. She asked for a half order of Chinese salad and black coffee, while Dean wanted eggs, bacon, homefries, a blueberry muffin, and a side of granola-topped yogurt.

"You and Noah need to go grocery shopping," Marlys said, marveling at the number of plates that the waitress had placed around him and the speed at which he was chowing down the food. "Last night it was beefsticks. This morning he didn't have anything to offer for breakfast?"

"Noah wasn't there this morning."

She hooted in surprise. "So the private got lucky last night! Who's the woman on gun-cleaning detail?"

His fork halfway to his mouth, he froze. His cool silver gaze seemed to slice right through her like an ice pick. "I don't know. What do you have against him anyway?"

Her plate of shredded cabbage, sliced almonds, and wonton strips required her full attention. "What makes you think I have something against him?"

"'Private'?"

Marlys squirmed. “It’s not meant to be a put-down. I don’t criticize soldiers—of any rank.”

“Mmm.”

Miffed, she glared at Dean. “I don’t!”

“Yeah, and that guy you tongue-kissed in your shop a little while back is your true soul mate.” He put down his fork and patted her fingers resting on the tabletop. “Don’t get worked up, angel. Not everyone appreciates the military life.”

Marlys jerked her hand from his touch and shoved it into the patch pocket of her cardigan where she fingered the silver amulet and played with the attached silver chain. “I lived on Army bases. I loved military life.”

“Yeah?” Dean pushed the last of his plates away. His eyebrows rose as he took in her expression. “I think you mean it.”

While she resented his apparent belief that he could read the truth on her face, she didn’t see any harm in reminiscing about the childhood she remembered as blissfully happy and incredibly secure.

“It was the best. I was an only child, but there were always other kids to play with. Our parents shopped at the same places, we went to the same schools, the focus of every family on my block was exactly the same. I loved the way that everything stopped on base when the flag was lowered at five P.M.” She had her hand out of her pocket and halfway to her heart before she realized what she was doing and, embarrassed, redirected it to her coffee cup.

Dean gave a little nod. “The way my sisters and brother and I were raised, our entire family was in the service, not just our father.”

“Exactly.” Marlys smiled. “I couldn’t wait until I turned ten and was eligible for my very own military I.D.”

Dean laughed. “I’d forgotten about that.”

“And instead of Barbies, I had a whole army of G.I. Joes.”

His brows rose again. “Which might explain your career in boutique-wear. You missed out on your girly years.”

“I didn’t miss out on anything.” Every day she’d walked

within those comforting gates, she'd known she'd belonged and she'd been secure.

Dean was shaking his head. "God, I felt like I did. When I turned fourteen, I wanted to be a civilian kid in the worst way, which only made my dad clamp down harder. My mom, too, telling me that every trouble report on me reached the base commander and reflected on my father, and my father's career. At seventeen, I bailed out of the whole thing and it took me a few years before I woke up, went back, and enlisted. I don't suppose growing up with that kind of pressure was any easier for you."

"My father was a general."

He shrugged. "Yeah? Only worse. My father didn't have near that kind of clout, and when I was a kid, he still pissed me off."

The amulet's silver chain strangled her forefinger. "I adored my father."

"I'm sure the feeling was mutual, though imagining Marlys Weston, teen angel, makes even a battle-scarred dude like me shiver a little. How'd the general deal?"

"The general didn't deal at all," Marlys heard herself confess. She whipped her hand from the silver tear in her pocket and flattened her fingers against the table as if it could flatten her own emotions. "My mom asked for a divorce when I was twelve."

Dean brushed her fingertips with his. "And?"

"If I recall correctly, he wasn't in the country at the time. He didn't protest. We moved off base, I lost my friends." *I lost my security, my place.* "I never spent any more time on a military base." The rare occasions she saw her father, they'd go to the mountains to ski or to the beach to swim. They never went anywhere and worked, *lived* like a family.

She'd never belonged anywhere again, she thought, staring off into space. Or belonged to anyone. Sometimes it made her so damn mad, and other times—

"Marlys? Angel?"

Blinking, she focused on Dean. He was tossing some

bills onto the little black tray that had come with the check, then he tucked his wallet in his back pocket.

Leaning across the table, he rubbed his thumb over her mouth. Her lips tingled. "I don't like to see you sad."

"Sad?" The word shocked her out of her reverie. It wasn't close to mad and sounded too much like serious. "Sad! Marlys Weston doesn't do sad. Marlys Weston is much too happy for sad."

"Whatever you say." He stood, then lifted her out of her chair. His posture was familiar, soldier-straight, and she had a sudden urge to see him in uniform. Crisp, correct, everything in its place. In the military, you knew the rules and you played within the fences.

It might sound weird to other people. Stifling, instead of comforting. But she could see herself in on-base housing again. It was a harmless little fantasy, just more playing, but she could see it. A house, with herself inside of it. The front door opened, and a uniformed man strode inside.

Not her father. Not some anonymous military man.

Dean. And her heart thrilled at the sight of him.

On the sidewalk outside the café in Santa Monica, he was gazing down at her. When he cupped her chin, their gazes met, and just like that, the chemistry experiment bubbling between them blew up in their faces. *Ka-boom.*

"Jesus," he said, all of him jerking away from her except for those fingers gripping her jaw. "Jesus, you do something to me."

Her heart jittered in reaction to the stark truth in his voice. This wasn't fun, or funny, or playful, or like the prank she'd played when she'd kissed Pharmaceutical Phil in his presence. This was weakness and want and everything she'd sworn that a man would never make her feel.

This was serious.

Juliet drove to Malibu & Ewe, eager to put distance between herself and Noah. He'd left her bedroom shortly after eleven, while she—what a chicken—pretended sleep. After a brief shower during which she acknowledged she could never look at those tiled walls the same again, she'd scampered to her car and instinctively headed for the first person she thought of.

Cassandra.

Her sister.

It was a notion still almost as unfamiliar as a man in her bed. But unlike that idea, it was a comfort to her, a promise of unequivocal support, and all she wanted right now was to sit on one of Cassandra's couches. In the other woman's calm, warm presence, she would draw out her needles and her yarn and work on the wrap she was making as a long-term substitute for a man's arms. In Malibu & Ewe, there would be time and quiet to get her bearings.

The parking lot the shop shared with Gabe's fish market/café was crowded, but she found a just-vacated spot and strode for Cassandra's place. It was another incredible day, November now, she realized, but the sun bounced so brightly off the ocean that she was forced to tent her hand over her eyes.

It wasn't so much easier in Malibu & Ewe, she discovered, as she pushed through the door. Colors came at her, clearer and brighter than she ever recalled, and not just from the bins of yarn around Cassandra's shop but from the outfits worn by the crowd of customers and in the tones of their upbeat, excited chatter.

By the register, Cassandra looked less calm than harried. A line had formed and she was obviously struggling to be efficient with the transactions while still answering the questions that were thrown her way from about the room. Juliet caught her eye, but she got barely a smile before her sister's attention was split by yet another request.

The couches were full, and in the chaos, no one but Juliet seemed to notice that ensconced in the middle of the cushions was One of the Most Famous Actresses in America. Oomfaa, her long, lean legs crossed at the knee, appeared to be knitting a red-and-white striped mitten. Juliet had to grin to herself. She wasn't the only woman who considered Cassandra's shop a haven. And apparently the paparazzi were as ignorant of Oomfaa's hobbies as they were of her home address.

A muffled, frustrated curse directed Juliet's attention back to Cassandra. She rolled her eyes heavenward. "Out of register tape," she muttered.

It wasn't clarity, but it was industry, and Juliet welcomed that almost as much. "Move aside," she ordered the shop owner. "I've got this."

She took care of more than inserting a new role of tape. Cassandra had been snagged by a customer when Juliet took over, so she stayed behind the register. It was the Accucount 480, and she knew how to work the thing. Yes, she had to call Cassandra back for a brief lesson on her preferred procedures for credit cards and checks, but even that was mostly familiar.

An hour and a half later, she was tidying the countertop. Her feet hurt, and she'd made zero inches of progress on her wrap, but a sense of satisfaction filled her anyway. Cassandra was moving about, returning skeins to their bins. Oomfaa and everyone else, for the moment, was gone.

Cassandra looked over. "I owe you, big. What would you like?"

*A game plan for what comes next with Noah.* Instead, she said, "That was crazy busy."

"My version of what Nikki calls the 'lunch rush' in restaurant speak. Everyone comes in before the kids get home from school or before the highway gets too bad with the commuter traffic. It's worse, for unknown reasons, on midweek afternoons." She sighed. "I suppose I should be looking for some part-time help. Strictly minimum wage plus discounts, but the location's stellar."

"You should hire me." The suggestion just popped out, and Juliet blinked, surprised by the thought. "Of course, you don't—" she started, and then swallowed the rest. She wanted the job, she decided—even at strictly minimum wage plus discounts—so why demur?

"Done." Cassandra grinned.

Juliet grinned back. Maybe it wasn't a career—finding that could come later—but this was a start.

My, wasn't this turning out to be an interesting day? Job in the afternoon, sex in the morning. Oh, that's right, there was that. Her mood dipped and she felt her smile die. Sex in the morning. Sex in the morning with Noah.

And now what?

He said he was moving out. Her stomach jittered a little at the thought, and she felt stupid at her dismay at the idea of him leaving.

It wasn't that she expected he'd stay forever. She knew he was going to move on, she'd said that to him herself. He'd move on, start his own life, find the woman he wanted to marry.

That wasn't her. For certain, that wasn't her.

Not only had she had her love-of-her-life and been wedded to him, but she wasn't sure she could satisfy a man like Noah, even for a little while. Because he'd said: *I'm no officer and gentleman outside the blankets or underneath them either. I'm a guy from the streets who likes his sex sweaty and raunchy and more intimate than you can imagine.*

Because he'd said that, and then, once they were in her bed he'd acted as if she were fragile. Delicate. Like a heart about to break.

"Uh-oh," Cassandra said, coming to the register. "Don't tell me it's nothing. Something's bothering you."

"It is," she said, nodding. "I came over here to ask your advice." There had to be someone who would tell her what to do when it came to Noah, and she was banking on this down-to-earth, warm-hearted woman.

Cassandra grabbed her hand and drew her toward the couches in the center of the room. "Sit down and tell me all about it."

As Juliet opened her mouth, the bells on the shop door rang out with an angry jangle. Her head turned in time to see Nikki storm through the door, her hands balled, her face and neck flushed, her blue and green eyes glittering like jewels.

Her gaze zeroed in on Cassandra as she stalked toward the center of the room. "Explain that e-mail," she spit out.

Juliet stared. Good God, the younger woman was steaming with fury. *That's how I'd look if I ever really let go*, Juliet thought to herself. *In passion* or *in anger*.

Nikki came to a stop in front of the shop owner and slammed her arms over her starched cook's tunic. "Cassandra—"

"Wait." She flicked a glance at Juliet. "Can't we . . ."

Juliet took the hint and jumped to her feet. "I'll just—"

"Sit right back down." Nikki pointed to the cushions. Then she addressed Cassandra once more. "What? You didn't e-mail big sister? You're keeping secrets from her just like you once kept them from me?"

A cold chill rolled down Juliet's back. "I don't like secrets."

"Cassandra's an expert at them."

"That's not fair!" Cassandra rubbed her palms against her flowing paisley skirt. "I apologized for that, for not telling you right away we're sisters. You know my reasons."

"What are your reasons now?" Nikki said, a brow rising over her one green eye. "Why would you consider contacting our sperm donor without—"

"Our *father*," Cassandra corrected, her voice rising, too. "The man fathered us."

Nikki's slashing gesture dismissed the idea. "Not me. Not Juliet. And not you either, Froot Loop."

The other woman's eyes now glittered, too. "Don't."

"Fathering goes beyond petri dishes and turkey basters. Even you should know that."

"And even you should know that every time you reach out a hand it won't be slapped."

Both fuming, they stared each other down and Juliet remembered she'd come to the shop for some calm. Before that, she recalled she'd been intrigued at being part of a trio. At the idea of sisters. But this was messier than she'd expected, not to mention—her train of thought derailed as the source of their argument finally sank in.

"Wait," she said. "You contacted our sperm donor?"

Cassandra glanced over. "Not yet. I just floated the possibility to you *both* in e-mail. I guess you haven't checked yours yet."

"I thought the donor process was anonymous," Juliet said.

"It was at the time," Cassandra answered. "But there are ways—"

"Sneaky ways," Nikki put in hotly. "The same sneaky ways you used to find me."

"It's not like I stole your identity," Cassandra shot back. "Thanks to my 'sneaky ways,' I gave you something. I gave you us, your sisters."

Nikki's mouth set in a stubborn line. "Well, fine. But I don't want or need anyone else. And we have no right to be poking into this man's life after all these years."

"Didn't you finish reading the e-mail?" Cassandra's gaze narrowed. "Oh, no, you didn't. You read the first line and then came stomping over here, breathing fire like a dragon."

Nikki didn't soften. "So what? What did I miss?"

"Donor 1714 registered on the website set up to connect biological fathers to their offspring. Once I provide the data I have, the site administrators will release his e-mail to me."

"Big whoop. You've known his name for months."

"A name?" Juliet realized she'd not asked enough questions of Cassandra and Nikki—or they'd been wary enough of her to hold some pieces of information back. It stung a little to think they hadn't trusted her with everything. "You know his name?"

"*I* do," Cassandra answered. "But Nikki—"

"Thinks knowing his donor number is knowledge enough," the younger woman finished.

Cassandra's eyes rolled. "You're such an ostrich sometimes."

"And you're such a meddler all of the time."

"Don't be childish," Cassandra snapped.

"Don't be judgmental."

"Judgmental?" Cassandra lifted her hands, let them fall. "You're a big snot, you know that?"

Nikki shrugged. "So says the Froot Loop."

Cassandra heaved in a short breath and took a fast step forward.

Nikki held her ground. "What are you going to do, poke me with a knitting needle or just pound me with a granola bar?"

Cassandra let out a strangled sound and her jaw tightened. "Nik—"

"Enough!" Goaded by their ridiculous behavior, Juliet stepped between the two of them—and into the fray. "Both of you cut it out."

The two women stared at her with round, startled eyes. Juliet crossed her arms and gave them a quelling look—something she didn't, before, realize she possessed. "I, for one, am thanking God right now that I wasn't around to referee your teenage spats over boyfriends and sweater-borrowing."

"Yeah." Nikki smirked and jerked her thumb at Cassandra. "Especially because the girls on that one would have overstretched any top we shared."

"Hey—" And then Cassandra laughed, the temper in her eyes cooling. "Okay, we sounded fifteen."

"Try thirteen," Juliet corrected. "So now let's all sit down and be civil like grown-ups."

In minutes she got the story straight. Cassandra visited a website where sperm donors could register information such as the fertility clinic where they donated, donation dates, and their identifying number in the hopes of connecting with offspring who were curious to learn more about that unknown half of their biological equation.

Cassandra was all for making contact.

Nikki was satisfied with sisters.

Juliet decided she was somewhere in the middle. At the moment, anyway.

But, surprise, surprise, she found the other two allowed her to negotiate their differences. Because she was the oldest sister? It didn't make sense to her, because she'd never been considered bossy in her life—dreamy, yes, agreeable, often—but it was obvious her sisters looked at her to take charge.

So she did.

With an assurance she hadn't called upon before, she got them both to agree to table the decision—as well as more discussion—for a few days so they could all think it through on their own. They were going to make contact, or not make contact, whichever the case might be, as a group. Given their burgeoning closeness, it didn't seem possible that one or two could get in touch with the man without compromising another sister's privacy.

Cassandra seemed mollified, Nikki satisfied, and Juliet felt . . . pretty darn good, actually. Even after Cassandra—with Juliet's permission—shared with her the name of their sperm donor after Nikki exited the shop. Knowing his identity didn't redirect the way her mind was running.

She'd fled to Malibu & Ewe so that someone could tell her what to do. That was her usual MO. After her parents' death, she'd looked to Wayne. After losing him, she'd relied on Noah to help ease her way. She'd too often placated as well—swallowing her thoughts so as not to upset the people in her life like Helen and Marlys.

But this afternoon, she hadn't needed direction. She hadn't rolled over, either. She'd stepped in, stepped up, and solved the problem.

This same sort of action would work in other areas of her life, too, she decided, as she drove back to her house.

Instead of faking sleep, she should have faced Noah and asked the questions she wanted answered.

*What now?*

And why had he treated her like she might break? Did he worry she couldn't stand up to a man's passion?

Without giving herself time to fret about the confrontation, she marched straight from her garage to the guesthouse. In the tiger's den, she'd take him on.

Its door opened the instant her knuckles left the wood. *Oh.* A dark-haired, gray-eyed man was on the other side.

*Oh, hell.* She'd forgotten about Dean. He stood gazing at her, and over his shoulder she saw Noah. He was looking at her, too, but she couldn't decipher the expression on his face. She could only remember the whiskery roughness of his kiss, the sure touch of his hand, the seductive sweetness of his dirty words: *I'm going to do you so good.*

Her knees wobbled and she had to grab the threshold of the door. What was her face telling him? she wondered.

But before she could come up with an answer, a familiar, yet unwelcome voice cut through the silence. "Stepmama! Hey, boys, it's going to be a foursome for our little barbecue after all."

# Thirteen

Gravitation cannot be held responsible for people falling in love.

—ALBERT EINSTEIN

Marlys planned on taking Dean to her bed. That's what she'd decided after their little late breakfast/early lunch rendezvous. So she'd showed up at his place after the boutique's closing hours and demanded to be fed. Later tonight, serious was going to be supplanted by sex.

Of course, she was going to torture him first by using all her skills to tease him out of his mind. She owed him the abuse for showing up in her ordered, man-free life and making her feel all female. Soft.

Sex would give her a hold over him.

To that end, she sat on the arm of his chair in Noah's small living area, while Juliet took a place on the nearby sofa. Marlys let her fingers run through the hair at the back of Dean's neck. The dark stuff was thick and bristly, but already longer than the day they'd met. He shot her a glance, and at her innocent smile, he grimaced and reached up for her hand. *Ticklish, huh?*

She bussed a little air kiss in his direction and was

satisfied to see his gaze drop to her mouth. *Yeah, baby, keep on looking.*

But she felt other eyes on her, too, and it was no surprise to find that her father's wife was staring, her weird, bicolored gaze betraying surprise. The goody-goody likely had her granny panties in a twist over Marlys's not-so-subtle signals that she intended to do the dirty with Dean, a man she'd known for only slightly longer than a couple of drinks at a dance club.

Fine, it surprised the hell out of her, too, because Marlys didn't easily shed her layers—of clothes, emotional armor, what have you—but it was either take Dean to her sheets or chance finding him someplace much more dangerous. Shameful as it was to admit—and unprecedented—she was afraid for her heart.

She slid her thumb from Dean's grasp and stroked the edge of her nail against the top of his hand. The long muscle on his forearm hardened, lifting against his skin in reaction. Smiling, she flicked him another suggestive glance, but the expression in his eyes snuffed her amusement. They were molten silver, and they seemed to promise wicked payback—when she was the one who was supposed to be holding all the weapons.

The skin at the back of her neck prickled, and with haste she redirected her attention, focusing on Noah, who had come from the kitchen with a round of cold beers. He passed one to Juliet—the perfect lady drank beer?—and then to Marlys.

After he handed over a bottle to Dean, he toasted the man with a clack of glass to glass. "Enjoy it while you can, friend."

"Planning an abstinence kick?" Marlys asked, then nudged Dean's ankle with her foot. "I hope you don't mean to extend that to other sorts of sins."

"He's off to Afghanistan," Noah answered. "Once his leave is over, he'll be heading to another danger zone."

"Oh." Juliet's mouth turned down in distress and her

gaze jumped to Noah's face and then back to Dean. "Give us your address," she said, "and we'll be sure to send care packages."

*We?* Though there was an uncomfortable chill rolling over Marlys's skin, that odd word registered. But then it was gone, as her body trembled with a full-on, this-sounds-like-trouble shiver. Afghanistan. Danger zone. Dean.

His hand squeezed her cold fingers. "What about you, angel? What will you send me?"

She made a grab for her composure and managed to lift the corners of her mouth. Then she leaned down to whisper. "Play your cards right, and I'll send you away with some very sexy memories."

This close, she could smell his skin. Her lashes falling, she drew in the scent, holding it deep in her lungs so she could focus on each note—and not anything else. Fresh, green—sage?—it made her think of clean snow and mountain air.

The mountains and cold of Afghanistan.

*Oh, God.* If she didn't get him in her bed and out of her system, something very bad could happen here. She might find herself destined to sick worry and hours glued to CNN.

"Marlys?"

She jerked back at the sound of his concerned voice and made another grand effort at an effortless smile. No way would she let him see her alarm, her dread at what might turn into a daily scouring of military websites and a fixation on counting down the days to the end of his deployment.

She couldn't care that much.

For the first time in her life, she felt an inkling of sympathy for her mother.

"When do you leave?" Juliet asked, leaning forward to put her bottle on the narrow coffee table.

Dean brushed back Marlys's bangs with his free hand, then turned to Juliet. *Whew.* And another first—a dollop of gratitude toward her evil stepmother.

"I'm off for another couple of weeks, but I have a few short visits to make here and there. Tacoma, maybe, before I report."

At his place beside Juliet on the couch, Noah froze, his beer halfway to his mouth. "Why Tacoma?"

"You know," Dean answered, his easy voice a distinct contrast to the other man's sudden palpable tension. "I thought I'd check on Tiny Tim."

"Tim?" Noah shot to his feet so fast, beer bubbled out of the bottle he held. "Why the hell would you do that? You know there's nothing to see."

Dean took a breath. "Noah—"

"Never mind. Shit." He ran his free hand over his face, then looked around at the startled company. "Shit," he said again, then he mumbled an apology and left the house, leaving the three of them staring in the direction of the slammed door.

"What's with the private?" Marlys asked, bewildered.

Juliet slid to the edge of her cushion and shifted her gaze to Dean. "His roommate in Iraq, right? He told me about him."

"Yeah?" Dean appeared surprised. "Noah's usually close-mouthed about that."

"He told me Tim's permanently disabled."

Dean grimaced. "A traumatic brain injury. In this case, an *extremely* traumatic brain injury."

Marlys's stomach jittered. She didn't know this Tim, but she kept abreast of military news. Brain injuries were common in this generation of soldiers. Surgeons managed to save their bodies, but couldn't restore damaged gray matter so much. Without thinking, she slid off the arm of the chair and into Dean's lap. She needed his heat and the reassurance that he was whole to ease her stomach-tumbling disquiet.

As if he read her mind once again, he wrapped an arm around her middle and drew her closer into the curve of his body. Marlys leaned her head against his shoulder, and despite how weak it showed her to be, she turned her cheek to press a kiss against his soft cotton sleeve. His arm gave her an answering squeeze and it was just silly how comforting she found it to be.

Juliet gazed toward the door again. "His friend's injuries hit Noah hard," she said, then frowned. "What a dumb thing to say. Of course they hit him hard."

"It's worse because of the promise he made."

"What promise?" Juliet's odd eyes went laser as they refocused on Dean's face.

"Before Tim transferred to our squad, he'd witnessed firsthand the result of an IED attack. Maybe he had a premonition, maybe it was just plain bad luck, but Tim agonized over ending up severely injured like this other guy he knew. So he forced a pact on Noah."

Juliet's hand crept toward her heart and pressed there, maybe to make sure it was still beating. "What kind of pact?"

"A promise that Noah wouldn't let him become a vegetable. That if his injuries looked serious, Noah would delay medical help and let him go in peace."

Juliet paled, and Marlys felt a little clammy herself. She pressed even closer to Dean. "That wasn't fair."

Dean shrugged. "Love and war, angel."

"So Noah feels like he failed his friend," Juliet mused. Color was returning to her face, and her eyes were so bright Marlys figured those were tears she was blinking away.

"Probably," Dean admitted. "But really, there was a medical officer on scene, so the choice was out of his hands. It was out of everyone's hands."

Setting her mouth in a line, Juliet pushed up from the couch. "I'll go talk to him."

Marlys turned to look at Dean. "Shouldn't it be you?"

His gaze on Juliet, he hugged Marlys close. "I think I'll stay here. Tell Noah I'll be ready to put my famous chicken on the barbecue in half an hour."

The new silence within the walls of the guesthouse only deepened Marlys's disquiet. Afghanistan. Promises. Injuries. Tears.

Damn it! This was all she didn't want.

Twisting on Dean's lap, she glared up at him. "I don't like feeling this way."

A smile kicked up one corner of his mouth. "And you think I do? That's out of our hands, too, angel."

No, it wasn't. Marlys had only been powerless twice before—when her parents divorced and when her father had died. Other than that, she took charge of her life, she owned it, and she dealt with its dilemmas with cold-blooded selfishness.

She always did what was right for Marlys Marie Weston, hang how it might affect anyone else.

And right now, Marlys Marie Weston needed to get back to her original plan. She needed to take this man to bed. This minute.

Winding her arms around Dean's neck, she pressed closer. "Who cares about your famous chicken?" she said against his mouth.

He put two inches between them and smiled. "I've had marinating breasts waiting in the refrigerator since three."

Marlys's fingers went to the tiny buttons that closed her sweater and she gave him a saucy smile. "Well, let me tell you how long my breasts have been waiting for—"

His kiss stole the last word from her. It stole her breath. Like every other time their flesh met, heat sparked, blood fired, the surface of her skin seemed to drum in time with her double-quick heartbeats. She dug her fingers into his thick biceps and hung on to ride out the thrill.

He lifted his head to stare down into her face. "Tell me again why I wanted to barbecue."

"Because I hadn't issued my much better invitation yet." Her second cat smile didn't seem to offend him.

He stood, keeping her close, and groaned as her body's

good parts touched all the hard ones of his. "Let me get my coat."

"And I'll bid adieu to the others for both of us." Yeah, this was the way to handle the situation. She'd sex him right out of her head, her life. Practically licking the cream from her lips, she poked her head out the guesthouse door.

Entwined figures were backlit by the greenish glow from the pool. Marlys blinked. Who the hell had invaded Juliet's backyard?

Then the man groaned, soft and low, and she recognized the couple. Oh, my God. She knew who the two sucking face were now.

Her mind reeled. She stumbled outside, her knees going soft, just as her mind honed to a razor's edge. Juliet and Noah. Her father's wife and her father's aide. *Juliet and Noah.*

She must have said it out loud, because they broke apart as if cleaved in two. Sickness filled her, making her mouth dry and causing her stomach to pitch and heave like an unmoored boat.

"You . . . you . . ." There were a dozen accusations she wanted to hurl at them, but her throat was too tight to release a single one.

"Marlys . . ." Juliet started.

"You whore!" She found the words and flung them toward the beautiful blonde, the perfect lady her father had adored beyond reason. Beyond Marlys. "You bitch."

Noah stepped forward. "That's enough, Marlys."

"Don't say a word to me, Private. You're no better."

"Neither of us has done anything to apologize for or be ashamed of," Noah said, his voice steely. "And now I think it's time you leave."

"I can't stand the sight of either one of you anyway," Marlys replied, striding past them to the side gate exit. There were hot tears in her eyes and she was glad the darkness hid them. Seeing her cry would make them think she was weak, but she was strong in her righteousness, in her sense of outrage on her father's behalf.

*Juliet and Noah.*

She whirled to glare at her father's wife. "How could you? You're still holding tight to my father's ashes and yet you're out here holding tight another man. Kissing him."

Juliet stayed cool as she delivered the sharpest blow of all. "The ashes are gone now, Marlys. As your father wanted, I released them into the ocean."

Marlys backed away, her hand creeping into her pocket to feel her silver pendant. Still there.

Dean emerged from the house. "Marlys?" His voice was puzzled. "What's going on? Are you leaving without me?"

Just the silhouetted shape of him made her ache. She didn't want to leave without him. She wanted what she'd wanted when she'd come to him that evening after work. She wanted him in her bed, wrapped around her. Worse, she wanted to run to him now, damn it. She wanted to fling herself into his arms and beg him to help her find her way clear of this tangle of treachery and grief. But that smacked of emotional dependence, and Marlys Marie Weston would never be so weak.

Later that night, Marlys's doorbell rang. She would have liked to ignore it, but Blackie was going nuts, jumping around just like her stomach and barking with fierce intent, communicating exactly what she wanted to: *I'm ruthless and strong and you should beware of bad, scary me.*

It was Dean outside, of course, she was as certain of that as she was certain he wouldn't easily give up if she pretended deafness and didn't answer the door. So she kneed Blackie aside and promised herself to get rid of him quickly.

When Dean stepped in, he greeted the dog with a brisk body rub. The caresses didn't quell the canine's excitement and he continued his sharp barks and excited leaps.

"Blackie," the man said, his voice hard. "Take it easy." The animal halted for a moment, then hopped about again, his yaps more demanding.

"Blackie." Dean eyed him with stern disappointment. "*No.*" Then he shifted his gaze from the dog and ignored him altogether. Blackie bounced his front paws off Dean's thighs, barked again, but then seemed to realize his antics were doomed to failure. His doggie eyes still trained on the man's face, he sat back on his haunches in sudden silence.

Dean immediately leaned down to rub Blackie's ears. "Good dog. Good boy." Then he straightened, and glanced around the shadowy, spacious foyer. "Big digs," he said to Marlys.

"Ancestral home." She was staring at her animal, who was cuddled up to Dean and doing his best—and first—imitation of man's best friend. "Blackie likes tunneling for the treasures that former Weston canines left behind."

With that, she turned to stroll through the dark house, toward the large kitchen that was the only room with lights blazing. Dean was behind her; she sensed his presence, but for such a large man he moved with an assured quiet.

She was halfway across the black-and-white tile floor when she turned to find that he'd halted in the kitchen doorway. Wearing a strange expression, he was staring at her.

"What?"

"That isn't . . . Good God, it is . . . It's the band Hanson on your robe."

Frowning, Marlys tugged the fleece lapels closer around her throat. She wasn't going to apologize for being in a pair of flannel pajama pants, a T-shirt, and one of her old robes. She hadn't invited him over. "Hanson memorabilia goes for a mint on eBay. This looks nearly brand-new and it's over ten years old. I'm thinking of putting it up for auction."

Dean looked beyond her to the dozens of cardboard boxes piled on the round kitchen table and the others stacked in a Jenga-like pile in a corner of the room. "Is that what you're searching for, angel? Items to sell on eBay?"

Marlys shoved her hand in the pocket of her robe and rubbed her thumb over the silver pendant. "I'm gathering together mementoes of my father's life. A friend of the family is putting on a big party to celebrate the publication of his autobiography. I said I'd provide his special keepsakes for exhibit."

"Juliet must have some, too."

Marlys knew the name would come up. She willed her expression to remain unchanged. "She's not invited to the event."

It was Dean who looked unruffled. "Family friend puts on a big do for the general's book and his widow's not invited?"

Beneath the fleece decorated with photos of Isaac, Taylor, and Zac, Marlys's spine steeled. "I asked Helen to keep her off the guest list."

"Christ, Marlys—"

"I have my reasons!" To her own ears, her voice sounded shrill. She swallowed, and tried smoothing out her tone, though obviously she had even better reasons to keep Juliet off the list now. "And Helen agreed with me."

He shook his head. "Marlys."

For a moment she felt like Blackie, not just chastised, but chagrined she'd disappointed him.

Fine! Let him be disappointed or disgusted or whatever that frown on his face meant. She hadn't invited him over. She wanted to be alone, anyway.

"I'm going to bed," she said. "You can see yourself out." The back staircase was just a few feet away, but his voice halted her at the bottom step.

"There was nothing between them while your father was alive, Marlys."

Again, betrayal bubbled and roiled in her stomach like bile. "Did they send you here to tell me that?"

"They didn't, nor did they have to." Dean's voice was

nearer now and she knew he was closing in on her. "Noah would never do that."

"Yeah? And you know this how?"

"I know *him*. Time in Iraq is often numbing boredom only broken up by mortar rounds and bloody battles. The soldiers standing with you are your saviors from death as well as from tedium. You get pretty damn close. So I'm certain Noah would never have shown such disrespect to your father."

"Maybe not while he was alive . . ."

Dean put his hands on her shoulders. "And now he's dead, Marlys."

Her body jerked away from his touch. "Thank you for that startling piece of information. Good night." She marched up the stairs, slapping her hand against her thigh. "C'mon, Blackie."

After a moment, the jingle of her dog's collar followed. She breathed a sigh of relief. Unless Dean was on his way out, she didn't think her fair-weather pet would have obeyed her command.

Her room was dim, lit only by the forty-watt bulb in the Sleeping Beauty lamp on her bedside table. It was another of her attic finds and she remembered it being in her room at Fort Bliss. She kneed her way across the mattress to pull at the spread covering the pillows. At the doorway, Blackie's collar jingled again.

Without glancing back, she pointed to his bed on the floor. "There you go, boy. Right there."

"I don't think I'll fit."

Marlys stiffened. Unless Blackie had suddenly done a reverse Dr. Dolittle on her, Dean hadn't left after all.

"I didn't invite you in here." Glancing back, she noted he was leaning his shoulder against the doorjamb and that Blackie's shoulder was leaning against his leg. She glared at them both. *Dogs.*

"I brought Blackie up. He didn't seem to be responding when you called him."

Like she'd thought before. *Dogs.*

"Thanks. You can go now." She snapped her fingers, and the dog pranced into the room, then he looked back at his new BFF, as if to say, *Hey, aren't you coming, too?*

"No, Blackie," she answered for him. "And don't even try begging for his company, either. Dean thinks we're spoiled enough as it is."

"That's not what I think," Dean corrected, crossing the rug toward the bed. "I don't think you're acting spoiled right now, Marlys. Like I told you earlier today, I think you're acting sad."

"And like *I* told *you* earlier today, I don't need cheering up." She jerked the covers back to expose her flower-sprigged sheets. As if he wasn't there, she yanked at the tie of her robe and tossed it away. Her toes slid down the icy cotton as she lay on her side and gathered the blankets around her.

"And now you're sad because of what Juliet told you." The mattress shifted as he sat in the space made by the C-curve of her body. "You're upset about the ashes."

"I don't give a shit about those ashes!" Blackie's head jerked up at the sharp edge of her voice. He whined.

Dean's big hand reached out to brush her bangs off her forehead. "Angel—"

"I have my own ashes." She snagged a piece of her robe and drew it across the bed toward her. From the pocket, she pulled the silver chain. "See? I carry around my own piece of my father."

The pendant swung from the chain clutched in her fingers. Dean caught it, held it against his palm for inspection. "A tear. Interesting choice. You wear it?"

"I don't wear it."

"You feel it?"

She'd had it with him. She wanted him out of her bedroom, out of her house, out of her mind, just out, before he could worm himself any further into her head. "Feel what?"

"Grief, angel. Anger and bitterness and sadness come off you in waves, Marlys, but I'm not getting grief."

She snorted. "I'm not giving you a single one of my emotions. Ever."

"Not even desire?"

"Believe me, the last thing I want to do with you right now is have sex."

"How about sleep?" He crawled over to curl around her on the mattress.

"What the hell do you think you're doing?" she asked, rising on her elbow.

"Holding you, Marlys. Holding you while you sleep." He pushed her against the pillows.

When she tried jerking up again, he stroked his hand down her arm. "Take it easy."

"You said that to the dog!"

"And look how he settled to my touch." Dean bunched the pillow beside hers and then pulled her more snugly against his body. He stroked her again. "Isn't this nice?"

On the floor beside her, Blackie dropped his head between his paws, sighed. "Are you a dog whisperer?" she asked.

He laughed, his breath warm against her neck. "If I said yes, you might take offense at the way that plays out."

"Bitch whisperer." Her head settled more deeply on the pillow. "You're right, I might take offense."

"So just take my touch, angel." His soothing hand had a soporific effect on her. So did his warmth. It stole through the covers that separated them. Her heart shuddered, but she squeezed shut her eyes and let her mind and her mood shut down for the night.

In the morning, she woke, panicked. She jerked upright, but found she was alone. Thank God. He'd only left behind an indentation on the pillow beside hers.

But her pulse wouldn't settle. She could still feel the

impression of his heat at her back and if she couldn't shake that, she was doomed. Somehow she had to push him away, because she couldn't risk wanting—no, *needing*—to belong to someone ever again.

Panic rising a second time, she jerked her gaze around the sheets and ran her hands over the cover. There. There. Her fingers found the silver tear. Holding the cold metal against her cheek to remind herself of her resolve, she spied a piece of paper half buried beneath the pillow he'd used. Pulling it free, she took in three sentences in masculine block letters.

HAVE TO BE GONE A FEW DAYS.

It was relief she felt. Yeah. Disappointment was for other women.

THINK OF ME.

Did she have any other choice?

BE GOOD.

Not on her life.

# Fourteen

The supreme art of war is to subdue the enemy without fighting.

—SUN TZU

She hadn't anticipated this was how or where she'd next confront Noah, Juliet thought, pacing the floor of the room designated as her home office. After Marlys had caught that impulsive moment of comfort on the patio, they'd separated without further discussion. Juliet had gone to her house and he'd returned to his place across the pool.

It wasn't clear who had avoided who in the thirty-six or so hours since, but it was fact that they hadn't caught sight of each other after that. By the next time they came face-to-face, she'd been hoping to have found some smooth and easy way of acknowledging what had happened between them in her bedroom—and then maybe moving on to those questions that had plagued her ever since.

Why had he treated her like she might break? Did he worry she couldn't stand up to a man's passion?

But she hadn't yet found her smooth and easy way into the discussion.

And they weren't yet eye to eye.

"Lucky the cable company finally hooked us up," Noah

said, from the other side of the closed office door. "Emergency call via e-mail. That's a first for me."

"I love technology," Juliet replied without enthusiasm.

"You should. It was like one of those little slips of paper you get in dessert at the end of a broccoli beef and chicken chow mein meal."

" 'Help, I'm locked inside a fortune cookie factory,' " Juliet muttered, and though he laughed, the humor escaped her. She was wearing a comfortable pair of cropped yoga pants, a simple T-shirt, and a pair of athletic shoes, but the casual attire had been no help. The tiny attached bath boasted a window only big enough for a loaf of bread to fit through. And without a phone in the room, and with her cell phone in her purse in the kitchen, she'd used the only means of communication open to her.

"Sorry it took me this long to get to you. I was out on an interview and didn't check my e-mail until just a few minutes ago."

There was a rattling sound. "I tried that," she said. "Jiggled the handle a dozen times." Four dozen times. Then pounded the paneled wood, kicked the doorjamb, silently screamed at the walls that had kept her captive since discovering that the lock had inconveniently jammed.

In her childhood home, there had been a downstairs powder room with a tricky door like this one. Unpredictable, unidentifiable elements would cause it to stick, stranding dinner guests on occasion, and confounding the handyman who'd been called to fix it a number of times. They'd eventually replaced the entire mechanism.

This baby was outta here as soon as today.

"What are you doing in there anyway?"

"That e-mail thing you mentioned." When she realized she'd missed Cassandra's message about their sperm donor, she'd figured it was past time she reconnected with the larger world. More progress, she'd thought, as during Wayne's illness and the months after his death she'd been unable to drum up any interest in such a thing as Internet access. "I spent the morning rearranging the furniture and setting up my computer."

And then spent the afternoon frustrated by her confinement . . . and the fact that she had to rely on a man—on Noah—to come to her rescue.

Still, she felt mostly relief when she heard the door pop open. Noah stood in the entry, his gaze taking her in. Then she stared, too. She'd never seen him look like this.

*Damn.* He was a stranger to her, and she'd had to appeal to him for aid.

In a well-tailored gray suit, Noah looked older, harder, more sophisticated than she could have imagined. Against the crisp shirt, opened at the collar, his tanned skin was smooth and golden, his eyes laser blue. There was a striped tie jammed into the breast pocket of his jacket and the note of an unfamiliar, yet delicious aftershave drifted toward her as he walked into the room.

She took a hasty step back.

He ignored her nervous twitch and turned to manipulate the knob of the open door, twisting it back, then forth, then back and forth again. As she figured it would—her luck was going that way—it moved freely, normally.

Embarrassed, she cleared her throat. "Really. I know how to operate a door. It *was* stuck." Shades of visiting the mechanic only to discover your car engine had abandoned its ominous clickety-clack-hum and returned to its usual steady purr.

Noah swung shut the door, fiddled with the handle again, paused. "I believe you."

"You do?"

"Yeah. I really do." He turned to face her, a half-apologetic smile on his face. "Because we're both stuck now."

"No!" She rushed for the door and when he moved out of the way, tested it herself, using both hands to try to free it from its frozen state. The four walls had been close enough when she was alone within them, but to share the small space with Noah . . . "Oh, no."

"Guess I shouldn't have taken the chance and shut it." He shrugged. "But don't worry, Dean's back in town. I'll call him on my cell and get him to star in Rescue Ranger Round Two."

Within moments, Noah had made contact, and in another few he flipped his phone shut. "Good news is, he didn't crash into another car while laughing his ass off. Bad news is, he's crosstown and with L.A. traffic, may be as many as a couple of hours from reaching us."

Frustrated, she went back to jerking on the knob. As she'd known, it didn't budge. Still, an annoyed grunt escaped her mouth and she didn't stay her impulse to give the door another sharp kick. "Stupid thing."

"Claustrophobic?"

"Not really." *I just didn't want to confront you quite yet.* And though she'd been all determination to do just that when she'd left Malibu & Ewe the other day, look how poorly that had turned out. She aimed another swift kick at the door.

"Juliet, you're surprising me again."

"Really?" Giving the knob a last ineffectual rattle, she figured she was out of excuses for avoiding eye contact and turned around. "What did I do now?"

He leaned against the back of the desk that she'd manhandled into the far left corner of the room. "Did you move all this stuff?"

"All by myself." She *was* a bit pleased about that. It had taken a lot of pushing and shoving, rocking and sliding, but not only had she moved the desk, she'd chosen a new place for the media armoire and the small loveseat, matching chair, and low round table that sat between them. She'd even hung a large antique mirror on the wall. Maybe it wasn't perfectly level, but she'd managed. "I'm stronger than I look."

"I should have known that." His head tilted as he regarded her with his vivid gaze. "You did a lot of things around the old house. More than once the general asked me to attend to something and you had gotten there before I could."

"I don't think he believed I was capable of even the most minor repair." Juliet smiled a little. "Or maybe he considered it unfeminine of me to show the slightest hint of handiness."

"No." Noah shook his head. "Unfeminine? Never that, no matter what."

"Are you sure? Because I don't know what else he'd think if he could see me kicking stubborn doors or cursing at the sky." She flushed, remembering exactly what that sky-cursing had been about.

Noah looked away as if to save her the embarrassment. "Still, strong or no, that armoire must have been a bitch to move on your own. You should have called me."

Right. The person she'd been so careful to avoid. "I knew you'd left early this morning. I, um, heard your car start," she added hastily, not wanting him to think she'd been keeping tabs on his comings and goings.

"Dean, then. He was here this morning." Noah shrugged out of his suit jacket and slung it across the desk, then went to work on the starched cuffs of his dress shirt.

"Oh." Juliet tried not to stare as he revealed his powerful forearms by rolling up his sleeve. The skin was tanned there, too, of course, and sprinkled with dark hair. She rubbed at the smoother skin of her own with the palms of her hands, trying to rub away a sudden chill. "I wouldn't bother Dean."

"Because you're embarrassed to face him?"

"Embarrassed?" It was Noah who she'd been so anxious to evade. "Why would I be embarrassed to face Dean?"

"Because he saw us kiss the other night." Noah focused on his shirt sleeve as he carefully rolled it to his elbow. "Because he knows, or guesses . . ."

She frowned. "He knows or guesses . . . what? What exactly are you getting at?"

Noah hesitated.

Giving her time to fill in the blanks.

"Are you saying Dean knows that we . . . that you . . ." His friend knew Noah had gone to bed with her and he expected she was distressed about it. Why?

Then it hit her. Heat crawled over her face.

"Why should I care that your friend knows you took pity on the dried up, lonely old widow across the pool?" She flung the question at him, in order to get the words away from herself. "I don't really know him, and you—well, in his eyes you likely just look like a nicer guy for doing the generous deed, don't you think?"

No wonder Noah had treated her like she'd break. Little old widows were frail like that.

Blinking at the burn that was in her eyes as well as on her face, she whirled back to the door, jerking on the knob and kicking the paneled bottom at the same time.

Incensed, she yelled at the stubborn thing. "Let me out!"

Arms wrapped around her from behind. She struggled against their hold, throwing herself from right, to left, then right again.

"Settle down," Noah said, tightening his embrace. "I don't want to hurt you."

Too late, she thought, still twisting. All her life she'd played the perfect lady, the composed hostess, the gentle wife, but the jagged emotions roiling inside of her were shattering that pose. "Leave me alone!"

He turned her easily, his arms still holding hers, fast, against her sides. "Not until we have this out."

She stiffened in affront, then went crafty instead, going limp in his grasp. Noah instantly relaxed, releasing her and stepping back.

Triumphant, Juliet whirled again to make another desperate attack on the door.

Noah was only a second behind. Once again he had her,

one arm banding her waist, the other around her chest, and as if it was no effort at all, he lifted her wiggling body off her feet to walk her toward the seating area she'd earlier arranged.

"No," she said through her teeth. "Don't do this."

"I'm not doing anything," he replied, his voice as tight as her own. "I just want to talk."

"But I have nothing to say." Her bottom bounced on the loveseat and then he dropped beside her, his hand like a vice around her upper arm. Fuming, she tried getting to her feet, but he held her against the cushions with just those five, implacable fingers.

"Stay put," he ordered.

Had she ever been this angry? A high whine buzzed in her ears and her blood was crashing through her system, hot and intoxicating like some kind of terrible drug. Under its influence, her right hand reached out, fast as a blink, and slapped him across his handsome face.

They both froze and she stared, horrified, fascinated, then horrified again at the faint red mark blooming on his lean cheek. Her blood halted its frenzied dash, her stomach tossed as if she'd thrown *it* into the ocean.

A single thought dominated her mind: *What* had she just done?

This time, when she got to her feet, he didn't try to hold her down. She took a step away from the loveseat, and then another, still staring at what her unfamiliar temper had wrought. "You bring out the worst in me," she said.

"You think?" His eyes narrowed and he slowly rose from the couch. "Maybe I bring out the best. Maybe I bring out what's real about you."

His taller figure towered over hers, and fear skittered down Juliet's spine. Not fear of Noah, even though she'd just slapped him. The one she was afraid of was herself: What might she be capable of next? When he moved closer, she placed her palms against his chest to keep a distance between them. "No."

The muscle in his jaw—his jaw that was still faintly red because she'd slapped him!—ticked. His gaze was trained on her face, the blue color hot as the center of a fire.

It burned her, so she looked away, and caught a glimpse of her reflection in that mirror she'd hung. Her usually straight hair was disheveled and a little wispy at the temples. A flush covered her from neck to forehead, making her own blue and green eyes stand out unnaturally bright. Her memory flashed to Nikki, stomping into Malibu & Ewe, intensity in every step, in every breath.

She'd thought then: *That's how I'd look if I ever really let go. In passion* or *in anger.*

Noah had said: *Maybe I bring out the best. Maybe I bring out what's real about you.*

In the mirror, she knew she had never so closely resembled her fiery little sister. And she marveled at the likeness. *Was* this Juliet at her best? Juliet . . . real?

Her gaze jumped back to Noah's.

One of his hands lifted and he traced a finger down her hot cheek. "Juliet . . ."

"What?" In the wake of his touch, her skin prickled with a heat that had nothing to do with anger.

He stroked again. "Pity is the last thing I feel for you."

"Is it?" It was that different Juliet, a tempestuous Juliet who was speaking through her lips, a carpe diem creature who curled her fingers and dug her nails into Noah's dress shirt in order to get to those hard muscles behind the cotton. Now it was passion that was crawling like a flame inside of her. She shivered, as sensible thoughts—they should discuss this, they shouldn't probably *do* this—evaporated in the heat.

"Well, me," she said, staring into his face where she could see the reflection of her own desire, "I just want to feel." Then, thrilled by her own audacity, she jerked her hands apart, tearing buttons from their moorings.

Revealing Noah's naked chest.

Dimly, she registered the buttons pinging against harder

surfaces. Vividly, she took in the view that had been distracting her since that first night when she'd caught him naked in her pool. His bare chest, bronzed, cut like a *Playgirl* centerfold, tempting with its heavy musculature and hard-tipped copper nipples.

If it was cold, she could fool herself and think it wasn't a reaction to her. To what she'd just done. But it wasn't the least bit cool in the room.

And she wasn't going to fool herself anymore.

She wanted to feel. She wanted passion and sensation and her skin against a man's skin.

No. *This* man's skin.

Without another thought, she stepped forward and took that tempting nipple into her mouth.

Noah's body tightened against hers. He groaned, and she didn't even bother deciphering the tone. She wanted to taste his skin, to suck that small pebble of flesh, to experience the heavy pound of his heart against her hands.

He groaned again, one of his palms rising to cup the back of her head and she flattened her tongue against his areola, her own pulse slamming in secret places. Her breasts swelled against her bra and her inner thighs tightened, trying to hold her erotic response close.

Warmth and wet flooded despite that.

But she didn't care. She ran the heel of her hand over his other tight nipple, rolled over it with the ball of her thumb, and Noah let her take the hard caress. With another groan, he let her own it.

Then she replaced her mouth with her other hand and lifted her head, demanding. He took the hint and dipped his lips to hers.

There was nothing gentle about their meeting.

His tongue thrust into her mouth, his penetration only a precursor to what she really wanted, and it was her time to groan because he knew what she needed. Hard, wet, invasion. Sensation.

This was real.

Him. She wanted all of him.

Yanking the dress shirt from the waist of his slacks, she pressed closer and let the kiss go wild. She bit at his bottom lip, sucked on this tongue, took his upper lip between hers to suckle it in hot, sweet, delight.

Did other women play like this?

She didn't know. She only knew she needed it, and that Noah was not ready to refuse her.

That knowledge sent her to her knees.

Amazing, yes? She'd never been this turned on, this ready to try anything, this determined to take every taste of life and passion available to her. Her hands fumbled at his belt and zipper, but she persisted, even though his head fell back and his groan rubbed like a calloused hand against her skin.

In the vee of his opened pants was the muted print of a pair of silky boxers. It was just a thin layer of satiny sensation between her hand and the heavy jut of his erection. She cradled it, letting the cup of her palm fold around his hard heat. He jerked into her touch and more wetness rushed between her thighs.

Hard. Heat. Wet.

Sensation piling upon sensation.

Who would have thought she'd need even more? That she'd push aside that silk so that his erection pushed toward her. Pushed toward her mouth.

And she wanted that sensation, too. She rubbed her cheek against him and reveled in the smooth heat that was softer than his lips and as hard as any of his other male muscles. His fingers slid into her hair—more dishevelment—but the light tug on her scalp sparked sensation all across her skin. She turned her cheek again and her lips found his soft skin. His erection jerked against the touch of her mouth, and his tense silence almost made her laugh.

Yes, this.

Of course, this.

She opened her lips and took him inside. The sleek head

rested on her tongue and she swirled around it, savoring him like ice cream in summer, then she stroked along his shaft as she would lick a peppermint stick in winter. His fingers scraped against her scalp and she tightened her own around his hard thighs as she slid her mouth back up to suck on the tip.

Noah groaned again, maybe it was her name, but her heartbeat pounded loud in her ears, distancing any other noise. Everything took second place to the virility of his hard thighs against her palms and the aggressive jut of his sex in her mouth.

Yet she controlled that aggression, even on her knees. She was the one with the power. It was exhilarating to have all this life at her mercy, when for so long she'd been at the mercy of slow death and suffocating grief. Leaning into his legs, she pressed her swelling breasts against him and took him deeper, finding a rhythm that worked in counterpoint to her pounding pulse.

The knuckles of one of his hands traced the fiery heat of her cheek and she lifted her gaze to his, seeing the blue irises almost eclipsed by the pupils. A shiver rolled down her back.

*I do this to him.*

Another shiver rocketed along her spine, and she slowed her rhythm to ratchet up his need. Then, without breaking eye contact, she stopped altogether, holding him gently in the wet cavern of her mouth. His chest expanded, but he didn't move otherwise.

"Whatever you need, baby," he said, his voice hoarse. "You take whatever you want, for however long you want."

But she wasn't an idiot. The tension in his frame made clear that despite his best intentions, he couldn't hold off forever. And there were places left to explore.

With a last reluctant tongue-stroke, she got to her feet—and found herself wrapped in his arms and her mouth busy once again . . . with his. She melted against him and let him take over for a moment, unable to resist the glorious feel of his chest pressed to hers. Her hands slid up his sides and she wiggled her fingers under the shoulders of his shirt to lift it off.

As it fluttered to the floor, he pushed her away. "Now you."

The ultra-sensitive skin over her rib cage twitched at the brush of his hands, but then her shirt was gone, too. Across the room, the mirror showed her breasts heaving over the cups of her bra and Noah glanced back to see what had snagged her attention.

He turned to her with a smile and his forefinger traced the upper edges of her bra. "Pretty. Can you blame me for my fascination?"

But *she* was fascinated again, as her attention shifted to the reflection of Noah's back. The powerful shoulders slimmed to narrow hips and she saw the flat planes of his muscles shift as he continued to caress the tops of her breasts with that maddening finger. "I want you naked," she said, her gaze still trained on the mirror. "I want to see everything."

The other morning, silly woman that she was, she'd spent too much time with her eyes squeezed shut. She'd wasted too much time worrying about what he thought and what she could possibly do for him. Now she wanted to see, touch, taste, experience for herself.

Without hesitation, Noah pushed away his slacks and boxers. Breath caught in her chest and heat flashed over her at the sight of his powerful curves and warm skin. Her hand seemed too heavy as she slid it around the hard flesh at his waist to cup one round, male cheek.

His grin blinked on. "Yeah, honey. Touch me."

And she did, not because she had his permission, but because it was what she needed, what she craved. She slid her hands over his high buttocks, down the back of his muscled thighs, around the front so that she could play between his legs and make him groan again. With every inch of skin she explored, with every new place she discovered, she went wilder herself, her blood burning under the surface of her flesh, her nipples hard beneath her bra, the place between her thighs clenching in anticipation of more.

Then she rolled her palm up his erection and the tide changed. His body tensed, his breath huffed out, his fingers tightened on her upper arms. He yanked her close, somehow dispensing with her bra before their chests met.

She moaned.

He sucked the sound away with his mouth, and then it was everywhere, on her cheek, her chin, running down her neck to nip at the curve of her shoulder. At the bite, her passion exploded.

Whether Noah sensed it or his own desires were driving him, she didn't know. And she didn't have the breath to ask because they went from upright to horizontal with one beat of her heart. Her yoga pants and bikini panties had melted from her body. Somehow he'd put on a condom. Noah made a place for himself between her legs, jerking her thighs apart and muscling his hips into the opening without the tender finesse of their last time together.

There was nothing of finesse now.

He entered her in one heavy stroke, but it wasn't enough, and she jerked her pelvis high to impale him farther. He grunted, reared back, and then invaded again.

Merciless, sweet invasion.

He started a ruthless rhythm, one she would have demanded had she known such perfection existed. Her hands crabbed for purchase against the soft area rug, digging in as he continued to fill her. Without breaking the tempo, he rested more heavily on his knees and caught the back of hers in his big hands. He pushed them into her chest, holding her open for him. Vulnerable and open.

Impassioned and liberated.

She bit her bottom lip to keep back her pleas. She didn't want to interrupt a moment of his rough possession of her. She didn't want anything to mar this proof that she, Juliet Weston, had driven a man to such abandon.

And then he abandoned her.

"What? No?" she cried out, but her voice turned into a strangled sob as he placed his mouth against her wet, swollen flesh.

"I have to go down on you," he muttered, his gaze flicking up to her face and his breath burned hotter against her than even the melting center of her body. "I have to have this."

And he had it, took it, licking, sucking, exploring with his tongue, finding another rhythm that made her mad with need. She was moaning, begging, surrendering to him with all that she had when he took pity. Lashing her clitoris with his tongue, he slid two big fingers inside her.

Her hips lifted, her body quaked, she couldn't find breath to let out the scream of delirious pleasure.

The next one was silent, too, because he didn't give her a chance to descend or even inhale before he replaced his fingers with his body. He had to force past her still-clenching muscles, but that was good, too, necessary, so she'd know that such ecstasy was real.

One thrust, two, and he went over, then made her tumble after by inserting his clever hand between them.

Minutes passed. His head was still buried against her neck when she felt his mouth move on her damp skin. "I don't dare ask you if I broke anything."

Juliet slid her hand up his back. "Just a few of my notions about myself."

He looked up, that killer smile tugging at his beautiful lips. "Sounds promising."

She'd been wanton—and that wasn't a bad thing. She'd been demanding—and that was just as thrilling, too. "I don't think I have to paint a picture, do I?"

"If you do, I'll be the first in line to make a purchase." He kissed the tip of her nose. "That was pretty spectacular for me. Thank you."

"You're welcome." Her eyes drifted closed and she wondered how long she would continue throbbing. There was a sweet, pulsing ache at the place where she'd been opened by him. The point where he'd bit her neck seemed to have its own heartbeat.

Her hand drifted over his back again. "Did you really want me like . . . like this before now? When . . ."

"When the general was alive?"

She nodded.

Still half-hard, he pushed into her again. "Since the first moment I saw you. Is that a problem?"

It boggled the mind a bit to think he'd felt desire when she was running out the door yelling like a banshee, but they said young men had sex on the brain just about all of the time. "It's not a problem."

It was flattering, of course, though she wanted to make clear she understood it wasn't a promise, either.

She took a breath in preparation for what else must be said. It didn't have to be this moment—as a matter of fact, this was probably the wrong moment, when his heart was still pounding against hers and their skin was sticking together as if their flesh had made a bond despite all the reasons why they should not—but . . .

The words stuttered out of her mouth. "Listen, I don't want you to think . . . to worry . . . I don't expect . . ."

Opening her eyes, she searched his face, because that was as close as she could come to communicating all her concerns.

"How about if neither of us expects anything?" Noah said. "That way we'll both be surprised by what happens next."

# *Fifteen*

All mankind loves a lover.

—RALPH WALDO EMERSON

Juliet slid into the passenger seat of Noah's truck. She brushed her hand against his arm. "Thank you for driving me to Knitters' Night. I didn't expect the dealer would have to keep my car until tomorrow."

"No problem." He slanted her a glance. "I hoped to have a hot date, but she made other plans."

"Cassandra's counting on me."

"You know I'm kidding." He started the car and headed off, then fiddled with the dashboard controls to warm the cab. "Chilly tonight."

Her hand touched him again, this time alighting on his thigh. "Is everything okay?"

He covered her fingers with his. Since their untamed interlude in her office a few days before, she touched him a lot. Often. God, he loved it like a soldier loves a cold beer at the end of a long day. When he was near, she would bump him with her shoulder, she would make sure their hands brushed when she passed him a cup or a plate, she played with his hair when he pulled her onto his lap.

And all those touches were nothing in comparison to the luxurious way she'd wiggle against him—naked to naked—when they were together in bed. The sex had been explosive each and every time, and when she'd whispered last night that she hated to shower his scent off her skin, he'd gone so hard that her tongue on his stiff flesh had been torture.

Juliet Weston was developing a very talented, very insatiable mouth.

Still, despite how good the physical was between them, uneasiness lingered at the edges of his mind, and it seemed to be creeping closer minute by minute, just like the coastal fog that stole inland every afternoon. He was living out fantasies he'd harbored for longer than he cared to admit, yet there existed alongside them a disquiet he was finding harder to ignore.

He wanted it gone, damn it, so he could enjoy all that boiling-hot sweetness that was sex and Juliet.

"Noah?" The disquiet had emigrated into her voice. "You're keeping something from me."

Oh, shit. Was that it? Those secrets he'd buried deep? But he was sure he'd come to terms with them a year ago.

"There *is* something," she said. Her doubt gave the still-cold air in the car a sharper edge.

Great. Dumbass. Why wasn't he counting his blessings instead of telegraphing his vague concerns? Now he'd have to dredge up some explanation . . . Well, there was something he'd been meaning to come clean about since that day she'd accused him of giving her a pity fuck.

He lifted her hand to his mouth and pressed a reassuring kiss against her fingers. "I should have told you right away. The other day in your office . . . that was all Jean Lindstrom's fault."

"In my office . . ." Her voice sounded puzzled. "Wait—we're blaming the rug burns gracing my backside on someone named Jean Lindstrom?"

Squeezing her fingers, he laughed. "Not that part. The

other part, when I suggested you might not want Dean to know . . ."

"You know I'm not embarrassed about being with you."

Noah kissed her fingers again. "I get that now. But Jean Lindstrom put a little chip on my shoulder—or more precisely, her father did. He was our high school principal."

"Uh-oh." Amusement filled her voice. "Let me guess. Your bad-boy self scared her daddy?"

"Got it in one." Noah smiled a little, feeling sorry for the street-smart, yet social dunce he'd been—a teenager full of wounded pride and rebellious bluster. "When I showed up at the winter dance with her on my arm, her father refused to let me in the gym."

"So you took Jean to the movies instead?"

"Ah, but then there'd be no chip on my shoulder, would there? She didn't protest Daddy's edict."

Juliet was silent a moment. "She went into the dance without you."

"Yep. Apparently Daddy's reaction opened her eyes. Now, instead of considering me good-for-rebelling, I was good-for-nothing. She took the ticket I bought for her and waltzed inside, never looking back."

"Little bitch."

It still surprised and amused him to hear Juliet Weston use anything less than high tea vocabulary. He laughed.

"I hope she dreams of you at night."

Laughing again, Noah shook his head. "Doubt it. She got knocked up by the president of the senior class and was married with a kid on the way before the ink was dry on her graduation diploma."

"Hmmph." Juliet flounced against her seat. "Then you're lucky. It could be you that was married to Mean Jean and the father of her babies."

"I never took that kind of risk with anyone." Not with Juliet, either. They'd used a condom every time. He was disease-free, and no doubt she was as well, but he'd never wanted to make a woman pregnant.

Except . . .

Except, God, it jumped into his head. The image of a child. A towhead with Juliet's uncommon eyes and his tall frame. Then another joined the first. *Two?* The second was a chubby, dark-haired toddler who could wrap a man around her little finger with just a flash of flirty lashes.

Juliet's voice popped the mental picture. "You're going quiet again. Are you feeling sick?"

"No." Crazy, maybe. Deluded.

"Good." She leaned closer and nuzzled his neck, then licked the edge of his jaw. "Mmm. Like sandpaper."

He rubbed the scratchiness with his palm. "I'll shave before—"

"I wish you wouldn't."

Uh-oh. Her voice took on this telltale throatiness every time she was thinking about steamy sex. He grinned, his lingering foreboding pushed off by the idea of ladylike Juliet with naughty plans of her own. "Why shouldn't I shave?"

Her voice lowered. "Because I like to feel your whiskers here"—she lifted their joined hands to draw them down her neck—"and *here*." His fingertips caught on the unmistakable jut of a hard nipple.

"Wait a minute." His grin widened as through her layers of shirt and bra he tweaked that sweet little berry already waiting to be tasted. "Ma'am, what's this?"

"Something we'll save for later, soldier boy."

"Later? But—"

"We're here," she said, a little breathless and a little smug sounding, and he realized they'd indeed arrived at Malibu & Ewe. He also realized Juliet had effectively defused his odd mood with thoughts of her creamy skin reddened by the rough caress of his five-o'clock shadow and the sensual promise of her already peaked breasts. Fact was, uneasy didn't stand a chance in hell against lust.

"How long did you say this knitting thing goes on?"

She pointedly put his hand back on his leg. Left it solo. "A couple of hours. But you're welcome to join us."

God, he was thinking about it. Even just watching her was preferable to his own horny company. "Well . . ."

"Nikki brings cookies."

That clinched it. The object of his desire, plus baked goods. A winning combination.

Or so he thought, until he walked in with Juliet and was the focus of twenty pairs of female eyes. Christ. But he'd been a soldier and trained to discern friends from enemies. Those bags they all had at their feet couldn't be big enough for grenade launchers. Still, he grabbed some cookies on a napkin and beat a path to a lone chair in a half-hidden corner of the room. From there, he planned to entertain himself by tripping out on sugar and sexy plans for the elegant woman across the room who hid her naughty soul from everyone but him.

Yeah, that cool fog billowing around the edges of his brain didn't stand a chance.

But he didn't get the opportunity to amuse himself with scenarios involving Juliet and the fastest way to let loose her inner sensation seeker. Because an obstacle to that arrived in the form of Cassandra, who approached his hiding place and then worked some sort of spell on him, as if she was a third of Macbeth's three weird sisters.

One minute he was swallowing a bite of cookie. The next he was holding knitting needles and a ball of yarn.

No. Really.

Noah looked at what she'd shoved in his hands and then up to her face. "What's this?"

"Something you should try." She smiled, that one so much like Juliet's.

Still, he tried to resist. "You some sort of wool evangelist?"

"Knitting's calming. You look like you could use calming."

Anxiety was showing on his face? "I don't know how—"

"I'll show you." She drew up a folding chair next to his.

"Look. I've already cast on the stitches. All you need to learn is how to knit."

Bemused, he looked down at the Army green stringy stuff. "What am I making?"

"That comes second. First you have to get a feel for it."

"Cassandra—"

"The first knitters were men. Are you going to tell me that the hero depicted in *Braveheart* wasn't manly?"

He frowned. "William Wallace was a knitter?"

"Between battles," Cassandra said, without a blink. "Where do you think those kilts came from?"

"Wait just a minute . . ." But Noah let the objection die as his eye caught Juliet's across the room. There was laughter in them, a sparkling, spontaneous happiness that he realized now she'd been without as long as he'd known her. Hell, he would shear a sheep himself to see that.

And knitting was easier than sheep-shearing . . . and easier than it looked. Clearly he wasn't creating anything more useful than a lopsided, tight-here, loose-there sort of caterpillar, but the actual under-over-slide-the-stitch-off-with-the-point-of-the-needle wasn't impossible, even for his big hands. He managed to finish his cookies while he fumbled with the yarn, and let his gaze wander on occasion to his lady, who occasionally abandoned her own yarn to work the register.

And laugh with the other knitters. Chatting, admiring their projects, rubbing elbows with other women in a comfortable way he wondered if she'd ever before experienced. In the last months of the general's life, there'd been occasional visitors, but they'd been interested in the sick man, not the lonely woman who had assigned herself his bedside post 24/7.

Except when Noah convinced her otherwise.

Guilt tried to rise, but he pushed it toward the back of his mind where those clouds lingered, and instead reveled in gladness at Juliet's obvious light heart.

"She's bewitched you," a male voice said.

Jerked from his thoughts, Noah nearly stabbed himself with one of the pencil-thick needles. It was Gabe, staring at him with an expression somewhere between queasy and astonished.

Noah glanced back at Juliet, then back at the man. "Uh . . ."

"Not her. I mean the Froot Loop. You must have let Cassandra whip out the eye of newt and wave her wand."

"I heard that." The yarn shop owner hurried over, her face a little pink and her quick breaths bringing her admittedly outstanding breasts into prominence.

Noah noticed that Gabe noticed, but the other man covered his interest so quickly that he didn't think Cassandra had a clue.

She frowned at him. "Some people find their sexuality isn't threatened by practicing a handcraft that's been around for centuries."

"Some people don't avoid their sexuality by practicing handcrafts as well as celibacy," Gabe retorted.

"Insults won't stop me from asking where you've been." Her voice lowered as she stepped closer. "Gabe, you've been out of touch for days. Did you go into your hole again?"

"If I did, it wasn't deep enough to avoid noticing the way your piece-of-shit veggie car isn't starting like it should. I'll take a look at it tomorrow."

"What do you know about cars that run on used vegetable oil?" she asked, hand on her hip.

"I know that it makes as much sense for a car to be fueled by what fried my onion rings as it does for a man to be fed by bran muffins instead of ones made from blueberries and cream cheese."

The woman gasped. "Onion rings? Cream cheese muffins? Have you no thought to your cholesterol, your heart?"

"My heart, Cassandra, is my own damn business."

The air crackled around the two as they continued their

familiar food argument. Noah rolled his eyes and then sent Juliet a pointed look across the room. *Can we just get them a room or something?*

Her mischievous smile messaged back. *Go ahead. You mention it and I'll dive beneath the couch to escape the fallout.*

He grinned—then felt the expression on his face die. Shit, that was strange. Of course he couldn't really read her mind, but it was odd enough to even imagine he could. There'd been times in combat when he was certain he knew what Tim or Dean was thinking, but that was training kicking in . . . not—not—

*Oh, God.*

"I thought it was just sex," he murmured to himself. "A purely hormonal kind of thing."

Next to him, someone snorted. "I could have told you it was much more than 'just sex' the first time I saw you with her."

Noah's head whipped around. Gabe. Last thing Noah remembered, Gabe had been engrossed in his tiff with the Malibu & Ewe owner, but now the other man stood alone, his gaze trained on Juliet and Cassandra who stood talking by the cash register.

Noah's chest hurt. "I called it—" *Lust*. "And I wanted to protect her." *I still want to protect her, hold her, support her, keep her safe.*

*Oh, God.*

Gabe offered no sympathy or solution, just turned his attention from the women to Noah. His expression was a mixture of pity and humor. "Life's a bitch, isn't it?"

*I could have told you it was much more than "just sex" the first time I saw you with her.*

Noah's vague disquiet billowed and strengthened, then rolled in from the corners of his mind to fill his head, cold and damp and damn uncomfortable.

He knew the reason for it now, at least, but had absolutely no idea what to do about it.

What to do about being in love with Juliet.

Hell. Hell. He looked with longing toward the balcony and the dark night outside. Could a little cold air cure him?

Juliet closed out the register, her mood as high as the receipts from Knitters' Night. Stretching her arms overhead, she eased the kinks out of her back and wondered how long such euphoria could last. Nothing remained forever, of course—and if she thought too hard she could feel guilty for such gladness—but though winter was coming on, her soul detected spring. She could feel herself unfurling toward a warm sun and growing roots in fertile soil.

Her sisters were the source of some of the feeling: They were the nourishing earth. As for the warm sun—she looked around for Noah, but he'd disappeared onto the deck outside with Gabe. So she called over to Cassandra, sprawled on one of the couches beside Nikki. "Great night."

When the last customer had left the shop at the conclusion of the Knitters' Night hours, her sister had kicked off her shoes. Now she had her feet propped on the low table in front of her. Inside her striped, handknit socks she wiggled her toes. "It's the time of year. Everyone has a project to finish, needs a project to distract her from the craziness that's coming with the season, or just wants a little personal downtime."

Like Juliet had done a few minutes before, Cassandra lifted her arms over her head. "I'm exhausted."

Nikki didn't look up from the sweater she was knitting for Jay. "I don't know why you should be. Juliet rang up all the customers."

"Best eight bucks and change an hour I ever spent." Cassandra said, her voice smug.

Nikki's needles dropped and her eyebrows lowered as she frowned at the middle sister. "You cheapskate! Is that even minimum wage?"

Juliet laughed. "But I get a deep discount, too." She dropped onto the couch opposite the others. "And I like having something to do."

"You want something to do, you can come work for me. I said 'yes' to a couple of private catering jobs and now I'm swamped. Everyone wants to host a holiday party this year."

Juliet's high-flying mood dipped. That's right. The holidays were coming. Last year, they'd come and gone without her even noticing, her grief so deep that not a whiff of turkey or a note of Christmas carol had penetrated.

This year, with the grief abating and her protective shell gone, too, loneliness would pierce her straight to the heart. At the thought, she felt her shoulders hunch forward a little, as if to ward off the chilliness invading her.

She looked up, a little desperate. "I want you at my house for Thanksgiving," she announced to her sisters. Her voice sounded a bit too loud, but at least the invitation was out there. She held her breath.

Was it too presumptuous? They'd only known each other a short time and it would be natural for the two to have already made other plans.

Nikki didn't pause in her knitting. "Thank God. I thought it was going to have to be me and Jay, and not only is he completely useless in the kitchen, but I have parties I'm catering the day before *and* the day after. I'll bring the turkey and the dressing, though."

Cassandra's head rested on the cushions and her eyes were closed. Her body didn't stir. "Sounds good to me. I volunteer for some vegetable side dishes."

Juliet released her air in a silent sigh as warmth blossomed inside her again. Her smile must be curving from ear to ear, she thought. "Great."

"Fine." Cassandra opened her eyes and beamed at Juliet, looking happy, too. "Really fine."

They shared a moment of pleased communion. Then

Cassandra crossed one ankle over the other. "And sign me up for pumpkin—"

"*No.*" Two voices—Nikki's and Gabe's—were adamant.

Juliet looked at her youngest sister, then glanced at Gabe who'd just come back inside the shop with Noah trailing behind. "Um . . ."

"Don't let her make pie," Gabe said. "She doesn't use real sugar. The flour has weevils ground in for extra nutrition."

Juliet blinked. *Ew.* "Well, then that leaves you, Gabe. You're our Thanksgiving pie man. My house, Turkey Day, two pies."

"Wait. Whoa—"

"Noah's going to come up with a special cocktail," she said over the sputtering Gabe.

"I am?"

All right, so she was planning on her personal spring lasting at least through the fourth Thursday in November. Was *that* presumptuous? Optimism and happiness seemed to go hand in hand and she didn't regret the pairing.

"I'll have Jay put together a special three-sisters soundtrack," Nikki offered. "And he'll bring the wine. So c'mon, Gabe, you're in, yes?"

"All right," he agreed, though he didn't look pleased.

Cassandra was regarding him with watchful eyes. Seeming satisfied, she relaxed into the cushions again. "Haven't heard your 'yes,' Noah. Have you got other plans?"

Juliet's heart clenched. She slid a look toward him, but his face was unreadable.

"I . . ." He glanced at Gabe, then his gaze settled on Juliet. "I give up," he said, a small—rueful?—smile curving his lips. "I'm in. I'm in all the way."

Juliet smiled back. Had she ever felt this joyful? Anticipation—of Thanksgiving and of the night ahead—carbonated the blood rushing through her veins. As if he was drawn to her good mood, Noah crossed to the couch and hitched his hip against the back of it, his hand making a soft pass down her hair. She shivered, as if the caress was tickling her naked skin.

Cassandra cleared her throat. "At the risk of nuking all this camaraderie and happy holiday planning, can we please make a decision regarding"—she hesitated as if searching for the correct term—"Donor 1714?"

Juliet's mood took an instant dip—but then the renewed argument threatening to rain on her beautiful spring didn't happen.

She tried explaining it to Noah as they left the Malibu & Ewe parking lot a few minutes later.

"Cassandra needs to see this all the way through. That's what I realized." To be truthful, Juliet was so pleased with her world that she wanted everyone else to get their fondest wishes, too. She would have done nearly anything to make her sister happy. "Maybe Jay's been working on Nikki to soften her up, or maybe the idea of our first family Thanksgiving gave her a new perspective. Whatever the case, Cassandra has the permission she needs now."

Noah took the turn that led them into the hills above Malibu. "Everyone was talking in code back there and I didn't want to stop the flow of conversation. Halfway through I walked out to help Gabe look over Cassandra's car. I don't know what agreement the three of you just made."

"Oh." She remembered, now, that the last time she'd discussed the subject with Cassandra and Nikki had been right before getting locked in her office with Noah. After that, discussing Donor 1714 had fallen low on her list of priorities. "It's about our biological father. He registered on a website of sperm donors looking for their progeny. We're going to make contact."

Noah pulled his truck into the driveway and she popped open her door. Before she could slip out, he was there, his hands up, ready to lift her off the high-perched seat. Smiling down at him, she hesitated, giving herself time to appreciate his rugged handsomeness in the moonlight. Giving herself time to marvel that he was hers.

For the moment, of course.

But it was going to be his body against her body when they got inside. His hands stroking her skin, stoking the fires she'd never known she had. This man, who treated her with such care, but who also treated her to his unchecked passion. In the morning, he'd point out a thumbprint bruise on her hip maybe, or perhaps a tiny bite on her inner thigh, but it wouldn't be to apologize or to show regret.

He'd point it out because he knew it turned her on—her body, her mind—to be with a man who found her woman enough, passionate enough, to mark with his untempered need.

A delicious shiver rolled over her skin and a knowing smile curved his luscious mouth as his hands closed around her waist. When he tugged her off the seat, he let her make a slow, intimate slide along his body until her feet touched the ground.

He was already on his way to arousal, his erection hardening against her belly. She lifted her face for his kiss.

His mouth took hers, his tongue painting the inside edge of her lower lip. Her fingers tightened on his shoulders and he eased up, giving a parting tug with his teeth on her upper lip. "You and your sister," he said. "Sorceresses. She can get me to knit and you can make me so hard so fast I'd do it in the back of the truck if it wasn't so damn cold out here."

She laughed, smug in her power over him. "You looked very cute in the shop, cowed by Cassandra's tutelage."

"Cute. Cowed." He spit the words out in disgust, but it only made her laugh more as he pushed her toward the front door. Once she had the key inserted in the lock, he turned it, then put her behind him as he went inside to deactivate the alarm. She smiled at his back, indulgent of his protective habits. Returning to her side, he took her hand, shut the door behind them, then led her toward the bedroom.

Already her breathing was shallow, her skin prickling with eagerness for his touch. As if he sensed her growing impatience, he gave her hand a reassuring squeeze. "Cassandra's going through some sort of third party to contact the donor, isn't she?"

Juliet shook her head, guessing he was trying to distract her with talk to draw out the anticipation. Fiddling with the top button of her shirt, she contemplated stripping her clothes before he had the chance. "She's known the donor's identity for months, and she's really eager to get on with it."

Noah halted a few feet in the bedroom and faced her, a frown on his face. "That's not a good idea, Juliet. Tell Cassandra—"

"Not Cassandra. Me."

"*You*?"

"It was Nikki's one condition. She still isn't certain she wants to have anything to do with him, and she thinks Cassandra will fall all over herself liking the man, no matter what. So, as the oldest, it's up to me." And it was funny how gratified she was by their trust and how natural the responsibility felt to her. "I'm going to get in touch with him and introduce myself."

Juliet Weston, former widow-made-of-glass, now was not only an industrious employee but the trusted oldest sister.

Noah dropped her hand. "Well, you can tell them it's not going to happen. Not right away. And not like that."

She stared at him. "What?"

"Use your head, Juliet. You don't contact someone and give them personal information about yourself. What if he's a liar—best case—or some sicko pervert?"

"I hadn't quite worked out the details in my mind

yet . . ." That was true. If she'd had more than a moment to think about it she would have come up with concerns on her own and discussed them with her sisters before proceeding.

"Don't bother your head with the details. You give me his name and I'll find out what you need to know and *if* he's someone you can safely speak to. If so, I'll contact him myself first."

Don't bother her head with the details? *Don't bother her head with the details?* Now a new fire raced over her skin—and this one wasn't kindled by need. Strange, how short a step it was to walk from the heat of desire into the inferno of anger. "You'll determine to whom I 'can safely speak?' "

Apparently she was the only one who heard the ominous edge to her voice, because Noah didn't hesitate. "Yes. I'll take care of it."

Her fingers balled into fists. Her throat went tight. "I don't need 'taking care of.' "

Wariness entered his expression. "Listen, honey—"

"Don't—"

"Juliet." His jaw went rock-hard and anger sparked in his eyes, too. "I can't let you—"

"I can do whatever I damn please." The words shot from her mouth, and she was so mad her hair felt like it was lifting from her scalp. Her palm itched to slap him silly again, but that had been a one-time deal. Struggling to control her fury, she slammed her arms across her chest. "Noah, you should go now."

"Forget it." His feet took root on the floor. "I refuse to allow you to do something foolish."

"Refuse? Allow?" Her voice was rising, she realized. And why not? The words needed to be yelled from a mountaintop if that's what it took for Noah to understand. "I don't need to be cared for like a child."

"Then don't act like one!" He voice was raised now, too. They were both breathing hard, chests heaving, as if they'd just broken apart in bed . . . instead of maybe just broken up.

But she was so incensed that the thought didn't bother her. "Jerk!" she said.

Noah threw up his hands, then heaved in a breath and tried visibly to take hold of his temper. "Honey, listen to me. You've been sheltered . . ."

A ceramic hairpin box from her dresser dashed to the ground with a shocking crash. Juliet stared at the mess of shards, aghast, baffled, and then more aghast and baffled when she realized it was her hand that had thrown the thing.

Noah took a step toward her. "What is the matter with you—"

*Smash!* The little tray she used to hold her earrings before she went to bed shattered into a hundred pieces between them. This time she wasn't surprised by what she'd done. "Leave."

He hauled in another quick breath, looking ready to refuse again, but then his gaze caught on her hand creeping toward a glass figurine that she'd never really liked.

"We'll talk when you calm yourself," he said through his teeth.

The figure hit the back of the bedroom door he closed behind him. She was never talking to him again.

This time when she caught sight of her reflection in the mirror over the dresser she wasn't surprised at the flush of color on her face or the bright color of her eyes. *This is how I look in passion and in anger.* A full circle. A complete person, not someone's idea of the perfect lady, or damsel in distress, or elegant hostess.

Juliet Weston, former widow made of glass, now was an industrious employee, a trusted oldest sister, a hot-blooded woman.

Okay, and maybe sometimes hot-tempered, but only when honestly provoked. It felt good, like spring verging on summer, to let her emotions have free reign.

The phone on her bedside table rang, and she snatched it up, not sure if she hoped or didn't hope that it was Noah.

It was Nikki.

And what she had to say chilled Juliet, an unwelcome and forcible reminder that winter was on its way.

# Sixteen

O peace! how many wars were waged in thy name.

—ALEXANDER POPE

When Nikki, Jay, and Cassandra arrived at the house, Juliet was already in the foyer, in the process of rolling her largest piece of luggage from the storage closet near the garage to her bedroom. Her youngest sister took one look at the wheeled suitcase and frowned. "Running away won't solve anything."

Juliet pushed it down the hallway, then turned to face the others. "Short of disappearing altogether, my preference, what other choice do I have?"

"Maybe it's not that bad," Cassandra suggested. "It's just some ridiculous celebrity gossip site . . ."

Jay lifted the laptop he had tucked under his arm. "Let's look at it together."

He set it up on the kitchen island, while Cassandra bustled around making tea. Beside Juliet, Nikki hovered impatiently. "Jay's e-mailed a weekly preview from a few of the celebrity rags and websites because *NYFM*'s online edition has a feature they call 'Rumor Roundup.' "

A few keystrokes, and there it was, in all its blazing

ugliness. "Happy Widow and Her Happier Pool Boy." A dull knife stabbed Juliet right through the heart.

The headline was more loathsome than the photo, which she recognized as she and Noah at The Coffee Bean & Tea Leaf on Halloween. They were physically close, thanks to the chain's tiny tables, but yes, they appeared emotionally close, too, their gazes focused on each other.

It looked bad.

The text of the article, brief though it was, contributed to the tawdriness. It was all there: Wayne, Juliet, Noah. Rife with innuendo, it said that the man she was pictured with had been her husband's aide during the last months and days of his life.

"The book's publication was supposed to put the focus back on Wayne's achievements," she said. The dull knife in her heart took another turn.

"The book's mentioned," Jay pointed out, scrolling down. "Look, here's a paragraph on the launch party being given by Helen Novack."

Nikki leaned down to squint at the screen. "The launch party you were specifically asked *not* to attend?" She straightened, and her gaze swung around to Juliet. "Is that true?"

She shrugged. "I didn't insist, how could I? And Noah was there beside me—"

"Which makes me wonder," Nikki said. "Who would have tipped the gossips about your relationship with him? Did it come from this Helen?"

"It's so unfair to Noah, too," Juliet said, sick all over again. "None of this is anyone's business."

"Damn straight," Nikki agreed.

But then Juliet remembered her argument with Noah, his ridiculous orders, the flare of her temper, and the way he'd marched out. "Especially when there's nothing between us anymore anyway."

Cassandra and Nikki exchanged glances, just as the

door leading to the pool opened. Of course it could only be one man who was letting himself into her kitchen.

"I heard that," Noah said. "We had a fight, that's all. And now there's 'nothing' between us?"

She couldn't meet his eyes. She didn't want to have to tell him about the dirty gossip soon to be hung on the public clothesline.

He came farther into the room and looked at her sisters and Jay. "She threw things at me."

Juliet had to defend herself now. "I didn't throw things *at* you. I just . . . threw things."

Her sisters were staring at her as if she'd gone mad. Then Nikki laughed. "Imagine that. The lady in beige is getting her bitch on. Awesome."

"Hey," Juliet defended herself. "I happen to be dressed in blue at the moment.

Cassandra nodded. "It's true, Nikki."

"Well, she's going to need her inner bitch in any case," the younger woman insisted. "Read that, Noah, and tell me I'm not right." Her hand indicated the open laptop.

Rubbing the pain in her chest, Juliet moved back so he could have a clear view of the screen while Jay filled him in on the how and the why of his sneak peek at the upcoming scandal sheets. Instead of watching him read it, she moved toward the windows and stared out at the pool.

Santa Fe? Seattle? Though she loved this house, she'd have to leave it, because there was at least one photographer who knew her address. Noah could stay if he wanted, though she supposed he'd distance himself from anything having to do with her ASAP.

God, why was he dragged into this ugliness? Cassandra and Nikki, too. She'd once called it infuriating, and it was, but now she felt a icier kind of anger building in her chest. Wrapping her arms around herself, she shivered.

Then heat enveloped her from behind. She was turned into Noah's familiar, broad chest. He pulled her tight, ignoring her protests, and held her to him, one hand cradling the back of her head, the other circling her waist. "I'm sorry," he murmured, tucking his cheek against hers. "I wish I could take it all away for you."

"I'm going to do that myself," she said, and when she stepped back, he let her go. "I figure if I leave town all this destructive gossip will leave with me."

Nikki was shaking her head. "I already told you, running doesn't do any good."

"And, um, as your boss, I think I should point out that you have a job." Cassandra passed her a cup of tea. "I'm expecting you at work tomorrow, and the day after that, and for every other shift that you've agreed to take."

"There's Thanksgiving, too," Nikki added. She slid her arm around her fiancé's waist. "Without you, we make Jay host and we'll be forced to feast on beer and blackened steak."

The man nodded. "It's the only two things I do well."

Noah stepped closer to brush Juliet's hair from her face. "Don't go."

She whirled to him. "Of course I have to go! Don't you see? I want this all to die down."

"But you have commitments now," he said. "Job, family, friends who are counting on you."

Juliet huffed out a sigh. "None of you understand. I made a promise to myself about the book. I vowed I'd do what it takes to make it a success. The world doesn't need to remember me right now, but the hero that Wayne was."

"The kind of hero who wouldn't flee from a fight," Noah pointed out.

"I don't see *how* to fight this." She squeezed shut her eyes, trying to calm herself and think. Was there a way? An idea flickered. "Unless . . ."

"Unless?" Noah prompted.

She opened her eyes to look at him. "What was the date of Helen's event?"

"The third week in November. That Saturday night."

"Okay, then, what if I use my newly kindled notoriety to bring attention to *General Matters*?" Juliet mused. "Am I crazy to think I could throw my own book launch, the week before hers?"

"Helen won't like it," Noah warned, a grin ghosting his mouth.

"I know Helen Novack," Jay put in. "She's a snobby pain in the ass."

"The man knows everybody," Nikki said. "I told you that."

Noah was nodding. "You put on your own party and tell the world about the general through your eyes, with your voice."

"I'm certainly sick and tired of the press telling my side of things for me," Juliet agreed. And a woman who didn't flinch at breaking a few things in anger wouldn't balk at facing down the media—and whoever else got in her way. "But would anyone come? And where would I have it? There's not enough room or parking here, and—"

"Lucky for you, you have family that can help with the details," Cassandra said. She'd found a paper napkin and had rolled it into a ring she was sliding on and off her thumb. "There's plenty of space for people and for cars at Malibu & Ewe. If Nikki doesn't have time to cater—"

"I'll make time."

"We can get Gabe to help out anyway."

Juliet protested. "We don't have to ask—"

"*I* can, and he needs reasons to emerge from his bat cave."

"And I'll put out the word," Jay offered. "I can get the press there and we'll distribute posters and flyers."

Juliet nodded, determination growing. "And I've reconsidered doing that interview for *NYFM*." She was nobody's delicate daisy. "I have a few things to say."

"I can have whatever those are online by as early as tomorrow," Jay promised, and then was drawn into Cassandra and Nikki's part of the planning

The room seemed to warm with all their positive energy.

Juliet let the talk flow around and then surround her, until their support felt as palpable as the cup of tea she held between her palms.

Winter went away again, and she didn't feel the cold night air, even as she walked her family—her *family,* how comforting was that?—out to their car. It was only when she walked back inside and faced Noah that she felt a renewed chill.

"I don't know what to say to you," she told him. "I want to protect you from all this."

Noah smiled, that beautiful, lady-killer smile of his, and he crossed the floor to cup her face in his big hands. "Then maybe you can forgive me for what happened earlier tonight. I just want to protect you, too."

Tears burned, but she hid them by closing her eyes as Noah's kiss drifted over her mouth. This wasn't the time for worries or regrets.

Right now, it was enough that he wanted her, and when they went into the bedroom, a different mood infused what before had been wild heat and needy passion.

*I want to protect you.*

*I just want to protect you, too.*

Equal impulses. Twin urges. Matching motivations.

Skin to skin, and closer than ever before.

Marlys sensed it was Dean in the shop the instant the door closed, ruffling the curtain that separated the supply alcove from the retail space. She kept her back turned to that curtain, but she was aware when he swept it aside, too.

With a steadiness she didn't feel, she kept to her crouch, continuing to unpack the box of holiday scarves that had arrived earlier that morning. "So . . . you're here again," she said.

"I told you I'd come back. In the note at your house that morning and in the messages I left here at the store. Funny how you were never available to talk to me. Funny how you never called back either. I left my cell number every time. I was here last week, just for the day, as I said in my message, but I still couldn't get a response from you."

"Been busy." *Busy working like hell to forget you. Busy hoping like hell it wouldn't be like this if you did come back.* Her hands were shaking and she had to fight herself not to jump up and bury herself against him.

"Stand up and let me touch you."

God, he could still read her mind! She shook her head, rejecting the idea and rejecting her need to do the very thing he ordered. Marlys Marie Weston couldn't want a man so much, because she remembered that whatever she'd wanted most she'd never gotten.

But hard hands grasped her waist and hauled her up, even when she stuttered a protest. Dean turned her, brought her flush against him, kissed her mouth as if he'd thought about her every day, every minute he'd been gone.

No, that was her.

Panicked, she wrenched away, though he only let her go so far, his hands still linked at the small of her back. Her heart was slamming against her chest. His breath soughed in and out like he'd been running for days.

No, again, that was her.

Running from *this*. How could one person become so important so fast? She didn't understand it. She could never trust it . . . could she?

He ran a thumb under her lower eyelashes. "Shadows, angel. You haven't been sleeping?"

"Don't call me that." Her voice was sharp, not cool as it should be, and she jerked out of his embrace. "I'm no angel." God knew that was true, and she didn't feel guilty about it either.

Regrets were for suckers. Same as this you're-the-one certitude that was pumping from Dean and trying to invade her. That way lay madness.

Sadness.

As Marlys had been avoiding that very feeling for

nearly a year, thank you very much, she was certainly not signing on for another potential source of the depressing emotion. Dean was going to Afghanistan, for heaven's sake. *A danger zone.* A woman would have to be crazy to want him enough to risk having to worry about him.

But her body betrayed her. Her feet carried her close again, her hands lifted to warm her palms against his chest. His heart beat against her flesh and her body trembled in return. How could she ache for something she so badly needed to reject?

And as usual, he could read her like a book. His palms cupped her face. "I won't hurt you."

He'd said that before. And again, she didn't want to give him the chance, but he was kissing her and she was letting him. More, she was reveling in giving over to him.

She wanted to give him everything, anything, all of her.

"Whoa." It was Dean who separated them this time, but he was smiling as he held her away. "Is it just me, or is it smoking in here?"

She laughed, he made her that giddy, and then she reached over to flick off the clothes steamer they used to dewrinkle the merchandise. "Hate to break it to your ego, but the mist is machine-made."

"Yeah? I think you should give this man another chance to prove himself."

Oh, God, she wanted to. She was going to. Marlys felt as feminine as a pair of marabou-trimmed satin mules when he curled his muscled forearm around her hips and pulled her even tighter to him. His silvery eyes burned and she unconsciously licked her upper lip, gratified when he groaned at the instinctive, seductive signal.

She laughed again, a purr that she'd never heard herself make, and threw caution to the wind as she wrapped one arm around his neck and slid her other hand into the back pocket of his jeans. Paper rattled.

He halted halfway to her mouth. "Oh," he said. "You make me forget everything."

"That's two of us," she murmured, drawing his head closer. At the moment, she couldn't care less about the condition. Another kiss would be worth a little amnesia.

But he broke from her hold to straighten and reach into his pocket himself. "I have something for you from Juliet. When I was restowing my gear in the guesthouse, she asked me to give it to you."

Marlys covered the quick sting she felt at the sound of the other woman's name. "Oh?" She shuffled back, then tucked her arms over her chest. "How is my evil stepmother?"

Dean's eyes narrowed, then he shrugged his shoulders as if dismissing an itch between the blades. "From what I understand, she's troubled by the latest crap in the tabloids and on the gossip sites."

Marlys didn't blink. "I heard about that."

"You know it isn't true. I told you that's not Noah."

"I don't really think that Keira Knightley made a baby with a martian, either, but they have a picture of it on the cover of *Gossip Universe*."

"The scandal hurts your father's reputation, too," Dean said.

Marlys didn't see it that way. "My father was a hero. He could have been President of the United States, but then he married *her*."

"Is that what you wanted?" Dean cocked his head. "A canopy bed in the White House?"

"No! My point is, if he hadn't married—"

"Marlys, he failed you long before he married his second wife."

"How can you say that?" She tightened her arms around herself. "My father's dead."

"Death doesn't make him a saint."

Marlys turned away, not wanting him to stir the embers of the emotions she'd been banking from the day her mother dragged her away from the last base she'd lived on. "My father's dead," she mumbled again.

"I know that. Have you accepted it?"

She shoved her hand in the pocket of her black pants, and finding the silver tear, squeezed it so tight it bit into her skin. "Dean . . ."

"Angel." He sighed. "All right, I'll let it go. But here." The paper he held out had been folded into quarters.

Marlys opened the sheet and stared at the slick-looking flyer. "What's this all about?" she asked, looking up at Dean.

"Juliet's throwing her own launch party for your father's book."

"There's already a party planned."

"One she isn't invited to attend, right?"

Marlys refused to feel the slightest pinch of shame. The only thing she felt bad about was that she'd confessed to Dean that Helen had left Juliet out at her request. "We've already been over that."

Dean sighed. "You're right. But Juliet wants to be sure you know that you're invited to the party she's throwing."

Marlys glanced back at the flyer. "What's this place? Malibu & Ewe?"

"A shop on the Pacific Coast Highway. I gather it has plenty of parking."

"Well, thanks for passing the info along." Marlys set the piece of paper aside, when she would have preferred to make a ball and send it straight to the round file.

"Unlike your friend's, this party is open to everyone," Dean said. "You could post the flyer in your window."

Incredulous, Marlys stared at the man. "You must have the totally wrong impression of me."

He shook his head. "I don't think so. I wouldn't feel like this if you were . . ."

"A stone-cold bitch?" she supplied helpfully.

He laughed. "I think you're scared. And it's my job to boost your morale."

"Oh, baby, I've got self-esteem to burn. Surely you can see that."

"I can see the future sometimes, you know, thanks to my Cherokee forefathers."

"Yeah?" She sauntered closer, intrigued despite herself. "My bullshit meter is quivering, but I'll play. What's this super-vision of yours foresee?"

He grabbed her close, grinning when she squeaked. "Me. I see me in your head, in your heart, and I'm burrowing deep, angel."

She rolled her eyes, trying not to panic at the thought. Burrowing deep? He was *deploying*. "I suppose you see me naked, too."

He looked off, apparently searching his inner crystal ball. "I guess it's going to let me get that picture all on my own. You *are* going to get naked for me, aren't you, angel?"

"Dean . . ." He kissed away whatever she'd been about to say. It was like every time before, which was like no time with anyone else. It was deep and wet and now she knew why they called it a soul kiss. He touched her there, her soul, and damn, she had one.

She stepped back, startled.

And worried a little, because it might mean she had a conscience as well.

"Why look so stricken?" Dean asked. His dark eyebrows drew together.

"How . . . why . . ." Her voice wouldn't rise above a whisper. "I don't think . . ."

"Stop thinking," Dean said, pulling her close to press his forehead to hers.

She breathed him in and already it was familiar, and the familiarity was as heady as the scent itself. "How do you know . . . ?"

"That this is right?"

Man could see both the future and read her thoughts. God. But she nodded.

"I just . . . do." He moved back but didn't let go of her, a crooked smile she'd never seen before making her stomach clench. "I have a rep, Marlys."

"You don't have to tell me you have a way with women—"

"Not that kind." He traced her mouth with two of his fingertips. "I'm known to be a little . . . impetuous."

She laughed. "You think?"

"Reckless."

The way he said the word was a clean kill to her laughter. "Reckless."

"There are guys—other soldiers I know—who are so damn careful. It used to make me kind of nuts, if you want to know the truth. Because I thought it took a certain kind of rashness to do what we do."

Her stomach clenched again. Impetuous. Reckless. Rash. Those were words she'd once used to describe herself.

"Before every mission, there are guys who whip out the photos of their girls and look at them like they're making promises and saying prayers at the same time."

Marlys was glad he was holding her up, because her knees were like pudding.

"When I opened my eyes that first day and I saw you standing there, I knew. I just knew. 'That's the picture I'll have in my head every time I go into battle,' I told myself."

*No*. She couldn't do it! That couldn't be her. She didn't want to live a life waiting for a man to come back, just like she'd waited all her childhood for her father to return and take her away. He hadn't, right? Instead, he'd left her with the lonely civilian childhood and the bitter woman that her mother had become. Marlys never got what she wanted most.

But she couldn't help herself. With a little whimper, she pulled Dean close and buried her face in his shoulder. She should be running from him, she wanted to run from him, but she wasn't strong enough to do it. Burrowing closer, she wondered how hard it would be to crawl inside his skin.

He drew her even nearer; they were pressed tight from chest to knee. Still, she moved into him.

"Ouch." Dean insinuated his hand between their bodies and felt the lump in her patch pocket. "What's this?"

Before she could stop him, he'd pulled free the silver pendant and chain. "Oh, Marlys."

The phone jangled in the shop, and she ignored it, her gaze fixed on the silver tear that was swinging between her and her soldier.

Leeza's voice reached her from the other side of the curtain. "Marlys, you need to take this. And don't forget you've got that appointment in fifteen minutes."

Marlys's gaze jerked from the necklace to Dean. "I have things I've got to do."

"I understand."

He would never understand. But really, she couldn't do this. That pendant proved the point. She couldn't, wouldn't fall in love with this man and she couldn't, wouldn't, let him fall in love with her.

He kissed her forehead, then looped the chain around her wrist.

"Wear this for me tonight, angel. When I get to your house, I'll take it off. Before we make love, I'll take all your tears away."

*Oh, God.* She had to figure out something to stop both.

There could be no love.

There would be no tears.

# Seventeen

> If it is your time, love will track you down like a cruise missile.
>
> —LYNDA BARRY

Blackie went ballistic when the doorbell rang as he always did. Marlys's heart reacted in the same way, slamming against her breastbone as she left her bedroom and made her way down the stairs. Before touching the doorknob, she cinched the belt of her robe more tightly. Then, with a last deep breath, she pulled open the door.

The dog rushed forward and his rambunctious greeting pushed Dean back a step, though he stayed well within the bright glow of the porch light. Then the man spoke in his usual firm tone, and Blackie obeyed, sitting as ordered, his gaze on his god's face. His furry body shivered with delight.

Dean grinned over Blackie's head at Marlys and she had to accept that he hadn't turned ugly in the few hours they'd been apart. There was the same studly soldier's body, the gleaming dark hair, the silver eyes. They narrowed, his smile dying, and then his gaze roamed over her, from her mussed hair and smudged lipstick, to the hint of bare legs exposed by the gap in her long flannel robe.

"I was planning on taking you out to dinner," he said.

She swallowed to lubricate her dry throat. "I'm not exactly dressed in my restaurant duds."

His gaze flicked over her again and he leaned a shoulder against the jamb. "Yeah, I see that. Everything okay?"

"Dandy." She took a quick glance over her shoulder and wiped her sweaty palms along her flannel-covered thighs. "I just, uh, sorta lost track of time."

"No problem. Why don't I go out and get some food for us to eat here. Thai okay?"

Marlys hadn't expected this to be so hard. The first part of her plan had been nothing, she'd divorced her mind from what was happening by thinking instead of how much safer she'd be when it was over. But damn, it wasn't over yet, and looking at Dean, at his handsome face and honest expression—

"No Thai?" he asked.

Helpless, she shook her head. There wasn't going to be a meal. Any second now he'd look at her with disgust instead of puzzlement and she'd go back to her man-free, emotionally strong life.

"My choice, then," Dean said.

"S-sure." It *was* going to be his choice. She'd known her unwanted but undeniable attachment to him meant that *she* couldn't have walked away, so she'd manipulated the situation to provide herself with the opportunity and him with the means to make the cold, clean break.

Except, God, it didn't feel clean at all. It felt dirty. She felt dirty. Her stomach roiled and placing her palm over it, she glanced up the stairs again. Shit, what was taking so long?

When she turned back, Dean was looking up the stairway, too, but there wasn't anything to see. Yet.

Damn it all.

Straightening, he shoved one hand in his pocket and she heard keys jangle. "I'm off then—"

"No!" He couldn't leave now. He'd miss the show and

she was certain she'd never manage a repeat performance. "No. Just a minute . . ."

And then it came. The sound of footsteps jogging down the carpet-covered stairs, the little jaunty whistle that used to make her nuts, but now just made her queasy.

"There you are!" Pharmaceutical Phil said, in the happy tones of a man who'd gotten lucky without having to work for it. His hair was damp from his shower—God, she'd forgotten how annoyingly long he liked his showers—and he had his suit jacket hooked over one finger. "I left my tie somewhere."

Marlys moved her gaze to Dean's face. "Try the kitchen counter."

"Good idea." Phil's stride hitched as he suddenly seemed to realize there was someone in her doorway. "Uh, hey."

"Hello." There wasn't a hint of heat or ice in Dean's response, but when no one moved to make introductions, Phil continued on his way, jaunty whistle restarting.

*He's such a sap*, Marlys thought. *I can't believe he bought a ring and ever thought I'd say yes.*

"He doesn't deserve you using him," Dean said.

Guilt had no place here. "Believe me, I don't think he'd complain."

Dean's eyebrows rose. "That good, huh?"

The cheerful whistle emerged from the kitchen and approached them again. Pharmaceutical Phil looked oblivious to the tension in the entryway—and damn self-satisfied, too. Marlys cast him a look, then sent a more pointed one at Dean. "What do you think?"

Phil leaned down to kiss her cheek. "Thanks for the . . ." He let the sentence trail off as if, again, he only now realized there was an audience.

Marlys rolled her eyes. "Boffing you was just what I needed this afternoon," she replied. "Good-bye, Phil."

Maybe, finally, the thick atmosphere registered in Phil's thick skull. "Good-bye, Marlys." He sketched a little wave, then ducked past the other man and headed toward the street where she'd instructed him to leave his car. She'd wanted to make this moment a complete surprise for Dean.

She squared her shoulders. "Would you like to come in?" she asked the man. Or he could do the big scene in the doorway. His pick.

"I think I'll stay right here, if you don't mind."

"Fine." Better than fine. Because in closer quarters they would both smell the scent of Phil's Armani cologne on her skin. She'd selected it for him herself, as she recalled, but now the fragrance was like rotting fish to her senses. Her palms slid over flannel again and she thought of the shower upstairs with longing. She wanted to wash in the worst way, but she'd put it off for just this reason.

And after Dean got through with her, she'd probably want to shower away his loathing, too.

But he wasn't gazing on her with revulsion like she'd planned. Instead, he was shaking his head and looking at her with . . . she didn't know what to call it. Pity?

"Angel. I knew you were scared, but this? Why didn't you just say something?"

"Say what? I don't know what you're talking about." Panic was fluttering in her belly, same as every time he kissed her, same as every time she thought of him soldiering in Afghanistan. Screwing Phil was supposed to put a stop to that! Screwing Phil was supposed to get Dean out of her life, but instead he seemed to have grown roots in her porch in order to give his X-ray vision another chance at looking inside her soul.

The one she didn't have, damn it.

"You're terrified," Dean said. "I had no idea how much this thing between us frightened you."

"Hah," she started, but then couldn't think of any follow-up that wouldn't sound desperate and hollow. "Hah," she said again, fainter. It was embarrassing as hell that tough-skinned, tough-talking Marlys Marie Weston couldn't come up with anything better than that.

"Oh, angel."

He was doing it again. Making her feel soft and vulnerable and female. Here she was, standing with some other man's smell on her and because Dean wasn't turning away, she was so ridiculously grateful she felt like crying.

Even though she knew there were only more tears in her future if she didn't get a hold of herself. If she let herself care for the man, this man going off to his soldier's world, she'd be powerless. He could forget about her, he could find someone else, he could . . . he could . . .

He could die.

And the thought of that just . . . just . . . She reached in her robe pocket and squeezed the small silver pendant. The thought of that just pissed her off.

Tightening her hold on the anger, she put steel in her spine. "Dean—"

"Hey!" Pharmaceutical Phil was loping back up the driveway to stand in the circle of the porch light. "I almost forgot."

She should have dumped him for his bad timing alone. "What? Your socks? Are your boxers under the bed?" Hearing herself, her face burned, but she couldn't take the words back now.

"No, no," Phil said. He reached in his jacket pocket and yanked out a small foil-covered box. "This was why I stopped by your boutique today, and then we got, um, sidetracked."

Marlys reached around Dean to take the small gift. "Phil, you shouldn't have."

He looked embarrassed. "I probably should do something for you, but this isn't from me. My brother asked me to give it to you. It's those chocolate truffles you like."

"Oh." Marlys shoved the box in her pocket, going cold and queasy again. "Thanks. Great. See you later, Phil."

"He had a message for you, too."

"I'll, um, get that from you later." Because she had an idea of where Phil was going with this, she would love to slam the door in his face. But Dean was on the other side of it, too, and she had to finish things with him. "I'm—we're kind of busy here," she said, trying to send him a "get along little doggie" message with her eyes.

"It won't take but a second. It's about that story tip you passed along to him."

Dense, dumb, thick-headed Phil. The only thing he was good for was a quick lay, no questions asked. "All right. Got it. See you later, Phil."

"He said to tell you that the Juliet-and-the-general's-aide thing was pure gold. November was turning into a real turkey—pun intended—in the gossip business until you dropped the juicy nugget." With that, he was loping back down the driveway.

Before now, she'd never experienced a deafening silence. But there it was, as loud as a jetliner's engines, roaring in her head with enough decibels to pop her eardrums.

Still, she could hear Dean's voice over the inferno. "You didn't."

"Of course I did." She swung her gaze toward him, defiant. "Just like I arranged for you to find me postcoital with some other man."

Wasn't that worse? But from the repulsion on his face, it looked like her little whisper to Phil's brother had been what triggered Dean's true ire.

His eyes glittered, his jaw was tense. "There were other ugly rumors, Noah told me. They called Juliet the Deal—"

"I had nothing to do with that," Marlys interrupted, but then remembered she *wanted* him to reject her. She folded her arms across her chest. "But maybe it was me who called my friend last year and told him that the general's widow had been getting a Finnish mudbath while he took his final breath."

"Jesus, Marlys." Dean shoved a hand through his hair. "Jesus."

She looked away. "I told you I was no angel."

"But this!" He made an impatient gesture that she

caught from the corner of her eye. "I thought . . . I thought you were like a friend of my younger sister's. In her teens, she used to cut herself—they said she did it to release the pent-up feelings inside of her. I thought that's what you'd done with that asshole this afternoon—that you'd turned self-destructive as a way of releasing your grief about your father and your fears about us."

What was she supposed to say to that? She only stood there, mute, trembling a little beneath her robe because there was an icy frost in the air that had nothing to do with the evening temperature.

"But hell, Marlys. I was wrong. It's not yourself that you injure. It's other people that you use to take out your pain. You hurt other people so you don't have to feel a goddamned thing."

With that, he swung around and started off, then he stopped. Without turning around, he asked, "Jesus, Marlys, how could you?"

The answer was so simple. "You said it yourself, Dean. All's fair in love and war."

Outside the door of Malibu & Ewe, Juliet glimpsed her reflection in the plateglass door and tugged on the jacket hem of her champagne-colored suit. The silk shell she wore underneath it was the same color and her only jewelry was the pearl choker that Wayne had given her for their first anniversary. It was an exquisite outfit and one of her husband's favorites. She'd worn it to his memorial service.

It had felt right to wear tonight at the book launch party.

But she didn't look right in it, she thought, frowning at herself in the glass.

Maybe it was too fussy for Malibu.

Maybe it was too formal for what was supposed to be a celebration.

But there wasn't time to drive home and restart the

wardrobe selection process. With a deep breath, she pushed open the door.

Cassandra and Nikki immediately looked over, but it was her youngest sister's disapproving expression that tripped her pulse. "What? What's gone wrong?"

Nikki shook her head. "It's just that you're so, uh . . . one-color."

*Oh, damn,* Juliet thought, looking down. *Beige.*

"Maybe that's good," she said, tugging at the jacket's hem again. "You know, 'Move along, nothing scandalous to see here.' "

"Your face is pale, too, though. Somehow the corpse bride thing isn't working for me."

Juliet groaned. "All right. I'll have to speed back and—"

"Relax." Cassandra came forward, a delicate confection of blue and green knitted yarn in her hands. "We can liven things up with this," she said, arranging the scarf over Juliet's shoulders. "There. That's better."

Chin to chest, Juliet tried assessing the change. "You think?"

"Beautiful," a man's voice pronounced.

Her head jerked up, a flush washing her body in heat. There went the pale problem, too, thanks to Noah. He'd come from the direction of the shop's small kitchen, carrying a silver beverage urn. Only a few hours had passed since he'd left her house, but it wasn't the afternoon she was recalling.

Instead, she was remembering the night before, when they'd filled the big tub in the master bath with hot water, bubbles, and then themselves. Hands slick with soap and water, she'd explored every inch of his skin in detail, even tracing the tattooed name, date of birth, and serial number inked on his sleek side under his arm, until he'd laughed and caught her hand. Then he'd reciprocated by inspecting every curve and fold of her flesh.

Now, his face clear of telltale expression—Was she the

only one who couldn't forget the sight of his hands sliding over her breasts to brush away the bubbles?—Noah just stared back at her. Then he quirked an eyebrow, and a shiver tickled down her center like the stroke of a calloused fingertip.

Nikki snickered. "Wouldn't I like to be a fly on the wall of her thoughts."

"Oh, stop," Cassandra scolded. "No teasing tonight."

"I don't think it's my teasing that's on our big sister's mind," Nikki retorted. "But I don't want to ruffle your celibate sensibilities, Froot Loop, so let's get back to work."

With a laugh, she ducked the skein of soft yarn that Cassandra tossed at her, and it sailed through the air only to land with a plop against the cardboard-backed photo Gabe was lugging in.

Everyone stared at the blowup of Wayne's photograph—the same that was on the back cover of the book. The colossal-sized blowup. In life, Wayne had been a lean five foot ten. In this cardboard version, he was closer to nine feet tall.

"Gabe!" Cassandra exclaimed. "What were you thinking? Inflate that thing and it could be one of the balloons for the Macy's Thanksgiving Day Parade."

Gabe propped it against a wall. "What's wrong with it?"

Astounded, Juliet stared into the one-dimensional eyes of her much-enlarged husband. Then she laughed. "Oh, my God." Her hand over her mouth, she couldn't stop more laughter from bubbling up.

The others watched her in wary silence.

Nervous hysteria, she figured they were thinking. It made her laugh even more. "No, no," she said, when she could breathe. "I'm sorry, it's just too good. Wayne would certainly approve."

Cassandra and Nikki exchanged another worried glance.

"Really. Noah, remember the flat-screen TV discussion?"

He frowned. "He wanted seventy inches. You thought—what?—thirty-two?"

She laughed again, she couldn't help herself.

Noah appeared perplexed. "I remember you snickering then, too, now that I think of it. What's so funny about that?"

Juliet looked over at her sisters. "The TV room at that house is something like twelve-by-twelve feet." Then she glanced at Noah. "But both you and Wayne insisted that bigger was far, far better."

Cassandra grinned. "And they say women think size matters."

Jay walked through the door at that moment, and his gaze snagged on the massive cardboard likeness. "Whoa," he said, taking a step back. Then he smiled in approval. "Looks perfect, Gabe."

When the three sisters failed to hold back their laughter, he frowned. "What?"

Looking bewildered, Gabe and Noah shook their heads and Cassandra, Nikki, and Juliet just laughed some more.

Perfect was right though, Juliet thought, as she continued smiling through the last of the party setup. The couches had been pushed to the edges of the room and they unfolded chairs to form rows that faced a podium backed by Wayne's hulking photograph. A table at the rear of the shop had been stocked with refreshments. The register was manned by a clerk from a local bookstore and she was surrounded by stacks of *General Matters*.

The party preparations looked perfect and the friendship and laughter Juliet shared with the people around her was going to make tonight her chance to sail through this turning point. The event would mark the moment she'd let go of her grief, she'd decided. Of course she'd always mourn Wayne and the time together they would never have, but after tonight she'd be able to move on from the past years of illness and sadness.

Across the room, Noah lifted a small table to shoulder level, the muscles in his back flexing as he carried it over a row of chairs to reposition it on the other side of the room.

Tonight she'd start saying her good-byes to Noah, too. When he left her—and it would be soon, just yesterday he'd told her he'd taken a position in the county D.A.'s office—she'd be able to let him go as well.

Cold swamped her skin, but she told herself it was just those nerves kicking in, because at that same instant the door to the shop opened and a group walked inside. The clock read seven on the dot.

After that, Malibu & Ewe filled almost as fast as the guests filled their plates with Nikki's appetizers and desserts. The bookstore clerk was busy, too, ringing up sales, and Cassandra and Jay, favored children of Malibu, chatted up the locals Juliet suspected they'd arm-twisted into attending. Even Gabe came out of the shadows long enough to lead a reporter and photographer from a coastal-living magazine over to her.

She tried not to appear stiff as she posed with a copy of Wayne's book and she was just leaning forward to answer the reporter's question when Cassandra drew her toward the podium. "It's time," she said, turning her to face the rows of occupied chairs. "Slay 'em, sister."

Cold washed over her again as she looked out at the crowd. Joining the locals she'd noticed before was a plethora of media types. Microphones bristled from the front of the podium. Two men with video cameras perched on their shoulders hovered at the rear of the room. Another stood at her left.

Jay had promised that the *NYFM* interview would trigger even more press attention and apparently he was right. On top of that, she knew he'd made some calls—she'd made a couple herself—that appeared to have paid off as well. Still, it must have been a slow SoCal news day, because this exceeded her highest expectations.

Or getting a glimpse of the Deal Breaker and the Happy Widow was more intriguing than she'd imagined.

Remembering the ugly nicknames froze her for a moment. Her mouth dried and her fingers curled around the copy of the book that was set on the podium. She clutched it as tightly as she'd wanted to hold Wayne in this life.

But then movement in her peripheral vision jerked her out of her paralysis. Nikki set a glass of water onto the podium beside Juliet's white-knuckled hands. "Page thirty-two," she whispered. "Noah says to start there."

Her gaze sought him out, standing at the back of the room. His expression serious, he looked like the ex-soldier he was, his legs braced, his arms crossed over his chest. He made a small gesture with his chin. *Go ahead.*

She'd sticky-noted a different section to read, but instead turned to page thirty-two. She smiled, recognizing the passage, and without making any opening remarks, she cleared her throat and began to read. It was a humorous account of Wayne's first day at a boot camp he'd attended in Junior ROTC. The people in Malibu & Ewe laughed at the appropriate moments, and she was gratified. Despite the humor, she didn't think they could miss what came through so clearly in Wayne's own words as well—the caliber and remarkable quality of the man himself.

When the passage ended, she closed the book and looked up. "Wayne always said that if he hadn't become a professional soldier, his second career choice would have been professional football quarterback. But those of us that knew him also know that 'quarterback' wouldn't have been enough for this man. He would have wanted to plan the plays, call the plays, *and* execute the plays. He was player, team leader, exacting coach, all rolled into one. Thank you for coming to help me honor 'America's Hero' and my beloved husband."

A smattering of applause broke out as she made to retreat, but then a reporter jumped up. "You'll take questions?"

Her heart jolted at his abrupt tone. Behind him, she registered that Noah moved forward, but then she did, too. "Of course," she said. This was the real test—and the real opportunity.

Gazing at the man, Juliet realized some of Cassandra's

knitters were in the audience as well. From her seat beside the aggressive reporter, a woman wiggled her needles at Juliet in a subtle greeting. It made her smile. "I'd be happy to address anything."

"What was his appeal to a young woman like yourself?" The implication she'd been a crass gold digger was clear in his tone. "Tell us what you thought the first time you met him."

Before big tests, she'd always over-prepared. Tonight was no different. In considering everything that might happen and anything that might come up, she'd brought along her diary. That very first diary. From the shelf beneath the podium's top surface, she drew the familiar little book, and placed it beside *General Matters*. The binding had broken long ago, and the front cover fell open easily.

"The time I first met my husband, he didn't give me a second thought. This is what I wrote about him, however." Juliet took a breath. "Dear Diary: Tonight I met the man I'm going to marry . . . ' "

As she read aloud, she remembered the next time she'd seen him. At twenty-three, she'd been at her parents' funeral, bewildered by the sudden loss. Then a uniformed man had appeared at her side, silver-haired and charismatic. His hands had been warm on hers as he drew her near to kiss her cheek.

Her knight in shining armor. That young woman she'd been had fallen for his handsome looks, his commanding presence, his bone-deep kindness.

Now, changed by her life with Wayne, his illness, his death, she was a different woman. Maybe that was why her oyster-colored outfit didn't seem to suit her any longer. The last year had changed her so much, too. Like an oyster, she'd worn a protective shell that she'd had to shed in order to find a new life for herself.

Now she had family. The start, at least, of some kind of career. And a lover. Thanks to him, Juliet had uncovered her true and passionate nature—the pearl within the shell.

Another of her diary entries came to mind, the one from the day of Wayne's funeral. She'd written, *I think no one, no man for certain, could ever make me . . . well, feel again.*

Her gaze drifted over the heads in the crowd and found Noah once more, still standing at the back of the room. She let her eyes run over him, and just that warmed her, buoyed her, made her heart beat fast, made her every cell feel alive.

Noah *had* made her feel.

Feel . . . Feel *love*. She was in love with Noah.

*Oh, God*, she thought. And God help her.

Because she suspected that there was no moving on from that.

# Eighteen

> Wars are not paid for in wartime, the bill comes later.
>
> —BENJAMIN FRANKLIN

Marlys followed a tall, very slender, and slightly familiar-looking woman toward the Malibu shop. As the other woman was about to pull open the door, she glanced back and then drew up short, causing Marlys to nearly collide with her skinny ass. She edged away as the tall female hooked a finger over the bridge of her pink-lensed glasses and gazed down at her in the light of the security fixtures.

"Hey, Marlys." She lowered her glasses farther down her perfectly sloped nose. "It's me."

Oomfaa. Familiarity explained. The actress frequented her boutique, though usually not garbed in sunglasses that made her eyes look like a rabbit's and with her hair stuffed into a black, floppy-brimmed, knitted hat.

Oomfaa tugged it toward her eyebrows. "I made it for when I want to go out incognito."

Oh-kay. Though combined with the pink sunglasses, Marlys would have thought it would attract more attention rather than less. "What are you doing here?"

Oomfaa smiled. "This is my LYS—little yarn shop. I'm friends with the owner and I come here to knit."

Marlys turned to look at the full parking lot and then turned back to Oomfaa, keeping her voice casual. "But it's not knitting tonight, right?" The other woman might be one of the most famous actresses in America, but she was also one of the biggest gossips in Southern California. The information she would spill during a short shopping spree could keep Marlys and her assistant, Leeza, entertained for days afterward.

And that's what Marlys was after tonight. Information.

She'd told herself she was going to stay away, but here she was anyway, albeit an hour past the publicized start time. Questions had plagued her until she'd given in to impulse and headed for Malibu.

What was Juliet up to with this party?

Why had she chosen some "little yarn shop" in Malibu as the event's location?

Was Dean inside?

A couple pushed through the door, and Oomfaa and Marlys had to step aside to let them pass. Each of them held her father's book. As if they were the cork popped from a bottle, a stream of exiting people followed, some of them obviously from the media, and most of them clutching their own copies of *General Matters* in one hand and a cup of delicious-smelling coffee in the other.

Oomfaa sniffed. "Nikki made coffee and I'm betting there's her food inside. That's reason enough to visit Malibu & Ewe."

"Nikki?"

"One of the three sisters," Oomfaa clarified, stepping back toward the door and then retreating again as another group wandered out. "Cassandra owns the yarn shop, Nikki's a personal chef and engaged to Jay Buchanan, and—"

The rest of what she was saying was swallowed by

the noise of the crowd in the shop as the tall woman walked inside. Even with Marlys at her heels, the words didn't reach her.

She took in the interior of the shop instead. Not only was it full of milling, chattering people, but there was color and texture to overwhelm her, too. Yarns overflowed built-in bins that were stacked against the walls. Knitted garments, from toe socks to campy lingerie, from fuzzy sweaters to elegant dresses, were displayed on the walls or hung from wooden coatracks tucked into corners.

As a woman who admired fashion and made her living from it, Marlys took a moment to appreciate the talent and skill that had gone into each piece. Not to mention the artistic eye that had placed them so strategically. She'd have to come back during regular shop hours, she decided, making her way toward the back table where platters of food and beverage urns were set.

She wanted to meet this Cassandra. It looked as if they might have a lot in common. Then she took her first bite of a spinach-and-cheese-filled pastry and her taste buds cried in happiness. Okay, she hadn't eaten much, not since that last encounter with Dean, but it wasn't only hunger that had her drooling in delight.

This was good, really good. Now she wanted to meet Nikki, too.

Marlys didn't have friends, not since her days as an Army brat, but maybe she could change that. She *would* change that, she decided, popping the rest of the small appetizer into her mouth, if only to prove Dean wrong. *It's other people that you use to take out your pain*, he'd said. Well, she'd prove to him that she could get close to people without hurting them.

Maybe then he would—

"What the hell are you doing here?"

The demand in the male voice had her whirling around and her stomach leaping toward her throat. Noah stared at her, his eyes narrowed. Noah, not Dean. Her stomach settled back to the bottom of her belly.

From the look on his face, she guessed his friend had passed along that she'd been passing along tips to the tabloids. "It's a free country, Private."

"You're not welcome here, Marlys."

She'd never taken rejection well, true. But it rankled even more as she remembered how she'd come on to him when they'd first met and how gently he'd tried letting her down. That gentleness was what she found so mortifying. Noah had treated her like she was breakable, and everyone—Dean included now—knew that wasn't true.

Marlys drew herself taller, and wished she was wearing higher heels. "It's a party for my father's book."

"The party's over for you." He took her elbow.

Her face went hot, and she yanked her arm from his hold. "I can see myself out." She meant to spin away and leave with dignity, but some stupid compulsion kept her glued to the spot. Call it curiosity. None of her questions had been answered, after all.

What was Juliet up to?

Why'd she have the party here?

"Where's Dean?" The two words tumbled out of Marlys's mouth. "Is Dean here?"

Noah's eyes narrowed. "You're toxic, Marlys."

The sharp edge in his voice had her stepping back. Noah had always seemed like such a nice guy, which had been a huge part of his appeal. The rough hunkiness and "do a good turn daily" demeanor was an unbeatable combination. But the Boy Scout was gone and all that looked to be left was the narrow-eyed, trained-to-kill soldier.

"I only—"

"Save it," he said, cutting her off. "Just get the hell out."

She took another step back, but found she couldn't go without knowing. "Please," she heard herself say, embarrassed further by the entreaty she could hear in her own voice. "Please, Noah. Dean—"

"Is gone," the other man said flatly. "He reported early. Happy now?"

Happy now? She couldn't breathe now. As the crowd moved around her, as Noah gave her a last look of condemnation and then moved on himself, Marlys stood where she was. Dean had reported early. Maybe he was in Afghanistan already.

In a danger zone.

She wouldn't think of it, she decided, turning and heading back toward the shop's door. Their short interlude wasn't something she should dwell upon. And she was good at letting go, remember? She was a military brat, a dandelion. Like them, she was resilient. Like them, she knew when it was time to let the breeze take her to the next place.

She was like a hardy dandelion that survived anywhere and that . . . Marlys's feet stuttered.

. . . that grew in unexpected places.

. . . and that—

She froze, then had to lean against the nearest wall to hold herself up. The other thing about dandelions, the thing she'd stupidly forgotten, is that their roots went so damn deep.

Just like her feelings for Dean. Unexpected, deeply held, *made to survive*.

And she'd done everything she could to turn him away from her.

Cold closed around her throat and she felt as if a wound opened inside her chest. She braced her hand on the plaster beside her because a shoulder wasn't enough. Who could stand when she'd so royally fucked up her life?

"Are you all right?"

She glanced up at Oomfaa. "Sure." No. *Never.*

The other woman gave a happy nod. "Party turned out great, it looks like. I know everyone's pleased."

"Everyone?" Marlys only spoke because it seemed to help her keep breathing. Dean. Oh, God. *Dean.*

"The sisters. Well, half sisters, I guess is more accurate. They're donor siblings, all products of the same sperm-donor father but different mothers who used the same fertility clinic."

"Oh." Closing her eyes, she thought of his face, those clean-edged features, the clear eyes that had seen into the soul she'd not been sure she had until him. *Dean.*

"I was the one who kind of spilled the beans to Nikki that she was related to Cassandra. I didn't realize she was at Knitters' Night, and I didn't know that while Cassandra had located one of her sisters, she hadn't told her right away they were related. But all's well that ends well, right?"

"Right." It wasn't going to end well for her though, was it?

"The story gets even better," Oomfaa said, bending closer to Marlys. "I overheard Cassandra talking about their biological father. He was a medical student when he was a sperm donor. You'll never guess who's the father of Cassandra, Nikki, and Juliet."

"Who?" she repeated obligingly. "Who's the father of Cassandra, Nikki, and—" *Juliet?*

"Dr. Frank Tucker," Oomfaa whispered. "You know. They call him Dr. Tuck on that show."

Marlys did know. Dr. Frank Tucker, who was called simply Dr. Tuck on the reality TV show he starred in, *Fountain of Youth*, was one of the most eminent plastic surgeons in the country. Dr. Tuck had been on *Oprah*. And he was Juliet's *father*? Juliet had *sisters*?

Something spilled into Marlys's chest from her new wound. It felt bitter and raw, like bile, and if it had a color she knew it would be an acid, ugly green. Juliet, the Deal Breaker, the Happy Widow, the woman who had taken Marlys's father from her and left her with nothing, now had her very own father, her very own family.

Before Marlys, the crowd parted, and there stood Juliet, in front of a blowup of General Wayne Weston. Noah stood close to her side, and Marlys noticed that while their shoulders remained a discreet distance apart, the backs of their hands were touching.

More poison leaked around her heart.

As she watched, two women closed in on the couple. One had a river of rippling brown hair and wore a beautiful, lacy, obviously hand-knit sweater. Cassandra, Marlys guessed. The other woman, who had shoulder-length, gold-streaked brown hair, glanced around the room. Her eyes were that same bicolor as Juliet's and she waved at a man standing nearby with a cup of coffee. Marlys recognized Jay Buchanan, well-known L.A. bachelor. Engaged to Nikki, Oomfaa had said.

So now she could identify them. Cassandra and Nikki, the two women who were supposed to be her friends, but who were instead Juliet's sisters. The chef said something, and Juliet laughed.

More acid leaked, burning inside Marlys's belly and fertilizing another ugly emotion growing inside of her. Two others approached the sisters, obviously a reporter and photographer. Without saying a word to Oomfaa, Marlys advanced on the group as the rest of the world fell away.

It was only the press she saw, the press who seemed less interested in Marlys's father, the general, a true hero, than the treacherous woman who'd married him. It was the press Marlys focused on, and also on the woman who now had a happy, supportive family and an adoring new lover. Her father's aide.

She heard the reporter say, "If I could ask another question, Mrs. Weston?"

And Marlys remembered she'd come tonight with questions, too, and they'd all been answered except for one that she'd never dared utter before, not even in the ear of her source at the tabloids. It came out of her mouth, though it wasn't much more than a whisper.

"Juliet, did you have something to do with my father's death?"

Noah's head turned at the sound of Marlys's voice. What the hell had she just said? She stood just outside their small circle of people—reporter, photographer, the three sisters, and himself. The majority of the launch party attendees had gone, but there were still a dozen or so left, enjoying the food or in line to buy the general's book. Juliet had handled the crowd like a pro, even taking on the most cutting press questions with unflappable cool.

A few media members continued to hang around—those standing beside them, and another photographer that Noah just now spied, tucked beside a beverage urn. He recognized the rat—that damn paparazzo he'd caught sneaking around Juliet's pool weeks ago.

Torn between throwing that guy out and not wanting to leave Juliet's side, he was still standing there when Marlys raised her voice and repeated her question for everyone's ears.

"*Did you have something to do with my father's death*?"

Jesus. "Of course she didn't," Noah ground out. Protecting Juliet was his number-one concern, and he should have known that meant getting rid of the general's daughter the moment he'd spotted her in the yarn shop. "I told you to get lost before, Marlys," he said, starting for her, "and it's time you listened."

Marlys evaded him by squirming between the reporter and photographer. From the corner of the room, Noah could hear the distinctive click of a camera shutter. He shot the other photographer, the one closer to the action, a searing look. *No pictures.*

Marlys's gaze remained on Juliet. "You played the doting wife in public and when my father's friends were in our family home, but when he was taking his last breaths, you were being pampered at a spa. How could you? How can you explain that?"

"Damn it, Marlys." Noah launched himself forward, but Juliet grabbed his arm and hauled him back.

"Don't," she said to him, then turned her attention to the other woman, her voice calm. "I've said this before, Marlys. I couldn't know it was that day, that hour—"

"He hadn't been eating."

"Your father—"

"He hadn't been drinking."

Juliet pushed back her hair. "His illness meant he didn't have much appetite—"

"Or was it that my father was refusing nourishment in order to hasten his death and you did nothing to stop him?"

Noah saw Juliet freeze. Shit. Shit, shit, shit. Her lips set and her eyes narrowed as her gaze slowly slid from Marlys to his face. Was she connecting some inconvenient dots?

The general's daughter's tone was shrill. "Juliet—"

"Knows nothing about anything like that," Noah interjected, his voice harsh and loud enough to reach all four walls of the store. He'd made a promise, but he couldn't let a public accusation such as this stand. "In the last weeks, the general didn't let anyone tend him during his meals but me."

"The both of you hinted it embarrassed him to have me see him struggle to feed himself," Juliet said slowly. "He flat-out refused to let me help. But neither of you told me how much he was eating and drinking. Or wasn't eating and drinking."

Noah knew the shit had hit the fan now. But with her looking at him like that, there was no way he could tell her anything less than the truth.

"He wasn't, not at the end. He really couldn't—it wasn't a matter of choice," he clarified. "But it was one of the general's last commands that I not let you know that."

"What? Why?"

Noah ignored the questions to pin Marlys with his glare. "Satisfied? Have you done enough?"

The general's daughter's face was pale. "What did *you* do?" she shot back.

"Christ, Marlys. Nothing like you're insinuating—hospice was there alongside me. When the general wasn't eating or drinking any longer, he asked us to keep the particulars quiet because it gave him a measure of control and self-respect. It gave him back a little dignity to think he was doing one last thing for his wife."

"What last thing?" Juliet's shaken voice made him ache.

"He didn't want you hovering at his bedside. He didn't want you making yourself sick while watching his every breath to determine if it was his last."

"Hover—!"

"He knew that would be torture for you and he wanted to protect you from the ordeal. The day he sensed was his last day . . ." Noah looked down, then back to the face of the woman he loved. He'd held this secret for so long, but it was out now, and he recognized with another sharp ache that the casualty of it could very well be the future with her he'd almost started to believe in. "On that day he asked me to convince you to spend it at the spa."

Juliet's hand rose to her throat. At her side, Cassandra put her arm around her older sister's shoulders.

Marlys made a strangled sound. "Why didn't you call me, if Juliet wasn't the one he wanted with him when he died?"

"Jesus Christ, Marlys. If he didn't want Juliet as a witness to that, he certainly didn't want you there either. He wanted to shield you, too."

"Shield me?" she repeated. "Why would my father want to shield me?"

Noah shook his head. "Because he loved you, Marlys."

She paled further, the angry expression on her face melting away. If he'd thought the little witch had a heart, he might have suspected it was broken. But he didn't believe she had a single soft organ inside her, and when she scrambled backward and then ran for the door, he could only be glad she was gone.

Leaving all the destruction that she'd wrought behind.

Silence settled over the room. There were a few last sales rung up at the register, a few last looks cast, but quickly the party was over, the shop empty of all but the sisters and the three men.

To Noah, the only one in the place was Juliet.

Even obviously upset, she'd never looked more beautiful—and more unattainable. Her sisters were close to her; Nikki had brought her coffee, but she hadn't taken a sip.

She hadn't looked at him.

Finally, she spoke, her gaze fixed on something only she could see. "That day, that day I went to the spa, you didn't really think it was Wayne's last day."

Juliet had been nearly impossible to pry from the general's side. She'd complied during mealtimes, but for months, the rest of her day—except that day—had been exclusively devoted to her husband. The spa certificate the general had bought for her last birthday was months old.

"Yeah, I did." Noah shut his eyes, remembering the wasted figure in the bed, the general's stoic attitude toward his pain, the calm way he'd come to terms with dying. On that day, his last desire had been to prevent his wife's further suffering and it had been what Noah wanted, too. "I did think it was."

"But it was you who persuaded me to have a day at that spa. I remember it perfectly. You encouraged me to leave Wayne's bedside. I wouldn't have gone if you hadn't insisted."

Noah opened his eyes and saw that Juliet had moved farther from him. If he put out his hand, it wouldn't reach her. "It was what he wanted."

"Wanted?" she snapped back. "It was that he considered me too fragile to handle it. And you, you thought he was right about that, too."

She'd gone from stunned to something else. Angry? Aching? Some miserable combination of the two? He didn't know how to fix it. Pushing a hand through his hair, he sighed. "That wasn't—"

"Don't give me that," she interrupted, her voice hot. "You could have reasoned with him; you could have refused. At the very least, you could have given me some sign of what you suspected would happen that day."

"Juliet . . ."

Her gaze narrowed on his face. "Did *you* think I was strong enough to stay at his side? Do you think Wayne was wrong?"

He thought it was the most heroic thing the general may have ever done—to meet the end of his life without the love of his life next to him. That wasn't what she wanted to hear, but her blue and green eyes were a bicolored lie detector and there was really nothing to be gained by bullshitting now. He'd already lost her. "No."

She jerked, as if the word was a blow.

At that sign of her pain, he found himself trying to leap the chasm between them anyway. "Juliet."

But she was already retreating farther from him, her outstretched hand shoring up the very air between them. "Don't touch me," she said. "Don't ever touch me again."

God help him, the insistence in her voice didn't stop him. He had to try one last time to reach her, he was that stupid in love. "Juliet, what we've had together—"

"Was nothing. Any warm body would do."

He ignored the sting of that and edged closer. "Juliet. *Honey.*"

"I said I don't want you near me."

"Fine." Halting, he shoved his hand through his hair again. "Later, when we're back at the house—"

"There won't be a later, Noah." Her expression was set, her beautiful mouth compressed in a tight line. "You're fired."

He froze. Two words. A single killing shot that dismissed him as well as the relationship they'd developed over these weeks of friendship and intimacy. *You're fired.*

Who the hell knew why it felt like such a damn surprise? Because no matter how he'd tried to fool himself otherwise, he'd never believed it would ever last—the officer's wife and the enlisted guy.

He raised stiff fingers to his forehead and sent her a military salute. "Yes, ma'am."

And like that, his tour of duty was over.

# *Nineteen*

In war, truth is the first casualty.

—AESCHYLUS

Juliet tidied the area around the cash register, Cassandra slid skeins into bins, and Nikki perused a stack of wedding magazines that she'd brought with her instead of her half-finished fiancé sweater. "I knew nobody would come tonight," she said, frowning at a slick page. "But still I had hope, even though it's almost Thanksgiving. I really need wedding advice and the knitters are always ready to offer some up."

"I considered canceling tonight," Cassandra admitted. "But then I thought—"

She broke off, but Juliet could finish the sentence for her. *But then I thought our older sister needed the distraction.* Today was the anniversary of Wayne's death, and Cassandra was right. She needed to be distracted. She didn't want to think about him. About him or Noah.

"Anyway," Cassandra continued. "I'm here, Juliet's here. We can help, though I thought you and Jay were pretty serious about the Vegas drive-through chapel on New Year's Eve."

"We figured his relatives would never forgive us, and then I thought . . . I realized . . ." Her cheeks pink, Nikki glanced up from her magazine to look at Cassandra across the room. "I have my own family now, too. I want you to stand up with me."

"Oh." Cassandra dropped the yarn she was holding, and then bent quickly to retrieve it. She stood again, grinning. "Oh, *yes*."

Nikki smiled in return, then glanced over at Juliet. "You'll have to cut cards for who gets to be maid of honor."

"What?" Juliet blinked. "Me, too? I don't know . . . a wedding . . ." Being involved in one might make it impossible for her to put from her mind the two men she'd loved and she was devoting every ounce of energy to just that very thing.

But there was her sister, her *sister*, looking at her with such expectation from eyes so very like her own. How could she refuse?

"Of course I'd be honored to be in your wedding party," she said quickly, and before her inner self could start howling, she forced out the next question. "And what kind of advice are you looking for?"

"A theme. That's what Jay's sister said. He, of course, immediately thought of 'sultan and harem,' but we managed to convince him that if he brought it up again he wouldn't live to see the wedding." The mischief on her face fled and her eyes flared wide. "Oh, God, I'm sorry. That's probably not so funny to you."

"What?" Juliet realized the turn her sister's thoughts had taken. "No, no. Don't worry about it."

"I've got such a big mouth. You don't need any offhand reminders that your husband has been gone a year, and . . ." She clapped her hand over her lips and mumbled from behind them. "Go ahead, kill me n—"

Cassandra clipped her on the side of the head, then dropped down onto the cushions beside the other woman. "Shut up, little sister."

With a groan, Nikki sank into the couch cushions. "I'm sorry. Someone should just shoot me and put me out of my miser—"

Cassandra's second clip wasn't quite so gentle. "Nikki? Seriously. Are you brain dead?"

Juliet's two sisters stared at each other, matching expressions appalled.

"It's not our fault," Nikki said. "It's just one of those things, where the subject you want to steer clear of most keeps making its way to the tip of your tongue."

Reaching for one of the magazines, Juliet gave a nod. "I understand. No problem. Don't worry about it."

"Thing is, no matter how hard I try, I have a terrible feeling I'm going to find myself talking about your husband's death—"

"Nik!"

She ignored Cassandra's protest and went on, like a dog with a bone. "—as well as how you're doing now that Noah's gone."

Juliet flipped a page of the magazine, staring unseeing at some glossy, frothy image. "I don't want to discuss either one."

"But that's the downside of this sister thing," Cassandra said gently. "You're stuck with our noses in your business."

They were ganging up on her. "I don't want—"

"And if nagging won't work, we'll use guilt," Nikki added. "Like, how could I possibly go forward with my wedding to Jay when you're so obviously unhappy?"

"Unhappy?" Juliet's hand froze, mid-page-turn. "I'm not unhappy. I'm *angry*." And if she dwelled too much on it, her mood might set fire to something.

Her sisters exchanged glances. Cassandra opened her mouth. "All right. Want to expand on that?"

"No." Juliet tossed the magazine to the table. "Can't you just let this go?"

"I could," Nikki responded. "But the granola girl here, she's just a big pain in the ass."

Cassandra huffed. "Snot."

"Froot Loop."

"Witch."

Nikki smirked. "Lightweight. Try bi—"

"All right!" Juliet dropped her head to her hands. "All right. If just to shut the two of you up."

"Hah." Nikki smiled, all good humor again as she elbowed Cassandra. "We cracked her. You said it might take margaritas."

"For God's sake, Nikki, we don't want to give away our plague-the-sister strategies," she replied, rolling her eyes. "What is wrong with you?"

"Nothing's wrong with me, Froot Loop—"

"Please stop calling me that."

Nikki's expression turned sly. "Why? Because it's Gabe's pet name for you?"

Juliet leaned forward, eager to nurture this new topic of conversation. "Yes, speaking of things a person is itching to find out . . ."

The two younger sisters stilled, then turned on her as one. "Nice try, but no banana," Nikki said.

Cassandra flipped a handful of wavy hair behind her right shoulder and then nodded. "We just want to help, Juliet. At the book party, what Noah said, help us understand . . ."

*Noah.* She tried pushing the man out of her mind, but it wasn't working. Wayne was there, too, front and center. "I can't believe they'd conspire to keep me away when my husband needed me most." The words tumbled out.

She rose from the couch, her voice rising, too, but she couldn't seem to modulate her tone. "It makes me furious to realize just exactly how frail they considered me to be." She held out her arms. "Do I look like a puff of air would blow me over?"

Cassandra appeared to think about it. "Well, kind of. No! No! Don't get all huffy. It's just that you do have that ethereal blonde thing going on. It's natural for people to respond to that in a certain way."

"And I don't think you've been eating enough," Nikki added. "I should make you a big dish of enchiladas."

Juliet dropped back to her seat, still frustrated. "Mexican food is not going to solve anything. As for people naturally responding to my kind of looks—these were two men who *knew* me. How could they have—What are you doing?"

She broke off as Nikki jumped from the couch to drag the oversized cutout of Wayne from the back room and over to the couches. Propped against the coffee table, all nine feet of him stared down at the three of them.

Nikki eyed the man right back, her arms crossed over her chest. "Just looking at him, he makes me want to enlist," she said. "Either that or confess I cheated on my U.S. History midterm exam."

Juliet could almost smile. "He had a way about him like that."

"So you knew him then," Nikki said.

"Of course."

"Like you wished he'd known you."

She narrowed her eyes at the other woman. "What are you getting at?"

"I hate to break big news, Juliet, but the man was old. Handsome and sexy, I'll give you that, yet of an entirely different generation. And he was a military man. A commander."

"But old," Juliet said wryly. Her elegant silver fox.

"Well, if you're aware of so much, can't you see that he very likely thought—as a man of his generation and inclination—that it was his duty to protect you? Hadn't he always tried to do that?"

"To a fault, yes, but he was *dying*, surely that meant—"

"I'll tell you something I know about people and about dying. I watched my mother die, my father, too. Nothing changes about a person when they come to their last days. The funny ones still make jokes, and the private ones don't suddenly reveal their souls."

Cassandra slid down the couch to move closer to Juliet as Nikki continued.

"If you ask me, the choices your husband made at the end of his life tell us something about him—that he was a proud and caring man—but they don't tell us anything about *you*."

Cassandra picked up the thread. "Nikki's right. They don't say that you're anything less than a woman loved with devotion by a well-intentioned, but perhaps pigheaded man."

Juliet stared at Cassandra, then shifted her gaze to Nikki. Were they right, that this wasn't about Juliet so much as it was about what Wayne needed to do for himself? And if so, how could her sisters possibly understand something so clearly that Juliet hadn't realized on her own?

*But wasn't that what family did?* she mused, looking up at Wayne's masterful—oh, yes, and macho-to-the-core—image. Family could offer up clarity because they cared. Her gaze drifted back to the two other women. She'd risked forging a bond with them to gain everything that was written across their faces at this moment: warmth, loyalty, caring.

Insight.

Her anger leached away as her gaze lifted once again to Wayne's photograph. *Stubborn cuss. Pigheaded, stubborn cuss. But maybe I understand now,* she conceded. Okay, she did understand now. *I forgive you.* She could almost swear she saw his black-and-white lips turn up in a little smile.

And if she forgave him . . .

But she wasn't extending that to the other man who was out of her life and who she was still trying so desperately to keep out of her mind. The one who—

The bells on the door to Malibu & Ewe clanged. Oomfaa came dashing through, her face flushed, her voice breathless. "Passed Jay on PCH. No cell reception. He said to tell you, come quick. Something about a man and a car crash."

The one who—Juliet finished the thought as dread filled her chest—was Noah, the man she still loved.

When they found Jay in the parking lot of Malibu's Surfrider beach, Juliet's dread seeped away. Her sisters had warned her that Oomfaa was as known for her hyperbole as her tendency to gossip and this "emergency" didn't look quite so dire and didn't involve Noah at all, though there was a tow truck, a crashed car, and a man—Gabe Kincaid.

The three women hurried from Juliet's sedan to join Jay, who was conferring with the tow truck driver underneath the propped-up hood of his vehicle. Apparently engine trouble had halted him in the process of towing a crumpled but classic Thunderbird convertible, complete with a drunken—and singing—man sprawled in its backseat.

"No matter where you go," Gabe sang at the top of his lungs, and though it wasn't top quality, Juliet thought she recognized the song.

"Beatles?" she asked the others.

Jay shook his head. "Badfinger. Common mistake, because McCartney wrote a big hit of theirs, 'Come and Get It,' and George Harrison produced one of their albums."

"I told you before he's a font of useless info," Nikki remarked.

"Useless?" Her fiancé grabbed her around the waist to yank her close. "That's not what you said last night when I showed you that technique to—"

"Can you guys stop playing around?" Cassandra interrupted, sounding strained. "Can't you see this is serious?"

Her voice seemed to penetrate Gabe's drunken fog. He pushed himself straighter on the backseat, cradling a tequila bottle close to his chest as he peered at their assembled group. "Hey, Froot Loop! Look, I found it!"

"Oh, Gabe." Cassandra's hand shook a little as she pushed her hair over her shoulder. "Surely this isn't *it*."

"Not *it*, it," he said, with an overemphatic shake of his head. "But like it, it. Going to restore this it. Bring it all back."

"Oh, Gabe," she responded again, as if her heart was breaking. She turned away from the man.

Juliet stepped nearer to her sister. "What's the matter? What's he doing?"

"I don't know what he's doing. Maybe what I've been worrying about all along," she said, her words nearly masked as Gabe renewed his loud cover of the Badfinger ballad.

"What's that?" Nikki said, she and Jay crowding close as well.

"Going completely crazy." Cassandra glanced back at the man, then wrapped her arms around herself as if there'd been a sudden temperature dive. "He had one of those cars before. A 1963 Thunderbird convertible. It was in an accident as well. A drunk driver T-boned it when his wife was driving. It killed her instantly, along with their five-year-old daughter."

"God." Nikki clutched Jay's arm. "God."

He cleared his throat. "We didn't know."

"Gabe doesn't talk about it unless he's drunk. Unless he's very, very drunk."

"Froot Loop!" Gabe interrupted his song to give a lusty yell. "Come over here."

With a sigh, she turned, then walked toward the car, the others trailing behind her. "Gabe . . ."

He frowned. "Whaz the matter?"

"I don't like this." She gestured to the convertible. "I don't like seeing you in there."

Juliet knew what her sister wasn't saying. It didn't take a giant leap of genius to wonder—to worry—that Gabe was placing himself in that same car because he was wishing he'd been with his wife and daughter at the time of their accident. That he was going to restore this Thunderbird so he could re-create the very same scenario.

"Come in wi' me," Gabe said to Cassandra, lurching for the door handle so that tequila spilled from the bottle he clutched. "We could fuck—"

"Gabe!"

"'Scuse me," he said, giving up on getting the door open and going back to his sprawl. "We could *make love* righ' here. Big backseat."

Cassandra groaned. "How can you—"

"Wha'?" He slapped the leather with his free hand. "Lynn . . . m'wife and me made Maddie righ' here."

"Gabe, I'm not—"

"Wha'?" He took a chug of tequila, then wiped his mouth with the back of his hand. "You don' want my babies?"

It was hard to tell if Cassandra wanted to cry or crack Gabe on the head with that tequila bottle. "I don't want you like this."

He didn't appear to hear her. "'S okay. I don't want babies either," he declared, then took another swig of liquor. "Proteshun. We'll use con . . . con . . . con . . ."

". . . doms," Jay put in. "Condoms. So why don't we get you out of that car, buddy, and I'll drive you home. We can discuss your favorite brand and preferred size on the way."

"Triple XL," Gabe said, getting to his feet so he stood on the back cushions, swaying.

Jay took his tequila and handed it off to Nikki, then he helped maneuver Gabe from the car.

On the asphalt, the drunken man gave the group a serious look and pounded his chest. "Hung like 'n elephant."

Cassandra rolled her eyes. "Dumbo, that's what I'm going to call him from now on."

"Hah." Gabe staggered to her and slung his arm around her neck. "Funny. Funny Froo' Loop. Still wanna do you, darlin'."

"Yeah. I'm sure." She started leading him in the direction of Jay's Porsche.

"Really." He looked over his shoulder, straight at Juliet. "Not like she said before. Any warm body won' do."

From what she could see of Juliet's expression through her car windshield, Marlys figured that finding her waiting in her Miata outside the Malibu house was the capper on an already crappy day. Instead of pulling into the garage, Juliet turned off her car in the driveway. Poised for a quick getaway?

As she exited her seat, Marlys's dog leaped out and ran for the driver's side of Juliet's where he hopped around like a pogo stick. When she emerged, Blackie threw himself against her.

Juliet shook her head as she made her way up the path to her front porch with seventy pounds of canine doing his unintentional best to trip her up. "Marlys, you need to put Blackie on a leash."

"He was hoping you were someone else."

Juliet's progress hitched a little, and Marlys cursed herself for the slip. She didn't want to think of Dean. She *really* didn't want Juliet thinking she was thinking of Dean.

Marlys wasn't weak like that. And she didn't pine after something she'd deliberately sabotaged. Marlys wasn't stupid like that either.

Tucking the box she carried under her arm, she followed the dog and Juliet into the house, then watched while the other woman turned on lights as she made her way through the shadowy interior. A routine she, too, was familiar with. Woman alone returns home to dark emptiness.

"Where's Noah?" she asked.

Juliet tossed her purse onto the kitchen counter then glanced over with her freaky, two-colored eyes. "He lives elsewhere. Why are you here?"

Ouch. Marlys's eyebrows rose. "Gloves are off?"

"What do you think? Dean told us what you've done.

Seeding the scandal sheets—good God. And of course you've read the latest on the websites about the book party and the ugly accusation you made there."

"Dean . . ." She wished she hadn't said the name. It lingered on her tongue, sweet, like a Lifesaver, though she didn't think its taste would ever melt away.

Juliet sighed. "Okay, I'm earning my heaven points by asking this, Marlys. Do you want to know how he's doing? Maybe Jay—"

Marlys snatched at the name. "Jay Buchanan?"

The other woman's face went watchful. Damn.

She tried her best to look innocent. "You know Jay Buchanan?"

"Yes." Juliet leaned back against a countertop and crossed her arms over her chest.

"I hear he's engaged now."

"Mmm."

"We went on a date once."

A smile crossed her evil stepmother's lips. "From what I hear, you and just about every woman in L.A. went on a date with Jay once."

Marlys grinned. "From what I hear, too. How'd you meet him?"

Juliet shrugged. "Malibu's a small place."

"So they say. Population thirteen thousand, feels more like three-hundred. But hey, none of L.A. is all that big. For example, I ran into Oomfaa at that yarn place the other night. I know her from the boutique."

And knew that though she was a notorious gossip, she wasn't always entirely reliable. Last month when she'd been trying on a selection of layered tees, she'd dished a bit about Katherine Heigl that had turned out to be totally untrue. Which meant Marlys had new questions. Donor siblings? Fathered by a celebrity plastic surgeon? If she was going to do something with the data, she needed more confirmation than Oomfaa's say-so.

Juliet wasn't taking the bait and it looked as if her brief moment of sympathy was gone, too. "Marlys, what do you want?"

The end of this pain. She'd been raw for a year, her father's death having reopened wounds she'd thought had healed over. And then Dean had come and then gone from her life and it was like acid everywhere.

Burn, burn, burn.

That Q & A at the book party hadn't changed a thing. The resulting talk of it so far had been, frankly, tepid. On a more personal note, sure, Noah had said that her father loved her, but that didn't alter the fact that Juliet had ruined his reputation. And Marlys still wanted payback.

Daddy issues much? Hell, yeah. But an awareness of them didn't blunt her resentment or her pain. So she produced her excuse, the cardboard box. "More mail from the Palisades house."

Grimacing, Juliet took the small box and dumped the contents onto the counter. A dozen or so envelopes dropped out. "I'm sorry for the trouble."

"No trouble." Not when she was after information. She watched the other woman reach for a knife to serve as a letter opener.

"You have Thanksgiving plans?" she asked.

Juliet paused, then drew out a sheet and started to unfold it. "I think so." Her hands slowed again.

Marlys hid her smirk, but she could see the goody-goody's good-mannered wheels turning. Did she think she was obligated to extend an invitation? Did she think Marlys was so hard up that she'd accept?

God, maybe she *was* getting soft because she couldn't stand the stupid tension emanating from the woman. "Don't worry. I'm not about to ask to bring my famous brussels sprouts in cream sauce to your holiday table."

Weird, how bitter she sounded. Juliet must have noticed it, too, because she looked up and sighed again. "Marlys, if you want—"

"Of course I don't want! I don't want anything to do with you. I don't need anything from you. You're not my family."

Something in her voice brought Blackie to her at a run. Sliding to a stop at her feet, he whined. She warmed her hand on the top of her head. "I'm going over to Helen's. Lots of dad's friends will be there."

Lie, lie, lie, but then, what did it matter? She hated turkey and she had a store-bought pumpkin pie in the freezer that she planned on baking and then nibbling on all day. Thanksgiving with Mrs. Smith.

Juliet moved on to the next piece of mail. "All right."

All was *so* not right. And Marlys didn't know how to cope except for in her usual way. *It's other people that you use to take out your pain. You hurt other people so you don't have to feel a goddamned thing.*

She hoped the man was right.

Juliet had opened another piece of correspondence. She unfolded a card, and then her eyes widened as she read. Her hand darted to the envelope and she turned it address-side up. "Speaking of Helen," she muttered.

Marlys perked up. "Problem?"

"No." Juliet stuffed the card back in the envelope. "Just that I've got an invitation to her party tomorrow night after all."

"You wouldn't dare go," Marlys said, bristling. That damn Helen.

Juliet narrowed her eyes. "Good-bye, Marlys."

Hell, she'd got the boot before she'd gotten her confirmation. Fingers drumming against her thigh, she was forced to follow her father's wife toward the front door.

She only needed a teeny, tiny sign. "I'm thinking of having some Botox injections," she mused aloud.

"You don't say." Clearly not caring, Juliet pulled open the front door.

"I'm thinking of seeing Dr. Frank Tucker."

Juliet jerked around to stare at Marlys. "*What?*"

Hah. This time Oomfaa had it right.

"I'll probably chicken out, though," Marlys continued, breezing by the other woman so that she and Blackie were over the threshold. "I've never liked needles."

Or pain.

Hand on Blackie's collar, she jogged to her car and tried to remember if she had Pharmaceutical Phil's brother's number in her cell phone's address book. For a moment she saw Dean in her mind's eye, and then heard his voice in her head. *Self-destructive,* he'd called her. *Fine.*

Bad Marlys.

But Blackie and being bad was all that she had left.

# Twenty

In war, there is no prize for the runner-up.

—GENERAL OMAR BRADLEY

Second thoughts? A heavy dose of guilt? Or just an oversight? Juliet couldn't know which had prompted the invitation she'd received to Helen Novack's private book party. Maybe Helen had sent it to the old house assuming Juliet would receive it too late.

But instead, Marlys had done her a favor in bringing it so promptly, and done her another favor by sending out a challenge she probably didn't even realize she'd voiced. *You wouldn't dare go.*

The Juliet Weston who had hidden behind her shell for eleven months wouldn't. But the Juliet Weston who had found a family, a job, a lover—the Juliet Weston who knew she was powerful and passionate—didn't dare not go. Not and still continue believing she wasn't the retiring rose that some still considered her.

Despite all that, her stomach played host to a standoff between fight or flight as she stood at the front door of Helen Novack's 1920s-era L.A. mansion. Her palms smoothed her dress, which was much more Malibu than Bel Air. At a flirty, above-the-knee length and constructed of slinky layers of blue and green knit, this dress didn't have a single beige thread.

And thank God Nikki hadn't delivered on her promise of enchiladas—the dress was that clingy. But Juliet was going to demand the dish, if she made it through tonight—not *if, when.*

Helen's houseman seemed pleased to see her. "Mrs. Weston!" If he was surprised, it didn't show.

Juliet waved her invitation anyway, then tucked it into her bag. "Miguel, it's good to see you."

He made a little bow. "Everyone is this way."

And everyone was. The crowd of a hundred-plus of Wayne's friends created clusters and knots throughout the living room and also spilled onto the courtyard with its bubbling fountain and strategic floodlights. Waiters in black and white moved about with trays of drinks and edibles. Here and there Juliet noticed attractive displays of old photos and medals—Marlys's distinctive touch.

But Juliet didn't see the younger woman anywhere. Instead, at the far end of the room, where stacks of books were being given away at a table, she found Helen Novack—who stood staring straight at Juliet.

Taking what she hoped was an invisible breath, she made her way toward her hostess. Whether the room went quiet or she just couldn't hear the chatter over the heartbeat in her ears, Juliet couldn't say. She didn't let the lack of sound stop her, though, even as along her path she caught the eye of people she'd known for eight years . . . and hadn't spoken to during the last twelve months.

With a nod, with a smile, she continued moving.

Until she felt another, different gaze on her. Her head jerked left, and there, coming through the doors to the courtyard, was Noah. In pale gray slacks, and a darker dress shirt and jacket, he looked more attorney than ex-soldier.

Had Helen's social secretary made a second screwup?

Whatever the answer, her feet halted as her traitorous heart tried climbing from her chest to her throat. Yet the traitor was him, damn it.

Turning her head away, she moved forward again, nodding at other acquaintances, murmuring greetings, but not hesitating until she was face-to-face with Helen. *I'm sorry*, she remembered saying the last time the two of them had met. Tonight, she would not be apologizing.

Stretching out her hand, she smiled at the other woman. "Helen." Now she knew the room had gone silent, and she raised her voice to carry to every corner. "Thank you so much for all the trouble you've gone to tonight. The party looks beautiful. Wayne would be so pleased. *I'm* pleased."

Helen's fingers were cool in hers, but Juliet didn't let that stop her from covering them with her second hand. "You've always been such a very good friend," she added.

Okay, to Wayne and not to Juliet, but that didn't matter anymore. They'd both lost a man who'd been important in their lives. As a photographer's flash went off, she moved even closer to the older woman and brushed her cheek with her own. "Let's give Wayne a little chuckle," she murmured for Helen's ears only. "And make the press look like idiots for reporting any ill will between us."

And it was Helen who chuckled, but that was good enough for Juliet. She pulled back to find herself surrounded by people. Whether they were well-wishers or ill-willers, she didn't bother deciphering. More smiles, more chat, more deep breaths later, she realized that like everything else in life, there was a balance of both in this crowd.

She made a lunch date, she overheard a catty remark, she stole away to a quiet corner with a glass of champagne. A man she'd never met trapped her there before she could make an escape. There was a platinum-and-steel watch on his left wrist and a heavy gold ring on his right pinky.

He introduced himself like she should know his name.

At a loss, she tossed out a guess. "You played golf with Wayne?"

He shook his head, his Einsteinian mass of hair waving. "No golf. Never had the pleasure of meeting the man. I make movies. Writer-director-producer. Last year's *Voyeur*? *Pop Art* three years before that?"

Juliet shrugged. "Sorry. I haven't been to the movies in a while."

"I have two Best Picture Oscars."

"Congratulations." What else could she say?

He nodded, as if coming to terms with his inability to impress her. "I came here tonight hoping to get a chance to talk with you. I was going to get Helen to introduce us, but I took it upon myself instead."

Apparently he was more informed about movies than society gossip, which upped his ante in Juliet's eyes.

"I wasn't sure if your bodyguard would let me get close, though," the writer-director-producer continued.

"What bodyguard?" She frowned.

"Intense young man in a dark jacket? He's been shadowing you all night."

Her heart made another leap for her throat and she found herself searching the crowd. *Damn*, she thought. Her feelings for him hadn't disappeared, had they? She still loved him so much.

But he wasn't anywhere in sight, she realized, as her heart settled back into her aching chest. If he'd had her under surveillance before, he was gone now, and she couldn't decide if it made her mad that he'd been watchful or glad he hadn't interfered.

She hadn't needed him to deal with Helen. Though she definitely needed some additional expertise, she decided, as her new Hollywood friend launched into his pitch. There was a chapter in Wayne's book about Gulf War I that screamed "movie" to the man. He wanted to option the autobiography.

Someone was noticing her husband had been a hero, after all.

An hour later, she made her good-byes and repeated her

thanks to her hostess. "I saw who you were talking to in the corner . . ." the older woman started.

"Yes," Juliet answered the unspoken question, and this time her smile was 100 percent genuine. "And I have a very good feeling, Helen, that after tonight they just might have to dub me the Deal*maker*." A deal that would put her late husband, America's Hero, in a worldwide spotlight for all posterity.

It was all she'd ever thought she'd want.

Around the corner from Helen's house, Noah leaned against the driver's side of Juliet's Mercedes and listened to her high heels tapping the asphalt as she approached. His gaze fixed on the ground at his feet and his fists dug in the pockets of his slacks, he tracked her unhesitating progress.

He'd watched her walk the gauntlet at the party and he wasn't surprised that her stride wouldn't hitch at the prospect of taking him on, either. Under her elegance, beauty, and poise, tonight he'd seen the toughness he hadn't given her credit for before now.

"What are you doing here?" she asked.

Instead of looking at her, he stared at the pointed toes of her high heels, stopped so close to his loafers. He shook his head and even that small movement hurt. His body felt like he'd been in a brawl and yet all he wanted was to find a convenient wall to pummel with his fists. "I really don't know why I'm here."

"Did you end up with an invitation, too?"

"I crashed the party. Cassandra told me where I could find you."

"What?" Juliet's voice was hostile. "You found out I was going to attend tonight and thought I needed a security detail?"

"No. You handled the crowd back there without a tremor. I admire the hell out of you for it." Maybe that was just another reason he was aching so damn bad. Juliet didn't need him.

"Then why, Noah? Why are you here?"

She'd already asked him once, and he was such a mess he didn't have a decent lie left in him. "To see you. I just had to see you tonight."

"What for? Do you have something to tell me?"

"Yeah." It came out then, things he should have said, things he shouldn't say, and then those he couldn't hold back. All of then tumbled out of his mouth, but none of them eased his pain. "I have to apologize. I have to say I should have given you the choice that day a year ago. I have to say that I love you, that I'm *in* love with you, and I have to tell—oh, hell, Juliet, I need to tell someone who would understand—Tim . . . My friend Tim died today."

"*Noah.*" There was a catch in her voice. "Noah, I'm so sorry."

He had no idea who moved first, but they were in each other's arms. She was warm and familiar, but beneath her willowy frame he sensed the resilience that had held her together through her great loss and into her new life. He breathed in her scent, he breathed in her strength, and it steadied him. His pain lessened as he felt his muscles relax for the first time since hearing the news.

*Tim*, he thought, closing his eyes to revel in this brief respite in her embrace, *I hope you're finding such peace wherever you're resting now.* He managed his first deep breath in hours. Then a second.

*All right*, he told himself, figuring he should let her go now. *All right*. He tried moving away but that toughness of hers came into play and her arms refused to release him.

"Wait a minute," she said, her gaze narrowed on his face. "Did I hear right? Did you just say you're in love with me?"

*Shit.* "You caught that, huh?" He kept his hands loose and relaxed at his sides. "I shouldn't have mentioned it."

He saw her swallow and in the glow of the streetlight he detected the flush rising on her cheeks. "Why not?"

Why not? No matter how closely they were pressed together, the reason why not stood between them, as big as if he was really the size of the cardboard cutout Gabe had made of his photo. Why not was America's high-class hero, General Wayne Weston. In comparison to her husband, Noah Smith, convict's son and soldier-from-the-sticks, had nothing to offer this woman. He'd known it from the start but for a few weeks had allowed himself to forget that fact.

"Because . . . because it made me really glad to hear it, Noah," she said.

*What?* Startled, he watched her swallow again.

"When I saw you just now, I knew . . . I knew . . ." She hesitated, then plunged on, "Well, I'm done with hiding away and hiding how I feel. I want you. I want you back in my life."

Despite his best intentions, his hands lifted, one to her hair, the other cupped that sweet indentation at her waist. "I can't . . . I don't . . ." Christ, what to say? She was dangling half a dream in front of him. He wanted everything with her, he wanted it all, but another, better man already filled her heart.

He dropped his arms and broke her hold, putting breathing room between them. "I can't come back into your world and start washing your windows again, Juliet." Christ, and it made his blood boil thinking about it, because he was afraid if she insisted that he'd settle for just that.

She stiffened. "That's not what I meant."

"And I also can't be the 'any warm body' in your bed when you feel like you want one of those."

"That's not what I meant either!" Hot color shot across her face. "You know I'm not asking for a servant. Or a gigolo. You know me better than that."

"Juliet . . ."

The three syllables seemed to incense her. Her body went rigid. " 'Juliet' what? You make me so mad! You're leading me on again, damn it, playing Mr. Hot-Then-Cold.

'I love you, I'm in love with you, I need you,' you said that, and then you back away." She crossed to her front tire and gave it a swift kick.

Noah winced, even as she took aim again. He grabbed her elbow and yanked her out of range before she could hurt herself. It only served to turn her ire back on him.

"Because that's what I want," she said hotly, wrenching her arm out of his hold. "A man who will love and need me in the same equal measure that I love and need him. I thought for a minute that was you."

Her eyes were bright with anger—or something else.

"But if you can't or won't be that man," she continued, "then eff . . . eff . . . No, let's make this simple and clear, Noah. If you won't be that man, then fuck you."

It was the F-bomb that finally got through to him. His head cleared for the first time since hearing about Tim, and Noah looked at her, really *looked* at her. Her face was red, her hair a little mussed, her fingers curled into tight fists. The Juliet who had been the general's wife was a lady, always controlled and composed. But this Juliet, *his* Juliet, was a woman with temper and passion.

Hah. He got it now. Really got it. This was what he had to offer her—himself, a man who brought out this woman, this real Juliet. And he would take pleasure in her every mood and every flame forever.

Except looking at her angry expression, he wasn't sure she'd let him.

"Okay," he told her, taking hold of her again. She tried jerking free, but he was firm. "You win. *We* win."

Her chin jerked upward and heat leaped in her eyes. "This isn't a game."

"Not a war either," he said. "Both sides can come out of this stronger. United."

He felt the tension in her muscles ease. "Noah. I don't want to fight you any longer," she whispered. "Not when I love you so much. Not when I need you so much."

The last of the wall he'd tried to put between them

crumbled. With those blue and green eyes on his, he knew, he finally believed there was a place inside her heart for him, too. And if she was strong enough to take the chance on him, he could do no less. "I love you, too," he said, his voice hoarse with emotion and hope. "I need you, too."

He hauled her closer and kissed her, unsurprised when fire flashed around them. It was only an imitation of the passion he felt for this incredible woman.

"Noah," she said against his mouth, and that brightness flashed once more, forcing him to look up. It wasn't only love lighting up their world, he realized, but that damn paparazzo who had been plaguing them for weeks.

"Get lost," Noah said, returning his gaze to Juliet, to *his* woman, the one who unbalanced and who steadied him, too, both in equal measure. "Get lost now."

"Or what?" the man asked, taking another photo.

"Or I'm going to sic the lady on you. She's tougher than she looks and I imagine she'll kick your ass."

Juliet laughed, her whole face alight with happiness. "I'll bet he's softer than that rubber tire."

"Just give me a quote and I'll go away," the tabloid guy offered.

"We're getting married." Noah lowered his forehead to touch Juliet's. "Yes?"

Her smile was brilliant. "Yes."

So brilliant that his heart ached to see it, because he owed her one more thing. Before he really let her make such a commitment to him, he owed this brave, generous woman who thought she loved him his very last, his very own secret.

"Juliet." He cupped her beloved face in his palms. "Listen for a minute. I'm not sure I deserve you. I—"

"What are you talking about?"

He blew out a breath. "I'm not the man you think. I'm not noble; you should know that. You should know what you're getting if you take me on."

Her hands closed around his wrists. "I *am* taking you

on," she said, her voice fierce. "Do I have to start throwing things to make you believe that?"

"I'm not like the general," he said, determined to get through his confession. "I'm not that kind of man. What I feel for you . . . oh, God." He thought of all he held in his hands and of all he could lose.

"Noah." Tears brightened the blue and green of her eyes. "What is it?"

"You have to know . . . I could never sacrifice like he did. I'll hold you to me with my last ounce of strength." He swallowed past his tight throat. "The way I love you . . . I want you beside me today and tomorrow and the next day after that and when I take my very last breath."

Tears spilled over to catch in her eyelashes.

"Is that all right?" he asked, as one of her hot tears rolled over his thumb. "Are you okay with that?"

She nodded as more tears fell. "It's what I needed to hear to make me the most okay ever. I want a partner, Noah, not a protector." Then she pressed closer and he gathered her against him. "But in regard to those 'lasts' you spoke about . . . I fully expect sixty blissful years first."

# Epilogue

Real love stories never have endings.

—RICHARD BACH

*One week later.*

Juliet loved Malibu & Ewe, especially on midweek late afternoons when it quieted down from the morning and lunchtime rush of shoppers. She wandered to the doors that led to the balcony overlooking the ocean. The bright sun glinted off the water, but the air was too cold to spend time outside unless she bundled up. So instead she stayed sheltered inside the shop, and looked northward through the glass toward Zuma where she'd laid Wayne's ashes to rest.

What a wonderful man he'd been.

How pleased he'd be for her now.

Cassandra wandered from the back. "What are you smiling about?"

"Nothing. Everything."

The front door banged open with a loud peal of the bells. Their sister burst into the shop, wearing starched chef gear and waving a newspaper. "How did this happen?" she demanded, her agitation disturbing the peaceful atmosphere.

The other two hurried to her, just as she slammed the

pages of a tabloid onto the table between the couches. "SURGEON'S SECRET!" the headline screamed. Right below it read: "Renowned Celebrity Doctor Fathers Beautiful Malibu Babes!"

It was all there. The three sisters, with names and photographs. Dr. Frank Tucker's photo was there, too, as well as a sidebar containing a list of his Hollywood clients and the procedures he'd allegedly performed on them.

"What do you think of that?" Nikki demanded again, waving her hand toward the tabloid.

Cassandra bent down and scanned the text. "I don't think Oomfaa really had a nose job."

"Cassandra!"

"Well, it's the first thing that came to my mind," she said. "That and 'Who the heck spilled the beans?' "

"I haven't even thought about contacting him," Juliet confessed. "My mind's been on other things since . . ." Her voice trailed off as she remembered that odd conversation with Marlys about Botox. Marlys the tabloid snitch. "Oh, brother."

"We've got a couple of those, by the way," Nikki said, gesturing to the paper again. "Dr. Tuck has two sons he adopted with his wife. She died a number of years ago."

Cassandra looked down at the photograph of the plastic surgeon. "What are we going to do now?" she asked, her gaze shifting to Juliet.

The oldest sibling role felt more natural than ever. Putting an arm around each sister, Juliet drew them close, trying to dispel the concern on their faces. "What we were going to do anyway. Have a lovely holiday dinner tomorrow and give thanks that we've found each other. As for the rest . . . we'll figure that out together."

At that moment, the door to Malibu & Ewe opened again and Noah walked through. She felt her own worry lift as he paced toward her with single-minded purpose. A kiss was already forming on his lips.

As she lifted her face for it, she composed a diary entry in her head.

*Dear Diary:*

*This afternoon, with my sisters by my side and the man I love in my sight, I know who I am. I know exactly who I am. I'm a very—wait for it, Diary—Happy Woman.*

Turn the page for a preview of the next book
in the Malibu & Ewe series by Christie Ridgway

*Dirty, Sexy Knitting*

*Coming soon from Berkley!*

"It's my party," Cassandra Riley told her companions as she wiped a tear from her cheek with the back of her hand. "I'll cry if I want to."

The pair on her couch didn't look up, and the one near the overstuffed chair in her living room continued toying with a small ball of soft yarn. It was leftover from the dress Cassandra had made for herself to wear to the celebration-that-wasn't, and she fingered the mohair-nylon-wool blend of the crocheted skirt, wishing its blue color mimicked the April sky. Staunching another tear, she pressed her nose to the glass sliding door that led to her backyard. Beyond the small pool with its graceful, arching footbridge, the green of the surrounding banana plants, sword ferns, and tropical shrubs looked lush against the dark storm clouds.

The rain hadn't let up.

And neither had Cassandra's low mood.

Thirty years old, she thought, feeling more wetness drip off her jaw, and she was all dressed up with no place to go.

That wasn't strictly true. Five miles away on the Pacific

Coast Highway, at her little yarn shop, Malibu & Ewe, the ingredients for a birthday bash were ready and waiting. But a spring deluge had hit overnight and before her landline phone connection had died, she'd been informed that the road at the end of her secluded lane was washed out. The narrow driveway beyond her place led to only one other residence.

She wouldn't be partying over there, even if the owner would let her through the doors. Even if he was inside his bat cave.

Though they'd been lovers for four weeks, he'd dumped her yesterday, hard. She suspected that following their public scene, he'd opted for one of his frequent vanishing acts cum ugly benders.

"That means we're alone, kids," she said over her shoulder. "Isolated."

All she'd never wanted by thirty.

She'd made contact with her donor sibling sisters because she wanted the family ties her sperm-inseminated, single mother had always eschewed. Cassandra had a real relationship with Nikki and Juliet now, even though she'd gone behind their backs and contacted their biological father and his adopted sons. Her sisters had forgiven her, understanding her need to cement the seams between them all so that she'd never feel lonely again.

And here she was, alone again. Lonely.

The rain picked up, drumming harder against the roof and all three "kids" jumped. She'd taken them in last year during a torrential storm, and they probably remembered what it was like to be wet and muddy and barely clinging to life.

She couldn't blame the cats for being spooked. Besides brokenhearted, Cassandra felt a little twitchy herself. Dark was approaching; the weather wasn't abating; and with the road gone already, she had to be on the lookout for more evidence of mudslides.

Blinking back another round of self-pity, she gazed over

her backyard again. At the rear was the first of the narrow flights of steps that led to the other house farther up the Malibu canyon. A creek ran through the northern end of the property, very picturesque, but if its banks overflowed, then water would come gushing down those stairs, just like—

Oh, God.

Just like it was doing right now.

She stared at the widening wash of muddy runoff tumbling Slinky-like down the cement steps. This wasn't good.

This wasn't supposed to happen on her birthday.

Or ever, for that matter.

Thumping sounds from the direction of her front porch caused her head to jerk around. Floodwaters behind her and who knows what on her porch? Her heart slammed against her chest and the cats jumped to their twelve feet and rushed toward the front door.

Surely only one person could get them moving with such haste. They loved him, though he paid them scant attention.

Could it be . . . ?

She crossed the room, almost beating the kids in the impromptu footrace. Their tails swished impatiently as she grasped the doorknob, then twisted and pulled.

In the deepening dusk, the visitor was just a dark figure in a sodden raincoat, a wide brimmed safari-style hat shadowing his face and leaking water at the edges like she'd been leaking tears a few minutes before.

Cassandra's heart smacked in an erratic, painful rhythm against her breastbone. Yesterday he'd walked away from her, and she'd wondered if she'd ever see him again.

The figure pushed aside the open edges of his long coat. The sleeve slid up, reminding her of the bandage he'd wound around his cut wrist just a few weeks before. She knew the skin was healed there now.

His hand appeared pale against the blackness of his clothes. She saw the gleam of something metallic shoved into the waistband of dark jeans.

Oh, God.

She'd known he was in a desperate frame of mind yesterday, especially after he'd told her why her birthday put him in no mood to celebrate. But even after the many times she'd rescued him from barroom floors, even after the numerous occasions he'd gone missing for days at a time, even after the skydiving and the hang gliding and the dangerous solo kayak ocean voyages, she'd never let herself think that he'd really . . .

"Gabe?" she whispered, her gaze lifting to the face beneath the hat's brim. "A gun?"

*Six weeks earlier*

The ring of the bedside phone jolted Cassandra from a fitful sleep. She jackknifed up, disturbing the snoozing cats. Her hand snatched the receiver from its base as adrenaline sluiced through her veins. "Gabe?" It was either him or about him. Her two a.m. calls were like that.

It was of the second variety. She assured the caller she was on her way, then dressed, the adrenaline hit she'd taken making her movements choppy. In cropped sweatpants, a T-shirt, and her yoga slip-ons, she let herself out of the house.

She didn't feel the chill in the spring night air.

She didn't feel the rough gravel under her thin-soled shoes.

She only felt relieved.

After three days without any sign of him, he'd turned up. This wasn't his longest time away and this wasn't the most worried she'd ever been, but still, she had to take deep breaths to calm her heartbeat on the short drive to the Beach Shack, notable for only two things: that in Malibu terms it was quite far from the beach, and that the owner kept Cassandra's number pinned on the corkboard next to the bar's house phone.

*Gabe's been found,* she told herself, pulling into the small, potholed parking lot. *We have another chance.*

There wasn't any "we," she knew that, but she used the word anyway, as if by doing so she could make him an active partner in this endeavor to keep him engaged in the world around him.

*Admit it, Cassandra,* an inner voice insisted as she pushed open the Beach Shack's door. *You really mean in this endeavor to keep him alive.*

And in jeans and a long-sleeved shirt he looked half-dead, that was a fact. His butt on the sticky floor, his back against the battered bar, Gabe had his head down. His black hair obscured his face as a little man wearing stained khakis and a greasy-looking Dodgers cap swept around his long, outstretched legs.

The baseball fan looked up. "Closed," he said, his Spanish accent thick.

She pointed her forefinger at the rag doll figure. "I'm here for him."

Another man bustled through a swinging door behind the bar. "That's becoming a bad habit, Cassandra," he said. His cap proclaimed him a Lakers devotee.

Shrugging, she smiled. "Hi, Mr. Mueller." She'd gone to elementary school with his daughter, and he'd never failed to attend the annual father-daughter luncheon. In second grade, she'd been assigned the seat next to his, and she'd pretended for forty-two blissful minutes that the pot-bellied man who smelled like Marlboros and deli pickles was her daddy.

Mr. Mueller wiped his hands on a dingy rag and then made his way around the bar to stand beside her. They both gazed down at Gabe.

"He showed up about eleven," the older man said.

"You could have called me then," she replied, frowning. "I would have—"

"He was with a woman."

The quick breath she took hurt her lungs. "Oh." Her face burned, and she pretended not to notice the sympathetic look he sent her. Malibu was like any other small town in the way that everyone knew everyone else's business.

Mr. Mueller grimaced. "If it helps any—"

"It doesn't matter," she interjected.

"—she looked like a two-bit . . ."

His voice drifted off as the man on the floor stirred. "I stink," Gabe mumbled.

"His, uh, friend threw up on him," the bar owner said to Cassandra. "After that, I called her a cab." He reached down to grab Gabe's arm. "Let's go, buddy. Your ride's here."

"Don' call her," Gabe said, his head swinging up to pin the other man with a bloodshot gaze. "Don' wan' her here."

"It's okay, fella," Mr. Mueller said, helping him to his feet. "A taxi took your date away."

Cassandra stepped forward to slide her arm around the drunk's lean waist. "Gabe means me."

To prove her true, he let out a long, low groan. "C'ssandra." When he shook his head, he stirred the air around him, bringing closer his disgusting smell.

Thanks to some other woman.

Gabe's date.

*She looked like a two-bit . . .* Cassandra suspected Gabe hadn't had to pay his evening's companion a thing. The dark spaces inside of him acted like a magnet for all kinds of women.

The wrong kind.

Even the smart kind.

Especially the kind who seemed to be lacking self-protective instincts.

"Let's go," she said, trying not to breathe through her nose as she led him outside the bar.

She spread an old beach towel she found in her trunk on the passenger seat then helped Mr. Mueller insert Gabe into the car. She buckled him in as his head lolled on the cushion and blessed the donut-and-chow-mein scent that rose in the air as she started the motor. Gabe always gave her grief about the odor of the used veggie oil that she put in her gas tank, but it smelled a heck of a lot better than he did.

She glanced over at him several times on the trip home. He'd passed out again, she decided, and that was a relief in its own way. After parking in the circular drive by his front entrance, she jogged around to open his door. Then it was up to her to search his pockets for his house keys. Better to get the front door open before trying to drag him up the steps and inside.

No need to instruct him to lift off the seat. Gabe carried his wallet and keys in his right front pocket. Leaning in, she inserted her fingers between layers of tight denim.

She shrieked when a hard hand clamped around her wrist. "Darlin'," Gabe said, apparently conscious again. "We fin'ly gonna do it?"

Rolling her eyes, she yanked on her hand, but he wouldn't release her. "Let go. Let go, you idiot."

"Liked where you were head'n."

Cassandra rolled her eyes again. There were twelve steps to self-recovery, so it shouldn't surprise her that there were steps to self-destruction, too. For Gabe, those had been tending to go like this: 1) a short-to-long disappearance 2) followed by a scene of public drunkenness 3) ending with demands for sex with Cassandra.

He never remembered them after he sobered up.

He never seemed interested in her that way after he sobered up either.

She yanked again, freeing her hand, then patted his thigh to check out the pocket from the outside. It seemed empty. "Gabe, where are your keys?"

"Dunno." Frowning, he managed to get his feet out of the car and then he stood, swaying as held on to the open door. His hands searched all four of his pockets. "C'ssandra. Do you have m'keys?"

"No." Thinking fast, she decided the best way to deal

was to run to her house and get the spare set. She'd dash through his front yard to the steps leading to her back patio. He'd be better off waiting here in the fresh air until she returned. "Stay," she told him, then made for her place.

It was the big splash that said he hadn't followed orders. At her back door, she whipped around to discover he'd fallen into her small pool. So small that she could lean over the side and grab his arm and tow his body to the side. "What are you doing, you fool?"

"Can't leave a girl 'lone in the dark." He grasped her waist to hoist himself up, lost his grip, then slipped back underwater. "Watchin' after you," he added wetly, as he broke the surface again. This time he dug his fingers into her hips and with her help managed to exit the pool. Standing up, he shook himself like a dog.

Dodging the spray, she decided that thanks to her good deeds there must be a cloud in heaven with her name already inscribed on it. And she hoped it was plenty fluffy, because handling Gabe was making her old before her time. She left him on her back patio and scurried for towels before he could get into more trouble.

Scurrying proved useless, however, because when she returned from the linen closet, he was standing in her small living area, stark naked.

Cassandra focused on his face. "What are you doing now?" she demanded.

He lifted his arms away from his lean, muscled body. The benders didn't seem to affect his fitness level. "Shortcut. I'm naked. Now you."

She threw the towel at his chest, but his reflexes were off and it fell to the floor after briefly catching on the impressive erection he was sporting. "I thought booze was supposed to make that impossible," she muttered.

He looked down at himself, palmed the thick flesh, then sent her a grin. "Hung like 'n' elephant. Did I tell you that?"

"Only every time you've been drinking." Except this

was the first time she'd seen the evidence for herself. Oh, and he had a nice ass, too, she noticed, as he turned and headed down the short hallway that led to a half-bath on the left and her bedroom on the right. She trailed his slow-moving figure, then had to yell out, "Left, left! You want to go left," as he veered into her bedroom.

Oh, fine. There was an attached bathroom there, too, complete with a shower.

But he didn't make it that far. Instead, he found her queen-sized mattress and fell on it, faceup. One of the cats tiptoed over and settled on the pillow around his head, just like a coonskin hat.

"My comatose Davy Crocket," she said, aware he'd sunk into drunken dreamland again. Resigned to an unexpected overnight visitor, she reached for the covers to pull them over his nakedness. Her gaze snagged on a thin strip of fabric tied with a clumsy knot around his left wrist. Watery bloodstains marred the white material.

Her stomach hollowed. A high whine rang in her ears and her spongy knees had her sinking to the mattress. She lifted his hand into her lap. His fingers were curled in relaxation, the skin warm, the callused palm scratchy under her thumbs. The bandage—

"Wha'?"

Her gaze jumped to Gabe's face. He was awake again, and staring at her.

"Your wrist," she said. "How did you get hurt?"

His gaze flicked down to the bandage and he looked at it, obviously bemused. Not alarmed. Alarmed was her.

"Accident." It was the first nonslurred word he'd spoken that evening.

Her alarm level rose. "What kind of 'accident'?" When he didn't respond, she shook his hand. "What kind of accident, Gabe?"

The same kind of "accident" that had led her to find him in his closed garage with his car's motor running? The same kind of "accident" that had led him to take a hunk of rope and coil it into a noose that she'd caught him tying from a beam in the gazebo in his backyard? She swallowed.

"*What kind of accident*?"

He frowned, as if thinking back. "Box cutter."

Box cutter. *Box cutter*.

"Gabe." She wanted to shake him, slap him, scream for mercy, but all she could do was say his name and hold tight to his hand. "Gabe."

He smiled, as charming as any angel seeking entrance into hell. It was obvious the discussion of the bandage and the box cutter was already forgotten. "Is so true, Froo' Loop. I so want to do you." Then he slipped his hand from hers so he could roll to his side and drop back into sleep.

Cassandra hastily stood, then stepped back, putting space between herself and the man she'd been trying to save for nearly two years. *I so don't want to do this anymore*, she thought. *I so can't do this anymore*. Because there was no longer a way to fool herself that there wouldn't come a day when she couldn't rescue him.

Backing up, she kept her eyes on his sleeping form sprawled across her bed. The cat at his head was snuggled against the nape of his neck now. The other two were draped across his limbs—one on his arm, one over his thigh—keeping him close like she'd always wanted to. Gabe was where she'd always imagined him in her deepest, darkest, sweetest fantasies, but it was going to be a one-time, no-touch night.

It had taken her two years to figure out, but now she knew that if she let him any closer to her heart his self-destructive bent was going to make her collateral damage.

Meaning it was past time for Cassandra Riley to rescue herself.